ATMOSPHERE

ATMOSPHERE

A Love Story

TAYLOR JENKINS REID

BALLANTINE BOOKS
NEW YORK

Ballantine Books
An imprint of Random House
A division of Penguin Random House LLC
1745 Broadway, New York, NY 10019
randomhousebooks.com
penguinrandomhouse.com

BALLANTINE BOOKS & colophon are registered trademarks of
Penguin Random House LLC.

Hardback ISBN 978-0-593-15871-5
International ISBN 978-0-593-98357-7
Ebook ISBN 978-0-593-15872-2

Printed in the United States of America on acid-free paper

2 4 6 8 9 7 5 3 1

First Edition

Book design by Susan Turner
Endpapers image by Getty Images

The authorized representative in the EU for product safety and compliance
is Penguin Random House Ireland, Morrison Chambers, 32 Nassau Street,
Dublin D02 YH68, Ireland. https://eu-contact.penguin.ie

To Paul Dye, the longest-serving flight director
at NASA and author of *Shuttle, Houston*.

Paul, I can see how you guided many a crew
home safely. This book would not exist without you.

AUTHOR'S NOTE

Dear Reader,

One night, last summer, after my daughter had gotten in bed, I walked outside, looked up at the night sky, and saw Venus in the distance.

It was brighter than any star, hanging low just above the trees. My daughter and I had been trying to spot Venus for a few days now. I knew that I should let her fall asleep, but instead, I snuck up to her room, opened the door, and whispered, "Come outside."

When we got to the backyard, I picked her up. She's far too big to be held anymore, but she still lets me do it when she's sleepy. I pointed toward Venus in front of us.

"There it is!" she said. "I see it." And, for a few moments, I held her in my arms as the two of us stared up at the night sky, filled with awe.

Before writing this novel, I could barely recognize the Big Dipper. But I wanted to make my main character, Joan, a passionate, excitable astronomer. So I downloaded an app, picked up some books, and began studying the stars. What started as my attempt to create an interesting backdrop for a love story became the beginning of me understanding my place in the world.

You see, once you start observing the night sky, you begin to orient yourself in time and space. You learn, for instance, that in the Northern Hemisphere, if you can spot Orion's belt, it's winter. You can learn to get a general idea of what time it is by where the constellation Cassiopeia is in relation to the star Polaris. My favorite thing I learned? If you can spot the stars Altair, Deneb, and Vega during the summer, you will see that they form a triangle. And that triangle always points south. If you are ever lost, you can find those three and know which way to go.

Something about that always seems to cure whatever ails me when my daughter and I walk out into the night. I know some of it is simply the joy of spending time with her and perhaps the thrill of new knowledge. But I think it is also the relief I feel that those stars are *immovable*.

Nothing you or I could do will ever alter them. They are so much bigger than us. And they will not change within our lifetime. We can succeed or fail, get it right or get it wrong, love and lose the ones we love, and still the Summer Triangle will point south. And in that way, I know everything will be some type of okay—as impossible as that can seem sometimes.

I hope, very much, that you enjoy this story. But I hope, even more, that Joan Goodwin can convince you to go outside tonight, after the stars have come out, and *look up*. I hope, with all my heart, Joan can convince you to be open to wonder.

—*Taylor Jenkins Reid*

ATMOSPHERE

DECEMBER 29, 1984

JOAN GOODWIN GETS TO THE JOHNSON SPACE CENTER WELL BEFORE nine, and Houston is already airless and muggy. Joan can feel the sweat collecting along her hairline as she walks across the campus to the Mission Control building. She knows it's the heat. But she also knows that's not all it is.

Her job today is one of her favorite parts of being an astronaut. She is CAPCOM on the Orion Flight Team for STS-LR9, the third flight of the shuttle *Navigator*.

The role of CAPCOM—the only person in Mission Control who speaks directly to the crew on the shuttle—is one of many that astronauts fill when they aren't on a mission.

This is something Joan often has to explain to people at the rare party she agrees to go to. That astronauts train to go up into space, yes. But they also help design the tools and experiments, test out food, prep the shuttle, educate students on what NASA can do, advocate for space travel in Washington, talk to the press, and more. It's an exhausting list.

Being an astronaut is not just about getting up there. It is about being a member of the team that gets the crew up there.

Plus, Joan has already been. She has, in her nightstand at home, that elusive talisman that every astronaut aches for: the gold pin. Evidence that she was one of the chosen few humans who have ever left this planet.

She has seen the spectacular shimmering blue of the seven oceans from two hundred miles away. *Cerulean? Cobalt? Ultramarine?* There was no shade vivid enough that she could name. Ninety-nine point nine percent of human beings who have ever lived have never seen that blue. And she has.

But now she is home, both feet on solid ground, and she has a job to do.

So when Joan walks into the Mission Control building that morning with a black coffee in her hand, she is at ease. She is not anxious or terrified or heartbroken.

All of that will come later.

JOAN ENTERS THE MISSION CONTROL room through the theater. She watches for a moment as the crew from the last shift prepares two of the mission specialists for their spacewalk.

Her boss—the flight director of Orion Flight, Jack Katowski—is down on the floor already, getting debriefed by the previous flight director.

Jack has a crew cut, graying temples, and a reputation for being *particularly stoic,* even in an organization known for its stoicism.

Still, he's long supported Joan in her role as CAPCOM. And they make a good team. That is something Joan prides herself on. That she is an excellent team player.

Especially with the crew on STS-LR9, which is composed almost entirely of astronauts from her class.

Commander Steve Hagen had been one of their instructors, but the rest of the crew—pilot Hank Redmond and mission specialists John Griffin, Lydia Danes, and Vanessa Ford—are the people Joan's come up with, trained with, learned how to do this job alongside.

They are more than just her friends; some of them are her family. And her complicated histories with each of them are part of what is going to make her the exact CAPCOM they need today, but also the very last person who should have to do the job.

The shuttle's mission is to launch the Arch-6, an Earth observation satellite for the U.S. Navy. However, yesterday, on day two of the flight, as the team prepared to deploy the Arch-6, the payload retention latches would not release.

This morning, they have been preparing Vanessa Ford and John Griffin for a spacewalk, so they can go into the payload bay and release the latches manually.

Joan joins the team in the flight control center. She waves good morning to Ray Stone, the flight surgeon, and nods at Greg Ullman, also known as EECOM—electrical, environmental, and consumables management.

The previous CAPCOM, Isaac Williams, reads her in, updating her on the telemetry and timeline. Ford and Griff are in their space suits. Their pre-breathe will be completed in six minutes.

Isaac leaves, and Joan takes her place at the console.

Jack gets on the flight loop—as do Joan, Ray, Greg, and the rest of the Orion Flight Team, which is made up of twenty members, each at their own stations on the floor, with a team of people in other rooms supporting them.

Ford and Griff complete the pre-breathe and get into the airlock, waiting for it to complete depressurization so that they can be ready to function within space.

The flight deck and the mid-deck—where the astronauts live and work on the shuttle—are pressurized to mimic the atmosphere on Earth's surface. But the payload bay—where the satellites are held until they are deployed—is not. It is exposed to the vacuum of space. Which means if Ford and Griff were to enter it without their space suits, all of the oxygen would be sucked out of their lungs and bloodstream instantly, causing them to pass out within fifteen seconds and be dead within two minutes.

The human body—intelligent as it is—was formed in response to the atmosphere of Earth.

It would be easy to make the case that humans are ill-equipped to be in space. *Whatever led to our design, it was not meant for this.* But Joan sees it as the exact opposite.

Human intelligence and curiosity, our persistence and resilience, our capacity for long-term planning, and our ability to collaborate have led the human race here.

In Joan's estimation, we are not ill-suited at all. We are exactly who should be out there. We are the only intelligent life-form that we know of in our galaxy who has become aware of the universe and worked to understand it.

We are so determined to learn what lies beyond our grasp that we have figured out how to ride a rocket out of the atmosphere. A thrilling ability that seems ripe to attract cowboys, but is best done by people like her. Nerds.

Everything about space exploration is about preparedness over impulsivity, calmness over boldness. For such an adventurous job, it can be achingly routine. All risks are carefully managed; no corners are cut. There are no cowboys here.

This is how NASA keeps everyone safe. Predictable models, prepared for every scenario.

When the airlock completes depressurization, Jack gives Joan the go-ahead and Joan punches in on the shuttle loop.

And now Joan is aware of her own breath, her own heart rate. Not because she is afraid of what this mission entails—there is no logical reason to be afraid yet—but because she gets nervous every time she talks to Vanessa Ford.

"*Navigator,* this is Houston," Joan says.

"Houston, we read you," Steve Hagen says.

Hank Redmond chimes in with his gruff Texan accent: "Good mornin', Goodwin."

"Exciting day today," Lydia Danes says.

"Indeed it is," Joan responds. "With a lot on the agenda, which is why I am happy to tell you, Griff and Ford, that you are cleared for the spacewalk."

"Roger that," Ford says.

"Yes, roger that, Goodwin," Griff says. "Nice to hear your voice."

These are the last forty-five minutes *before*.

VANESSA FORD HAS HAD BIOMEDICAL SENSORS ALL OVER HER BODY FOR hours. They have been sending her vitals down to the flight surgeon, who monitors every breath she takes. But even well before the electrodes were placed on her body, Vanessa has been aware that someone on the ground is always watching.

Mission Control knows everything that happens on the shuttle—every temperature, every coordinate, the status of every switch. Everywhere Vanessa turns, there is Houston, hearing and sensing everything around her.

This does not seem to bother anyone else on the crew as much as it bothers her. But knowing that everyone can see her heart rate—that they can see how her body reacts every time Houston speaks up—makes her feel like she has nowhere to hide.

"Nice to hear your voice, too, Griff," Joan says. "Good start to the day here."

She can hear Joan smiling. She can hear it in the lilt of her voice.

Vanessa reaches out and puts her gloved hands on the airlock hatch to the payload bay. She feels a vibration in her chest. With the payload bay doors already open, this is all that stands between her and space.

There's no data on the airlock hatch. It is one of the few things on the shuttle that doesn't send its own signal. Which means one of them has to notify Houston that they are about to open it.

Vanessa looks at Griff. She's glad she's doing this alongside him. She's always liked him. Not just because they are both from New England, although it helps.

"Houston, we are opening the airlock," Griff says.

Vanessa begins to open the hatch. She tries to keep her heart rate steady. She's been working toward this moment for five years, dreaming of it most of her life.

Space.

She and Griff both inhale when they can see through the hatch.

They've looked through the window, but nothing quite prepares them for the sight of it now.

Vanessa's mind goes blank. There are bright lights from the ship, but beyond that everything is black. There is no horizon, only the edge of *Navigator* and then nothingness with the brilliant colors of Earth in the distance.

"Wow," Vanessa says. She looks to Griff. He's lost in the vision of it himself.

She lets go of the ship and moves through the hatch, to take her first step into space. Her legs feel steady as she wades into the darkness. Her eyes widen at the intensity of it, a void unlike anything she's ever seen.

She looks up, past the payload bay doors, to see Earth in the distance. Clouds streak across the deserts of North Africa. For a moment, Vanessa stops and looks at the Indian Ocean.

For so long, she has loved to be above the clouds. But to be this far above them knocks her breath from her chest.

"My God," Griff says.

Vanessa turns toward him. They are both tethered to the ship, and Griff pushes away.

She follows, headed straight for the payload. The view is spectacular, but the real reason she's here is because she wants nothing more than to tinker with a machine two hundred and eighteen miles above Earth's atmosphere.

They get to the payload, and each takes their position. There are four latches, two on each side of the satellite.

"Take it slow, Ford," Griff says. "I'm going to be very upset if we set the record for the shortest spacewalk."

"There's not really much time we can milk out of this," she says. "It's just releasing a few clamps. But all right."

Using a socket wrench, Vanessa cranks open one of the latches on her side, then moves to the other. Once her second latch is open, she waits a brief moment for Griff to get his second one released, too.

When he's done, he sighs. "Houston, the clamps have been released, in no small part thanks to the brilliantly efficient Vanessa Ford."

"Copy that, *Navigator*. Good job," Joan says. And then, after a moment: "*Navigator,* we've got hours left on these suits, so better to keep you in the airlock as we deploy, in case we need you again."

"Awww," Griff says. "Now you're just being nice."

"Well," Joan says, "we've got a soft spot for you down here."

"Back at ya, Houston," he says. "Roger that. Ford and I will stay in the airlock."

They float back. Griff lets Vanessa in first and then joins her. He goes to shut the hatch. But then he stops and looks at Vanessa. He lifts his eyebrows.

Protocol is to close that hatch. But if they leave it open, they will be able to watch the satellite deploy.

Vanessa does not want to lie to Houston. Still, a smile escapes from her.

Griff smiles back and takes his hand off the hatch. He does not close it.

"Houston, we are in the airlock," he says.

They both turn their attention to the open hatch. They watch as the tilt table is raised into position to release the satellite.

"Houston, we are happy with the degree of the sat," Vanessa can hear Steve say.

She thinks about their last night before the mission, when they were quarantined at Cape Canaveral. Steve had spent an hour on the phone with Helene. Hank was annoyed because he'd been waiting to call Donna. But Steve had just stood there, leaning against the kitchen counter, making jokes with his wife, his bright blue eyes crinkling as he laughed. Vanessa had listened more than she probably should have. It seemed so easy for Steve to be both sides of himself at the same time—the man he is on the ground and the commander he has to be up here. For her, those two roles have always been in conflict. "Are we cleared to deploy?"

"Affirmative, *Navigator*," Joan says. "You are cleared to deploy."

Lydia is on the remote manipulator system, the RMS. She will release the satellite.

"Roger that, Houston," Lydia says. "Preparing to deploy."

"Copy that, *Navigator*."

There are two explosive cords holding the Arch-6 in the payload bay. Vanessa and Griff watch as one is detonated according to plan.

But then, swiftly, the second cord explodes in a flash unlike anything Vanessa has ever seen before. It looks nothing like their simulations. The explosions tear the metal bands around the satellite into pieces. Debris goes flying in every direction.

Vanessa cannot tell what has happened. All she can see is the flash of metal, and then a grunt comes out of Griff, like the air has been knocked out of his lungs.

She turns to see a gash below the waist ring in his suit. Within seconds, the exposure will kill him. He puts his hand on his suit to cover the hole.

"I'm okay," he says to her. They both know that his hand on his suit is enough to save him for now. But his voice is a rocky, thin whisper, as if he has spent all of his breath.

Then an alarm begins to sound, one that Vanessa recognizes but cannot place. And it is only once Steve, Hank, and Lydia all begin to shout that she understands there has been a second hit.

AS THE ALARM RINGS, JOAN BREATHES DEEPLY, TRYING TO THINK clearly. When Greg stands up, her stomach falls.

"Flight, this is EECOM. We are seeing a negative dP/dT. Pressure is dropping rapidly."

Jack: "What are we at?"

Before Greg can answer, Hank's voice comes through the loop, level but sharp: "Houston, this is *Navigator*. We have a cabin leak. We can feel the rapid depress."

"Copy that, *Navigator*," Joan says. She keeps her voice calm, but this is a choice she has to make. She looks to Jack.

Jack turns to her, eyes focused. "Tell them they have a hole. Judging from the depressure rate, it could be as big as half an inch. It's punctured the skin somewhere on that aft wall, most likely—mid-deck or flight deck. Do they have a visual?"

Joan relays.

"Negative, Houston," Hank says. "We see no hole."

Jack: "Tell them to pull everything off the walls, lockers, close-out panels, anything they can get off to expose the skin—pull it all off!"

"Roger that," Joan says.

Jack continues: "Keep Ford and Griff in the airlock but start pressurizing as quick as possible. Tell *Navigator* they need to flow in oxygen and open up nitrogen systems 1 and 2 to the cabin to feed the leak until we find that hole!"

Joan updates the crew. Clear, concise, calm. *This is NASA. We have a plan for this.*

"Roger that," Hank says as the crew gets to work. "Already on it."

Greg: "Flight, EECOM—we aren't seeing a positive change in the leak rate. Pressure is still dropping."

Joan knows that Hank is the one most likely feeding the oxygen and nitrogen while Steve and Lydia are pulling everything off the walls—the layers of wires, the sleeping bags—as fast as they can. There is so much lining the limited space of the orbiter, and they are tearing it all away, looking for that hole. Each second that goes by stuns her.

She looks at Jack. But Jack is looking at Greg.

"It's not in the aft of the flight deck!" Steve says.

"I'm pulling the lockers off the mid-deck!" Lydia calls.

Greg looks up at Jack and shakes his head.

Jack slams his hand onto the top of the console and looks at Sean Gutterson, who is in charge of the mechanical systems. "RMU, what do you have? What are they not seeing? I need something! We have seconds!"

Everyone is up out of their seats. Joan can barely hear herself think.

She has been through simulations like this, with the pressure dropping rapidly and no way to stabilize it.

They have ended only when the leak is found.

Or the crew dies.

This is NASA. We have a plan for this.

VANESSA HAS CLOSED THE HATCH, AND THE AIRLOCK IS PRESSURIZING.

But as Vanessa watches Griff, she can see that he is losing consciousness. She slips her hand under his, presses it against the hole in his suit, and applies pressure to his lower stomach.

"Griff, Griff," she says. No response. "John Griffin, do you hear me?"

When he blinks, she cannot tell if it is purposeful. "I've got it," she says to him. "I've got you."

She cannot pinpoint the exact moment he passes out. Only that soon, his hand falls away and now her hand is the only thing keeping him alive until the cabin pressure in the airlock returns. She checks for any indication of blood under his suit. She sees none.

She can hear the commotion and the voices of her crewmates as they try to coordinate. Steve's voice calms her, but Lydia's is starting to rise in pitch.

She realizes she has not heard Hank speak in at least thirty seconds.

That moment grows longer and longer. And Vanessa gets a sinking feeling.

When she was six years old, her mother told her that her father died. Vanessa does not remember what her mother said. She only remembers that before her mother said anything, her mother looked at her but could not speak. It was a brief moment, no more than a second. But Vanessa knew something bad had happened. And it was not by what her mother had said, but the silence that had preceded it.

Vanessa thinks of that silence now.

RAY STANDS UP. "FLIGHT, THIS IS SURGEON. JOHN GRIFFIN'S HEART RATE is dropping."

Joan has been working to slow down her breathing.

"Hank has lost consciousness," Lydia says through the loop. And then: "I think Steve has, too."

Jack goes pale. He looks to Joan. "Stay on Danes."

"Copy that, *Navigator,*" Joan says on the loop, each word feeling heavy in her mouth. "We read you."

Jack: "Keep Danes on the leak. But she also has to make sure the N_2 is all the way up. Keep Ford on Griff in the airlock."

"Roger," Joan says, and then she gets back on the loop. "*Navigator,* Houston. Danes, we need you to find that leak as soon as possible. We are reading that the N_2 is funneling in, but we are not seeing an increase in cabin pressure."

"I think I—" Lydia's voice cuts out.

"*Navigator? Navigator,* this is Houston, do you read?" Joan says.

Nothing.

"Lydia Danes, do you read me?"

There is no answer. This feels inevitable to Joan now, even though just one second ago she would have said it was nearly impossible. Losing all three in the cabin was something to *pretend* was a real fear, but it would never actually happen.

Joan leans forward. "*Navigator,* this is Houston, come in."

Ray: "Flight, this is Surgeon. Given the rate the pressure has been dropping, Hagen, Redmond, and Danes are certainly unconscious, suffering from the bends. But, given the length of exposure, I believe they may be dead."

Joan can feel the mass of this moment as it takes hold in her brain stem, making her neck stiff, her head heavy.

Greg: "Flight, EECOM—the cabin pressure is rising."

Jack: "Rising? Confirm you said rising."

"Rising, sir. PSIA returning to normal levels."

"Danes found the hole," Jack mutters.

Joan gets back on the loop. "*Navigator,* this is Houston. Can you confirm you have found the hole and patched it?"

Ray: "She's not going to be able to answer."

"Lydia, come in," Joan says again.

Nothing.

Nothing.

Nothing.

And then Vanessa's voice.

"Houston," she says. "I think I am the only one left."

SEVEN YEARS EARLIER

JOAN'S YOUNGER SISTER, BARBARA, HAD CALLED HER ONE MORNING TO tell her about a commercial she'd seen on TV late the previous night.

"It said, 'This is your NASA.'"

"What?" Joan said. She was in her kitchen, pouring herself a cup of coffee, the phone held between her shoulder and her ear. She was about to head to the car. Her first class of the day at Rice University was a survey course on the cosmos, offered to freshmen of all majors. Although she had a PhD focusing on an analysis of magnetic structures in the solar corona, she was spending her expertise teaching eighteen-year-olds the definition of a parsec. But, as her department chair had pointed out when she'd gently asked for a different assignment, "someone has to do it." Apparently that someone just so happened to be the only woman in the department.

"What do you mean, 'This is your NASA?'"

"That's what she said, the woman from *Star Trek*. Hold on, I wrote it down somewhere. I saw the commercial just before putting Frances to bed, but I was able to grab a pen before it was over. Here it is: 'This is your NASA, a space agency embarked on a mission to improve the quality of life on planet Earth right now.' It was Nichelle

Nichols—that's her name! That was driving me crazy. They are re-cruiting astronauts. Scientists. To go up into space. They specifically said they wanted women."

Joan put the lid on her coffee. "They said female scientists?"

When Joan was twelve, she had read a newspaper article men-tioning the FLATs—First Lady Astronaut Trainees, involved in what was known as the Women in Space Program. That group of thirteen women had been privately tested and trained by William Randolph Lovelace II, the same physician who had helped select the Mercury program astronauts. He'd done it on his own, outside of NASA, in hopes that the organization might recognize the potential of female candidates.

But the article where Joan first read about the program was the same article in which she learned of its demise. The FLATs needed NASA's approval in order to be granted permission to complete their testing at the Naval School of Aviation Medicine. Days before they were scheduled to arrive, they were notified that NASA would not approve the request.

A congressional hearing in which many of the women testified about gender discrimination did nothing to change the NASA ad-ministrator's mind. John Glenn had even been quoted as saying that women not being accepted as astronauts was "a fact of our social order."

Joan had spent a lifetime of looking up at the stars, but had not imagined herself in a space suit in a very long time.

"They definitely said 'scientist' and they definitely said 'women,'" Barbara told her.

Joan put down her coffee and took the phone from her shoulder into her hand. "You really think I could be an astronaut?" Joan said.

"You study the stars. Who else could they possibly be asking for?"

"I don't know. I . . . You really think I should apply?" Joan asked.

Barbara sighed. "Oh, forget it. You've zapped all the fun out of it," she said and hung up.

As the dial tone kicked in, Joan took the phone from her ear,

slowly put it in its cradle, and kept her hand on it for a moment, staring at the receiver.

Two weeks later, without telling Barbara, she requested an application.

As she filled it out, she could barely look at it directly. *Me, an
astronaut.* And yet. She went to the library to xerox her documenta-
tion, then stuffed it all into a nine-by-twelve envelope—a summary,
thus far, of everything she'd accomplished on Earth.

She walked to the post office and, without allowing herself to
agonize any further, dropped it into the mail slot.

That January, Joan walked out her front door on the way to teach
another introductory-level course and saw a newspaper in the apartment complex's driveway. She picked it up and noticed the headline
below the fold.

"NASA CHOOSES 35 NEW ASTRONAUT CANDIDATES, INCLUDING SIX
WOMEN."

Joan swallowed hard as her eyes began to sting. She got into her
car, threw the newspaper onto the passenger seat, and stared at the
steering wheel for seventeen minutes.

It was the only time in her career she had been late to a class.

A YEAR LATER, IN 1979, Joan was walking into the lounge when she
overheard Dr. Siskin, her department chair, mention to a fellow professor that NASA had opened up its astronaut applications again—and
that they were specifically looking for astronomers and astrophysi-
cists.

She pretended to be searching in the refrigerator for her lunch
but, instead, considered her options. Ten minutes later, she was at
her desk, writing to request another application.

That year, one hundred and twenty-one applicants were invited—
in groups of twenty—for a week of interviews at the Johnson Space
Center.

This time, one of them was Joan.

The first night, Joan checked into the Sheraton Kings Inn and got settled in her room. She was ten minutes early for the evening orientation.

She was the third person to sit down. The two already seated were men, and both looked to be military. Then, just behind Joan, another woman walked into the room.

The woman had curly brown hair and light brown eyes, which looked especially striking with the olive-green button-up shirt she was wearing. There was a thin gold chain around her neck.

She sat down just a few seats away from Joan. This woman did not smile or say hello. Joan had no particular reason to feel a connection to her except that, now, Joan was no longer the only woman in the room.

Joan watched as more people filed in. Soon a set of classifications emerged in her mind: scientist and military. Later, Steve Hagen would make it even simpler: "The astronaut corps has two types: dorks and soldiers." Still, that evening, Joan could not classify the woman in the olive-green shirt.

A man at the front cleared his throat. He had salt-and-pepper hair, closely cropped and combed to the side, with a mustache that was beginning to gray as well.

"I am Antonio Lima, the director of flight at the Astronaut Office," he said. "Welcome, everyone."

Joan looked around, seeing them all from what she imagined of his perspective. They all must seem so green.

"If you made it here today, you are one of the select few applicants who we believe may be an asset to NASA and to this nation. Over the course of the next week, you will be assessed in terms of your unique abilities and how they may be a benefit to the larger astronaut corps. Our astronaut candidates—those of you who are fortunate enough to be chosen to join the training here at NASA—must be physically fit and mentally sound, as well as superlatively prepared for the task that lies ahead."

Just then, a man snuck into the room, taking the chair closest to the door. Joan looked at her watch. He was two minutes late. Certainly this man knew that he was done for.

"You are here," Antonio continued, "because NASA is about to embark on its greatest and most groundbreaking enterprise yet: the space shuttle program. Until now, space exploration has been exceptional. It has been rare. Soon it will become routine."

Antonio lifted the cover off the easel and showed a blueprint of a spacecraft. Everyone in the room leaned forward. Joan was familiar with the concept of the shuttle, but learning this level of detail about how it would work made her pulse quicken.

"The shuttles are the first spacecraft in NASA history designed to be reusable," he said. "With a fleet of shuttles, we can fly into low space orbit over and over again. Launches will happen monthly, even weekly. We will carry cargo to deploy to space. We will perform experiments. Eventually, we believe, we will establish a permanent presence in space, including a space station and manned flights to Mars, built by the shuttle missions we are developing today."

Antonio grabbed the pointer from the easel.

"This is the orbiter," he said, pointing to the bulk of the shuttle. "It will launch with an external tank and two solid rocket boosters, one on each side." He removed the top diagram to show another, more complex one.

"Once the shuttle is launched, the external gas tank and the solid rocket boosters will fall away. And the orbiter will enter low-Earth orbit. As for the crew . . ." He pointed to the nose of the orbiter. "They will occupy the flight deck here and the mid-deck here."

The flight and mid-decks were tiny compared to the rest of the orbiter. Joan was starting to get a sense of scale, and she could not keep a smile from escaping.

"Once in orbit, the shuttle will be traveling at approximately five miles a second at a typical altitude of around two hundred miles, circling Earth every ninety minutes. After the astronauts have com-

pleted their mission, they will return to Earth. Unlike previous pro-
grams here at NASA, we will not be using a splashdown landing in
the water. Instead, upon successful reentry into the atmosphere, the
shuttle will fly—much like an airplane—and land, wheels down, at
one of our bases."

Antonio stepped back and allowed everyone to take that in. Then
he resumed his introduction:

"By now I hope you have surmised that you are looking at a spacecraft unlike anything we've seen before. The shuttle is not one piece
of machinery. It is three. On launch, it is a rocket. In orbit, it is a
spaceship. On landing, it is an airplane. This is what will allow us to
usher in the future of space exploration."

Joan felt a flutter in her belly. It was the same feeling she'd gotten
the first time she saw the glowing band of the Milky Way when her
parents took her to Joshua Tree as a child.

"Our missions here at NASA are not without risk," Antonio said.
"You will put your life into the hands of your directors and your fellow
astronauts, as well as the researchers and engineers who make space
exploration possible. But, if chosen, you may become one of a very
small number of people who can say they have left the Earth and
who can report back to the rest of us on what our planet looks like
from afar. You will usher us into the future. I can assure you that this
will be the greatest technological achievement in the history of
NASA. It may well be the greatest endeavor in the history of man-
kind."

Joan tried to process just how close this opportunity was to her
grasp, but as she did, her eyes met those of the woman with the curly
hair, a few seats away. The two of them held each other's gaze for a
moment.

Was this really happening?

That week, she sat for heart-rate monitoring, hearing and vision
tests, blood draws, and full assessments from the flight surgeons.
Her body was poked and prodded in ways that shocked her.

But she was determined to show all of her NASA evaluators that what she had to offer was exactly what they needed: determined, stoic composure.

She stepped onto a treadmill connected to electrodes and ran for over five miles before even beginning to slow down.

She sat for interviews in which the intense tone made even a question like "Would you like me to turn down the thermostat?" seem complicated to answer. She spoke calmly and clearly as she answered each one.

Joan's favorite part of the week was when she was put in a suit and instructed to climb into a three-foot-wide white fabric ball. Her only source of air was an oxygen tank. She was ordered to stay in there for fifteen minutes. The moment Joan got in and could feel the quiet solitude of the ball, she understood.

It wasn't a test of dexterity or mechanical aptitude. They wanted to see if she'd freak out, unable to stand the sensory deprivation and claustrophobia. She smiled to herself. Piece of cake.

She fell asleep.

ONE EVENING TWO MONTHS LATER, the phone in her apartment rang. Joan was eating Chinese food and sketching a portrait of Frances to give Barbara as a birthday present. She put the pencil down and walked to the phone.

It was Antonio. "Are you still interested in joining the astronaut corps at NASA?" he said.

Joan looked up at the ceiling and steadied her voice. It was the closest thing she'd ever felt to the way women look in the movies when they are proposed to. "Yes," she said. "Absolutely yes."

"Good, we are lucky to have you on board, Joan. There are sixteen of you who will be joining us here in Group 9. Eight candidate pilots and eight candidate mission specialists, such as yourself. I am not sure if you got to know Vanessa Ford during your time here at JSC, but she was in the same interview group with you. She also made the cut and has accepted. You two are the only finalists to make it through from that session."

"No men from our group, huh?" Joan asked, and then could not quite believe she'd let that slip.

But Antonio laughed. "No," he said. "I am afraid they were not up to snuff."

SUMMER 1980

IN THE MONTHS AFTER LEARNING SHE WOULD BE JOINING THE ASTRO-
naut corps, Joan did three things.

First, she gave notice at Rice.

On her last day, the Physics and Astronomy Department threw
her a going-away party. By the punch bowl, Dr. Siskin asked—in a
way that struck Joan as remarkably transparent—how she'd managed
to pull this off. Joan said, "Luck, I guess," and then regretted it.

Joan knew that Dr. Siskin, and most men like him, had never
taken a good look at her. She was used to it. After all, she was not
Barbara. She had never commanded the attention of the entire room
with how great she looked in a dress or how well she delivered a
comeback. Once, when Joan was a teenager, her mother told her that
she and her sister each had their own strengths. She said that Barbara's were loud and Joan's were quiet, but both were powerful in
their own way. When her mother said this, Joan hugged her.

Joan knew she was easy to overlook. She was average height and a
bit stocky. She dressed simply. Her light brown hair was just past her
shoulders, but she didn't wear it feathered like some other women did.
Instead, she pulled it back loosely. Sometimes, when Joan saw herself

in photographs, she was struck by how beautiful her smile was, her dimples making her face seem friendly and bright. In high school, Adam Hawkins had said so. But she didn't expect other people to notice.

She also didn't expect other people to ask what she did in her spare time (she was a classically trained pianist, had run two marathons, was an avid reader and an amateur portraitist, among other things). When people came into her office and saw some of the sketches on her wall, she knew they'd assume she'd bought them somewhere. When someone admired them, she never bothered to tell them she'd drawn them. The praise was never the point. In any case, no one in a long time had asked her about herself enough to know any of this. And Joan found a familiar peace in going unnoticed.

So it came as a huge shock to the men in the department, many of whom fancied themselves secretly destined for victory, to see that the woman they'd overlooked was lapping them in a race they did not know had started.

Joan looked around the room, put her drink down, and left her own goodbye party early.

THE SECOND THING JOAN DID was tell her family she was going to be an astronaut candidate.

"It's all because you suggested I apply," Joan said to Barbara over the phone.

"I did?"

"Because of the commercial."

"Oh, right," Barbara said. "Well, you're welcome."

Her mother and father flew out from Pasadena. They all went out to a celebratory dinner, at which Barbara mentioned multiple times that she hoped this didn't mean Joan was moving to Clear Lake. After all, Frances needed her close by. Joan explained three separate times that it *did* mean she was moving to Clear Lake. There were apartments right next to the Johnson Space Center. It was only thirty minutes south of her current place, and regardless, she would never in a million years miss a second she could spend with Frances.

And then Joan leaned over to Frances and kissed the part in her hair at the top of her head.

There were things Joan had done with Frances since Frances was a baby—turning her upside down, carrying her on her shoulders, throwing her on the bed—that Frances was too big for now. But Joan would always be able to kiss the top of her head. Even if she had to get on a stool, one day, to do it.

When Joan and Barbara were little, they'd played make-believe for hours. Joan was always a doctor or a nurse or a teacher. Barbara would pretend to be a singer, a ballet dancer, or a figure skater. But once Barbara could see adolescence approaching, there was no more pretending. She went out in search of things Joan knew nothing about.

Though four years younger, Barbara snuck out to her first party before Joan, had her first kiss before Joan, had her first drink before Joan. What could Joan offer someone so much more worldly than her? How could Barbara look up to someone so far behind?

A few years later, when Joan was pursuing her PhD at Caltech and Barbara was in her junior year of college at the University of Houston, Barbara called Joan late one night, sobbing.

She'd gotten pregnant.

"You're the only one I could call," Barbara said.

Joan could barely believe what she was hearing. Not that Barbara had found herself here—in fact, Barbara had already gotten pregnant and miscarried once as a teenager. The shock was that Barbara had called *Joan.*

"What do I do?" Barbara asked.

Joan stayed on the phone with her for three hours, talking it through. She gleaned a lot of surprising information from that conversation. Namely, that there was more than one possible father, that Barbara was unwilling to suffer the indignity of trying to figure out which it was, that she was intent on hiding this as long as possible from their parents, and that she'd stopped going to classes weeks ago.

Joan was trying to find the words for how to respond to the last bit of information when Barbara's roommate came in and Barbara rushed off the phone.

Then Barbara called again two days later, this time with a clarity of purpose.

She had realized this was a great thing! This pregnancy was the answer to a question Barbara had been asking herself for years. *What was she meant to do with her life? This!* The reason she had yet to find a passion was because she'd been waiting for this child to give her life a shape.

Joan knew that Barbara did not understand the full weight of the task. But there was little to be done about it now.

"Do you think I'll be a good mother?" Barbara asked Joan.

Joan had a hard time imagining Barbara as someone's mother, but the simplest way of looking at it seemed true. "You've always been incredible at anything you've put effort into, Barb."

"Thank you, Joan. That means a lot."

After that, Barbara kept calling. Barbara needed money for an apartment. Barbara needed help finding out if she could get her tuition money refunded now that she was officially dropping out. Barbara needed Joan there when she finally told Mom and Dad. *Barbara needed Barbara needed Barbara needed.*

When their parents were upset that Barbara was single, pregnant, and dropping out of college, Barbara called on Joan to defend her.

When their mother offered to be with her when the baby was born, Barbara asked for Joan instead.

When Frances was born that May, this gorgeous gangly thing, it was Joan who held her first. It was Joan who handed her over to their mother to hold, Joan who filled out Frances's birth certificate.

Frances Emerson Goodwin.

Joan spent months sleeping on the sofa in Barbara's new one-bedroom apartment in Houston. She had to. Frances needed someone to arrange her checkups. Frances needed someone to rock her. Frances needed someone to feed her when Barbara was too tired to wake up. *Frances needed Frances needed Frances needed.*

It felt weird to Joan—holding a baby. She always felt as if she was going to break her, always worried she wasn't supporting her head enough. Frances was colicky the first few months; there were times when she would not stop crying, no matter how much Joan held her. Joan sometimes could not hear her own thoughts above the screaming.

And Joan wondered how she'd gotten here. This was not the life she'd seen for herself, caring for a baby.

Joan's bright, sharp brain—her most beautiful muscle—turned to mush from too little sleep. Sometimes, unsure what else to do, Joan would take Frances out of the apartment, stare up at the night sky, and talk to her about the phases of the moon. Frances often cooed then. It was probably just the cool night air, but Joan also suspected that Frances was starting to focus, perhaps even taking in Joan's finger, bright against a dark sky. *Maybe this was who she could be to Frances. Maybe this was their language.*

But that clarity was fleeting. The rest of the time, caring for Frances felt like trudging through mud up to the knees.

Still, as soon as Joan could, she did what Barbara asked and applied to transfer to Rice to be close to Barbara and Frances.

"I do not understand why it has to be you," her mother said to Joan when Joan was accepted and began to plan her move. "Why it can't be me? Why can't I help with my own grandchild?"

Joan did not know how to say to her mother what they all already knew: Barbara had chosen Joan, and Barbara always got what she wanted.

Looking back on it, Joan could see that the universe had unfolded just as she had needed it to. It had given her something she had not even been smart enough to have wanted. Because those tiny moments with Frances—in the courtyard showing her a waxing gibbous moon, blowing bubbles and teaching her shapes, tickling her under her chin and making her laugh—came more and more often, each day. They grew longer, settled in deeper. Until one day, years ago, Joan took Frances to the playground and, as she watched Frances befriend another kid on the slide, realized that she could not envision a good week where she did not at least once get to brush her thumb against Frances's soft, dewy cheeks. To tickle Frances's chin—and hear that laugh—was to need it forever.

The night of their dinner, Frances looked up at Joan and smiled. She was six years old. Her light brown, shoulder-length hair was no longer baby fine. Her bright blue eyes picked up on more of what was going on around her than ever before. She'd stopped wearing Mary Janes and dresses last year. Now she wore corduroy pants and T-shirts most of the time. She'd begun using words Joan was surprised she knew, like "horrid" and "pivotal." She did not have a "great" day but a "splendid" one; when she tasted a new food, it did not taste "bad" but "peculiar." She'd already skipped a grade in school.

Frances had been born just yesterday; Joan was sure of it. And yet, Frances was going into second grade and Joan was going to be an astronaut.

"Joanie?"

"Yes, Franny?"

"Wait! You're the only one who calls me Franny!"

"And you're the only one who calls me Joanie!"

Frances laughed. "When you get a new place to live, can I come visit?"

"She's not getting a new place," Barbara said.

THAT WAS THE THIRD THING Joan did. Days later, she stopped by Barbara's with a pound cake from the bakery on the corner and explained to her sister one final time that she was, in fact, moving.

"Well, fine," Barbara said. "But you still need to take Frances on the weekends. I can't afford a babysitter."

"I will see Frances on the weekends, just like I do now."

"You're really excited about this astronaut thing, huh?" Barbara said. She pushed the pound cake away, and Joan recognized this as her punishment.

"Yeah, I am. And I'm scared, but in a way I've never really been before. Which I think is good. It's exciting."

"You're really lucky," Barbara said, her voice lightening. "That you are free to do something like this. No kid or husband or anything holding you back. I always think about where I would go if I could. And I think London or Paris . . . but you're going to the stars. You're thinking so much bigger."

Joan felt a swelling in her throat.

Later that week, Joan packed up her entire apartment. When the moving company arrived, they took all of her stuff and drove off. Less than an hour later, she opened the door to her new place. It smelled like fresh paint.

That night, she went out for a walk in her new neighborhood and ran into Donna Fitzgerald and John Griffin, two of the other mission specialists who were a part of Group 9. She recognized them from the day NASA had gathered them for a photo of the incoming class.

Donna had blue eyes and dark brown hair that was thick and bouncy, so much so that Joan thought she looked like she could be in an ad for shampoo. And John—with such an easy smile and eyes that crinkled—had the most soothing voice Joan had ever heard. It was low and gravelly and made Joan like him the moment she heard him speak.

"I guess we're all predictable as shit, huh?" Donna said. "Join the astronaut corps and get a one-bedroom apartment by the campus the week before training starts."

Joan laughed. "Well, I don't know. Maybe John got a two-bedroom."

"Sorry to disappoint," he said. "It's a one-bedroom, just like yours. Pretty sure Lydia Danes is in the building, too. I think I saw her."

"Ah, well," Joan said. "So much for being original."

Joan would remember this moment for weeks to come. Because within days, Donna and Griff would come to feel like such close friends that she laughed to think she'd ever called Griff "John."

THE MORNING OF THE FIRST ALL-ASTRONAUTS MEETING, JOAN, DONNA, and Griff walked over to JSC together, already cracking up at their own inside jokes, overusing their new punch line: *"But that's not going to happen here."*

Griff had said it the first time a few days prior, talking about how he'd been the big man on campus at his New England prep school: valedictorian, class president, and captain of the lacrosse team. When Donna arched her eyebrows, implying that maybe he expected to be just as big a deal at NASA, he quickly added, "But that's not going to happen here." And all three of them laughed.

Donna then used the line not even a half hour later, when talking about her previously dramatic and volatile love life.

Then Joan told them about how she'd been considered an astronomy nerd by almost everyone she'd ever known and added, in a sarcastic tone that surprised her in how well she nailed the joke, "But I bet that's not going to happen here."

As they made their way onto campus that morning, they spotted Lydia Danes up ahead. She was slight—no taller than five-two, her body wiry—but to Joan there was something terrifyingly invincible about her. Perhaps it was the way she moved with such intense focus. As if enjoying the walk would threaten to waste her time.

The night before, Donna had asked Lydia if she wanted to walk over with them in the morning. Lydia had never given her an answer.

"There's always one in a group who thinks their shit doesn't stink," Donna said.

"Oh, but Donna . . ." Griff said.

"Don't!" Joan said.

"That's not going to happen here," he said.

Joan shook her head and smiled.

"I'm telling you," Donna said. "She's rude."

Joan watched Lydia walk ahead of them. "You can't take it personally," Griff said.

"She thinks she's better than everyone else," Donna said. "As evidenced by the way she keeps clarifying for people that I'm only an ER doctor, but she is a *trauma surgeon.*"

As Donna spoke, Joan began taking in the architecture around the campus. All brutalist, boxlike buildings made of windows and concrete. Somehow dated, and yet timelessly plain.

But as she glanced at the Mission Control building, something buzzed inside her. It had a personality to it, a spark of the '60s Apollo program flair. And Joan nearly froze in her tracks.

I'm at NASA.

They got to the conference room one minute early, which Joan considered four minutes late.

The three of them crammed in along the sides of the room, obeying the clear and unspoken hierarchy that the chairs were only for the astronauts, and the candidates would remain standing on the periphery. There was already a tension in the room that Joan could not name. Some of the astronauts were seated with their legs extended, taking up as much floor space as possible, making no attempt to create room for the new candidates. Joan, Donna, and Griff stood wordlessly along the wall. Lydia barely looked at the rest of them. The last person to dash in, just before Antonio began to speak, was Vanessa Ford.

Her curly hair was pulled back, her posture was tall and straight, her shoulders broad. She took off her sunglasses and tucked them into her shirt pocket, with her eyes narrow, her jaw tight. Then she clasped both hands behind her back and faced forward, her full attention on Antonio, at the front of the room.

And the thought that went through Joan's head was: *That's* an astronaut.

· · ·

LATER THAT NIGHT, GRIFF AND Donna headed out with some of the other astronaut candidates—which Joan now understood was what everyone meant when they said "ASCANs"—for drinks. They invited Joan, but she declined. She'd promised Frances she'd call her to tell her all about her first day, so she headed straight back to her apartment.

"Did you know that there are two pins I might get eventually?" Joan said to Frances over the phone.

"Like my Mickey Mouse pin?" Frances said.

"Yeah, close to that. But these pins are shaped like a star with three rays behind it, coming out of a halo. One is silver and one is gold."

"And they give you them for being an astronaut?"

"Hopefully, but not yet," Joan said. She was pulling at the twisted telephone cord in the kitchen, unraveling it as she spoke. Just two weeks ago, the phone had been brand-new. Now it was already tangled from use.

"A year or so from now, if I pass this program, they will make me an astronaut. And they will give me that silver pin, which means I am ready to fly. And then one day when I get chosen for a mission, and go up there and come back, that's when they'll give me the gold one. To symbolize that I have flown in space."

"I can't believe my aunt is going to space."

"Maybe one day," Joan said. "Yeah."

Joan kept the phone between her shoulder and her ear as she pulled a frozen dinner out of the freezer and popped it into the oven.

"I want to be an astronaut," Frances said.

What a time Joan lived in. To be able to tell her niece that she could be an astronaut.

"If you work hard at it, then you will," Joan said. "Now go brush your teeth. Every quadrant. You remember what the dentist said now that your molars have come in."

"I know," Frances said. "I will."

Once Joan hung up, she looked in the oven at her still-half-frozen dinner and felt a familiar sadness creeping over her. She turned off the oven, put the food in the fridge, and headed out to Frenchie's for dinner on her own.

She walked straight up to the bar and ordered a Caesar salad and the chicken marsala, then grabbed a book from her bag and began reading. But before she even got to the second paragraph on the page, someone sat down next to her.

Joan knew who it was before she saw her face. She also knew there was a scientific explanation for these moments in which she felt she could sense the future. Information was being received at such a rapid speed that it felt as if the reaction was coming in before the stimulus. But the sensation was eerie, nonetheless. She understood why people got confused sometimes, started calling things fate.

"Hi," Vanessa said.

"Oh." Joan put away her book. "Hi. I'm Joan. I've seen you around, but I don't think we've officially met."

"Vanessa."

Joan looked at Vanessa and tried not to stare. Vanessa's eyes were light golden brown, almost amber. Her hair was such a dark shade of brown it was verging on black. And there was so much of it, the curls taking up so much space.

"It is nice to formally meet you," Vanessa said.

Vanessa seemed more stoic than Donna, less high-strung than Lydia. Joan started to wonder what she must seem like to Vanessa. *Bookish.*

"No one has really introduced themselves to me," Vanessa said. "But you all seem to know each other already."

"Oh," Joan said. "It's because we all met about a week and a half ago. We moved into the same apartment complex."

"The one right next to campus?" Vanessa said, nodding. "Makes sense."

"Where do you live?"

"A bit further out."

"Didn't want to bunk with the rest of us?"

"No, it's not that," Vanessa said. She smiled out of the left side of her mouth and then laughed. "Or maybe it is. I like my privacy. Not sure I'm going to be good at this whole 'living in a fishbowl' thing."

Joan laughed as the bartender brought her salad and put it down in front of her. "Thank you," she said to him.

Vanessa leaned forward, gestured to the bartender. "Can I have a glass of cabernet and a steak, medium rare?"

Joan's salad seemed so boring now.

"I really am sorry none of us have spoken to you," Joan said. "It wasn't on purpose, but I regret it."

Vanessa sat back on the barstool, waved her off. "It's perfectly all right. I figured it was up to me to say hello. So, hello."

"Hello," Joan said. She speared a piece of romaine on her fork. It was disarming—a little confusing, maybe—to think of Vanessa as in want of company. She was the sort of woman who seemed like she could have any friend she wanted. Didn't the world revolve around women like her? She was tall and lean, with big eyes. Her hair was so shiny. That way she smiled out of the side of her mouth—certainly that pulled people in.

"Settling in okay?" Joan asked.

Vanessa shrugged as her glass of wine arrived. "I mean, it's hot as hell out here. But otherwise, it's going okay."

Joan nodded. "July is the worst of it. The humidity is brutal. You get used to it."

"Do you?"

Joan laughed. "No, I don't know why I said that. It's miserable."

Vanessa chuckled and sipped her wine.

This made no sense at all. Vanessa was the one who had come up to her and said hello. But now, somehow, it was Joan leaning toward her, as Vanessa sat there, cool in every sense of the world.

Detached. Effortless. Aloof.

Joan thought about Paul Newman in *Cool Hand Luke*—and got the sense that it would not end well for her if she challenged Vanessa to eat fifty eggs. If she challenged Vanessa to anything at all.

"How about you?" Vanessa asked. "How is it for Miss Popular over here?"

Joan laughed so loud that it startled the man a few seats down. She covered her mouth. Vanessa reached over and gently took her by the wrist, pulling her hand away from her mouth. Joan looked at Vanessa's fingers on her.

"You did him a favor," Vanessa said. "He was falling asleep in his beer. But, really, how are you settling in?"

"Well, wildly incorrect assumptions about my social status aside . . ." Joan said. "It's going all right."

"Glad to hear it."

Joan wasn't sure why she was still talking—what she was thinking, saying this out loud? "Though . . ."

"Hm?"

"Did you sense an . . . *undercurrent* today?" Joan asked, turning toward Vanessa. "When talking to almost anyone in the astronaut corps?"

"You mean the feeling that any of them would slit your throat for ten bucks?"

Joan laughed, this time at a completely reasonable volume. "Exactly!"

"Yeah, I suspect we have a horse race ahead of us," Vanessa said.

"Am I supposed to compete with you?" Joan asked. "And Donna and Griff and everyone? It seems like a lot of work, to do all that and still put all my time into training."

Vanessa raised her eyebrows. "Spoken like a real killer."

Their food arrived at the same time, and as Joan looked at her chicken, she wished she'd ordered Vanessa's steak.

"For what it's worth, I don't think you and I are going to have a problem," Vanessa said. "I don't think anyone's going to put us up against each other like they would Donna and Lydia. I mean, I'm an aeronautical engineer. But . . . you're the astrophysicist, right?" Vanessa said.

Joan corrected her: "Astronomer."

"What's the difference?"

Joan shook her head. "There barely is one."

"But there is a difference, clearly."

"An astrophysicist studies the physics of space, whereas my focus is on space itself, the sun in particular. Then again, you can't study space without studying the physics of space. And time. Or math. Or anthropology and the history of humans' understanding of the stars. Or mythology and theology, for that matter. It's all connected."

Vanessa nodded. "And that's why you like it."

"Hm?"

"You're smiling as you're talking."

"I am?"

Vanessa grinned out of the side of her mouth again, and Joan wondered if it was one of those quirks she was born with or if she'd practiced it, knowing how captivating it would be.

"Yes," Vanessa said. "You are. I love that. I love when people love what they do."

"I do love what I do. I have been . . . I don't know . . . obsessed with the stars since I was in elementary school. During the winter, when it got dark out early enough, I would lie in the backyard and look up at the night sky, just aching to touch the stars. I'd sit there with my hand stretched out as far as I could reach, trying to convince myself I could scoop them into my hand. I begged my parents to buy me a Unitron telescope for my twelfth birthday. I had never made a fuss about anything before, never asked for so much as a doll, I don't think. But I had to have that telescope. I had to see the stars up close. And that was before we landed on the moon, mind you."

"You're like the girls who liked the Beatles before they went on *Ed Sullivan*."

Joan laughed. "Yes, the moon landing was, for us space nerds, exactly like the Beatles on *Ed Sullivan*! I liked the moon first."

"Good for you."

"But I cannot claim to be cool enough to have liked the Beatles first. I barely like the Beatles at all."

"You don't like the Beatles?"

"I am . . . indifferent to the Beatles."

Vanessa's eyes went wide.

"Oh, it's not that big a deal," Joan said.

"It's . . . an illegal opinion to have."

Joan laughed. "The melodies are good, obviously. It's good music. But . . . it was a little simplistic, don't you think? I don't understand why it worked so well."

"Why what worked so well?"

"The pandering. To what little girls think love is like. It was just a bit much. 'I Want to Hold Your Hand' and 'All You Need Is Love.' 'Blackbird' is a great song. And 'Eleanor Rigby.' But the cheesy stuff just struck me as, well, cheesy."

Vanessa finished her steak. "You are a curious one, Joan."

"Am I?"

"Yes, it's all very interesting."

Joan wasn't sure if Vanessa was making fun of her. But her gut said she wasn't.

"So, obviously, you like the Beatles," Joan said.

"I liked the Beatles when I was a young girl, hopelessly in love. . . . They explained it better than I could."

Joan looked away and sipped her water. What was she thinking, going on and on like this? Was it really that intoxicating, being asked about herself?

"So, we aren't going to have to compete," Joan said, changing the subject. "Me and you. You and me, I mean."

"Well, look, anything's possible. But they want us for different purposes, if I had to guess. They'll want you for designing and running experiments in space. They'll want me to help build the payloads. They aren't going to be measuring you against me, or vice versa."

Joan nodded. "I like that theory."

Vanessa nodded and then looked Joan in the eye. "Did it kind of kill you today?" she asked. "To be so close to it all? It killed me. I want to get up there almost as much as I want to breathe."

Something about the openness of Vanessa's face made Joan realize that, sitting on her barstool, her feet didn't touch the floor.

Joan blinked. "Yeah," she said. "I think it did kill me a little."

"I want to fly the fucking thing," Vanessa said. "Though God knows, since I've only flown privately, and not as a military pilot, it's going to be an uphill battle. But I want to go somewhere so few people have ever gone that you could name them all—and when people do name them, I want them to name me."

"I understand that," Joan said. "I understand that completely."

Vanessa looked at her, her gaze intense. "You do?"

"Absolutely. To do something so few people have ever done? No one will ever be able to take that away from us. If we do it, if we leave the planet, we will carry that with us into every room we enter for the rest of our lives."

Vanessa's shoulders relaxed. "Yes," she said. "Yes, that's . . ." She shook her head and exhaled. "That's exactly it." She grew more animated by the second. "Every time Antonio talks about the program, I can feel this ache in my chest. Like I'd die to get that chance. Like nothing on Earth will ever matter to me as much as getting up there. It's what I was born to do."

Vanessa was so lit up that Joan forgot for a moment that she was right there next to her, that Vanessa was not onstage in a play or on a TV show.

"I want to make my niece proud," Joan said when she remembered herself. "I want her to know that she can do anything."

"See, even if I did want to screw you over to get assigned before you, I certainly can't now. You're too noble," Vanessa said.

Joan laughed. "No, please, I insist you take the opportunity if it presents itself."

Vanessa pretended to consider this. Then she said, "I mean, joking aside, if it does come down to you versus me, or me versus that guy Griff, or whatever—I hope I don't do it with both elbows out, knocking everyone down. I hope I wait until I fully earn it instead of trying to steal the chance out from under someone. I want it bad, but still, I hope I do it right."

"You know, my mom used to say something to me when I was a kid," Joan said. "That you're reminding me of."

"What?"

"I always had the top grade in the class. And I would come home and brag about how I helped this boy who sat next to me who was struggling with times tables. Or I helped this girl with her spelling. Then one day, this boy joins our class and he's really good at math. Not as good as me, but almost. And he asks me for help. And I told him I'd think about it. But . . . I didn't want to. Bobby Simpson. I was so scared that he'd take the top score from me. I told my mom that I wasn't going to help him, and my mom said that if I was going to be proud of myself for being generous, that I had to do it even when it meant I might lose something. She said, 'You have to have something on the line, for it to be called character.'"

Vanessa looked at her. Joan shrugged. "Maybe that's you. Character when it counts."

"So I have character?" Vanessa said. "That's a nice thought. Not sure I've been accused of that before."

Joan smiled. "Well, let's see what you do, then. Just how honorable you turn out to be."

"What did you do?"

"Hm?"

"With Bobby Simpson."

"Oh, I helped him," Joan said.

"And did he beat you?"

Joan laughed. "No." And then: "I am very, very good at math."

Vanessa threw her head back and cackled, and Joan blushed at the attention it drew. But when Vanessa raised her hand to give her a high five, Joan laughed and returned it.

TWO DAYS LATER, JOAN WALKED into the first class on the space shuttle's design to see that Donna and Lydia were sitting at the front. Griff was talking to naval pilot Hank Redmond and mission specialist Harrison Moreau. There were more guys she didn't know well yet, mingling in the center. Vanessa was seated in the back.

"This seat free?" Joan asked her.

Vanessa barely looked up as she opened her notebook and grabbed her pen. "Wide open. You're my only friend so far, Goodwin, you know that."

"Well, as your friend, don't call me Goodwin."

Vanessa glanced up at her. "Oh, c'mon."

Joan sat down. "Goodwin feels like . . ." Joan said, trying to explain it. "I'm not sure."

There was a part that Joan was going to have to play at NASA. She understood that. Wearing the navy polos and khaki chinos she and Donna had gone out and bought together to fit in. Going out drinking together most nights. Hanging with the guys. Entertaining the posturing from the military side. Fine. She could sense what was expected of her. She was ready for it. But for it to extend to what should be the more honest moments . . .

"It feels like I'm pretending to be somebody else. I call people by their first names. I'd be playacting calling you Ford," she said. "When really, you're a full person, with a first name."

Vanessa put down her pen. "Are you always this earnest?"

Joan had not meant to be particularly earnest, but this *was* what she was like. "Yes, I believe so."

Vanessa shook her head and laughed.

"Look, I'll call you Ford when it's appropriate," Joan said. "I'm not entirely opposed to it. I just . . . you know, if we're going to be friends, let's be friends."

"All right," Vanessa said with a smile. "Fine, Jo, if that's what you want, that's what you got."

Joan shook her head and rolled her eyes, ready to tell Vanessa that she didn't go by Jo. That no one had ever called her Jo in her life. But she couldn't quite make it come off her tongue.

THERE IS A THEATER ABOVE MISSION CONTROL THAT LOOMS OVER THE flight center like a mezzanine hovering over an orchestra. And when Joan first walked in and saw, through the glass, the consoles lined up in rows along the floor and the telemetry up on the screens, she felt a great sense of occasion.

There had been a lot of thrilling firsts lately. The first time on the campus, the first night the entire group of ASCANs went to the Outpost Tavern together, the first time seeing the Saturn V rocket and the space suits used during the Apollo program.

But walking into Mission Control created a pull she felt deep down in the layers of her skin. It was the same feeling she'd had when she'd first seen the belts of Jupiter through her telescope. The same one as when she'd convinced her parents to take her to Death Valley the summer before her senior year and—with the clearest view of the sky she'd ever yet seen—she'd spotted the Andromeda Galaxy, two and a half million light-years away.

Astronomy was history. Because space was time. And that was the thing she loved most about the universe itself. When you look at the red star Antares in the southern sky, you are looking over thirty-three hundred trillion miles away. But you are also looking more than five hundred and fifty years *into the past*. Antares is so far away that its light takes five hundred and fifty years to reach your eye on Earth. Five hundred and fifty light-years away. So when you look out at the sky, the farther you can see, the further back you are looking in time. The space between you and the star *is time*.

And yet, most of the stars have been there for so long, burning so bright, that every human generation could have looked up and seen them. When you gaze up at the sky and you see Antares, with its red-

dish hue, in the middle of the constellation Scorpius, you are looking
at the same star the Babylonians cataloged as early as 1100 B.C.E.

To look up at the nighttime sky is to become a part of a long line
of people throughout human history who looked above at that same
set of stars. It is to witness time unfolding.

That was the stuff that made her knees buckle.

Standing there in the theater of Mission Control, Joan felt excep-
tionally aware that she was not just embarking on a grand adventure.
She was also joining the succession of those dedicating their life to
working to understand this Earth, and the galaxy around it, for the
betterment of all of humanity. She was part of something that had
started well before recorded history and continued through the times
of Aristotle and Aryabhata and al-Sufi and Shoujing and Copernicus,
through Galileo and Kepler and Rømer and Newton, the Herschels
and Leavitt and Rubin and Einstein and Hubble and beyond.

She knew her name would never be on that list. She had no desire to add her name to a list like that, in part because the idea that
astronomy advances because of any one great mind struck her as
simplistic. It was a collective pursuit, groups and cultures building
upon and learning from what came before them.

But standing there at Mission Control, looking at the same com-
puters they had used to put astronauts on the moon, Joan knew that
even if she had erred here and there on her journey through life, she
was on the right path now. Because she was now contributing, in
such a thrillingly direct way, to the larger goal.

To learn what lies out there and, in so doing, perhaps how we got
here.

As everyone took their seats, Griff sat down next to her.

"Morning," he said.

"Morning."

"I overslept. Can you tell?"

The back of his tie hung lower than the front, he'd missed a belt
loop, and the roots of his hair were damp with sweat.

"The truth?" Joan asked.

"That bad, huh?" Griff said.

Joan waved him off. "You're handsome enough," she said. "They forgive handsome men anything."

Griff laughed. "I had no idea you were such a charmer," he said.

Joan laughed, too. "Honestly, neither did I."

Donna came into the room. Joan waved, but Donna didn't see her. Joan watched as Donna began to take a seat next to Hank. As Donna sat down, Hank smiled at her. Donna smiled back and then looked around. Then, suddenly, Donna stood up and took a seat three seats away, by herself. Vanessa ended up taking the seat next to Hank.

Joan turned toward the front and bit her lip. She'd known Donna for only a few weeks but knew her well enough. Joan shook her head. *Already!*

Being completely immune to romantic rituals herself, Joan could spot them better than almost anyone. It was true, she had never had a real boyfriend. Had been on only a few dates. She had been kissed, a few times, by Adam Hawkins. And she had not cared for it. She was not offended or grossed out. But it felt, to her, like people were making a very big deal out of what was, essentially, no different from eating a cracker.

Of course, she did not discuss this with anyone anymore. Because every time she'd come close, it became clear no one would understand.

Not her mother, not her father, not Barbara (certainly not Barbara). Her girlfriends from undergrad kept assuming the issue was that she was shy or afraid. When the reality was much simpler: she was not like them. Why was it so hard for them to imagine that she had more interesting ways to spend her time? They mystified her just as she mystified them.

But there was one giant silver lining of being on the outside of it all. From afar, Joan could spot what everyone else could not see up close. Like how botanists know more about leaves than trees do.

Case in point: it was clear to her that Donna and Hank were sleeping together.

Joan tried to hold back a sly smile. Not being interested in romance herself didn't make it any less intriguing. *Donna and Hank. Huh.* She wouldn't have predicted that one.

Lydia ducked in at the last moment and snagged the seat behind Joan. She leaned in toward Joan's ear.

"Did I miss anything?"

Joan shook her head. "You're fine."

"I heard today is about Apollo 1," Lydia said.

Joan and Griff both turned to look at her.

"Really?" Griff said.

"Yeah," Lydia answered.

"Oh, gosh. I'm not sure I . . ." Joan said.

"You're not sure what? That you can handle it?" Lydia said. "Because if not, then you should probably leave the program."

Joan and Griff turned to the front of the room, and as they did, Griff raised his eyebrows at her. But Joan didn't engage. Lydia was entirely right.

The instructor, a man with a crew cut who, Joan learned, was Jack Katowski, walked to the front of the room.

"It's important that you understand what's at stake here," he said. "For those of you coming from the military, this will be less of a surprise. But for you civilians, this may be the first time in which you have embarked on an endeavor with this magnitude of risk. Going into space is not for the faint of heart. Great men have died in the pursuit of space exploration. If you are not prepared to face the sacrifices that may be required in order to serve this country in this unprecedented undertaking, it is best that you realize that now."

Joan could hear people shifting in their seats, leaning forward.

"We have lost nine men here at NASA over the last twenty years. All but one during training or testing. Here today, I'd like to talk to you about the weight of what you are signing up for. And I'd like to start by making sure you all understand the significance of the Apollo 1 fire."

Joan looked at Griff and took a deep breath. She felt Lydia's hand, ever so briefly, on her shoulder. And then it was gone. When Joan turned to acknowledge her, Lydia frowned and gestured for her to pay attention.

"As you are all aware, Apollo 1 was supposed to be the first crewed mission of the Apollo program, originally designated as AS-204. But in January 1967, a fire erupted in the cabin during a launch rehearsal. All three astronauts—Gus Grissom, Ed White, and Roger Chaffee— were locked inside. None of them survived. At NASA, we honor the people we have lost by referring to them as being 'on an eternal mission.' But please do not let the euphemism soften what happened here—and what you all risk, by being a part of this program."

He pressed a button. Within seconds, Joan realized he was playing the recorded audio from inside the cabin of Apollo 1.

"Flames!"

"We've got a fire in the cockpit. It—"

Every muscle in Joan's body tensed as she heard a man screaming. And then another and another.

Joan could feel the tension in the room as they listened to the men's increasingly desperate voices. Joan could hear their movements as they scrambled to get out. She could see it, could feel it. What it must have felt like to be trapped there, knowing they were going to die.

Joan could not get Frances out of her mind. How would Barbara explain it to her if something like that happened to Joan? How might Frances be forever changed by a tragedy like that?

Joan was not afraid to die. She had always felt that she was prepared for the nothingness that awaited her. She was happy, in some ways, to know that her body would decompose. That she would give back to the Earth all she had taken from it.

But Frances.

She might be fine with dying, but she was not fine with leaving Frances.

The transmission ended after only seventeen seconds. Everyone in the room knew what that meant. Joan's entire body felt heavy, her legs concrete, her head a magnet pulled to her chest. She could not look at Griff. But when she managed to raise her head, briefly, she saw that he could not look at anyone, either.

"Most of our days here at NASA are good ones. We achieve things once believed to be impossible. But there have been some days that we never see coming. Days that stick with us forever. That may cost some of us our lives. If you cannot accept that this risk lies ahead in all we do here," Jack said, "now is your chance to make a different choice. To choose a different life for yourself. A safer one."

The theater was quiet. There was no shuffling of feet. No one fiddled with papers. For a moment, Joan felt a strong sense that this entire undertaking was a mistake. Perhaps humans should not do this. The shuttle was nothing more than a pair of wax wings.

When Joan finally exhaled and looked up, Griff was pinching the bridge of his nose, and Hank was staring straight forward. Donna's chest visibly rose and fell. Vanessa was so lost in thought, Joan could not even catch her eye.

Then Joan turned to look at Lydia. The color was gone from her face. The two of them looked each other in the eye. *Could they do this? Could they really stay here in this room knowing what it might one day mean?*

Not a single person left.

DAYS LATER, EVERY MEMBER OF GROUP 9 STOOD ON THE TARMAC AT EL-lington Field in front of a fleet of Northrop T-38 Talons—white jet trainers with glass cockpits barely big enough for two people. The T-38s were *supersonic,* meaning they could fly faster than the speed of sound. And they could go ten thousand feet higher than a commercial airplane.

As the ASCANs stood in front of the jets, Joan began to understand just how large the disparity was between the military astronauts and the mission specialists. She had not noticed the difference in the classroom, where it favored her. But here, in a flight suit on the airfield, with the wind drying out her eyes, the gap between them felt vast, its edges sharp.

"As you know, if you are not a military pilot," the instructor said, "you will be a backseater for the entire time you fly here at NASA."

Joan had already known she'd be relegated to the backseat and was grateful for it. But when she looked over at the rest of her colleagues, she could see that Vanessa's jaw was clenched.

Soon the group was divided, and the military guys made their way to the other side of the tarmac.

Joan could not think of a single pilot she had gotten to know. Some of them, like Hank, seemed nice enough. But a lot of them kept making the kinds of cracks that irritated her.

At first it was things like "I've never been so up close and personal with so many women," at the gym on campus. And then it was a comment one of them made about the women's "sturdiness" during one of the facility tours. There were innuendos about skirts, cracks about penis envy.

Just yesterday, Lydia had been bemoaning the fact that they'd have to meet on the tarmac so early in the day, instead of easing in with classroom instruction first. Joan had disagreed and said that she was "glad to get the hard part done first."

At which point, one of the pilots, Jimmy Hayman, said, "I've got a hard part you can do first."

Joan stared right at him, unsure how to respond. But then Lydia *laughed*. And in the moment, Joan wanted to slap her.

Didn't Lydia understand that if one of them made it seem like it was okay, the rest of them would be sidelined as humorless? Didn't Lydia get that this was how the men kept them separate and underestimated? With these small jokes that made them look petty if they got upset? Couldn't Lydia see how it worked?

"Hayman," Griff had said as he walked into the room, "cut that out."

Jimmy shut up then. Joan knew she was supposed to be grateful, though she resented the need for it at all.

"Thank you," she whispered to Griff when she sat down.

He shook his head. "Don't thank me for doing the bare minimum," he said. "It does a disservice to us both."

Obviously, the mission specialists weren't immune to bad taste, but they weren't as overt about it. And so Joan preferred it when she was grouped with Vanessa, Donna, and Griff. Even Lydia, Harrison, and the others were all right.

The instructor refocused on them as the pilots left.

"As mission specialists, you will be required to gain significant flying experience here at NASA, fifteen hours of flight time a month, for the length of your time in the corps. You will not take off and land the jet yourselves," he said. "But you will learn a lot from that backseat—including how to navigate and, occasionally, how to handle the aircraft while in the air.

"As you know, flying is not without its myriad risks. Today we will start slow. You will watch the pilots from the ground as they take off, barrel-roll, and land," he said. "Think of it as a flight show, knowing that in the future, you'll ride shotgun."

Joan looked to Vanessa, whose face showed nothing. But Joan already knew what she was thinking.

The flight instructor had to raise his voice over the sound of the engines starting.

"Before you are allowed in the planes," he shouted, "you will have to learn how to survive being thrown out of one. First thing tomorrow you will be leaving for water survival training."

IN THE SWAMPY AUGUST HEAT, Joan, Griff, Donna, Vanessa, Lydia, Harrison, and the other two mission specialists, Ted Geiger and Marty Dixon, had departed for Homestead Air Force Base, in Florida, for three days to learn how to bail out over the ocean.

In their first test, they'd been strapped to a parachute and then tied to the back of a speedboat. One by one, each of them had been dragged through the ocean while attempting to keep their head above water for as long as possible. They'd had mixed results. Vanessa and Lydia kept calm. Marty almost drowned and had to take a rest on the boat. Donna and Griff ended up somewhere in the middle. And Joan took so much water into her stomach and lungs that she was burping for hours afterward. Her head was thrashed so hard by the chop of the waves that she still had a headache the next morning.

But still, she had done it.

The next day, in the open water, she had successfully swum beneath her floating parachute, come up for air on the other side, and inflated her life vest. It had taken her a few tries—and one full moment in which she thought she might be drowning—but again, she succeeded.

But today was the biggest test. One she was not sure she could pass.

They would start on the deck of a large boat, connected to both a parachute and a harness that were attached to a speedboat. When the speedboat accelerated, they would run off the edge of the first boat and let the wind catch their parasail, the speedboat pulling them high over the ocean.

When they were hundreds of feet in the air, they would disconnect their harness from the tether to the speedboat. This would send them crashing into the water, where they'd have to get themselves to the surface, inflate a life raft, and then crawl into it.

If, until this point, Joan had been able to convince herself that being an astronaut was a cerebral affair, she was cured of it now as she sat on a boat just off Biscayne Bay with a harness on, preparing to crash-land in the ocean.

She wiped the sweat off her forehead. She kept imagining the moment when she was supposed to disconnect from the boat.

Griff was guzzling water like his life depended on it. Donna was chattering away, as if talking nonstop would dispel her terror. Vanessa was silent, watching the wake behind the boat.

"There are sharks in the water," Griff said to Joan under his breath. "Just because we didn't see them the past two days doesn't mean they aren't there. Right?"

"Here, mostly hammerheads and tiger sharks," Marty said. "I'd be surprised if we saw a great white, but it's certainly possible. Maybe some bull sharks."

"So then just say yes," Lydia said. "Nobody needs a list."

Donna had told Joan that Marty and Lydia had slept together that first Friday they'd all gone out to the Outpost. This had made perfect sense to Joan. Both of them were more in love with the sound of their own voices than listening to anyone else. She pictured them carrying on two conversations at once, talking only to themselves, and having the most wonderful time.

But today, Marty said something about Atlantic water currents and Joan saw Lydia roll her eyes. So, unless Joan was mistaken, it seemed probable that Lydia had ended it.

People say opposites attract, but Joan had found this to almost never be true. People just couldn't see the ways they were drawn to exactly who they feared—or hoped—they might be.

Lydia and Marty were now quarreling, Griff and Ted looked seasick, and Joan could not stand to listen to Donna talk anymore.

She turned to Vanessa. With her hair pulled back, it was easier to see that Vanessa's cheeks were a little rosy, her skin smooth without any makeup. Joan had always worn a little mascara, a little powder. She'd been beaten into it by Barbara's taunts as a teenager. *Plain Joan.*

"You're not afraid," Joan said to Vanessa. She'd meant it as a question, but it came out as an observation.

"I am," Vanessa said. "Specifically of the part where we have to get out from under the parachute."

"But you seem so calm."

Vanessa nodded. "Yeah, I suppose I am."

"Braver than me," Joan said.

"No, not braver than you."

Their boat slowed as it met up with the speedboat.

"I'm . . ." Joan blew all the air from her lungs. "I'm terrified," she said. "It doesn't even make any sense. I passed the other two tests well enough. But today, I . . ." She would swear her hands were shaking except that she could see they were completely still.

"Do you know the difference between bravery and courage?" Vanessa said.

Joan considered the question. "I don't think so."

"My dad taught me when I was little. Bravery is being unafraid of something other people are afraid of. Courage is being afraid, but strong enough to do it anyway."

"Oh," Joan said.

"Neither of us are particularly brave right now," Vanessa said. "But both of us are going to be courageous."

Joan again imagined herself disconnecting from the boat.

"Okay," she said. "Okay."

Griff went first.

Joan watched every second. The sun blinded her as he got higher, but she could not look away. He detached from the speedboat and drifted on his parachute down to the open water. And then he was gone under the surface. She kept watching, holding her breath, waiting for him to pop up.

A second went by. Then another. And then there he was.

Joan inhaled.

She watched as he inflated his raft. It took him a few attempts before he could get himself onto it, but on the fourth try, he managed it. A second later, he put his fist up in the air.

"If he can do it, you can do it," Vanessa said.

Joan nodded, unsure.

When it was Joan's turn, she took a deep breath.

"Don't think about it," Vanessa said. "Just go do it. And then you can tell your niece how courageous you were."

"Frances," Joan said.

"Yeah, you can tell Frances."

Joan got into position. They connected her harness to the speedboat. Her heart started to race. She stood on the edge of the deck, waiting for the go-ahead. She pictured telling Frances she had parachuted into the ocean from behind a speedboat. She laughed to think of it.

Okay, she thought, *here we go.*

When she got the thumbs-up, she took off, running as fast as she could. She felt the catch of the air as the speedboat accelerated. For a moment, she fought against the fear in her body. But then she gave in to it. She let herself feel the horror, and then it passed through her.

In fact, for a few slow seconds, Joan could feel nothing but the ocean air on her face. The smell of the brine of the sea overtook her nose and filled her lungs.

When she looked down, she could see the expanse of the dark blue ocean, how quiet it was, how steady, cut by the strong wake behind the boat.

When they gave her the signal, she put her hand on the latch of her harness and closed her eyes.

She disconnected.

Her parachute slowed her down, softened her descent enough that it felt like being cradled more than falling. And the view of the ocean drawing nearer felt a little mesmerizing. By the time her whole body landed in the water, she'd forgotten to panic.

Suddenly she was underwater, her ears clogged, her vision cloudy, her body dragged down by the weight of everything she was tied to. Her parachute darkened the ocean above her. She managed to get herself free from it and then twisted and turned, looking for the light of the sky. Soon she found it, just to her left, the sunshine diffused across the surface. She swam for it.

When she broke out into the air, she gasped and choked on the water. But when the breath rushed into her lungs, she wondered if anything had ever felt so good as breathing.

She inflated the raft and then managed to throw one leg over the side of it.

She dragged herself onto the raft swiftly, her back soon resting against the bottom, feeling the current of the ocean. She coughed up the salt water in her nose and her throat. She pushed her hair out of her face.

And then she looked up at the clouds, raised her hand in a thumbs-up, and smiled.

My God, she thought, *what else can I do?*

WHEN THE T-38 ASSIGNMENTS CAME IN, JOAN WAS GRATEFUL TO FIND out she'd be flying with Hank.

He was tall and broad-shouldered, with a Texas accent. He'd come out of Top Gun, the naval flight school in San Diego, so he and Joan shared some of the same Southern California references. Breakfast burritos, fruit trees, how cold the Pacific was. Joan also liked his sunglasses. He wore dark-tinted aviators that made him look like a movie star.

"Come on, girl," he said to her as they got in the jet. "Let's go fly a plane."

"All right, *boy*, let's go," she said.

He laughed as they got in. That was another thing she liked about him: he laughed at women's jokes.

Joan fit tight into the backseat, the weight of her helmet and harness already bearing down on her before he'd shot them into the sky. She could swear they were perpendicular to the Earth. She tried not to focus on how sick she felt in her belly as they reached higher and higher. She did her best to ignore the force of the air in her ears. She closed her eyes, trying to ward off the intensity of the headache. It reminded her of riding the Round Up as a kid when the carnival came to town, fighting the centrifugal acceleration flattening her body.

It reached a fever pitch, and she was not sure she could withstand the pressure.

But then they leveled out above the clouds and Joan gasped. The beauty of the pale pink puffs—soft blankets against the sky—startled her into focus. The steady hum of the wind drowned out almost everything except the sound of her own voice inside her mind. Which was such a gift. She had always been her greatest friend, her greatest guide.

Up here, all she could hear was that voice. The kindest version of her. *Look at the clouds, take a breath, do you see how pale the blue of the sky can be?*

Suddenly Hank's voice crackled in her helmet: "Tell me that's not the heavens."

"YOU ARE NEVER GOING TO believe this, but I was thirty thousand feet into the air!" Joan said that evening, holding Frances's hand as the two of them and Barbara walked into Joan's apartment. "And on Monday, we're going to fly upside down."

"*Upside down?*"

"Upside down! And by the way, I almost puked just going right side up! So who knows what's going to happen."

"Oh my *gosh*, you can't puke, Joanie!"

"I am obviously going to try not to!" Joan said. "But I might not be able to control it. I might just go, 'Oh no,' and then *blaaach*." Joan mimicked puking right over Frances's head. Frances laughed so loudly that Barbara asked her to please use a normal tone of voice and then looked at Joan with reproach.

As they settled in, Barbara told Joan how great the apartment looked and Frances immediately gravitated toward all of the portraits Joan had been working on when she couldn't sleep at night. There were a few of Frances with her big eyes and long eyelashes, one of Barbara, one of their father.

"You have to do Grandma," Frances said.

"I know, I really do," Joan said. "For some reason, I find it hard to draw Grandma."

Barbara looked at the portrait of herself, which was sitting on the nightstand. Joan saw a small smile on her face, even though Barbara tried to hide it. This was Joan's favorite part. To be able to show someone what they should love about themselves.

Barbara put the picture down, gently. "It's because you look like Mom."

"What?" Joan said.

"You look like Mom. I look like Dad. And you can't draw Mom because you don't like to draw yourself."

"I could draw myself."

"Oh," Barbara said. "Well, you don't ever draw yourself, so I just figured you didn't want to."

Joan considered this. "I just . . . don't find myself all that interesting, I suppose."

"Joanie, I think your face is *very* interesting," Frances said. "I like how you have tiny light freckles all over it and you have three gray hairs on the side of your head."

Joan laughed. "Thank you, my love." And then: "I ordered pizza for dinner." Barbara offered a tense smile, but Joan knew she wouldn't complain. Joan always paid, ordered too much, and sent Barbara home with the leftovers.

"Did you get pepperoni?" Frances asked.

"Yeah, and with extra anchovies because I know how much you love them."

"Noooooo!" Frances said, and Joan grabbed her and tickled her ribs. Barbara set the plates for dinner.

After dinner, Barbara sent Frances to get ready for bed. She was spending the night at Joan's, and the two of them were going shopping for back-to-school clothes the next day. It was their annual tradition. As Joan walked Barbara out, she handed her the leftover pizza. Then Barbara pulled Joan into the hallway.

"You seem happier," Barbara said. "Lighter."

"I do?" Joan felt a little jolt go through her.

"Yeah," Barbara said. "It's nice."

"Well, I guess . . ." Joan thought of that feeling up in the jet. The pale pink of the clouds. "I guess I am a little lighter."

"You've met someone," Barbara said.

"What? No!"

"I thought for sure that's what all this was. That glee in your voice."

"Barbara," Joan said. "No."

Barbara sighed. "I swear, Joan, every time I think I understand you, I'm more wrong than the time before."

"I'm not that hard to understand, Barb. I love my new job. It's . . . the coolest thing I've ever, ever, ever done."

Barbara looked at her, and Joan could feel the distance between them growing. She'd been just an arm's length away a second ago, but she was gone now.

"If only I could find something I love half as much as you love talking about stars."

Joan said good night to Barbara and went back inside her apartment with a smile still on her face. She could hear the condescension in her sister's voice, but she could not be angry.

Joan so loved the beauty in this world: showing people the stars, spotting the fuzzy glimmer of the Orion Nebula with just her eyes, the rare moments when auroras are visible even in the southern states because of intense geomagnetic storms, trying one more time to really nail Rachmaninoff's Prelude in C-sharp Minor, rereading *The Awakening*, listening to Joni Mitchell and Kate Bush, drawing for so long, so late into the night that her palm cramped, running so far that she forgot to think, taking Frances for ice cream and watching how long she deliberated over which flavor to choose, the smell of Frances's hair . . .

That was the stuff that made life worth living. And she worried Barbara didn't see that.

"All right, babe," Joan said once Frances was done with her shower. "Are we watching TV or reading a book?"

"Reading a book!" Frances said.

Joan began taking the throw pillows off the sofa. "Okay, if you're sure . . ." It was the easiest trick with Frances: if you let her choose, she'd choose the responsible option. But if you told Frances she couldn't do something, you'd get a battle for the ages. Joan had tried to explain this to Barbara, but Barbara didn't want to hear it.

Joan extended the sofa bed, and Frances got settled in, grabbing her book.

"Joanie," Frances said. "I love your new apartment. I wish I lived here."

"Aw, babe, you can stay here anytime you want. It's your place, too. Always."

Joan kissed her on the forehead and turned out the lights in the living room. She went into her bedroom.

And then, instead of grabbing her own book, she grabbed her sketchpad and a pencil. For the next hour, she tried to draw her own face.

IT WAS LATE AUGUST AND JOAN WAS STANDING BY HERSELF IN STEVE and Helene's backyard, watching Steve turn off the smoker while his daughters ran around the yard trying to catch fireflies. On the table next to her were the very few leftovers from the spread of brisket, macaroni salad, coleslaw, baked beans, and biscuits. People had not yet cut into the buttermilk pies or the Texas sheet cake. Joan was trying to remember the last time she'd eaten dinner alone. It had been far too long.

In their training, they had been split into two teams. The Red Team, led by a military pilot ASCAN named Duke Patterson, consisted of Donna, Harrison, Vanessa, Marty, and some of the pilots Joan still did not know well yet.

Joan's team, the Blue Team, was captained by Hank and included her, Griff, Lydia, Ted, and their own group of pilots, including Jimmy Hayman, whom Joan disliked more every time she spoke to him.

The Red Team would have instruction in the classroom in the morning and then head out in the T-38s in the afternoon. Joan's team would do the opposite.

Their days were packed. Between the lessons on engineering, oceanography, geography, anatomy, and other topics, Joan was absorbing so much information alongside her fellow ASCANs that it only made sense to study after hours with them, too. She and Griff had spent so many nights in his apartment, going over country borders and emergency medical procedures, that they now knew each other's takeout orders without having to ask. Every other evening there was some get-together, either at the Outpost or Frenchie's. Joan couldn't remember, even in college, being out so late, so often, with so many people.

The only thing she was actually enjoying right now at this party was the nearly empty beer bottle in her hand. She'd never tried a beer until Donna and Griff insisted. She'd been surprised to find that Coors Light was delicious.

Joan took a last sip and looked around. Most people seemed occupied. Maybe she could sneak out without anyone noticing.

But a moment later, Vanessa strolled up to her and handed her another beer. "You look like you're counting down the minutes until you can leave."

Joan laughed. "I think I've had my share of socializing for now," she said as they stood on the edge of Steve and Helene's pool. "Present company excluded from my complaining, of course."

Hank walked into the backyard, hours late to the BBQ. Everyone cheered, even Joan. They'd gone up in the T-38s four more times together since that first ride. Each time, Hank had let her take more control of the jet than the time before.

She found Donna's mooning over him to be a bit much. But she had to admit, he was one of the good ones. She thought of him the way she thought young children must think of Willy Wonka. Here was the door to all the magic and danger.

"I mean, Griff and Donna are great. Hank, I like. You're great. But some of these other guys, I could do without. No offense, but I could be at home right now with a good book."

Vanessa laughed and sipped her beer. "You're awfully grumpy."

"I am not *grumpy.*"

"It's a good thing."

"How is it a good thing? To be grumpy?"

"It gives you some much-needed dirt on your clothes."

"What?"

"Otherwise, you're a little too perfect," Vanessa said. "Smart, well-rounded, always five minutes early, nice to everyone. A little edge to you is good."

Joan turned to look at her. "I have plenty of edge to me."

"I know. You're grumpy and a little antisocial," Vanessa said, sipping her beer again. "So am I. It's nice to see."

Joan frowned.

"It's a compliment. You're like Marlon Brando," Vanessa said as she leaned in and shoved her shoulder into Joan's.

Joan tried to maintain her frown, but it wasn't working. "How am I anything like Marlon Brando?"

Vanessa put her beer down on a folding table covered with a vinyl tablecloth.

"Okay, so . . ." Vanessa said. "Before *Streetcar*, Marlon Brando was gorgeous, sure. But almost too beautiful. Maybe a little . . . boringly beautiful? But then, during the run of the play, he's goofing around, boxing some guys backstage. He gets decked in the face, right across the nose. Pow!"

Vanessa mimicked somebody getting knocked out. Joan was trying to stay irritated, but it was a helium balloon and she was losing her grip on the string.

"Breaks his nose. He's rushed to the hospital. The doctor does a shit job resetting it. It's totally crooked. And the producer, I don't remember her name, but it's this woman and she goes to the hospital and she says, 'Oh, no, Marlon, they've ruined your face.' But he doesn't care. He never gets it fixed. And he goes on to be a major star, bigger than anyone ever thought he'd be. And years later, she takes it back. It didn't ruin his face, it enhanced his face. Somehow, with that crooked nose, he was *more* handsome. He had been too perfect before. Now he had a flaw. Now he was somebody you could touch. He looked like the most handsome real man that ever lived, instead of some beautiful doll."

"It made him interesting," Joan said.

Vanessa snapped her fingers. "Exactly—it made him interesting."

"So my not liking this party is my crooked nose?"

"When somebody's too smooth, there's nothing to grab on to. Now that you've got a little edge to you, I can hang on."

"You didn't like me before?"

"I have always liked you, Jo," Vanessa said, picking up her beer. "You know that. I just like you more now."

Joan nodded. "Well, thank you for comparing me to Brando, I guess. No one's ever done that before."

"You also look a little like Ingrid Bergman—not that you asked," she said.

Joan tried to picture Ingrid Bergman.

"From *Casablanca*," Vanessa said.

"Oh," Joan said. And then: "Oh, wow, that's . . . that's very nice. I'm not sure I see it, but thank you." Joan just kept talking now, couldn't stop herself. "First time I really met you, I thought you seemed like Cool Hand Luke. Not that you're a man. Just . . . the attitude, maybe. Sorry, this is coming out wrong."

Vanessa put her hand on Joan's arm as if to stop her. "Joan," she said.

Joan looked at her.

"That's the nicest thing anyone's ever said to me."

Joan laughed. "It is?"

"Yes, it is. Thank you."

"Oh, well, you're welcome."

"I love Paul Newman. Who wouldn't want to be Paul Newman?"

Joan shrugged and laughed. "I mean, yeah, when you put it that way. Who wouldn't?"

Why had she been annoyed? She couldn't remember.

Duke's wife, Kris, opened the sliding glass doors to the living room and Steve's dog, a blue heeler named Apollo, came running out and pawing at Vanessa's leg.

"Oops!" Kris said. "Sorry!"

"No," Vanessa said, crouching down to pet him. "You're all right, aren't ya, buddy?"

Apollo rolled onto his back, and Vanessa scratched his belly.

"Apollo, you make me wish I could have a dog," she said.

"Why can't you?" Joan asked.

Vanessa looked up at her. "One day soon, I'm hoping to strap myself to a rocket and bounce out of the atmosphere. I'm not going to be able to take care of a dog."

"Oh," Joan said. "Okay. But couldn't you just get a dog sitter when you go on a mission?"

"I'm not going to put a dog through that. I'll just come over here and pet Apollo," Vanessa said and then rubbed his back and gave him a good pat.

"Vanessa!" Steve called from the side yard. "We need you! Antonio's Dodge is stalled."

Vanessa raised her eyebrows. "Come on, boy," she said. And then she smiled at Joan. "Bye, Jo."

Joan laughed as they walked away. She could leave now. But instead, she sat on the rough concrete, pulled her long skirt up to her knees, and put her feet in the pool. It was so warm, it felt like stepping into a bath.

She watched as Lydia floated by her with her eyes closed, hogging the only pool float. Lydia had refused to share with anyone enough times that no one asked anymore.

Griff swam up to Joan. "I have obtained very important, very confidential *insider* information," he said as he pushed his hair back off his face. "And if you play your cards right, I will read you in."

Joan looked at him. She'd long ago noticed he was objectively handsome. But she could see now that he'd probably had to grow into his features. And she wondered if that had made him an ugly duckling. She loved ugly ducklings.

"Lay it on me," Joan said. Maybe she had a bit of a buzz. She must have.

"Do you know Duke's real name?"

"I did suspect it wasn't Duke."

"It's *Chris*," Griff said. The pool lights had kicked on a few moments ago, just as the sun was setting. Griff's smile was lit from below.

"Oh, wow," Joan said.

"Yeah, so they are Chris and Kris," Griff said, pulling closer to the pool's edge, hovering close to her.

"So he let her be Kris," Joan said. "And he took on a nickname.

That is . . . that is very touching." She looked up at Duke and Kris, standing by the sliding glass doors with Steve's wife, Helene.

It was obvious how well Duke and Kris fit together. Duke was quiet and strong. Kris was small and spirited, with big hair. Duke told the stories and Kris hit the punch lines.

"No, she knew what she was doing," Duke was saying, with a smile.

"Oh, I absolutely did!" Kris added.

Helene laughed.

Joan was always curious what it was like on the inside of a marriage. What happened when it was just the two of them at home, Duke and Kris? Did she have to ask him for permission to buy new clothes? Did he sometimes tell her he didn't like what she made for dinner? Joan tried to ward off the sadness that always came when she pictured a marriage—any marriage.

Her parents' marriage seemed fine to her. Good, even. They still loved each other. Her mother, basically a vegetarian, made her father's favorite meatloaf most weekends with a joy that Joan had scrutinized for years but found completely sincere. Still, when she thought about it, a gloom dared to take over. You could develop your personality your entire life—pursue the things you wanted to learn, discover the most interesting parts of yourself, hold yourself to a certain standard—and then you marry a man and suddenly his personality, his wants, his standards subsume your own?

Joan knew that society was changing and some men were changing with it. Some of them now understood that a woman's career, her life, her passions were just as important as their own. But still, all Joan could think was that it was now just *two* people cutting off parts of themselves to make themselves fit together. A world of vegetarians cooking meatloaf.

"Goodwin, do you read me?" Griff said.

"Sorry, what?"

"I said, I'm going to head out in a minute. Do you want a ride?"

Joan had come with Donna, but any second now Donna was going to ditch her for Hank.

"Sure," she said, standing up.

Griff dried off and they said their goodbyes, including to Antonio and his wife, Jeanie.

When they got to the driveway, Vanessa had her head underneath the car's engine, next to Steve. Ted and Harrison were watching. Apollo was now at Steve's feet.

"How's it going on the Dodge?" Griff said.

The path to get by the car was narrow, and there was a hose on the ground. Joan saw where to step, but Griff put his hand on the small of her back to guide her. When Joan turned to look at him, he smiled sweetly at her.

She had been here before—not often, but enough to recognize it for what it was. The glances that lasted just a bit too long, the softer tone of voice directed only at her. It almost never ended easily. There was always a thrash or two, when she tried to kill it.

Joan moved forward quickly, away from his touch.

"Looks like Steve's got it," Harrison said. "I certainly couldn't figure it out."

"Actually, Vanessa spotted it," Steve said. "It was the vacuum pull-off on the choke."

Vanessa stood up slowly and wiped her hands on a rag. "A team effort."

Steve laughed, and then Vanessa saw Joan there, with Griff. "Off to read your book?"

"Caught red-handed."

"Well, good night, Brando."

Joan shook her head, "Yeah, yeah, yeah. Good night, Newman."

DECEMBER 29, 1984

FIRST GRIFF'S VOICE GONE.

Then Hank's.

Then Steve's.

Now Lydia's.

"Ford, we read you," Joan says.

Joan is now all Vanessa can hear, all that lies between her and isolation.

With the hand that's not pressed to Griff's suit, Vanessa bangs on the side of the airlock, trying to get someone's attention and wake them up. The force of it pushes her backward. She rights herself.

"LYDIA!" she screams. "STEVE! HANK! SOMEONE!"

The ghostly quiet of the shuttle overwhelms her. Suddenly she becomes aware of her body floating in microgravity. The slowness, the absence of both feet on the ground. She has never felt the full scope and terror of floating the way she does in this moment, tethered to nothing, unable to move.

"Ford, the cabin pressure has returned to safe levels and the airlock is fully pressurized. We want you to bring Griff out of the airlock."

Vanessa closes her eyes. This is another thing she learned as a child. That the world beyond the edges of her eyelids can and will be a dangerous place. But that she can hide from it for whole seconds at a time when she closes her eyes. So she stays there, and breathes. In once, out once.

When she opens her eyes again, she is surprised by the steadiness of her voice. "Copy that, Houston. Preparing to enter the cabin."

She takes her hand off Griff's stomach; it's no longer needed to protect him from the lack of pressure. And then she starts to open the hatch.

Once it's open, she begins to swim out of the hatch to the middeck with Griff in tow. She takes off both of their helmets.

She can work her way out of the pants of the space suit. But it is hard to maneuver the torso piece without assistance. The suits are designed for crew members to assist each other when getting in and out.

Vanessa begins to panic, claustrophobia setting in. She thrashes against the suit, which only makes it worse. She cannot lose control of herself right now. She counts her breaths and then she moves her shoulder in a way that feels unnatural, as if her collarbone might snap.

But then she stops.

Because there, floating toward her, is Hank. His entire body is swollen. His face is mottled, his skin covered in a rash so severe that for a moment, she thinks it is blood. But she realizes the blood is under his skin. She wants to ask him if he's okay.

But there's no doubt.

Hank is dead.

She closes her eyes and screams, breaking herself out of the rest of her suit. She has never heard her voice do this: it is a raw screeching sound. When she finally gets the suit over her shoulders, it catches against her forehead and scrapes the skin above her eye.

But then she slithers out of it.

She manages to remove Griff's suit, too, with somewhat less agony. Then she pulls down his cooling suit, exposing his chest and stomach, so she can assess his injuries. The shrapnel did not break through his skin, but there is already visible bruising across his lower

stomach, extending up into his chest. He must be bleeding inter-
nally. There is no way to know, right now, just how bad it is.

She should have told him not to leave the airlock hatch open.
One small shake of her head would have prevented this.

She could not have stopped the leak. That would have happened
no matter what. But she could have prevented the blow to his chest
if only she hadn't gone along with his stupid fucking idea. Instead, he
is floating in front of her, unconscious.

Vanessa looks down to see Hank underneath her. She closes her
eyes. *Do not think of Donna pregnant this past summer. Do not think of
the smile on Donna's face the night they announced they were engaged.*

Vanessa sees another pair of feet between the mid-deck and the
flight deck. She moves toward them.

When she gets to Steve, she holds in a yelp. He is lifeless, drift-
ing. *Dead man's float.*

There are droplets of blood in the air around him, which he must
have coughed up. She puts her hand to his neck and checks his pulse
without an ounce of hope, confirming what she already knows.

How can her heart sink in microgravity? But it does.

She does not want to think of Helene and the girls. Her stomach
turns as she imagines Apollo waiting by the door.

She does not want to think of just how alone she herself will be
in this world without him to guide her. In this ship, out in space, inside her own head.

She inhales. "Houston, this is *Navigator.* Astronauts Steve Hagen
and Hank Redmond are dead. John Griffin has suffered potentially
critical internal injuries but is breathing. Do you read?"

She can't fall down in microgravity, but the idea sounds so nice,
right now. To let go and land on her knees and throw herself onto the
ground.

"Roger that," Joan says, her voice so gentle that Vanessa wants to
cry. "We read that Hagen and Redmond have died. We have vitals on
Griff. We believe Danes is alive as well. Please confirm."

If Donna and Helene are listening in on the loop from their

homes, Vanessa just told them their husbands are dead. Her throat constricts and goes sour. She swallows hard.

She looks to her left and then her right, and then, finally, up. That's when she sees that Lydia is floating near the ceiling, one arm stretched out. Vanessa finds her way to her and places two fingers on her neck.

"Houston, I can confirm Lydia Danes is alive," Vanessa says.

"Copy that, *Navigator*," Joan says. And then, her tone almost breathless: "Thank you."

Vanessa looks past Lydia and sees where the hole was. She can barely stand to look at it. Such a fragile, cheap repair, and yet—if applied seconds earlier—might have saved them all.

"Houston, Danes found the leak and sealed it with a clipboard and duct tape."

Joan is quiet for a moment. Vanessa is now hanging on her every word.

"Roger that," Joan says. "Cabin pressure is now approaching 10.2 psi. We believe that with monitoring, we can keep it stable long enough for you to get everyone home."

"It was the last thing Lydia did before she passed out," Vanessa says.

"Yes, *Navigator*," Joan says. "That is our conclusion as well."

It was Lydia, of all people, who had saved them. Saved her. Vanessa laughs for a moment—the sound has a dark tinge to it, an uncontrolled terror. She knows that if she keeps laughing, it will be exactly like crying. It will take over her body—her horror shaking within her to get out—and she will not stop until it is far too late. She is teetering on the edge of mania, and it is so tempting to give in to it, to lose all touch with what is happening and let her mind leave her.

But she can't.

"Lydia has the bends," Vanessa says.

"That is our estimation, yes," Joan says.

"How long does that give her?"

"She needs treatment within ten hours," Joan says. "Griff maybe sooner. We cannot be certain due to the internal nature of his injuries, but we are tracking his vitals and we are formulating a plan. We believe it is possible to have you home in as little as three revs."

"Four and a half hours? Is that even possible?"

"We believe it is. We will begin deorbit as soon as we can."

Vanessa closes her eyes. "How soon until you have the deorbit plan?"

"Confirming landing sites, back to you ASAP. In the meantime, we ask that you prepare the deorbit checklist and, as you do, that you leave the biomedical sensors on Griff and attach a set to Danes as well, so that we can monitor her vitals from here alongside his."

"Roger that," Vanessa says. And then she cannot help herself but to confess. "Houston . . . we . . . we left the hatch open."

"Copy that," Joan says. "We already suspected that was how Griff was hit. We are just glad you were not. We need you up there. Back to you soon with our contingency deorbit plan."

"Copy."

Vanessa takes in a full deep breath and looks around the ship. An entire crew unconscious or dead.

She is a mission specialist. But she has been begging to be given a chance to pilot this thing for years. And now, ironically, she will finally get what she's asked for.

She can do this. She has never landed a space shuttle before—not even in a simulation—but she will do it today.

And so, as Mission Control comes up with the plan, Vanessa grabs the deorbit procedure checklist and reads it.

She has to stabilize everything in the orbiter—nothing can be free-floating, all must be strapped down. This usually refers to things like microphones and sleeping bags and binders, the items the crew needs. She had never, until this moment, realized it would ever refer to the crew themselves. She has to strap them in.

She considers the seats in the flight deck. After all, there are four of them. But she needs full use of the flight deck to land.

And so, for Steve and Hank, she settles on the airlock.

She nods, swallowing. A droplet of blood floats past her, and she pulls away. She grabs a Huggies wipe from the stash that has been ripped off the wall. She takes the wipe, opens it fully, and touches the corner of it to the blood droplet as it passes through the cabin. It absorbs into the sheet, gone from the air.

She begins with Steve. She tucks the wipe into the front pocket of his shirt and then grabs his hand. She can't imagine not talking to him every day. Not calling him when she's afraid she's screwed something up. She has always understood that Steve being ten years older than her has allowed her to put more faith in him than he probably ever asked for.

But now, looking at his face, she regrets so sharply that she never told him how much his guidance meant to her. She had just left it for him to glean from her high fives and thank-yous.

"Steve," she whispers to him. "I have to put you in the airlock, okay?"

Her throat catches as she sees his expressionless face. But there is no time for that. She pulls his body toward hers and swims slowly through the mid-deck.

She pushes him inside the airlock and knows that she will need to shut the inner hatch to keep him from floating back into the mid-deck. Before she does, she wants to tell him that he's the best commander she ever had. But she knows what he would say to that: *I'm the only commander you've ever had.*

Anyway, it would feel awfully final. It doesn't need to be like that. She closes the door.

Afterward, she takes Hank and pulls him toward the airlock, the same as she did with Steve. She tells him that his joke earlier about getting home in time to watch *M*A*S*H* was funny. But she cannot bring herself to reassure him about Donna and Thea. All she can think of is Donna bringing Thea to the Outpost last month, Hank showing his baby girl off the entire night.

Vanessa snaps herself out of it. This is not something she can indulge right now.

When she gets to Lydia, she looks at her face. It is swollen but peaceful, without any of Lydia's usual consternation. In this one acute moment, Vanessa regrets not trying to understand Lydia better when they were both on Earth. Joan was the only one who had ever really tried, the only one who had ever seen what Lydia was capable of. Joan had tried to tell her. Vanessa sees that now.

Carefully, Vanessa unzips the top of Lydia's flight suit and applies the sensors for respiration, temperature, and heart rate. She zips it back up and takes Lydia's hand in hers for a moment. She squeezes. Wordlessly, she pulls Lydia to the flight deck and puts her in the chair behind the commander's seat. She buckles her in.

Then Vanessa takes Griff in her arms and carries him to the flight deck, putting him in the seat next to Lydia. And in a moment that she does not know is happening until it is over, she leans forward and kisses him on the temple.

"*Navigator,* this is Houston." Joan. Finally, Joan is back.

"Copy."

"Prepare for a contingency deorbit. We can land at Edwards in three revs. They have full trauma center capabilities. We are going to begin the deorbit checklist."

All on her own, Vanessa will need to stow away all the equipment—including everything that was torn off the walls—and shut the payload doors. Then she will have to get in the pilot's seat and begin the process of reentry.

She has been through enough in her life to know that there is no value in long-term thinking right now. In a crisis of this magnitude, you are best served by evaluating second by second.

So Vanessa does not imagine herself back on Earth. She does not imagine landing this shuttle. She does not imagine preparing for reentry.

Instead, she imagines strapping the lockers back onto the walls.

That, she can do.

ALMOST ANYONE WHO IS CLEARED TO BE IN THE FLIGHT CONTROL ROOM is there. The director's suite is filled with men in jackets and ties. The simulation supervisors' room is packed.

Joan can tell, just based on the hum within the room, that the theater behind her is filling up.

She cannot turn around, and she cannot consider just how many people are listening in on the main loop right now. It is accessible to almost three thousand people, across the Johnson Space Center and the wider Houston area, including the astronauts' homes and news organizations.

On a normal day, most of them would not be listening. Now they almost certainly all are. This accident has, most likely, already been reported all over the world.

Which means that Donna and Helene know. Even if they weren't listening earlier, they know by now.

In fact, because of the way some of the men keep glancing behind themselves, Joan suspects that either Donna or Helene is in the theater now. Most likely Helene. Donna is the sort of person who needs to be alone in a situation like this. She has most likely handed Thea over to someone and locked herself in her bedroom or bathroom, refusing to respond to anyone. Helene, on the other hand, is the sort of person who needs to see what is happening for herself. It is almost certainly Helene.

Joan keeps her gaze forward.

The commotion around her is distracting, but the din of murmurs and whispers within Mission Control forms a calming reminder that NASA is not merely a collection of individuals. NASA is a team. Joan had never before in her life felt the sense of belonging that she has with the people here at NASA.

If they get the shuttle home with Vanessa, Lydia, and Griff still alive, the entire campus will share in the relief. And if tragedy strikes further today, Joan knows this team will carry that burden together.

Still, there is a burden that Joan will carry alone.

Joan watches Jack. His shoulders are hunched, his fists tight. Joan opens and closes her own hands, trying to make space in the bones.

Since the end of November, Joan has been having dreams in which her life is less complicated than it really is. When she wakes in the morning, she always has to take a moment to understand that the dream wasn't real.

But today, she keeps forgetting that this *is* real.

Steve and Hank are dead. Griff and Lydia might not make it.

At least Vanessa is safe right now.

"Houston, the galley has been deactivated."

Jack: "Let's prep her to close the payload doors."

Joan on the loop: "Copy, Houston. We want you to begin to close the payload doors."

"Roger that," Vanessa says.

"Let's go to the deorbit checklist, page two-dash-fifteen. You will be running a deorbit burn soon."

"Copy that," Vanessa says. And then, more quietly: "Okay. I can do this."

Joan knows that tone in Vanessa's voice. The tiny waver.

"Ford," she says. There is so much she wants to say to Vanessa that she can't. "Everyone here believes that you have the ability to land *Navigator* safely today on your own."

Joan believes this. Even though no one in the history of NASA has ever had to do it before.

Vanessa does not respond for a moment. Then: "Thank you, Houston. After a certain point, the shuttle can land itself. We just need to get to that point as quick as we can. I'm going to get started."

What if Joan got on the loop and said what she was really thinking? What if she told Vanessa everything she needed her to know?

ATMOSPHERE

Watching the telemetry monitors, Joan can see that Vanessa has thrown the first switch to close the payload bay doors. The left one has closed. As Vanessa begins to close the right, Sean Gutterson stands up.

Sean: "Flight, this is RMU. The latches on the right forward bulkhead aren't closing. We think the PLBDs were hit in the explosion."

Jack stares ahead and blinks.

"Houston," Vanessa says. "I'm getting a malfunction signal on the right forward bulkhead gang."

"Roger that," Joan says and looks to Jack.

Jack holds his pen, clicking it over and over, grasping it so tight his fist is red and his knuckles turn white. He closes his eyes and inhales, shaking his head. "Ford's going to have to do it manually." He opens his eyes. "If she's going back into the payload bay, that means she has to get into the suit on her own. She can do that, right, EVA?"

Chuck Peterson, the man assigned to extra-vehicular activity, stands. "The suits were not designed that way. But she got out of it by herself, so we believe she can get into it by herself."

"If you tell her she has to do it," Joan says, "she will."

Jack nods. "EECOM, are we still at 10.2 psi?"

"Affirmative."

"What does that give us for a pre-breathe?"

Greg does not answer Jack at first, still calculating. Jack stands up, tosses the pen onto his desk. "C'mon! What does that give us for a pre-breathe?"

Greg: "We believe seventy-five minutes. The team is evaluating whether we can shorten it."

Jack leans onto the desk in front of him. "Either way, when you add in the time to get in the suit, and get the latches closed, and get back in and start the deorbit, we've lost a rev, maybe two."

He looks across the room to Tony Gallo, the flight dynamics officer. "FIDO, get us landing site options."

FIDO: "Copy that."

Ray: "Flight, Surgeon. Based on Griff's vitals, he may have more time than Danes. But if we don't get them home in the next seven hours, one or both may not make it."

Jack: "The shuttle cannot land without the payload bay doors shut. It will burn up on reentry."

Ray: "Yes, but Griff and Danes may not survive the time it takes for her to get into the payload bay."

Jack: "None of them will survive reentry if she doesn't."

FIDO: "We can still land at Edwards on the next rev, but then the closest opportunity after that will be twelve hours after."

Jack closes his eyes and nods. "Then let's hope she can do it within ninety minutes. CAPCOM, prepare her for EVA."

Joan: "Roger that. *Navigator,* Houston. You will need to close the payload bay doors manually. Please prepare to get into the EMU."

"Copy, Houston."

And then, more quietly, Vanessa says, "I . . . I don't know how to get into the suit without help. It was hard enough getting it off."

"Understood," Joan says. "Tell me what you need from us."

"You can't help me," Vanessa says. "No one can."

Joan does not know what to say. "Copy that," she says, finally. It is so useless.

Joan can see the future for a moment—everything that happens if this doesn't work.

"I'm going to start the oxygen for the pre-breathe," Vanessa says. "And then figure out how to get in the damn suit again. I hope you all can talk me through how to put my shoulder back in the socket if I dislocate it."

Joan considers how to respond, but then Vanessa speaks up again.

"I'll have to get Hank and Steve out of the airlock. Then I'll get in there and depressurize again. Then I'll figure out what's wrong with the latches and come back in here and start deorbit and land this thing. And somehow do it in less than four revolutions."

Joan waits an extra moment, to make sure Vanessa is done.

"You and I . . ." Joan says. "We will do this together."

"I'm . . ." Vanessa says. "I'm grateful you're the one in that chair today, Goodwin. I'm glad it's you."

Joan stares forward, worried she might catch someone's eye. She is good at this, understanding what Vanessa means. So this is enough for now.

She closes her eyes and begs the unfolding cosmos: *Please. Please don't take Vanessa.*

FALL 1980

IT WAS AFTER ELEVEN ON SATURDAY NIGHT. JOAN SHOULD HAVE BEEN IN bed, but she could not tear her fingers away from the piano.

After a long week of classes, her brain was fried. The lingo at NASA was going to kill her, especially the abbreviations. OMS, RCS, EVA, EMU, FIDO, GPCs. Joan was attentive and ready. But the terms were coming at her so fast that often it felt less like science and more like French.

She needed a break. So instead of going out to a bar, she'd gone on a long run, come home, taken a shower, and sat down at her keyboard. She did not know how long she'd been at it, but she'd played so much and just kept playing. Tchaikovsky, Chopin, Shostakovich, and now, Satie's "Gnossienne No. 1."

It was exactly what she needed: one of those moments when she forgot where she was or even *who* she was. It was what she had loved about the piano as a child, why she had kept with it even after deciding she would never try to become a professional. It let her mind leave her body, let her body speak for her.

Everything else in Joan's life was thinking thinking thinking

thinking. But when she picked up that pencil to draw or put her hands on the cool keys, the thinking stopped.

The knock at the door startled her. She yelped so high and so loud that she cringed to hear it.

Two possibilities flashed across her mind of who it might be, neither good: her neighbor, angry about the loud noise, or Griff.

"Jo?" she heard through the door, just before she could unlock it. Vanessa.

"Hi," Joan said as she opened the door.

"You screamed very loudly just now," Vanessa said at the doorway. "It sounded so dainty and helpless. I worry you'll set women back centuries if any man hears it."

Joan frowned. "Thank you for your excellent notes on how I can be scared in a less vulnerable way."

Vanessa smiled. "Can I come in?"

Joan opened the door farther, and Vanessa followed her into the room. "What are you doing here?"

"Nice to see you, too."

Joan raised an eyebrow.

"I just dropped off Donna—she's drunk as a skunk. I was going to ask you if you'd check on her in the morning."

"Oh," Joan said. "Of course I will."

"I wasn't even going to stop by. I assumed you'd be asleep, but then I could hear you playing when I passed your door."

"Is it that loud?"

Vanessa shook her head. "You'd have to be walking by, hoping you were up, to notice." And then she added, "You are very good, by the way."

"Oh, thank you," Joan said. "I just like to play to clear my mind. I'm not anything to write home about."

"Are you doing that thing where you're like, 'Oh, I'm not that good' and then I have to tell you that you're great?"

"What? No. I don't do that. I'm competent at a lot of things and am honest with myself about my talents. But I am an amateur classical pianist. I don't practice enough to be superlative. I do it because I enjoy it."

Vanessa hid that smile, the lopsided one.

"What's so funny?" Joan asked.

"You have a very high standard," Vanessa said. "That's all."

Joan pursed her lips, trying not to frown or smile.

"Anyway, listen—I had a secondary reason for coming over here," Vanessa said.

"I'm listening."

"I need . . . I need help with something. And you're . . . sort of the only person that can help me. I guess I'm asking a favor."

"Are you . . . nervous?"

"I'm embarrassed," Vanessa said.

"What on earth is it?"

Vanessa laughed. "It's actually not on Earth."

Joan shook her head and smiled.

"I'm not able to orient myself in the night sky as well as some of the others. Lydia can spot every constellation, and she's incredibly smug about it. But I'm having trouble recognizing them consistently. Especially in a dark sky."

"Okay, what *can* you spot?"

"Well, I can find Polaris. And I have a handle on Vega, Deneb, and Altair. So I can always find north and south. But I'd love to feel more confident about the dimmer constellations."

"Then you've come to the right place. Of course I'll show you."

"Thank you," Vanessa said, her eyes warmer than Joan had ever seen them.

"You're an astronaut who doesn't recognize most of the stars," Joan said, "That's pretty funny."

"I'm a pilot who applied to NASA because I want to fly out of the atmosphere," she said. "And I'm willing to learn anything I have to in order to do it."

"Okay," Joan said. "I would love to teach you. Tomorrow night. We can head out of the city. I can even bring my telescope."

"Yeah?" Vanessa said.

"Yeah, it will be fun."

JOAN ARRIVED AT VANESSA'S FRONT door one minute before six o'clock. She waited two full minutes to ring the doorbell so that Vanessa could see she was perfectly capable of being late.

Vanessa's bungalow was painted teal with a red door, a curved archway at her front porch. Joan could hear the doorbell ring inside the house.

Vanessa appeared with a cooler in her hand. She was wearing jeans and a dark gray T-shirt with the sleeves rolled up, her hair still a tad wet. In a flash, Joan went from liking the dress and jean jacket she was wearing to feeling mortifyingly overdressed. And why had she never thought to roll her sleeves up like that?

"I made sandwiches and brought us sodas and beers," Vanessa said, gesturing to the cooler.

"That's great. Thank you."

"Well," she said. "I like to pull my own weight. Thank you for helping me."

Joan waved her off. "It's a good excuse to do a little stargazing myself. I don't make time for it as often as I'd like. So, really, you're doing me a favor, too. Keeping me company."

Joan started walking to her Volkswagen, but Vanessa stopped her. "We can take my car," she said. "You can just tell me where we're going."

"You're sure? It's a bit of a drive."

"It will be nice," Vanessa said. "Wait here, I'll pull out of the garage."

Joan grabbed her binoculars, telescope, and blanket out of the back of her car and then stood on the lawn and looked up at the sky as the sun began to set. It would be a good night to take a little sky tour around Hercules.

Vanessa backed out of the driveway in a cream convertible with a red interior.

"Wow," Joan said, putting her things in the back.

Vanessa laughed. "I like cars."

Joan opened the car door and got in. "It's nice."

Vanessa pulled away from the curb. "Where are we going?"

"Brazos Bend."

"I don't know it."

"It's far outside of town. But the view is incredible. Turn left here—we're going to head to 288."

As Vanessa's car picked up speed, Joan's hair began to float behind her, the wind on her shoulders.

"I used to take Frances there when she wouldn't fall asleep."

"How old is she, again?"

"She's six now," Joan said. "It was a long time ago. My sister would lose her mind after so many nights not sleeping and so I'd take Frances and just drive. Usually out to Brazos. Most of the time, she'd be asleep by the time we got to the park, but sometimes, she'd still be wide awake, so I'd lay her on a blanket and show her the stars."

"Raising the next generation of astronauts," Vanessa said.

"Frances has said she wants to be an astronaut," Joan said. "I don't know if she really will, but it's a nice idea that . . . you know . . ." Joan seized up, very aware of the lump in her throat. It'd snuck up on her.

"Girls today might look at us or the women in Group 8," Vanessa said. "And know they can do it, too."

Joan looked at Vanessa as Vanessa watched the road. The wind ran through Vanessa's hair. Joan had been trying to control hers, holding it back. But Vanessa just let it fly. Joan put her hands down, let hers go.

"I mean, pretty soon, they are going to put a woman in space," Vanessa said.

"Have you heard anything about who they might choose?"

"No," Vanessa said. "You know how they are about that stuff. It's like we're not even supposed to admit we're curious."

The first American woman in space would be one of the women from Group 8, the first round that Joan had applied to, when she hadn't been called back. She was grateful for it, in hindsight. Being the very first would have been so much to hold on her shoulders.

As they got onto the highway, the wind was too loud for either of them to say anything and so Joan closed her eyes and felt the air run over her.

"This *is* far," Vanessa said once they took the exit and the wind quieted down.

"I know," Joan said. "But trust me. It's worth it."

Vanessa kept her eyes on the road. "Donna and Hank are fucking, right?"

Joan's shoulders came up to her ears. "I think they are sleeping together, yes. But I don't care for that word."

Vanessa laughed. "You're a little bit of a prude."

"No, I'm not," Joan said, in a tone that she knew undercut her point.

"What's the worst thing you've ever done?" Vanessa asked.

Joan tried to think of something, but her mind was blank. "I mean, when I was six years old, I stole a pack of cards from the five-and-dime." She could already tell it was a dud. "Forget that one— I ended up returning them anyway."

Vanessa smiled. "Okay, you can try again."

"I let kids in high school cheat off my tests for about two months before I lost my patience and told them all to study on their own."

"And which is the bad part? Cheating or eventually telling them no?"

Joan laughed. "Cheating! Obviously."

Vanessa shook her head. "Sorry, try again. I'm asking you to look deep down in the ugly parts of your soul, Jo. Come on, now. What's the thing you're the most ashamed of having done?"

"I assume you're going to answer, too?"

"Of course. I'll go first if you want. I've got loads to choose from."

"No, no, I'll think of something."

Joan was not sure why she was so *willing*. "Oh," she said finally.

"You got it?"

"I . . . yes. I have the thing I regret the most," Joan said. "I'm not sure how terrible you'll find it. But I do."

"I'm ready."

"When my sister was seventeen, I was home from college, and I heard her sneak out her window to go see some boy. I woke up my parents and told them. They pulled her back in the house and she was grounded for months."

"Why'd you do that?"

"She'd gotten pregnant the year before. She'd miscarried early, before she'd even figured out she was pregnant. She never told our parents. I was worried it would happen again, and I didn't know what else to do."

Vanessa thought this over. "There were better ways to go about it, maybe. But I don't know . . ."

"You didn't let me finish."

"Oh, well then, by all means . . ."

"When my sister came to my room the next morning complaining about being grounded, I pretended I knew nothing about it. I told her Dad must have heard her climbing out the window."

Vanessa raised her eyebrow and bit her lip. "Why not tell the truth?"

"Barbara is . . . very delicate. If you so much as look at her the wrong way, she might just say the worst things you can think of. And mean each and every one of them. We all just tiptoe around her. We always have. I am not . . . I am not honest with her. Maybe ever. I don't even know what that would look like. And I hate it about myself."

Vanessa put her hand on Joan's shoulder.

"Forget I said that. You go," Joan said.

Vanessa stopped at the red light. "Wait, I feel like there is a lot to discuss there."

"No, no, you go. Please."

"Okay." Vanessa shifted her head from side to side. "Oh, what to pick, what to pick. There are so many. Even as a teenager," Vanessa said, "I stole money out of the vending machines by taking them apart. I hot-wired a car for a friend of mine. I drank too much. I slept around."

That last one made Joan take her eyes off the red light to look at Vanessa. She turned back only when she remembered herself.

"I did too many drugs."

"Drugs? What drugs?"

"I smoked pot at first, did LSD." Vanessa looked at her and considered whether to go on. "Tried heroin."

The sound Joan made was somewhere between a gasp and a gulp.

The light turned green, and Vanessa pressed her foot on the gas. Suddenly Joan hated the way her own confession had sounded coming out of her mouth.

"Please don't read too much into my story," Joan said. They were approaching the park.

"What do you mean?"

"About ratting out my sister. Just . . . please don't think that I can't be trusted, or I ruin people's fun, or I'm a coward, or anything like that. I'm not."

"I know."

"Okay, it's just, with my sister, it was . . . I always feel like I'm trying to do the right thing and getting it wrong. I don't know why I told you that story. You're right, I am a prude. And always early. And all the things you think I am."

"I don't think of you any differently than I did when you got in the car," Vanessa said. "You are what you are, and I like what you are. Anyway, nobody is one thing all the time. Maybe you've been a Goody Two-shoes up until now. But anything can happen," she said, laughing, as she pulled into the parking lot. "The night is young, and you're out with a bad girl."

IT WAS DARK NOW, WITH hundreds of stars visible. They put down a blanket, and Joan set up the telescope as Vanessa stood on the grass and stared up at the sky.

"We might be up there one day," she said.

Joan looked through the eyepiece. "I know." She could show Vanessa the constellations without it. But the truth was, Joan relished any moment to show people certain stars up close. How else could she tempt them to fall in love? Joan got Rasalgethi, the head of Hercules, into view. She looked at Vanessa.

"Okay, come look."

Vanessa moved over Joan's shoulder, and Joan backed away to give Vanessa a chance to look. As Vanessa brushed up against her, Joan noticed that she smelled like baby powder. Joan now felt gauche, wearing perfume.

Vanessa peered into the eyepiece.

"That is Alpha Herculis, or Rasalgethi, which is Arabic for 'Head of the Kneeler.' It's almost four hundred years into the past you're looking. It appears to be one star to the naked eye, but it's—"

"Is it a binary?"

"It's actually a triple star system."

"Okay."

"Hercules has no first- or second-magnitude stars, so it's a great place to start expanding your celestial landmarks. It's not like Lyra or Cygnus, or even something like Boötes or Auriga, which we can see tonight on the horizon. Hercules doesn't have a bright star that draws your eye to it. Though a lot of the stars are magnitude four, which is decent. The brightest star is actually called Beta Herculis, not Alpha. Don't get me started on that."

Vanessa laughed, and Joan gently pulled her away from the

telescope. "Can you see Rasalgethi now with your eyes? As I point to it?"

Vanessa's sight line followed Joan's finger. Joan watched Vanessa's face for any sign of recognition.

"I think so," Vanessa says.

"Okay, now to the right and farther toward the zenith, you should see a star a little brighter than Rasalgethi—do you see it?"

"Yeah, I got it."

"That's Beta Herc, also known as Kornephoros—the 'club bearer.' Now we're looking at Hercules upside down. Rasalgethi represents the head and Kornephoros one of his shoulders. From there, you should be able to make out the four stars that are the torso. They are called the Keystone asterism. One star at each point of his shoulders and hips. With two arms coming off it. The one off of Kornephoros goes up, almost like he's throwing a football. The other arm goes out to the side, as if he's pointing."

"I can see that," Vanessa said.

"All right, so follow it down, you've got his pelvis, in this asterism there, and then two legs."

"He looks like he's running," Vanessa said, smiling.

"Exactly. He's standing or dancing—or, as most commonly interpreted, kneeling—on Draco's head. Draco being the representation of the dragon Ladon, who Hercules defeated outside the garden of Hesperides."

Vanessa took her eyes off the sky. "Placed there by Zeus, I assume. Almost all the constellations are placed by Zeus."

Joan smiled. "Well, most of the northern constellations. At least in Western cultures. They say that when Hercules—or Heracles, I should say, since that was the Greek name—was poisoned by Hydra's venom, the human part of him died but the immortal part of him joined his father and the other gods on Mount Olympus. And Zeus had the image of both him and Draco placed in the night sky, to honor him."

Vanessa looked at Joan. "The mythology always struck me as a little trivial."

"Oh, no. I disagree. That's part of what I love about astronomy. When we learn about the constellations, we also learn how earlier generations made sense of the world. The stars are connected to so many other elements of our life. It's the gray areas that are most fascinating: 'Is this astronomy or history?' 'Is this time or space?'"

Vanessa looked back up at the sky. "I can still see it—Hercules. Now that you've pointed it out, I can see it so clearly. And then just beyond it is Ursa Major and then Ursa Minor, with Polaris."

Joan nodded. "That's what made me fall in love with astronomy as a kid," she said. "That the night sky is a map, and once you know how to read it, it will always be there. You'll never be lost."

Vanessa smiled at her. And it made something in Joan want to keep talking. "I've always felt like, when I look at the stars, I am reminded that I am never alone," she said.

"Really?" Vanessa said. "How?"

"Well, we are the stars," Joan said. "And the stars are us. Every atom in our bodies was once out there. Was once a part of them. To look at the night sky is to look at parts of who you once were, who you may one day be." As she said it, Joan could tell how lonely it must sound. To find companionship with the stars. But what she meant was bigger than that.

Being human was such a lonely endeavor. We alone have consciousness; we are the only intelligent life force that we know of in the galaxy. We have no one but one another. Joan was always moved by the fact that everything—all matter on Earth and beyond, up past the atmosphere, going as far as the edges of the universe, as it expands farther and farther away from us—is made from the same elements. We are made of the same things as the stars and the planets. Remembering that connection brought Joan comfort. It also brought her some sense of responsibility. And what was kinship but that? Comfort and responsibility. "It sounds stupid, I know," she said.

"No," Vanessa said. "It doesn't. It's fascinating. I love hearing why you became an astronomer. I don't know if I have that clarity."

"About why you wanted to be a pilot?"

"I mean, what am I doing at NASA? I know they want me because I'm an aeronautical engineer. But that's my day job. The real me is a pilot. That's who I am. And they won't let me fly the shuttle."

"You don't know that."

"I do, actually. I got into a fight about it with Antonio when everyone went up in the T-38s for the first time."

"Oh."

"They won't let me get fully checked out in the T-38 because I'm a commercial pilot, not military. So I'll always be a backseater. And if I can't fly the T-38, they won't let me fly the shuttle. I signed up as a mission specialist. I get that. But I did think that it would be open for discussion, at least. That once they saw what I could do, it would be something to work toward. Which was naïve, in hindsight. They said that they absolutely cannot bend or change the rules."

"That's not true," Joan said.

"What's not true?"

"They have excused the college-degree requirement for certain members of the military. So why can't they excuse the military requirement for certain civilians?"

Vanessa looked at her. "I mean, you already know the answer."

Joan frowned. "Why didn't you join the military?"

"Women couldn't join the military as pilots, and now NASA will only take military pilots. Ergo, women can't be NASA pilots. It's a nice little work-around they've got themselves there. It's not like I could go to the Naval Academy, like my father did."

"Your father was in the military?"

"He flew in the Korean War." Vanessa looked up at the sky. "I think most of my life I've been both drawn to and terrified of the idea of being just like him."

Before Joan could respond, Vanessa said, "Will you show me another one?"

"Of course." Joan gazed through the scope and set it on the next star, far out along the horizon line. "Do you see Scorpius just with your eye? It looks like, well, a scorpion or maybe a fishhook. Try to find the bright star that has a bit of a reddish hue."

"I see it—looks a bit like Mars, right?"

"It does. It's a red giant star, Antares. Ant-Ares. Rival of Ares, the Greek name for Mars. Here, I have it in the viewfinder."

Vanessa leaned in. "Okay, I see it."

"Now come look at the sky. It's low in the distance."

Vanessa pulled back, Joan now right behind her shoulder. Joan pointed toward Antares and then out. "Antares is in the body of the scorpion, with two stars flanking it. Behind it is the tail. It creates an S shape. But on the other side of Antares are three stars in a line. Those represent the head and the claws. Do you see those?"

"I'm not sure."

Joan stood closer behind her, trying to align their eyes as much as she could. She pointed again.

"I see them," Vanessa said. And then she was quiet as she looked further. "I see the whole thing, the whole scorpion now." And then: "My father died flying an F9F Panther over Sui-ho Dam. I didn't mention that part."

"I'm so sorry."

"I was six."

"I can't imagine how hard that must have been."

Vanessa turned back to the stars. "What is the cluster of stars between Hercules and Scorpius? It is not Sagittarius, right?"

"It does look a little like Sagittarius, but Sagittarius is smaller and closer to the horizon. That's Ophiuchus," Joan said. "It almost looks like a rounded triangle—as a kid, I thought it looked like a stingray. But it's said to be a god holding or fighting off snakes. It might even represent the Mesopotamian serpent-god Nirah. Try to find the two winding arms coming off each side."

"Okay."

"Did your mother remarry?" Joan asked.

Vanessa nodded, softly, as she looked. "About a year later."

"And you didn't like him?"

"I see them. Those are the Serpens, right?"

"Very good."

"I liked him fine. He's a nice enough guy. Taught me to drive a car."

"But he wasn't your dad."

"Hard to compete with a war hero."

"Sure."

Vanessa looked at Joan. "Sometimes I don't know if I knew my dad or I just created a man out of thin air, as a god to pray to."

"Well." Joan sat down on the blanket. She opened the cooler and grabbed a beer. "Maybe it's both and maybe that's okay."

Vanessa joined her, and Joan handed the beer over, grabbing another one.

"I made chicken salad," Vanessa said. "I hope that's okay."

"More than okay," Joan said, pulling out the sandwiches. "It's so thoughtful."

Joan took a bite and realized, at that moment, how hungry she was. "This is very good."

Vanessa shrugged. "I dry-poached the chicken, and I put a lot of tarragon in the chicken salad. I think that's the big thing. That, and people never use enough salt."

"It's *so* good."

Vanessa laughed and took a sip of her beer. "I'm glad you like it. I really appreciate you doing this. Helping me."

"It's nothing," Joan said.

"You only think that because of how you are," Vanessa said.

Joan took another sip of her beer, and the thought went through her mind that everything about this moment was perfect. The breeze that cut the humidity, the salty chicken salad, the cold beer, the stars.

"Tell me more about your dad," Joan said. "If you want to."

Vanessa looked away. She picked at the bread on her sandwich, which she had yet to touch. "You know how I was talking about bravery versus courage?"

Joan nodded.

"I always thought he was really courageous. That he must have been. And kind, and quiet. Just based on the stories my mom and uncles told me. He died doing something very few people could do. And he gave up his life to do it, to serve his country. I hope he felt conflicted about it. I hope he knew that he was needed back home. But I think he did it. . . . I think he flew that jet with a sense of duty. So, in that way, I think or I hope that he was okay that that's how he went."

Joan reached out and touched her shoulder. Vanessa looked at her, surprised. And Joan pulled her hand away, unsure of what line she'd crossed.

"How old was he?" Joan asked. "When he died."

"Thirty-eight."

"So young."

"It seemed so old to me when I was little."

"So he's why you became a pilot," Joan said.

Vanessa sighed. "I think he's why I did a lot of things, honestly. Lashed out at my mom, cut school. I gravitated toward people I knew were bad news. I remember knowing exactly how stupid it was, what I was doing, and doing it anyway."

"You were lost."

"I don't think I was lost. I think I was trying to lose myself."

Joan nodded.

"I'm assuming that's where the heroin comes in?"

Vanessa laughed. "It's not funny, but it is funny hearing it come out of your mouth."

Joan threw her napkin at her.

"I think I just wanted to feel something other than sad," Vanessa said.

Joan did not look away. "Did it work?"

Vanessa inhaled. "Yes, that's the problem. If you find a way to make yourself absolutely terrified, there's no room for any other feeling."

Joan nodded. "Makes sense."

Vanessa laughed. "You're the first person to tell me I'm making sense."

Joan laughed, too. "Well, maybe people aren't listening. But it makes perfect sense to me. You make yourself afraid so you don't feel sad. But the more you put yourself in terrifying situations, the braver you become. So you have to put yourself in more and more danger until . . ." Joan regarded Vanessa expectantly. "Until what? Tell me. How did you stop?"

Vanessa considered this. "I don't know. My uncle Bill—my dad's best friend from the navy—never gave up on me. I think that was part of it. I remember turning eight years old and asking for a model plane for my birthday. My mom didn't get it for me. But that night, Bill came over with one. He used to take me out in his prop plane. My mom and I would be in some huge fight, and she'd call Bill and he'd come over and ask if I wanted to go flying. I think I was seventeen when he pushed me to fly by myself. And when I did, I just . . ." She laughed. "At first I thought I had just found something dangerous that was more fun than stealing or having sex . . ."

Joan blushed and looked at her hands.

"But that wasn't it," Vanessa said. "I think flying that plane, glancing at the ground below me, watching the horizon ahead . . . it was the first time I remember feeling . . . peace."

Vanessa relaxed back on the blanket, her hair spread all around her, and looked up at the stars. Joan, after a moment, joined her.

"That's Cygnus, right?" Vanessa said.

Joan moved closer, following her finger as she pointed to the sky. "Yeah, very good."

"I only know it because of Deneb," Vanessa said.

"Still, it's harder to spot when there are so many stars in the sky, like tonight. Easier in the city," Joan said. "There are a lot of stories about it, but my favorite is that Orpheus was transformed into a swan after he was murdered and placed next to his lyre, which is Lyra, right next to Cygnus."

"I'm going to guess he was placed there by Zeus," Vanessa said.

Joan laughed. "You know, I'm not sure. It could have been Apollo. But, yeah, I mean, for much of recorded history, humans have looked at the stars and believed there are gods up there."

Joan did not believe there were gods up there, but she did believe that God was there. Was everywhere. The wonder of the night sky was as good a place to connect with it as the smell of a grapefruit or the warmth of a pocket of sun.

"Of course we look for the gods there," Vanessa said. "And if we make it up there, we're going to have to fight against that sneaking suspicion that we might just be gods ourselves."

If Joan could have been pressed harder into the Earth, if gravity was variable, this would have flattened her.

Did Vanessa know that, on some level, Joan could not resist the idea that to go up there would be to touch God? That Joan could not help but wonder if, among the stars, there would be answers to questions no human had yet found?

It seemed so clear to Joan, as crazy as it might be, that the meaning of life had to be up there, somewhere.

JOAN HAD RESCHEDULED FRANCES'S SLEEPOVERS THE PAST FEW WEEKS because, for a short period of time during the training, all of the AS-CANs had to hop into a fleet of T-38s and travel all over the United States, visiting NASA centers and contractors.

They visited the Kennedy Space Center to see the launchpads and Boeing to tour the facility and boost morale. They went to the Goddard Space Flight Center and Edwards Air Force Base. Soon they would tour Marshall, to check out the development of the shuttle rockets and payloads.

Joan began to see firsthand what being in the astronaut corps, even as candidates, meant in the eyes of the public. They gave talks at schools all over Houston and were met by reporters as they stepped off the bus. Every person they came in contact with seemed to stand a little straighter in their presence and regarded them with a respect that Joan had never received before. Most people's smiles were a little more intense, when Joan shook their hand, than she had expected. It wasn't personal. It was the aura of being an astronaut. It was the promise she held. That one day, anyone who shook her hand might be able to say with pride, "I met her."

After a while, Joan started standing a little straighter, too.

THIS FRIDAY NIGHT, JOAN HANDED Frances a magnet from Washington, D.C., where she had gone with the ASCANs and some astronauts to meet lawmakers at a state dinner. Joan had not said much at the event. She let some less reserved members of the group take center stage. But she was surprised to see just how easy it was for Lydia to step into the spotlight. Joan watched as she explained the mechanics of the space shuttle to a senator with such focus and verve that Joan realized Lydia could be a very good instructor one day, long after her astronaut career was over.

"I also got you a replica of the Apollo LEM, but it shattered in my bag on the way back," Joan told Frances.

"You skipped two Fridays in a row," Barbara said. "We miss you."

"I missed you, too. But I will be here for the next few weeks, all right? So no one needs to worry about me being away for a little while."

Frances ate her Chinese food. "And I can come over every week again?"

"If she can find time in her very busy schedule," Barbara said.

Joan tried to catch her eye, but Barbara wasn't looking at her.

"Okay," Frances said.

Frances never pushed Joan, never tried to make her feel guilty. Joan was not sure if that was because Frances was nothing like Barbara, or if she just hadn't figured out the power she held yet. But there was something about Frances that made Joan believe she was better—held more goodness—than anyone she had ever met. That kind of faith was a lot to put on a six-year-old girl. Joan tried to keep it in check. To be ready to accept all the ways that Frances would grow and change and blossom into her full imperfection.

Joan would love her no matter what. Even if she grew up to be exactly like Barbara. Joan would love her then, too. Without hesitation. Whether she had to work at it or not, she would do it forever.

"We learned about gravity in school," Frances said. "My teacher said that astronauts float, and I told her she was wrong. I said, 'My aunt is an astronaut, and she doesn't float.'"

"Frances, that's not—" Barbara started.

Joan looked at Frances. "You're right, I don't. But if I go up into space, I will."

"You'll float?"

"Have they taught you yet in school how gravity works?"

"It pushes us down?"

"It *pulls* us. Everything that has mass has some amount of gravitational pull. So think about this—Actually, wait, come with me."

Joan got up from the table and walked into her bedroom, looking for something heavy. She wanted a bowling ball but settled for a few rolls of quarters. She tore the comforter off her bed.

"What are you doing?" Barbara said. Frances was smiling.

"Okay, look." Joan threw the rolls of quarters onto the mattress. "The quarters are heavy, right? They have mass."

Frances nodded, but then Barbara did, too, and it stopped Joan for a second.

"Okay, look at the mattress over here," Joan said, pointing to an empty space. "It's flat. It's a flat plane, right?"

"Right," Barbara said.

"But look over here, by the quarters," Joan said. She pointed to the indentation the quarters made in the mattress, the way the rolls sank into the mattress around them in a circle. "If the mattress is the fabric of space, do you see how the mass of the quarters bends the space around it? It's creating gravity. Hold on."

She searched in her freezer and found a bag of peas. She opened it up and took one out and returned to Barbara and Frances.

"So if I put a pea where it's flat, what happens?"

"Nothing," Frances said.

"Right, it stays put. Nothing near it has *enough mass* to pull it anywhere. But now," Joan said, placing a pea just outside the quarters. "What happens when I put one within the gravitational force of the quarters?"

The pea rolled toward the quarters.

"It rolls."

"It's being pulled," Joan said. "Right."

"So the quarters are the Earth, and we are the pea," Barbara said.

Joan nodded. "Yep, the pea is all of us and all the trees and all the dust and all the dirt and every animal and all the—"

"We get it."

"Okay, sure," Joan said. "So right now, we're the pea right here. If I get chosen to go up into space one day, I'll be the pea here."

She put it back on the flat plane of the mattress. "Nothing will be pulling me down, at least not at the rate that Earth can. So if I'm not being pulled toward the Earth, what's going to happen?"

"You're gonna float," Frances said.

"I'm gonna float."

THEY CALLED IT THE VOMIT Comet—a Boeing KC-135 Stratotanker. It was designed as a refueler, but at NASA, it had a much different job. It was a cargo plane—with no seats, only padding—used to simulate weightlessness.

With the ASCANs as passengers, the pilot would fly a series of parabolas that would lift the ASCANs into the air with extra gravitational forces, then lower them back down, allowing them to enter free fall. In between these moments of intense lift and fall, there were pockets of time—less than a minute—in which the ASCANs would float in midair.

The parabolas, when executed properly, simulated microgravity.

They also made a lot of people sick. Especially Joan.

On the KC-135 with Lydia, Hank, Teddy, and Jimmy, Joan seemed to be the only one calculating how quickly she could grab the barf bag from her pocket.

It was her first time on the plane, and they were approaching the third moment of weightlessness. The first two times, she had barely kept her food down. Putting on her blue flight suit that morning, she had felt like an astronaut. But now, as she lay flat on the floor of the aircraft as it ascended again, she felt like a child.

"Maybe we should land so Joan can get off." Lydia was seated in the corner, her knees drawn up to her chest. "She seems a little pale."

Joan wanted so badly to understand Lydia. She always corrected everyone, always had some way to cut Joan or Donna or Vanessa down. But even if it was a competitive strategy, there was no need for it. Lydia was already a clear favorite of Antonio's—Donna and Joan had seen Antonio out with Lydia and Griff for dinner more than once. And she was picking up every class lesson quickly, not just those in her field of study. If anyone was pulling ahead of the class, it was Lydia.

"I am fine, Lydia, thank you," Joan said.

Jimmy huffed. "She'll have to be a big girl."

"I said, I've got it," Joan said.

Jimmy put his hands up as if she were about to shoot.

She tried not to roll her eyes, or he'd make a comment about that, too. But he didn't have to say anything else. The subtext was clear: *This is why women don't belong on the shuttle.* Last week, he'd asked Lydia if she was going to be bitchy if she got her period in space. Lydia had laughed, and Joan had had to clench her jaw to keep it shut.

"I almost puked my first time," Hank said to Joan. "No shame in it."

Joan closed her eyes. Bless Hank for trying. But she did not need to be consoled, either. She just needed everyone to shut up.

As the plane began to rise once more, Joan felt the air gain heft underneath her, and her stomach somersaulted.

Her body rose into the air. As she lifted farther, Joan closed her eyes like she had all of the other times. She'd thought that weight-lessness would feel like floating in a pool. But to her, it felt more like being thrashed around in the ocean. She braced against it, but that didn't work. She tried to think of it differently, to remember the times she'd swum past the breakers and felt the ocean lift her briefly as the waves surged and then gently brought her back down. She thought of being in the ocean with Barbara as a kid, the way Barbara had clung to her, and Joan would tell her she was okay.

Her stomach began to roil.

Joan gave up on that idea and opened her eyes. She looked at her legs and pulled them into her chest. Her stomach calmed.

"You're gettin' it," Hank said.

Seconds later, the plane began to level out, but she kept her eyes open. As the weight of the air landed on her back, she looked at Jimmy. He was holding on to the padding on the side of the plane, and as he began to drop, his eyes went wide and blinked over and over again, his chest rising and falling rapidly as his breath became shallow.

Joan realized he was terrified.

And it did not excuse his attitude. But she understood, finally.

Jimmy had been told from a young age that fear and failing and trying and wanting and openness and kindness and sincerity made him weak. And because he had believed it, he'd learned to suppress all of those things. And when he saw those traits in others, he hated them because he hated himself.

Jimmy was *hiding*. That's what Jimmy was doing. Lydia was, too—because she was trying to prove she could be like Jimmy. And Joan was falling for it.

She was trying to prove that she could be just like a man to all of them. To Jimmy. To Lydia. Because the world had decided that to be soft was to be weak, even though in Joan's experience being soft and flexible was always more durable than being hard and brittle. Admitting you were afraid always took more guts than pretending you weren't. Being willing to make a mistake got you further than never trying. The world had decided that to be fallible was weak. But we are all fallible. The strong ones are the ones who accept it.

Joan had let men like Jimmy set the terms.

But the terms were false, even to him. He was just as scared as anybody else.

Bravery, Joan suspected, *is almost always a lie. Courage is all we have.*

She didn't want to lower herself to the game men played.

As the plane turned toward the sky, her stomach dropped hard and fast before her torso caught up.

Joan grabbed the barf bag from her pocket. And puked.

"WHO WANTS ANOTHER BEER?" HANK CALLED OUT FROM HIS KITCHEN at just after eleven o'clock on New Year's Eve. His high-end stereo was blaring the Eagles. It was supposed to be a small party, but as word spread, more and more of the astronauts arrived. Hank's place was now packed. Harrison and Marty had already made two additional runs for more beers and ice.

Someone made a joke about needing to turn water into wine. But to Joan, it felt more like high school juniors getting incredibly excited when the seniors showed up.

Griff called out, "Another round for everybody!" and everyone cheered.

Joan downed the rest of her bottle. She was two beers deep in a buzz that felt less like the consequence of the alcohol and more like the genuine promise of 1981.

The first shuttle mission was scheduled for just over three months away.

Originally predicted to launch as early as 1977, the inaugural orbital flight had been delayed multiple times. The development of the shuttle had not been without its challenges. There were issues with the main engines during testing. The shuttle's complicated carbon and silica thermal tiles were so temperamental that entire portions of them had repeatedly fallen off. But the engineers kept at it.

Two days ago, the space shuttle *Columbia* had left the Vehicle Assembly Building to be ushered over to the launchpad at Kennedy Space Center.

STS-1 was on the horizon.

Hank was pulling bottles out of the coolers and ice buckets and passing them around as if he hadn't a care in the world.

One of the many things Joan had learned during their flights was that Hank was the recipient of a very large trust fund. It was a fact that Hank wore with complexity.

He had mentioned it on one of their flights, after they'd landed in Nevada somewhere and were getting a bite to eat at a roadside stand. Joan had asked him why he'd joined the military in the first place.

"I think I wanted to do something no man in my family had done before," he'd said, biting into his sandwich.

"No one in your family served in either of the World Wars? Or even Vietnam?"

Hank shook his head. "They found a way out."

Joan raised her eyebrows. "And here you are," she said. "About to fly to space with your own two hands."

"God willing, I suppose so."

It was easier and easier for Joan to understand why Donna would love him. But the further she got into her training, the harder it got for Joan to understand why Donna would tie herself down to someone at all.

"My father is a mathematician," Joan told Hank. "Very left-brained and analytical. So I'm not sure I fell as far from the tree as you did."

"But I bet your mother was a homemaker," Hank said.

"She was, she is," Joan said.

"So you've carved a new path for yourself, too."

"Yeah, maybe that is true." Joan finished her sandwich. "Hey, I wanted to say thank you."

"What for?"

"It's not easy to get a pilot to give consistent time to us backseaters," Joan said.

Hank nodded.

"I know you're helping out Donna, too," she added, and then, so he didn't have to respond, she kept going: "Vanessa's got Steve, but Lydia, Harrison, and Griff aren't having an easy time getting their hours in. So I just wanted to say thank you. You've been a great teacher."

Hank smiled. "Well, I'm glad for it. I enjoy these rides with you, Goodwin. You're one of the good nerds."

Joan laughed.

"No, I mean it," Hank said. "A lot of these eggheads have come in here and acted like they're smarter than everyone else. And talking to that Marty fellow requires propping your eyes open with toothpicks. But you—you're easy to talk to. And you're trying. I'm on the other side of it, tryin' like hell, too. My mother always said, 'I like a try-hard.' I agree with her. I like somebody scrappy. Man or woman, I don't care." Joan detected that Hank was affording himself a sense of magnanimity with this statement, but she let it go. "You're scrappy, Goodwin. I'll always stick my neck out for that."

Joan smiled. "Well, thank you. I hope you know that I feel the same about you. If you need anything, I hope you'll ask."

Hank nodded and put his hand in his jacket pocket.

"I do have something for you, partner," Hank said.

Joan laughed. "Oh?"

At that moment, Hank pulled out his aviator sunglasses and put them on. He then pulled out another pair for her.

"Pilot to pilot," he said. "You need to look the part."

Joan took them and laughed. "Oh, this is great," she said. She slipped them on and then tightened her face, clenched her jaw, and removed all hint of a smile from her face.

"Atta girl!" Hank said.

Joan put her helmet on and, later, took over the controls as they flew home. She got them back to the base, and then Hank took over and landed them.

After she had gotten in her car to drive home that day, she'd picked up the glasses again and put them on. When she had looked in the mirror, it had no longer seemed like a joke.

"Coors Light for Goodwin," Griff said now, as he handed Joan a beer.

Everyone beat their hands on the tables to thank Hank for circulating another round. Joan started moving through the crowd toward an open window for some air.

She watched as Donna hung back, across the room from Hank. Vanessa was laughing with Steve about something, and Joan wondered what it could be that made Vanessa laugh that hard. She wondered if maybe Vanessa had a thing for Steve.

"Do you think Hank's in the lead to get the first assignment out of our group?" Lydia asked. Joan had not realized Lydia was behind her.

Vanessa caught Joan's eye and smiled. Joan instinctually looked away. Did Vanessa know how beautiful she was? Her beauty seemed so obvious to Joan, but no one ever reacted to Vanessa the way they reacted to most beautiful women.

"Are you listening to me, Goodwin?" Lydia asked. "Hank seems like the favorite out of the Group 9 pilots, don't you think?"

Joan turned to her. Lydia was dressed for a party—she was wearing a blue dress and the sides of her hair were pulled back with two tortoiseshell combs—but her eyes were narrow, her lips pursed tight. Joan realized that *being* at a party and *partying* were two different things. "I don't know," Joan said. "It's hard to gauge."

Once NASA had one successful shuttle mission, they were going to start scheduling many more. Everyone wanted to be chosen for a crew as soon as possible.

Already there seemed to be an unspoken hierarchy emerging, with favorites and leaders, long shots and outsiders.

Hank, Teddy, Duke, and Jimmy were training to fly chase—to be the pilots who guided the shuttle to the landing site once it reentered the atmosphere. Vanessa and Griff were spending a lot of time in the dunk tank, experimenting with what was possible on spacewalks.

Lydia and Harrison had been added to the team working on the thermal protection system—the shuttle's complex protective skin of tiles and blankets—which meant they had the most hands-on time with the spacecraft itself. And Donna, Marty, and Joan had been assigned to Spacelab, an orbital science laboratory designed by NASA's European counterparts.

Donna was studying the effects of weightlessness on the human body, for which Joan was immensely grateful. She was still puking in microgravity.

Joan, herself, was preparing for ultraviolet and X-ray astronomical observations from space. She'd helped design experiments for a set of planned solar instruments, and soon would begin making calls to geologists and physicists she'd known in her time in academia to get their ideas about potential shuttle experiments in those fields, too.

Despite how necessary each of these jobs was, Antonio was partial to certain people in Group 9, and he showed it. He favored Lydia, Griff, Harrison, and Hank. He gave them more scheduled time on the most relevant and urgent skills that one would need to fly.

So, yes, Hank probably was the favorite of the pilots. But this was not something Joan was particularly interested in talking about at 11:30 on the last day of the year, when everyone was trying to—for one small moment of their lives—let go.

"I think Hank will get assigned first," Lydia said.

"Can we talk about this another time?"

Lydia sighed. "Sorry for trying to remain focused on the objective."

"I'm just saying that you could back off a little," Joan said.

"Do you honestly not realize that everyone here is clocking everyone else? That Antonio is going to hear about everything that happens here tonight? Someone gets drunk and passes out in the bathroom and trust me, all of JSC is going to hear about it and there'll be a little mark next to their name."

Joan knew this was true for all of them, herself included. Who she was, what she did in her spare time, how she chose to conduct herself . . . it all mattered. It would be weighed in terms of passing training and would be a factor in what roles she was assigned. It would no doubt be considered when—or if—they put her on a mission.

"Look, Joan, you want to get up there as much as I do. So do

Donna and Vanessa. And you know damn well they aren't going to put two of us on a mission together at first. They are going to assign one woman at a time, because we're novelties to them still. We're not the same as a male astronaut until one of us or two of us or even three of us have gone up there and proven that we are. So if I want to get assigned, it means I have to wait out all of the women in Group 8, most likely. And then I have to make sure Antonio chooses me over you or Donna or Vanessa. So go ahead and blow off steam and take your eye off the ball—I don't care. Because the first crew assignment for our class, you can bet your ass I'm going to be on it. If it means I need to curry favor with Hank so he wants me to be on his crew, I will. Especially because I know he's more likely to push for Donna, since they're sleeping together."

There was nothing Lydia was saying that Joan didn't already know. "Lydia, you have to do what you have to do," Joan said. "Just leave me alone tonight, please."

"I really don't get you, Joan," Lydia said.

"What's not to get?"

"I see you working harder than almost anybody else out there except me," Lydia said. "You're up in the T-38s all the time, you're puking in microgravity and going right back up the moment they give you a chance, you're studying like hell for these classes, asking more questions than anybody. When the astronauts are running the simulations, you're always there in Mission Control, always watching, keeping notes, just like I am. You look like you're just as desperate to get into that seat as I am. The only other thing you have to focus on is politics, and you're not doing it."

Lydia was right about the simulations. They weren't letting any of the ASCANs on them yet, but whenever Joan heard that any of the astronaut crews were doing one, she made sure to be there. She watched as the simulation supervisors threw every possible problem at them. It was one of her favorite parts of the job, being on that floor, watching it all unfold.

One of the jets starts leaking and you don't understand how to close the manifold while properly accounting for the other lost jets? The crew dies.

One, two, three buses go down and you can't figure out if you've lost critical redundancies in time to act? The crew dies.

A radiator inside the payload bay doors has a blockage at the same time the flash evaporator is low on water, which means the heat of the spacecraft is not dispersing, and you can't fix it? The orbiter burns up and the crew dies.

Any one of the ASCANs who was chosen would be putting their lives in the hands of their fellow crew members and everyone down in Mission Control. Hank, she knew, would do anything to save her life. Donna, she was confident, would, too. Griff would. Vanessa surely would.

Would Lydia?

It suddenly seemed too full of risk to ignore Lydia. Or Jimmy. Or Marty, or any of the ASCANs she didn't get along with. Success would be found together or not at all.

"Hear me out, Lydia," Joan said. She grabbed an unopened beer from the cooler next to them and handed it to Lydia. "You're not just an astronaut—do you get that?"

"Well, not yet," Lydia said.

"No, I mean . . . this isn't all that you are."

Lydia looked at Joan as if she were the stupidest person she'd ever met.

"Come on," Joan said. "You have hobbies."

"No, I don't."

"You have friends."

"Are you making fun of me?"

"You have your family."

"My parents like my brother's wife more than me. They all go on skiing trips together and don't invite me. My dad still hangs out with my ex-husband."

"I bet it's because you're too . . . ." Joan hiccuped and covered her mouth. "Busy."

Lydia frowned and gave up. "Sure."

Joan took the beer back out of Lydia's hand and opened it.

"What are you doing, Goodwin?"

"The clock is going to strike midnight soon. I'm not going to kiss anybody—are you?"

Lydia glared at her. "Do you see any man knocking down my door?"

"Right, okay. So have a beer with me. We can ring in the new year together. You need to take a load off for a moment."

Lydia inhaled sharply and then took the beer. "Just until midnight."

"Great: for fourteen minutes, try to calm down, and then you can go right back to shoving coal up your butt and pulling out diamonds."

Joan was drunk. Even she knew it now. But it was fun! She should do this more often. Why had she spent so much time with her nose in a book up until now? She liked going to parties!

Lydia stared at her. "That wasn't funny."

SPRING 1981

JOAN WAS STANDING ON TOP OF THE LAUNCH CONTROL CENTER AT KEN- nedy Space Center with her aviator sunglasses on and her bomber jacket unzipped, revealing her blue polo shirt and khakis. It was Sun- day, April 12, and while it would grow warmer during the day, it was not yet seven in the morning and there was still a chill in the air.

STS-1, the inaugural mission of the space shuttle program, was about to launch. Almost all of the astronauts had been assigned some role that day, like flying chase or search and rescue. Others had been made available for interviews with TV and radio news anchors. But Joan and the majority of the Group 9 ASCANs were there just to observe.

There were so many people at Cape Canaveral that morning that the surrounding beaches were packed. The launch was being broad- cast on multiple channels.

It felt as if the whole world were watching.

Frances would be watching on TV, too. And Joan kept thinking of her as she looked over at the *Columbia* shuttle: a monumental bright white symbol of progress. The orbiter was positioned with its nose in the air, twin solid rocket boosters, one on either side of the external tank. Any minute now, the main engines would ignite, and everyone would watch liftoff.

If Joan had thought Barbara would listen to her, she would have told her not to let Frances watch.

"Joan, I'm nervous," Vanessa said.

Joan looked around, to see if any of the many astronauts, AS-CANs, NASA officials, or admins on that rooftop with them were listening.

"It's going to be fine," Joan said.

Vanessa looked at her. "You're not nervous?"

"I didn't say that. I just said it is going to be fine."

Vanessa lightened up slightly.

"Goodwin," Griff said as he approached Joan, not seeing Vanessa on the other side of her. "Want to grab breakfast after this?"

Joan's stomach churned. "Yes, sure."

Griff nodded and walked away.

"He's got a thing for you," Vanessa said.

"Stop it. People don't understand that men and women can be friends," Joan said.

"Or maybe you don't understand when someone is giving you signals that they're interested."

Joan looked at Vanessa. "You are nervous about the launch, and it's making you edgy," she said. "Shake it out."

"Shake it out?" Vanessa said, smiling out of the corner of her mouth.

"Yeah," Joan said. Joan shimmied her shoulders, shook her hands and arms.

"You look ridiculous."

"Well, the tightness is gone from my shoulders, and I'm feeling better about this launch already, but if you're too cool for it, be my guest. That is kind of your thing."

"You think I'm cool?"

Joan squinted at her. "Now you're pretending you don't try to act cool?"

"I just didn't know you thought I was cool."

Joan rolled her eyes. "Stop fishing for compliments."

Vanessa smiled just as the crowd quieted and a low buzz overtook Joan's body.

"T minus five minutes and counting," the flight controller said.

Joan turned her attention to the *Columbia*. She pictured John Young and Bob Crippen strapped into their chairs, lying back, parallel to the ground. Were they as scared as she was? Or was it like a hurricane? Those outside of it were caught up in the chaos, but inside—right in the eye of it—there was calm.

All around the country, little boys were dreaming of their futures today. Little boys who, when asked what they wanted to be when they grew up, would proudly declare, "Astronaut!" and would dress up as one for Halloween.

She wondered if, soon, there might be a woman up there. Joan hadn't needed to see a woman in that ship in order to believe in herself enough to apply. But she had also never dressed up as an astronaut for Halloween. Not once. For some reason, this made her acutely furious.

"T minus three minutes and forty-five seconds and counting."

Joan looked at Vanessa, whose eyes were focused on the shuttle. She wanted to tell Vanessa that she knew she would fly it one day. That if any of them got up there, it would be her. But she wasn't sure about anything after this moment.

There were now plumes of white smoke coming out of the engines.

"T minus one minute and ten seconds and counting."

Joan prayed that Barbara hadn't turned on the TV.

"T minus twenty-seven seconds."

Joan took a breath. She and Vanessa exchanged a look.

And then: "Seven . . . six . . . five . . ." Joan had heard the flight controller count down before, but it had never felt like this. "We've gone for main engine start. We have main engine start."

Joan reached out, unaware of herself, filled with terror, to grab

Vanessa's hand. And Vanessa clutched hers tightly in return, as if her hand had been searching for Joan's just the same.

The rockets lit up. Fire and smoke emanated from the bottom of the shuttle. Joan felt the bone-crushing pressure of Vanessa's fingers around hers. The billow of smoke was so big that Joan thought for a moment something had gone wrong. But just as quickly as the smoke arrived, the startlingly bright fire underneath the shuttle erupted into a blaze and the whole thing began to move.

"We have liftoff of America's first space shuttle, and the shuttle has cleared the tower!"

Joan's eyes followed the blaze up into the air. She could no longer hear the flight controller or the countdown. All she could hear was the burning of that fire as it rose higher into the sky, the shuttle getting smaller with every passing moment.

At one hundred and thirty-two seconds after launch, the two rocket boosters fell away. Joan took a breath. By now the *Columbia* had likely reached over seventeen thousand miles an hour. Soon it would hit main engine cutoff. The external tank would fall away, too. As Joan waited for that moment, she realized she was still holding on to Vanessa.

She took her hand away.

"Sorry," she said. "Got a little more scared there than I anticipated."

Vanessa nodded and said nothing. Joan could not bring herself to look at her. Instead, she looked up again at the sky. She could barely see the shuttle anymore. Success was a white dot getting smaller and smaller.

They'd done it. They'd launched up into orbit.

There was nothing to be afraid of.

She felt so silly.

JOAN WAS COMING HOME WITH A BAG OF GROCERIES—ALMOST EN-
tirely cereals for Frances to try that weekend—when she saw Vanessa and Griff talking in the parking lot.

Vanessa was laughing at a joke Griff must have made. Joan was
starting to wonder if Vanessa laughed that way with everyone.

"Hi," she said.

They both turned and looked at her. "Hey," Vanessa said. "I came
by looking for you."

Griff headed toward his car but pointed at Joan. "Are we still
headed to Frenchie's for dinner later?"

"Yeah, I'll find you," Joan said.

And then he was gone.

"You're going to dinner together?" Vanessa asked.

Joan started walking toward the building, and Vanessa followed
her.

"Yeah, why don't you come?" Joan said.

Vanessa held the building door open for her. "No, thanks."

"Uh-huh."

"What's that mean?" Vanessa had a smile on her face that Joan
didn't care for. "*Uh-huh.*"

"It means I knew you wouldn't come," Joan said, walking into her
apartment. "But you really should. We'd have fun."

"I wouldn't want to interrupt your *date*," Vanessa said, following
her in.

"You know it's not a date," Joan said. "And you know calling it a
date will get me nervous that he thinks it's a date. You know exactly
what you're doing."

"Are we fighting right now? Are you mad at me?" Vanessa asked,
as if it thrilled her.

"Of course not." Joan started putting the cereal boxes—all bright and covered in cartoon characters—into the cupboard. Vanessa reached into the bag and loaded the milk and fruit into the refrigerator. Joan watched as she paused to look at the sketch of Frances hanging on the refrigerator door. Vanessa took the magnet off it and held it for a moment.

"Is this Frances?"

Joan nodded.

"She's beautiful."

"She really is."

Vanessa put the sketch back. "Griff does have a crush on you, though," she said as she shut the refrigerator door.

"Would you stop it?"

"It's obvious," she said. "And why wouldn't he? You're smart and gorgeous and about ten other things."

"So are you. Does he have a crush on you?"

"Joan, c'mon."

Joan looked at her but did not say anything. Vanessa reached out and touched Joan's shoulder. "Hey, I'm sorry I called it a date, okay?"

Joan looked away. "Thank you," she said. "I'm sorry I'm sensitive."

Vanessa jumped up and sat on the counter. "I'm probably looking to pick a fight."

"Why? What happened?" Joan said, leaning against the opposite countertop.

Vanessa sighed. "Antonio's going to tell us tomorrow that Lydia is being sent to Toronto to be the first of us to study the RMS." This was the robotic arm that could be manipulated from inside the orbiter to deploy and control payloads. Operating it was one of the most important skills a mission specialist could be assigned.

"How do you know that?"

"Because he told Lydia last night," Vanessa said. "And you know that smug little shit can't keep anything a secret."

"She probably looked quite self-satisfied."

"She pretended she 'hated to break it to me.' I cannot stand her. I truly cannot stand her."

"Well, look, we knew she was the favorite, right? And she's not as bad as you're making it out."

"You're the only one she's halfway nice to."

"I'm the only one who tries with her."

"How am I supposed to try? If I caught fire, Lydia would consider whether she could use me to warm her hands before deciding to put the flames out."

Joan laughed. "Well, you got me there . . . I think that's probably true," she admitted.

Vanessa laughed, her head thrown back. And Joan wished she hadn't seen her laugh like that with other people. So that she could take more pride in eliciting the response now.

"But I do think," Joan said, "that if we included her more she'd put your fire out faster."

Vanessa squinted at her. "Are your parents divorced?"

"What? No, you know that."

"I'm just wondering when you became a peacemaker."

Joan frowned. "Maybe I'm just a nice person," she said.

Vanessa shook her head. "No, I bet it was because of all the drama with Barbara."

Joan blinked. "Would you like me to psychoanalyze you?"

"It would be too easy—I'm too rich a subject."

"Well, don't do it to me."

"Fine. What time is it?"

Joan looked at her watch. "A little after five."

"Blow off Griff and come get a beer with me."

"Why won't you just join us?"

"Because I just want to get a beer with you."

Joan considered this. "I don't know . . ."

"Doesn't seem like that big a deal to me to just leave a note on his door saying you need a rain check," Vanessa said.

Joan bit her lip, unsure. "Okay," she said finally, with the spirited verve of someone agreeing to break the law.

Vanessa popped down off the counter and pulled Joan toward the door. "I'm driving."

VANESSA TOOK JOAN TO A dive bar outside the city with a dirt parking lot, sticky tables, and dollar bills pinned to the ceiling. Someone was feeding coins to the jukebox to keep it playing Willie Nelson.

They'd been there a couple of hours and had had a few beers. Which was why Joan was tipsy enough to tell Vanessa about Adam Hawkins, the neighborhood boy who wanted to marry her.

"He was good-looking?" Vanessa asked.

"Yeah." Joan shrugged. "I guess. I don't know. Barbara always thought he was cute. We went out on dates here and there, to the movies and some parties together. He was fine."

"Did you like him?"

"I don't know. I couldn't tell. Which I think means no."

"Did you sleep with him?"

"Oh, my gosh, no."

"But the two of you kissed?"

"Sometimes, sure."

"So he was your boyfriend."

"I don't know about that. He was a boy I dated, and it was clear our parents wanted us to get married. And he did, too."

"How is that not a boyfriend?"

"I think of a boyfriend as someone you love. I never loved him. I would know if I'd fallen in love."

"Have you ever?"

"What?"

"Have you ever fallen in love?"

Joan glanced down at her fingernails. "No," she said, looking back up.

Vanessa nodded, absorbing it all. "Because you haven't met the right person?"

"I don't know. Or . . . maybe it's just not my thing."

"What's not your thing?"

"Falling in love, getting married."

Vanessa cocked her head and finished her beer. "So there's this nice, handsome guy, and your family liked him. And he asks if you could see yourself marrying him and you said no?"

"Yes?"

"If a different boy had asked, would your answer have been the same?"

"I think so."

"I'm impressed, Joan Goodwin."

"What? Why?"

"It puts you in a different context, that's all," she said. She wasn't slurring her words, but there was a laziness to her mouth.

The table was a mess. The empty beer pitcher—the foam drying along the sides—hadn't been cleared. What was left of their burgers sat off to the side. The air smelled acrid. The bar was quiet for a moment as the song changed over. When a new one started, Joan recognized it as "Mamas Don't Let Your Babies Grow Up to Be Cowboys."

Vanessa started humming along.

Joan realized she was sweating. "What *context* does it add?" she asked.

"You could have married a nice handsome guy and had some kids. Happily ever after and all that. It would have been easier than all this," she said, gesturing to the restaurant around her as if it were NASA itself. "But you didn't go that route."

"Neither did you."

"Well, right, but . . . I never could have. Whereas it seems like you had the option."

Joan gazed down at the remains of her meal. "You're making a lot of assumptions."

Vanessa looked at her, inviting her to explain.

"Marrying Adam Hawkins and being a wife? Waiting at home and making dinner every night? My mom is so good at that stuff, but I never looked at her and saw myself. I know that hurt her feelings. I know that me choosing a different life didn't quite make sense to her at first. But I think choosing that other life, her life, would have been *very hard.* I think it would have been one of the hardest things I'd had to do. I chose the only life I knew how to choose."

"I was trying to compliment you," Vanessa said. "But you look insulted."

Joan shook her head. "No, I just . . . Don't make it out like life in the suburbs is easy. Life's not easy for anybody, first of all. And second of all, I've never fit in there. That life, in particular, would not have been natural for me at all."

Joan could feel Vanessa studying her face. But then Vanessa pulled back and put her arm on the back of her chair. She sat slumped ever so slightly, with her knees apart. When she sat like this in bars or buses, Joan cringed a bit.

"Sometimes I think you and I are having one conversation and then I realize we've been having an entirely different one the whole time, you know that?" Vanessa asked.

"No," Joan said. "I think we're on the same page."

Vanessa considered this. "I admire you," she said finally.

Joan scoffed. "That's a little silly."

"Why is that silly?"

"Because you're just as accomplished as me. In some ways more so."

Vanessa leaned forward. "I can fly a plane better than you. Fix a plane better than you."

"See? There you go."

"But I can't play the piano the way you do."

Joan waved her off.

"You can try to deny it, but I've heard you play," she said.

Joan caught her eye and then looked away.

"And I don't know the history of the stars. Or how to take care of a kid—stock my kitchen with food they'd like and say all the right things, like you do with Frances. Lord knows, I can't draw at all," she said.

"Yeah, how terribly accomplished of me. I doodle."

"Why are you calling them doodles? Why are you doing that? All I'm trying to tell you is that I've only ever really loved one thing. Being in the sky. But I look at you, and you are so curious about everything. Not just about the planets and galaxies and the stars. But Earth. About the people on it. That's what I admire."

"My curiosity?"

"Your commitment to the world around you. How much you care. You are so thoughtful. About everything."

Joan suspected that liking the view of herself through Vanessa's eyes was dangerous. She just wasn't sure how.

"Why are you telling me this?" Joan said.

"Because I understand why it isn't me who is in the lead for the first mission of our group," she said. "But I don't know why it isn't you."

"I think sometimes you . . ."

"Sometimes I what?" Vanessa said, leaning forward, daring her to finish.

"I'm not as great as you think I am," Joan said.

Vanessa smiled. "Don't do that."

"Don't do what?"

"Don't kill my dream. Let me think you're the best astronaut in the class. Can you give me that? Let me think that right now, the wrong woman won, okay? Let the world be as I see it for just tonight. Without too many gray areas and caveats. Where I know I'm mortal but I'm not sure that you're not a god," she said. And then her voice got barely above a whisper as she leaned in. "Can you do that for me?"

And what escaped Joan's lips was "Yes."

JUNE 1981

THE WHOLE GROUP OF ASCANS TRAVELED TO THE NATIONAL SPACE Technology Laboratories in Mississippi. On the way back, they opted to spend the night in New Orleans.

Joan had wanted to get back to Houston to see if she could pick Frances up from school on Monday, but she had been outvoted. She called Barbara from a pay phone in the lobby of the hotel to let her know.

"I swear, Joan," Barbara said. "It's like I don't even know you anymore."

Joan sighed. "C'mon. Because I'm staying an extra night on a work trip? Don't you think you're overstating it?" She looked at the buttons on the phone, the deep grime of the numbers, the one and the zero worn down more than the others. "Just let Frances know I'll pick her up Tuesday, okay?"

"I mean, fine. But she's struggling, Joan. I know she doesn't say it, but she misses you. She's been very crabby lately, a little rude, honestly."

"Okay," Joan said. "Well, I will see her Tuesday. Please tell her when she gets home from school."

When Joan walked away from the pay phone, Vanessa was standing in the lobby.

"You're coming with us to Bourbon Street," Vanessa said.

"Do I have to?"

"That's the spirit," Vanessa said. "Donna wants to go shopping before we go out. And specifically requested our attendance."

Joan considered this.

"You think *I* want to go look at dresses?" Vanessa said. "But we can't leave her with Lydia. You're coming."

JOAN STOOD IN THE ESPRIT store—looking in the full-length mirror at herself in the blue floral dress Donna had insisted she try on—completely taken aback.

"Joan?" Donna called from the other side of the fitting room door.

"Yeah?"

"How does it look?"

"I don't know."

"Show me."

Joan looked at herself one more time and then came out of the dressing room.

Donna gasped. "Jesus jumped-up Christ."

When she was off the clock, Donna had taken to teasing her hair so it was big and voluminous. She was wearing a red denim skirt with a high slit and a white-and-yellow strapless top. She'd put it on in the dressing room, then handed the saleslady the tags and asked her to bag up her old clothes. "You have to buy that," Donna said.

"I do?" Joan looked at the price tag. She could just hear her father's outrage at the audacity.

"Have you had those tits this whole time, Joan? My God."

"Stop it. Please stop that."

"You have to buy it! Wear it out of the store like I am. Let's have fun! We're only in New Orleans for one night."

Joan looked down at the way the dress hit her body. The hem was so short. She could feel herself curving inward. "It's too much," she said. "It's so flashy."

"You're buying the goddamn dress."

Donna grabbed her arm and led her out past the other fitting rooms. She ripped the tag off the dress.

"Donna!" Joan said.

"*I'll* pay for it if I have to."

Lydia walked over, trying on a jean jacket. "Joan, you look really pretty."

"Wow," Donna said under her breath. "Hot enough to melt the ice queen."

Vanessa was at the front, looking at men's striped shirts. She glanced up, scanning the store, and saw them. When her eyes landed on Joan, Joan flushed. She put her hands to her opposite shoulders, as if she could cover up the blush of her skin. Vanessa shook her head and smiled. And then caught Joan's eye and mouthed, "You look great."

"Excuse me, miss?" Donna said to the saleslady.

When the woman turned to them, it was Joan who spoke up: "I'll take this."

THE AIR WAS STICKY, AND the light pollution on Bourbon Street was so terrible that you could barely see a star in the sky. Joan was sweating on her upper lip and at the base of her collarbone.

Duke and Hank had each bought her a beer earlier. Harrison bought her a fruity drink that tasted like candy. She'd never had this much attention from them, and she'd had more to drink tonight than she'd ever had in her life. Griff bought her a flower, and she took it and laughed.

Vanessa and Harrison were up ahead, trying to talk Donna out of getting a tarot reading. She imagined Donna asking questions about her future, as if the answers weren't obvious. Joan saw it all: she was going to marry Hank, and be the second astronaut in that marriage.

"Astronauts shouldn't fall in love with each other," Joan said aloud and then looked around and realized she was walking side by side with Griff. *When had that happened?*

"What?" Griff said.

"We all have bizarre priorities and, let's be honest, probably God complexes," Joan said. "There should only be one of us in a relationship. The other person has to make up for all the other things we lack. No, it's a bad idea to fall in love with one of us. If you're one of us."

"I don't know about that," Griff said, smiling at her in a way she'd forgotten she didn't like. They walked past Donna, Vanessa, and Harrison.

"No, I'm right about this," Joan said. "I think about it a lot."

"You think about it a lot, huh?" Griff pushed his shoulder into hers. "I think you're wrong. Who else would put up with us except each other? Who else is going to understand why we might have to miss our kid's recital or can't be home on Christmas, or why we're risking our lives?"

Joan looked at him, considering. She could not ever miss Christmas with Frances. Not ever.

"It doesn't matter anyway," she said.

"Why not?"

"Because people never fall in love with who they should. This whole world is full of stories of people falling in love with exactly who they weren't supposed to."

"I had no idea you were such a romantic," Griff said.

Joan rolled her eyes. "I don't believe in love," she said. "For me. So how can I be a romantic?"

Griff considered her. "What do you mean?"

Up ahead, Lydia was waving everyone over. Duke, Hank, Marty, Teddy, and Jimmy were all walking into a club. Donna ran past Joan and Griff.

Joan felt a hand on her shoulder before she heard Vanessa's voice. "What are you two talking about?"

"Ford, don't you think that Joan might just be a secret romantic?"

"I want to stop talking about this," Joan said.

Vanessa looked at her with a smile Joan couldn't decipher. "I think Joan still has a lot of things to figure out."

Joan tightened her jaw. "You can be very condescending," she said finally. "Has anyone ever told you that?"

Vanessa laughed. "No, actually."

Griff stopped in place suddenly. "Oh, no."

"What?"

Joan looked up at the sign, which said, "CONTINUOUS ALL GIRL SHOWS." There were neon outlines of half-naked women all over the storefront.

"Everyone went into a strip club?" Joan asked.

"Joan's not going to a strip club," Vanessa said.

Donna pulled at them. "Come on, everybody, it's only fun if we all do it."

Joan looked at the club door. The hairs on the back of her neck started to rise.

"I'll do it," Joan said.

"What?" Vanessa and Griff said at the same time.

But before anyone could say anything else, Joan walked through the front door.

JOAN HAD SEEN WOMEN NAKED in locker rooms.

But she'd never seen this.

There were six or seven women all dancing on the stages. Some with bras on, some without. Some teasingly pulling on the string of their bikini bottoms.

At first, Joan had not known where to look. But now, whether it was the drinks or watching Donna and Lydia put dollars in the strippers' G-strings, something in her was settling. Her body was becoming softer, her muscles liquid, her belly warm.

And she began to watch.

She watched the way they moved. The way they curved and flowed.

Just watching them, Joan liked her own body more. As she saw Duke tip a topless waitress, Joan made so much more sense to herself for one crystal-clear moment. Of course men were uninteresting to her. They were fundamentally uninteresting.

We are interesting.

Joan's eye drifted onstage to a woman to her right, who called herself Raven, no doubt a reference to her dark curly hair.

Raven rolled her hips in front of Joan and Joan knew she was staring but could not stop. Joan watched Raven as she took her bikini top off. She felt a rush of something as she saw Raven topless. Joan kept watching as Raven smiled at her and began to play to her, writhing in front of her.

The world clicked into place for Joan then: why men were so obsessed with women's bodies, why they made so many mistakes just to get closer to one.

"Here," Donna said.

"What?"

Joan looked over to see that Donna was handing her a dollar bill. "Put it in her bikini to tip her!" Donna shouted. "It's fun!"

"Oh." Joan took the dollar bill and looked back at Raven. There was something so gentle about Raven's smile. So peaceful it was dangerous.

"Hi," Raven said as she turned her hip toward Joan. Joan leaned over and slipped the dollar into the string of her bikini. Her skin was so soft. How could Joan get her skin that soft? How could Joan move within her body the way Raven did? How could Joan be just like her? Had Joan ever held that much power in her whole life?

As Joan looked around, everyone was starting to leave. So she got up and nodded at Raven and waved goodbye. It took her a second to remember how to put one foot in front of the other. How to pretend to be normal.

How to act like she hadn't just found something everyone else had discovered long ago.

When her eyes hit the neon signs of Bourbon Street, Joan could feel the lightness in her head that would feel heavy tomorrow. She knew she should call it a night. But instead, she said, "Where's Vanessa?"

"She went back to the hotel after, like, two minutes in there," Lydia said.

"Oh," Joan said. "I should head back, too."

"Do you want me to walk back with you?" Griff asked.

Joan looked at him. He was so handsome. And kind. And patient.

"You don't have to," she said.

"At least let me put you in a cab," he said.

The next thing Joan knew, they were walking arm in arm away from the crowd.

When they were out of sight of the others, Griff took her hand for a moment. Joan loved the warmth of his skin on hers, the feeling of another hand entangled with her own. "It's been a wild night," he said.

"Yeah. Pretty crazy."

Griff smiled at her. "You're drunk."

"Not really." But even she didn't buy it.

He looked at her. His eyes were light brown, so soft. Why couldn't she love him? Maybe she could. She leaned toward him, giving in—to what she did not know.

But he pulled away from her. "I've wanted to kiss you for months now," he said.

Joan opened her eyes.

"But not when you're drunk."

"But I want to," Joan said. "Right now, I want to. And I may not want to tomorrow."

Griff smiled, but his eyes were sad. She could see that.

"Then we shouldn't," Griff said.

Joan had seen enough movies to know what to do. She grabbed

the lapels of his jacket and pulled him toward her, pulled him against her, her body pressed against the brick wall behind her.

He gave in to her then, put his hands on the wall and pushed against her. He kissed her back.

He tasted like rum, and she wanted to gag. The roughness of his chin. The smell of him. She hated it as much as she'd known she would.

She pushed him away—she had to.

"I shouldn't have done that," she said. "I don't think we are . . . like this."

He frowned, but she felt such relief. She had finally said it. He could stop trying to love her now. Because she did not want him. She wanted something, she wanted it so badly. In her bones and her legs. But she did not want him at all.

He backed away a step, and then he laughed to himself in a way that wasn't funny. "It's okay," he said. "I had a feeling this would happen. It's why I haven't made a move."

"I'm sorry, Griff," she said. "It's just . . . it's complicated."

Griff nodded. "I thought it might be. I thought you might be."

Joan did not want to know what he meant.

A taxi came down their side of the road. Griff hailed it and opened the door for Joan. He put her in the backseat and gave the driver the name of the hotel.

"Thank you," Joan said, her hand on the edge of the open window. She was overwhelmed with love for him. Love in the sense that she trusted him, and saw all the good in his heart, and cared about him and wanted only good things to ever happen to him. Love in the sense that she would always be on his side, even if he was wrong, in the sense that he was one of the people on this Earth she believed in. And in that moment, the swelling in her heart was unbearable. Absolutely unbearable.

"I'm sorry," she said.

He shook his head. "No, don't be. I'll be okay. Give me a little while and I'll be just fine."

She nodded.

"You looked gorgeous tonight, Joan," he said. And then he tapped the cab's roof. And off she went.

As the cab drove away, Joan touched her lips. Her lipstick was smeared. And her lips felt as if they were tender, buzzing not with satisfaction but with longing.

That night, Joan dreamt of things she'd never dreamt of before.

SHE WOKE UP TO THE fog of morning. The bright sun coming through the window was a shock to her cloudy vision. She reached for her sunglasses on the nightstand and put them on. A loud pounding on her door forced her to finally get out of bed.

She was naked, which surprised her. She grabbed a robe from the closet and then turned to see that the bed was covered in sketches. She'd used up the entire hotel stationery pad. Joan looked at them, trying to remember drawing them.

Every single sketch was of Raven.

Raven smiling at her. Raven dancing. Raven with her top off. Raven's hips and her stomach.

Joan gathered them all up frantically as the pounding continued. "Be right there!"

"Open up, Joan! You're late for the bus." *Vanessa.*

"I'm coming!" Joan stuffed all of the sketches in the nightstand.

"Everyone can't wait to see what you look like hungover," Vanessa said loudly out in the hall.

Joan cringed. "Please be quiet until I get to the door!"

Finally, she opened it.

Vanessa turned to see her and only then did Joan realize she had not yet looked in the mirror. She glanced down. Her robe was loose, a deep V showing the borders of her chest. Vanessa looked at it and then back up at Joan's face. Joan pulled her robe tighter.

"It's worse than I thought," Vanessa said, smirking.

Joan smoothed her hair down and let her in.

"Oh, your hair's not the half of it," Vanessa said as she followed Joan into the room. Joan started throwing her things into her suitcase. Vanessa began helping her.

"Everyone decided to go grab breakfast while we wait for you. Donna and Jimmy really wanted grits anyway."

Joan tossed her new dress into her bag. "This is so embarrassing."

Vanessa shook her head. "Everyone's charmed. Joan Goodwin cut loose."

"Everyone bought me too many drinks!" she said.

"It happens to pretty girls a lot. I'm surprised you're not used to it."

Joan looked up at her, but Vanessa was already walking to the bathroom. When she came out, she handed Joan a toothbrush with toothpaste already on it.

"Here you go, slugger."

Joan took it and brushed her teeth. "I feel like I might vomit," she said through the foam of the toothpaste.

Vanessa nodded. "You've been hungover before. It will pass."

Joan headed into the bathroom, Vanessa following her. "I've had a headache before. This is . . . disgusting."

Vanessa nodded again as Joan spit the toothpaste out. "Yeah, that's because you usually drink wine or beer. Last night, you drank those hurricanes everyone was buying. Donna already puked this morning."

Joan's stomach turned. Vanessa wet a washcloth and then put a little bit of Vaseline on it. "Your face looks like a Jackson Pollock. Come here."

Joan held her hand out for the washcloth. But Vanessa either didn't notice or ignored her. "Close your eyes."

Joan looked at her for a moment and then slowly complied. She swallowed hard.

Vanessa put the washcloth on Joan's cheekbone. She rubbed gently, and with her other hand she held Joan's chin. The washcloth was so warm that Joan could have fallen asleep right there. And she was once again so close to Vanessa that she could smell the soft, sweet scent of baby powder.

Vanessa started in on Joan's eyes, her hand gentle but firm. Joan could feel her skin getting cleaner under Vanessa's touch, her stomach settling.

Vanessa rubbed Joan's eyebrows, and then her forehead and down her jawline. And then she stopped.

Joan opened her eyes.

"You're . . . um, you should probably do your lips," she said, handing Joan the cloth.

"Oh, okay, thanks," Joan said. She took the cloth and wiped the lipstick off as quickly as she could. "Good?"

Vanessa nodded. "Yeah, you look like yourself again."

"I didn't look like myself last night?"

"I don't know, Jo. I'm still trying to figure out if you know who you are."

"Do *you* know who I am?" Joan asked her. It came out with an edge, but Joan desperately hoped she'd say yes.

Vanessa shook her head. "I'm hoping I do. Only you can say for sure."

Joan could feel the space between them grow thicker.

"I kissed Griff last night," Joan said. "After the strip club." She studied Vanessa's face for any reaction. It showed nothing.

"You seemed to be having quite a nice time at that club," Vanessa said.

"I didn't enjoy it," Joan told her. "Kissing Griff."

Vanessa nodded. "No, I had suspected you wouldn't."

"I liked the club, though."

Vanessa was quiet, but she held Joan's gaze. Then she looked away and nodded again, this time with a little smirk. "Yeah, I suspected you would."

"Did you enjoy it?" Joan asked. "The club?"

"What do you think?" Vanessa said.

"I don't know. You left early. I couldn't tell."

Vanessa didn't say anything.

"You say I don't know who I am, but do you know who *you* are?" Joan asked her.

Vanessa laughed. Joan cringed.

"Yes, Joan, I do. And you know who I am, too. If you're honest with yourself."

Oh, they were much too close to the sun.

"I think we should . . . I mean . . . we're already so late! Can you grab my sunglasses? I'll get dressed."

Vanessa looked at her for a moment longer and then said, "Okay."

Joan shut the bathroom door and put on her clothes. She fixed her hair. When she came out, Vanessa was holding her sunglasses and her wallet. She was standing right by the nightstand. Joan's cheeks grew hot, as she worried Vanessa had opened the drawer. But she showed no signs of having seen anything.

Vanessa started to walk past the bed, toward Joan and the door, but then she stopped and leaned over. "Oh, looks like you left something," she said as she grabbed a piece of paper, half-buried in the sheets.

"It's nothing," Joan said. "Don't look at it. You don't need to."

But Vanessa did look at it, and then she smiled. "Oh, I do know you," she said. "I know you so well. I know you exactly, Joan Goodwin."

Joan could feel her cheeks warming. She was on the thinnest edge of something. But, somehow, she knew she was okay.

"All right, Ford," she said. "Let's go."

THE FOLLOWING WEEKEND, JOAN HAD MADE PLANS TO PICK FRANCES
up on Sunday morning at ten, but she woke up almost half an hour
late.

She'd been doing that lately. Unable to sleep, then unable to
wake up, her mind scattered, her body falling behind. She called the
house but no one answered, so she threw on a dress and got in the
car. She made up some of the time by cutting through corner gas stations to avoid red lights—painfully aware that the maneuver was illegal.

When she pulled into Barbara's driveway, Frances was outside
sitting on the stoop. She was in cream overalls, her hair in two braids
she'd clearly done herself.

"Hey, babe," Joan said. "Sorry I'm late."

It was eleven minutes after ten.

"It's okay," Frances said, getting up.

"Where's your mom?"

"With Scott."

Joan did not know who Scott was, but she could figure well enough.

Frances walked toward Joan's car, but Joan stood on the lawn for
a moment.

"Your mom's not home?"

"No, she left about a half hour ago, to go pick him up. She said to
wait out here until you came."

"Why not in the house?" Joan said.

Frances shrugged. "She locked the door when she left."

Joan could not tell if this was as big a deal as it seemed to her.

"Are we going out to breakfast?" Frances said as she got into the
front seat. "I already had Lucky Charms, but I'm still hungry."

Joan opened her own car door and got in.

"If you want to, sure."

Joan drove them to the diner by her apartment building and they got a table. When the food arrived, Frances scarfed down both her pancakes in about three minutes flat.

"Franny, c'mon, eat your eggs," Joan said.

"I really don't want to," Frances said.

"You promised that you would," Joan reminded her.

"I'm not hungry anymore," Frances said.

This worked with Barbara. Joan was sure of it. "Eating an egg is not going to kill you," she said, entirely unamused. "I don't want you to get all hopped up on sugar and no protein."

Frances frowned, but then she picked up her fork and began eating.

"What are we doing today?" Joan asked. "Movies or shopping?"

Frances considered her options. "How much money will I get for shopping?"

"The exact cost of a movie ticket—you know that."

Frances nodded. "What if I said I wanted to see a movie tonight, would you take me?"

"Of course, my love. If it is okay with your mom."

"But those tickets are more expensive."

"Right, but that's fine."

"So if we go shopping now, can I have the same price as an evening movie ticket?"

Joan laughed just as Frances did. "You little trickster," Joan said.

Frances's eyes crinkled and she curled her shoulders up, so pleased with herself. "You did say . . ."

"Okay," Joan said, pointing at her. "That trick will work this time. I'll give you the money because I admire your moxie. But next time, I'll be on to you."

Frances shrugged. "It's okay," she said. "I want to go see a movie anyway."

Joan laughed. "You're going to be a lawyer when you grow up," she said. "Or a hostage negotiator."

"What's a hostage negotiator?"

"Don't worry about it. All right," Joan said. "Which is it? *Great Muppet Caper* or *Superman II*?"

Joan did not hear Frances's answer because she was distracted by Griff walking into the diner, headed for the counter.

He was picking up a takeout order. He saw her the moment she saw him, and he smiled at her, albeit forlornly. She wanted to go up and talk to him. But he'd been keeping his distance, walking over to JSC on his own even when they had the same schedule, declining dinner invitations from the group. She did wonder when things would go back to normal, but as she looked at him at the counter, he waved to her with such a sweet curtness that she understood it wasn't normal yet.

"Joanie?"

"Hm?"

"I said I want to see *The Great Muppet Caper*."

"Okay, babe," Joan said. "Finish your plate and let's head out."

"Do I really have to?"

Joan wondered why she couldn't be the cool aunt who let Frances eat chocolate cake with whipped cream for breakfast and stay up late and learn all the swear words. She didn't know if that was her fault or Barbara's fault. Or maybe it had always been inevitable.

"Yes," Joan said. "You have to."

THAT AFTERNOON, JOAN PULLED INTO the driveway to bring Frances home, as planned. Joan had rebraided her hair, but otherwise, Frances was worse for wear, with maple syrup on her overall bib and popcorn butter on her pants.

"Can I spend the night at your house?" Frances said before she got out of the car.

Joan turned off the engine. "I don't know about that, babe," Joan said. "You have day camp tomorrow."

"But you could take me," Frances said. "I was thinking if you would take me to camp, or even school, in the morning sometimes, I could stay at your place more often."

Joan nodded. "Why don't we talk about it with your mom at some point?" she said. "But not tonight, okay?"

Frances nodded. "But you know she's going to say yes," she said. "She doesn't care if I'm here."

"Of course she does," Joan said. "Your mother wants you with her all the time."

Frances looked at Joan with a disappointed frown.

When they got to the front door, Barbara was cleaning the kitchen and there was music coming from the record player. Joan could hear a man's voice in the backyard and smell the smoke of the grill.

"Hello, family," Barbara said. She walked over to the front door and pulled Frances close to her. "Joan, do you want to stay for dinner? Scott is making ribs."

"I can't," Joan said. "But can we talk for a moment?"

"Can I go watch TV?" Frances asked.

"Sure, honey," Barbara said. "Go ahead."

Even with Frances gone, Joan whispered as low as she could. "Why did you leave Frances outside by herself this morning?"

"What are you talking about?"

"You shut her outside and left."

"You were picking her up."

"She was alone outside by herself for more than a half hour."

"Well, it's not my fault you weren't here on time. I assumed she'd only be there for a few minutes. And anyway, she's fine, isn't she?"

"Barbara, she's seven years old."

"I know how old my daughter is, thank you very much."

"I'm just saying, maybe don't lock her out. What if I hadn't shown up?"

"I'd have been back in an hour. I just went to pick up Scott," she said. "She's a smart kid. She would have gone around to the backyard and played until we got here."

"Barbara—"

"You consistently underestimate how smart and capable she is. You baby her."

"I don't baby her. I watch out for her."

"Oh, screw you, Joan. Screw you. And don't look at me like that."

Joan was not sure how she was looking at her, but already the confusion was settling in.

Barbara often accused Joan of *thinking* things, claiming that Joan didn't even have to speak, because of how clear her disdain was from her body language.

And the fact was that yes, sometimes Joan worried that Barbara was careless. Sometimes Joan was concerned about Barbara's inability to consider other people, to think things through from any perspective other than her own.

But Joan worked so hard to stay on Barbara's side.

Still, Joan was often snapped at for things she'd never said, accused of taking positions she had not yet even committed to within her own mind.

Was Barbara being unfair? Or was Joan indeed judgmental? And maybe her sister was the only person close enough to confront her about it? Joan wasn't sure, knew that she might not ever be sure.

"I'm not looking at you like anything," Joan said finally.

"Yes, you are—you think I'm a bad mother."

"No, I don't."

"But you don't know the first thing about being someone's mother, Joan."

"I know that."

"And certainly not how hard it is to do it by myself. With no one helping me."

Joan nodded, unsure what to say to that.

"So mind your own business."

Joan looked past Barbara to where Frances was watching TV and playing with two of her dolls. She was laughing. She was completely fine. Right?

"I'm sorry," Joan said. "You're right."

"Thank you," Barbara said. "That's very big of you. Thank you."

Joan kissed Frances's forehead on the way out. "I'll see you soon. Okay, sweetheart?"

Frances nodded and said, "Yep. Bye, Joanie."

JULY 1981

AT THE ONE-YEAR MARK OF THE ASCANS' TRAINING, THERE WAS A CAMP-
ing trip at the lake. Astronauts, instructors, and the ASCANs and
their families were all invited.

Joan had invited Frances to join her. When Joan arrived to pick
her up, Frances was standing in the front yard with Barbara. She was
wearing a fisherman's vest and an adult-sized camping backpack.

Joan tried not to laugh as Frances's body sank under the weight
of it all.

"I can carry that, babe," she said, taking the backpack off.

"I didn't know what she'd need for camping," Barbara said.

Joan held back a smile. "You did great. I've borrowed a tent from
Harrison, who can't go. And I have sleeping bags from when we
would lie out under the stars at Brazos. So we are all set. But all of
this is helpful, too."

"It's too much!" Frances exclaimed as she took off her vest and
got into Joan's front seat.

Barbara whispered so low that Joan had to lean in to hear her:
"This is the sort of stuff I worry about. She doesn't know how to
camp. She doesn't know any of this stuff. Without a father around."

Joan was unsure of the details, but apparently Scott was already out of the picture. She'd heard as much from Frances.

"Oh, Barbara, she'll be fine. Really."

"I just don't want her to miss out on anything, or feel left behind," Barbara said.

"Hey, you and me, we got her, all right?" Joan said. "We always have, always will."

Barbara nodded. "Yeah, and maybe Dad should fly out more, spend more time with her."

"I think that's a great idea—I think both Mom and Dad would love that."

Barbara waved goodbye to Frances and then made her put down her window so she could give her a kiss. "Don't roll your eyes," Barbara said. "I have given up my entire life to raise you. You can give me one damn kiss."

"Sorry, Mom," Frances said. She kissed Barbara on the cheek and then said, to both Barbara and Joan, "Can we go now?"

DONNA AND JOAN SET UP Joan's tent while Lydia set up her own. Most of the kids were playing nearby, while others were on the fishing dock. Frances had already run off with Duke and Kris's oldest daughter, Julie, and Steve and Helene's eleven-year-old, Patty. Patty was teaching the younger girls how to stain rocks by crushing flower petals on them.

As Joan pressed a stake into the ground, she tried to pretend she didn't hear Vanessa's voice behind her, coming up from the parking lot. Vanessa was with Steve, unloading food from the back of Duke's truck. Joan could not bring herself to turn and look at her. For the past few weeks, Joan had not been able to look Vanessa in the eye.

"You need to shove that stake in more or this whole thing's gonna blow over with a fart," Donna said.

Joan rolled her eyes and stomped on the stake, driving it farther into the ground.

"Thanks for the tip."

"You're lucky I love you and put up with all your half-assed tent making," Donna said.

"You're lucky I love you and put up with your foul mouth."

Donna considered Joan's comment. "Yes, I suppose I am."

They finished just as Lydia's tent fell over.

"Come on," Joan said.

Donna sighed. "Do I have to help her?"

"Yes."

"Even though she lobbied for more time on the RMS so badly that they pulled me off to give it to her?"

"If you're not gonna help her, I'll do it myself."

"Well, you aren't gonna do shit," Donna said, marching ahead of her. "You barely put up your own."

When they approached Lydia, she said, "I've got it. Don't touch it!"

Donna shot a look at Joan.

"Lydia, let us help you," Joan said.

"Just give me some space to move—jeez."

"Hey, how many chicks does it take to pitch a tent?" Marty said. Jimmy was with him, already laughing before Marty even delivered the punch line.

Joan closed her eyes, her chest rising. Donna shook her head.

"Doesn't matter! Any of you can pitch my tent!" Marty said.

Lydia cracked up and gave Marty a low five.

"Just fuck off, Marty," Donna said.

Jimmy muttered, "So touchy," and then he and Marty walked on.

When they were out of earshot, Joan turned to Lydia. "Why do you do that?"

"Do what?"

"Laugh at those stupid jokes. I hate it when you encourage them."

"I think maybe you just need to lighten up."

"You sound like them," Donna said.

"Well, isn't that sort of the point?" Lydia said, dropping the center of the tent onto the ground and giving up. "If you'd just go with the flow, they'd stop eventually. And see that we're just like them."

"I don't want to be like them," Joan said.

"We have to be like them," Lydia said. "That's why they are letting women into the program. Because we have finally convinced them we are just as good as them."

"She has a point," Donna said, sighing. "No one at NASA is thinking, 'Let's see how women do it.' They're thinking, 'Maybe we should give them a chance to prove they are just like us.'"

"I mean, it's 1981, Joan," Lydia said. "It's time to stop getting upset at stupid jokes and start getting stuff done."

"I would say the exact opposite to you," Joan countered, her breathing shallow. "It's 1981, and I'm done pretending sexist jokes are funny just so men will give me a chance at something I'm probably better at than they are."

Lydia shook her head. "You just don't get it. It infuriates me sometimes. Before Group 8, there wasn't a single woman in this program. All men, and every man who's been assigned a mission has been white."

"I obviously know that."

"Group 8 they let in six white women, three Black men, and an Asian man. The rest of the thirty-five? All white men."

"I know that, too," Joan said.

"She's saying we're outnumbered," Donna said. Joan looked at her. "NASA is run primarily by men. If we want to go up there, we have to convince a *man* to choose us. We have to be somebody *the men* here want to work with. We have to be smart."

Studying Donna, Joan realized that she was actually fully aware of how people saw her. That Donna knew *they all knew* she was dating Hank. And that her coyness about it, her complete denial of it in front of any of them, was her only shot at self-preservation. It was Donna, then, who was keeping it a secret. Not Hank.

And if Donna was smart enough to know that seeing Hank would hurt her career and did it anyway, well, Donna must really love him.

"I will never be Jimmy," Joan said. "Or Marty. Or Teddy. I don't want to tell jokes at other people's expense, and pretend I'm never afraid, and refuse to ask for help. I don't want to hold in how I feel, or hide it if I've been hurt, or try to prove to anyone that I don't cry. Because I do cry sometimes."

"Oh, me too, hon," Donna said. "But you know we can't show that."

"We can never, ever show that," Lydia said.

"I . . ." Joan shook her head. "I don't want to prove I can be like them. I don't want to be like them. I'm not going to do it."

"But what you do affects all of us," Lydia said. "Because they are looking at every woman here. There aren't enough of us in this program yet for us to only represent ourselves. You cry in front of them and they are going to say, 'Women can't handle being in the hot seat.' And then *I* get screwed over. You're not just here for you, Joan—we all succeed or fail together."

"I don't know if that's true," Joan said.

"It is true," Donna said. "I don't know exactly what to do about it. But it is true."

"So, we let them say crude things about us and we don't push back?"

"I mean, I tell them to fuck off," Donna said. "You should try it."

"But Lydia laughs like it's funny."

"Sometimes it *is* funny," Lydia said.

"The only reason you think it's funny is because we've been told our whole lives it's okay to make fun of us," Joan said. "But I'm not doing it. You want to talk about how it reflects on all of us the way one of us behaves? You laughing at those jokes makes them think it's okay to keep doing it."

Lydia sighed. "I don't want to keep talking about this," she said.

"Well, me neither."

Joan thought of Vanessa then, still talking to Steve. She wondered if Vanessa would agree with her. And whether she would see that Joan wasn't being a peacemaker now.

"All right, let's dust it off," Donna said. "We all agree on the root problem here. We just don't know how to solve it."

"There is no one way to solve it," Joan said.

Lydia nodded. "No, you're right about that."

"But me fighting with you certainly isn't it," Joan admitted.

"Yeah," Lydia said.

"I'm so annoyed," Joan said.

"At me?" Lydia asked, with such a childlike vulnerability that it softened Joan's heart.

"No, at them. It's their fault we are fighting at all. I am actually mad at them, but instead I'm blaming you."

"Well, as you know," Lydia said, smiling, "women can be very irrational."

Joan laughed, despite herself.

"Lydia Danes, as I live and breathe," Donna said. "Did you just make a good joke?"

"I can be funny, you know."

"No," Donna said. "Nobody knew that."

AFTER DINNER, KRIS WAVED JOAN over to one of the tents and showed her that Frances had fallen asleep with Julie in Julie's sleeping bag. They were still in their day clothes, covered in dirt. Frances's hair was in knots, chocolate on her cheeks.

Joan watched Frances snore with her mouth open, her little hand holding Julie's as they slept. It passed through her mind that she wasn't sure how often Frances got to see her friends outside of school.

"Do you want me to carry her over to your tent?" a voice said softly, from behind her.

Joan turned to see Griff.

"They're okay," Kris said. "Let her sleep. Julie does this all the time with her cousin Linda. She thinks she's being sneaky, but it's the only time she puts herself to bed."

Joan laughed. "Okay, you sure? You want to come get me in the morning when she wakes up?"

"They'll be fine," Kris said.

Griff nodded toward the lakefront, and Joan followed him. The night air was warm, but there was an easy breeze. The sky was clear, the tops of Cygnus and Aquila straight ahead of them, behind the trees.

In the distance, Joan watched Vanessa, on the edge of the dock, having a beer with Steve. Joan felt like a moth that knew what a flame could do to it.

When Joan turned away from the sight of Vanessa, she saw Griff watching her.

He was quiet until they were farther away from the group.

"I wanted to tell you that it's okay. I'm good, you don't need to give me space anymore," Griff said.

"Are you sure?" Joan asked. "I'll do anything you need."

Griff nodded, appreciatively. "Have you ever been in love?" he asked.

Joan could not look at him. "No, I don't think so."

"Well, it's like a bad cold: it's miserable and then, one day, it's gone."

Joan laughed.

"All I'm saying is, let's put it behind us."

"Put what behind us?" Joan said, smiling.

Griff laughed. "Thank you."

"You really are the best guy I've ever known," Joan said.

"Well, let's not start with that," Griff said.

"No, I just mean . . ." Joan said. "There aren't many men in my life, really. Aside from my father and the rest of . . . these guys. But you are good. You're a good one."

"Well, I try to be."

"I know you do. And I'm honored to be your friend. I really mean that. I'm honored to work with you."

"I feel the same."

"So can we go back to walking over to JSC together?"

"Yeah, I'd like that."

"And we can get dinner?"

Griff raised his palm up. "One thing at a time, Goodwin."

Joan smiled when she heard him call her that. But she did recognize that something had been lost between them that would never come back.

They walked on, farther from the campsite, before eventually heading back.

"Can I say one more thing?" Griff asked, just before they approached the camp. "That is not my place to say?"

"Of course."

"I'm not going to pretend to know what's in your heart. But you've said a few things, here and there, and I've . . . sensed a few things, maybe . . . and . . ."

He stopped and turned toward her. "If you do have feelings for someone—if that's something that's on your mind . . . I worry that you're in a tough spot. Because as wrong as I think their position is, there are some things NASA doesn't officially condone for astronauts. From what I've heard."

Joan couldn't breathe for a full second, her body forgetting how to let the air out of her lungs.

"You okay?" he said.

She nodded. "Thank you, Griff. For looking out. But I . . . I'm not sure what any of that has to do with me."

"Okay," he said. "I just . . . I will go to bat for you. If you need it. I just wanted you to know that. Regardless of you completely decimating my ego back in New Orleans . . ." he added, laughing.

"Would you stop?"

He kept laughing. "I'm just saying . . . my wounded pride wouldn't affect what I believe to be right. Everyone should be free to live their lives, love anyone they choose. I've got your back, Goodwin. Okay? That's what I'm trying to say."

"Thank you, Griff, really," Joan said. "But I have no idea what you're talking about."

JOAN WENT BACK TO HER tent but, finding herself all alone in there without Frances, she couldn't sleep. She could not quiet her mind— but also could not ignore the small splashes she kept hearing from time to time, some fish or bird out there in the lake. With a huff of frustration, she got out of her sleeping bag, unzipped her tent, and stood up.

There, on the dock, was Vanessa. She was skipping stones across the lake's surface.

Joan looked up at the sky. Just based on where Vega hung, Joan suspected it was earlier than two A.M.

She could have returned to her tent and tried to fall asleep again. But the back of Vanessa's body was lit by the brightness of the moon, and Joan walked to her.

Vanessa must have heard her footsteps, because she turned and, upon seeing Joan, smiled big and wide. Vanessa's smile was so beautiful, the way it was lopsided, but the rest of her face was always perfectly symmetrical. The curls of her hair were the most gorgeous thing Joan had ever seen in her life, and she wanted to reach out and run her hand through them. To pull her closer.

"Look," Vanessa said, pointing up toward the western edge of the sky. "Hercules."

Joan did not speak.

"The whole sky makes sense to me now," Vanessa said. "Because of you."

And Joan thought, *Oh no. Oh no. Oh no. Oh no.*

DECEMBER 29, 1984

NOW IN HER SPACE SUIT, VANESSA ENTERS THE PAYLOAD BAY, TETHERED to the ship. She moves toward the forward bulkhead to inspect the right-side latches. She tries not to think about Hank. She tries not to think about what Donna must be going through right now. She tries not to think of baby Thea and the fact that Thea will never remember the way Hank held her on Thanksgiving. The way Donna kept asking to take her, and Hank always shook his head. "No," she'd heard Hank say. "Please don't. Let me have her." Thea will never remember the way it felt to be in her father's arms like that. Her father will be some-one people tell Thea about.

She can't stand to think of it.

She thinks, instead, of Griff. She thinks of Lydia.

And she thinks of Joan.

When she gets to the forward bulkhead, a shudder runs through her. She can see the other side of the hole on the forward bulkhead. But then, in addition, the payload bay door is bent. It took a hit, most likely from the debris that flew from the explosive cords.

"Houston, the right payload bay door is warped. I am going to attempt to manually latch it closed, but I am not positive I can get the edges to make contact."

Joan's voice comes through: "*Navigator,* copy. The PLBDs can withstand some measure of variation. We would like you to get started so we can assess."

Vanessa looks around. The doors make the shape of a capital I on the top of the payload bay, and when closed, they are held together with a total of thirty-two latches. Eight on the forward bulkhead, eight on the aft bulkhead, and sixteen down the centerline. First, she's going to pull the forward bulkhead latches closed as best she can.

The left set of four have been closed electronically. So she moves to the right set, beginning with the one farthest from the center. The first has jammed, but she knows what to do. In almost any other scenario up here, this might even be Vanessa's shining moment. This is what she's here for. The mechanics.

She grabs the tool kit from behind the thermal blanket and floats back to the first latch. She takes out the ratchet wrench. There can be no rushing in space, really. And in this moment, she is grateful that she is forced to work through the problem methodically. She has trained for this moment. Back on Earth, she learned where to put her right hand, where to put her left hand, how to get into the foot restraints, and how to brace herself for maximum leverage. She gets into position and begins.

How is she going to be an astronaut without Steve? How is she going to get home without him? She can't. She can't do any of this. She's going to fuck this up and they are all going to die. She can't do this.

Vanessa inhales sharply.

Maybe rushing would be better. Maybe, if she didn't have a moment to think, it would all be easier. Gravity is underrated. It gives us something to fight against.

She tries to clear her mind. She aligns the ratchet wrench to the gearbox and begins to turn.

Steve had told Vanessa, at one point, that even though he was the younger of two brothers, it felt like *she* was his little sister.

Vanessa had replied that she, too, felt like a little sister, always the focus of the attention between them, always asking too much of him. But Steve had corrected her. He said he got something out of it, too. "Talking to you, hearing what you're going through, it makes me realize how far I've come since I was your age. And hell, I might be a great astronaut. But if all I'm doing with what I've learned is using it for myself, what kind of legacy is that?

"This way, I'll help you, and you'll help another ASCAN, and she'll help another, and on it will go. And then one day, decades from now, when we get to Mars, I'll be long gone. But I'll still be a part of it."

She turns the gearbox, pulling it as tight as she can. The four latches close. The firm connection of the latches feels good in her hand.

"*Navigator,* we see the first gang of four is done. Thank you."

Vanessa looks up. The bend in the door is preventing the doors from making total contact. She puts the ratchet wrench back on the gearbox and tries to turn it farther, pulling the door in as much as possible.

If the gap between the doors is sizable enough, the shuttle will burn up upon reentry into the atmosphere. Vanessa will never see Joan again.

She tries to release her jaw and focuses on her breathing. *In for four. Hold for four. Out for four.* She knows if she repeats the same pattern of breath, she can occupy her mind enough to stop her from thinking about the rest of it.

In for four. Hold for four. Out for four.
In for four. Hold for four. Out for four.

She continues turning.

It is dark inside the payload bay, and there is still much to be done.

JOAN IS NOT GOING TO SAY IT OUT LOUD. NO ONE IS. BUT IF THE FOR-
ward bulkhead latches cannot pull the door flat, things are going to
take a turn.

Ray stands up. "Flight, Surgeon. I'm concerned about Griff's
heart rate."

This is the fourth time Ray has noted this, but now his tone is
calmer and less animated, which has an inverse effect. Joan turns to
him. She can tell from his pale face and wide eyes that he's exerting
a lot of effort to control himself.

Jack: "What are we at?"

"Twenty-one bpm and it is growing more irregular."

"How irregular?"

Ray checks the instruments again and swallows.

As Ray begins to speak—his face somber—it is as if someone has
turned down the volume of Joan's world. Every word exchanged between Ray and Jack feels muted—muffled and unreal. She can see
Ray frown. She can see Jack slam his hand down on the top of his
console.

But she cannot make out a single word.

Later, she will realize that she actually did hear all of this. That
she stored it away to process when she could face it. It will come
back to her in flashes much later.

"His temperature has fallen." "We've lost heart-rate signals." "Do
not tell Ford." "Even if she got to him in the next thirty seconds, I
don't believe—"

But right now, it is as if Joan has left her body. Her view is from
ten feet up in the air.

She can see herself in her chair. Her hair falling out of her ponytail, her eyes bloodshot.

Now everything is moving backward. She can see herself coming in to work this morning, then going to bed last night. She can see herself waving goodbye to Griff in the parking lot at JSC before he went into quarantine. She can see him talking to her in the pool at Steve's house, swimming up to her. She can see him greeting her that first day at the apartment complex.

She can see the past, but it is now tinged with the excruciating inevitability of the present moment.

How has she never seen where this was headed, when it was so painfully obvious?

You absolute child, she thinks. *He was hit with shrapnel from an explosion two hundred miles above Earth, and you thought he'd survive?*

An abrupt and violent silence crashes into the room, and she snaps back into the moment.

She sees the blood drain out of Ray's face. "Flight, Surgeon. John Griffin is dead."

Joan can feel the liquid iron core of the Earth pulling her toward it, down into the depths of a hell she does not believe in.

Hank is gone. Steve is gone. Now Griff is gone, too.

He'd once told her she was a romantic, and she hadn't believed him. How had he known her better than she'd known herself? The Joan he saw that day had been closer to who she was than the Joan she had seen in the mirror her entire life.

Vanessa's voice comes in clear: "Houston, this is Ford. I have attempted to tighten the latches but cannot pull the doors flush. We have an approximately one-centimeter gap."

Joan closes her eyes. She can't understand how she's going to get past this moment.

She squeezes the pen in her hand so hard it cracks, the sharp edge cutting into her palm.

She has her whole life to grieve. She has just a few more hours here at this console.

"Houston, come in. This is *Navigator,* do you read?" Vanessa says.

Pull it together, Goodwin.

Joan has never called herself Goodwin in her own head before. And now she wonders who's speaking to her.

"Don't tell her," Jack says. "We have to focus on the latches."

Joan looks at him. She knows it is Vanessa's only chance at staying focused enough to save herself and Lydia. It's what has to be done.

But she's not sure she can bear to do it.

Let's fucking go.

"*Navigator,* this is Houston," she says. "We believe you should move on, given the time constraints. Assuming the rest of the latches connect down the line, we believe we have viability."

"I disagree, Houston. I believe that I should keep trying to—"

"*Navigator,* move on. We do not have time."

"Are you okay, Goodwin?" Vanessa says. "You do not sound well."

Jack looks at Joan. He shakes his head. "Our job is not to tell her the truth, our job is to get her home."

"*Navigator,* yes. We are still confident about the PLBDs at this time. Please continue to the eight aft bulkhead latches."

Joan can feel that her soul has gone dormant. Her mouth is moving, but her heart is not here anymore. She knows she will get through this—these hours will pass with one outcome or another, and she will physically survive it. But she is not sure, when it is all over, if she will ever come back to herself.

VANESSA CAN HEAR THE UNSTEADINESS IN JOAN'S VOICE. BUT IF JOAN does not want to tell her what's causing it, there's a reason.

"Roger that," Vanessa says.

Vanessa maneuvers over to the aft bulkhead.

Each one of the eight latches snaps into place sequentially. That is sixteen of thirty-two down. Both the top and bottom bars of the capital I are done, however imperfectly.

She imagines the feel of her feet on the tarmac, the relief of seeing the doctors rush into the flight deck to save Griff and Lydia. She thinks of the way the air will smell to her, full of dirt and fuel.

Steve had told Vanessa that getting off the ship was like walking into your house after a long vacation. That you will get that rare moment of smelling the familiar scent of Earth, before you grow too used to it again to sense it.

She'd been looking forward to that.

She scoffs to think of how much she'd been looking forward to this entire mission. How she'd protested against being "only" a mission specialist. How she'd begged for the chance to be a pilot.

But, of course, it had been Steve who had told her she'd deserved the chance to fly the shuttle someday. Steve who'd lobbied for her. Who'd told her he would keep at it until Antonio understood.

She moves on to the centerline latches. Thankfully, the first four close easily. She continues to the next four.

Steve had cheated on his wife ten years ago. It was one time. He'd been drunk. He never forgave himself for it, even though, after he confessed to Helene, she gave him a chance to make it up to her. And he did. Make it up to her.

Vanessa didn't quite understand either side of it—the betrayal of someone or the forgiveness possible. But Steve had said that over time, she would understand both. Once she'd loved someone long enough, she'd understand that anything is possible, that she was capable of worse and greater acts than she knew.

He'd taught her that, too.

She closes the last latch in the gang. Twenty-four down. Eight to go. If she can get all eight done, it is reasonable to assume that the shuttle can withstand the issue with the forward bulkhead as its only weak point. She moves on to the next set of four, the centerline latches up by the forward bulkhead.

Quickly, she can see that the gearbox has cracked, hit by the debris.

"Houston, how many latches can we lose?" Vanessa asks. "The shuttle was designed to withstand what level of failure?"

She looks down the line to the final set of four latches, all the way at the forward bulkhead. She can see, for the second time, that the door is bent.

"*Navigator,* we believe it is possible that, even with the forward bulkhead latches not lying flat, the orbiter may be able to withstand some unpredictability with the centerline latches."

"How much? I may have eight latches that do not connect at all, in addition to the gap in the door."

"Roger that, *Navigator.* We are calculating."

Vanessa already knows the answer is not *The Shuttle can withstand reentry with eight latches open and a one-centimeter gap at the forward bulkhead.* But if she can get this gearbox to turn and close this gang of four latches, it might pull the payload bay doors tight enough on the aft bulkhead end. Which means that even if she can't get the rest of the latches closed, they still have a chance of making it.

She does her best to get a good grip on the ratchet wrench and applies it to the gearbox. But it doesn't move. She twists as hard as she can, but the harder she tries, the more microgravity pushes her away from the latch, so that she has to brace herself with one arm and one foot against the payload bay door, using her own body as counterforce to keep her leverage. She bears down as hard as she can, pushing against the door with every muscle in her body. She can feel it through her limbs and into her back and abdomen. She tenses her jaw so hard she thinks she might crack a tooth.

It's not budging.

"*Navigator,* we believe four latches on the centerline could go unlatched and we would be okay."

That's not enough—she's got eight to go, plus the warped door. She has to get this group of four. Or none of them will survive.

Vanessa tries to leverage the tool in again. *Nothing.*

She tries again. The same thing.

Again.

And again.

And again.

"Goddammit!" She stops pressing against the door and loses her footing. She has to pull herself back into position. *Fuck.*

"Ford, we believe you should move on. Confirm, please."

Vanessa can't speak. She will scream.

"*Navigator,* please confirm you will move on."

She wants to throw the fucking wrench across the payload bay and take off her helmet and wail. But she needs that tool to get home, if she so much as *unlocks* her helmet she will die within seconds, and even if she could scream, no one would hear her up here. The sound won't go anywhere.

"None of these four will close! If I move on, it means I have to secure all the rest, which appear, from here, to be busted. Are you sure I should move on to the last four?"

"Given the time constraints, we believe it is best."

"Roger that, Houston," Vanessa says. She closes her eyes and exhales.

She moves to the last group of four, down by the aft bulkhead.

But she's right. Not only has the door warped in this spot, too, but the torque shaft is damaged.

She fits the ratchet wrench onto the gearbox, but it won't turn the latches. She grabs the three-point latch tool and tries to secure each latch individually, but none of them will zip closed. She breathes in and focuses on the first latch of the four. She back-drives the three-point latch tool into the active latch and tries to turn it.

Finally, it turns one millimeter toward her. Her whole body lights up. She pulls harder and harder. Her arm is killing her. Her back aches. She has to keep going.

It turns another millimeter. And then, just as it seems like she might get the latch to catch, the torque shaft cracks further. She closes her eyes.

She just needs the payload bay doors to stay closed upon reentry. *Is that so fucking much to ask?*

Donna once told her that if one of them had to die, between her and Hank, she hoped it would be her. Vanessa didn't believe her, but Donna insisted. "And it's not for some stupid-ass reason like I can't live without him," Donna said. "I can. I did for thirty years before I met the son of a bitch. It's because he's the better parent. He loves our baby more. I know you can't compare love, but I love her so much and he loves her even more, Vanessa."

Vanessa doesn't want to think about Donna anymore. But she does want to get Hank's body home, because every time she went to her father's gravestone, she knew her father's body wasn't really there. And it always mattered to her.

She tries to pull the second latch closed enough to apply the latch tool, but it won't move.

She slams her glove against her helmet. Again. And again. And again.

"Houston, I don't know what to do."

"*Navigator,*" Joan says. "We are waiting to see if you are able to get the last four latches closed."

"And if I can't? What's the contingency?"

Joan doesn't speak for a moment. Vanessa has lived so long with this feeling, the full obliteration of everything except Joan's voice, the need to hang on her every word. "Houston, do you read?"

"We read you, *Navigator*. We are seeing on our end that all four latches are not closed."

"I do not believe they will close, Goodwin."

"Roger that," Joan says.

"Can the ship survive reentry with eight latches out and two gaps, one each toward the forward and aft bulkheads? By visual assessment, we have at least a centimeter vulnerability along the centerline."

It's quiet again. But Vanessa understands it all perfectly. Joan does not want to lie to her.

"*Navigator*," Joan says after a while, in a tone that is terrifyingly firm. "We are not confident that the shuttle is viable with that many latches out. We do not believe it will withstand the heat of reentry. We need you to start from the beginning again, tightening each latch as much as possible, starting with the forward bulkhead latches. We believe that some degree of tightening at the beginning will offer significant potential to pull the doors back into alignment."

Vanessa's heart begins to race. "Houston, if I start over and try to tighten each latch again, we are going to miss our deorbit opportunity."

"*Navigator*, that is correct."

"Can Griff and Lydia make it another rev?" Vanessa asks.

She is met with silence.

"Houston, do you read? When is the next deorbit opportunity? Will Griff and Lydia make it if we miss this one?"

"*Navigator*," Joan says finally. "We need to update you about the crew."

THERE IS A SENSE OF AGONY WITHIN MISSION CONTROL—NO ONE IS saying very much. Jack is standing right behind her, and Antonio is standing to the side of the entrance. Everyone else is slumped in their seats. Joan cannot bear to meet anyone's eye.

"Which one of them is it, Goodwin?" Vanessa asks, her voice rising.

Joan can't get the words out of her mouth.

"Is it Griff or Lydia?" Vanessa asks again.

Griff had once told Joan that he had worried he'd peaked too early. That he'd been too popular in high school. And didn't that mean that it was all downhill from there? Joan had laughed and put her head on his shoulder. "Maybe you're just going to keep getting better," she'd said. "Did you ever think of that?" "No," he'd said. "I don't buy it."

"It's Griff," Joan says into her headset. "He died seventeen minutes ago."

Vanessa says nothing.

"Ford . . ." Joan says. "We're so sorry."

I'm so sorry. I'm so scared of what happens next.

"Goodwin," Vanessa says, finally. "Are you okay?"

"I . . . I . . ." Joan remembers herself. "No, I am not. All of us here on the ground are heartbroken. But we are, at this moment, most concerned about how to support you in the objective to land the shuttle in an attempt to get all surviving astronauts home."

Vanessa does not respond.

The seconds unfold, one after another. Seconds they do not have.

But then Vanessa's voice comes through: "He was one of the best astronauts we have," she says.

Joan tries to maintain her composure. "Affirmative" is all she can choke out.

"If I keep working on the doors," Vanessa says, "what will happen to Lydia?"

Joan looks to Ray, who frowns. Then she turns to Jack. He nods at her.

"*Navigator,* Edwards is our last opportunity until we have a shot at KSC, twelve hours after."

"Copy that, Houston. How much time does Lydia have?" Vanessa asks.

"We can't lie to her about this," Jack says.

Joan nods.

"Tell her," he says. "It's time."

AUGUST 1981

THE ALL-ASTRONAUTS MEETING THAT MONDAY LOOKED LIKE ANY OTHER. The astronauts and directors were seated at the conference table and around the room. The ASCANs were lined up against the wall, Joan, Griff, Lydia, and Vanessa crammed into a corner.

Donna and Hank slipped in quietly at the last minute and took up the remaining spots by the door.

Then Antonio walked in.

Joan knew something out of the ordinary was about to happen. And while other people might have called this a sixth sense, Joan recognized it for what it was: perception. Antonio was carrying himself differently, walking slower, and holding back a smile.

"Today is a day that I know the astronauts in this room remember fondly from their own time as ASCANs," he said.

Joan looked at Griff, and he raised his eyebrows.

"In the fall of 1979, we received three thousand one hundred and twenty-two applications for the astronaut program. In the early winter of 1980, we interviewed one hundred and twenty-one finalists and selected the top eighteen to become astronaut candidates."

Lydia caught Joan's eye.

"Today, one year and one month after we began this training and evaluation, I can confidently say that the eighteen members of NASA Astronaut Group 9 have proven themselves to be some of the finest candidates NASA has ever had the pleasure to train. And it is my honor to declare that you are no longer ASCANs. Gentlemen—and ladies—we are immensely proud to call you, as of this moment, astronauts. Congratulations."

Everyone started cheering. Joan caught Vanessa's eye and, this time, could not bring herself to look away. Vanessa smiled.

LATER THAT DAY, AFTER ELEMENTARY school was out, Joan picked up the phone at her desk at NASA and called Barbara.

"Can you put Frances on, too?" Joan asked.

Barbara called Frances to the phone, and when Joan could hear both of them, she told them the news.

"Did you get the silver pin?" Frances asked.

Joan was holding it in the palm of her hand. It was small and sharp. *Ready to fly.* "I am looking at it right now."

Frances hollered, "Joanie! I am so proud of you!"

It unnerved Joan, just how quickly that made her choke up. She cleared her throat. "Thank you, babe," she said.

"Well, how do you like that?" Barbara said. "My big sister is an astronaut."

EVERYONE WENT TO THE OUTPOST that night to celebrate. Hank and Jimmy were buying rounds of beers, people were trickling in. It was early still, but getting rowdy quickly. When Duke offered to get a round for the whole bar, everyone in the place cheered, and then Hank turned to Donna and kissed her.

Lydia looked at Joan with her eyes wide. Joan laughed.

"So this is out in the open now?" Jimmy said.

Hank shrugged.

But Donna was beaming. When Donna caught her eye, Joan smiled at her, despite being filled with absolute terror. That one day she might smile like that, so unguarded.

"I suppose it is," Hank said. And then, just above a shout: "We're getting married. We thought y'all might as well know."

The group cheered so loud Joan's eardrums vibrated.

"Well, knock me over with a feather," Jimmy said. "Hank giving up on happiness and tying his boat to a dock." Jimmy laughed. "Good luck having a good time ever again!"

"Real nice, Jimmy," Donna said.

"I'm just kidding!" Jimmy said. "Hank, get your girl to take a joke."

"She takes a joke just fine, Jimmy."

Vanessa arrived just then and came up next to Joan. "Why is everyone cheering?" she said. "The silver pins?"

Joan shook her head. "Hank and Donna are engaged."

"Wow," Vanessa said.

"It's wonderful," Joan said, but she couldn't make her voice sound enthusiastic. Donna was hanging on to Hank's arm, curling right into the space of his shoulder. Joan was mortified for her. "I guess."

"You aren't happy for her?" Vanessa said.

"I . . . they just think they're very cute, don't they? Two astronauts in love."

Vanessa laughed. "Yeah, how awful. Two astronauts in love."

HOURS LATER, THE BAR HAD mostly cleared out. Griff, Lydia, Joan, and Vanessa were the only ones left.

"We did it," Lydia said. "We actually *did it.*"

"We did," Vanessa said.

"I didn't think either of you would make it," Lydia said, pointing at Vanessa and Joan.

"All right, Lydia," Vanessa said.

"No." Lydia shook her head with a fluidity that made Joan realize she was absolutely hammered. "I'm saying . . . I'm saying . . . listen to me."

"Why don't I make sure you get home?" Griff said.

"Yes, fine, but wait," Lydia said. "I had good reason to be worried. I mean, Vanessa is a glorified mechanic, okay? Don't get upset."

"No," Vanessa said. "Why ever would I be upset by that?"

"Right, you get it. I'm not being offensive," Lydia said. "And Joan, at first you were so meek. You were like a tiny little baby mouse and I thought, 'She's never even going to make it out of parachute training.' But look at you!"

"Let's move on to your larger point," Joan said.

Lydia sighed. "I didn't think I had much to learn. I mean, I've always been the smartest girl in the room," she said. "My whole life. Do you know what that's like? When it's *all* you have? Neither of you probably do."

Vanessa rolled her eyes. "Lydia, I swear to God. You may be smarter than me, but you're not smarter than Joan, so drop it. Just drop it. I've tried to be cool, but you're really pressing on my nerves," she said.

"It's fine," Joan said. "She's fine."

"She's not, actually," Vanessa said. And then she looked at Lydia. "You're not."

"You don't like me. I get it," Lydia said. "I'm *used to it*. Not many people like me. And I understand why, because I don't care about you as much as I care about myself and it's obvious. I don't even know how to hide it."

Vanessa shook her head. Griff buried his face in his hands and sighed. Joan kept listening.

"I'm just trying to tell you that I understand that you must have something going for you that I don't have," Lydia said. "Something I could learn from. I don't know how to do that yet, but I do see it. I do see how great you two are. You have skills I am lacking. And I need to listen to you."

Joan smiled at her. You had to keep the bar low with Lydia, but if you did, she would eventually surprise you.

"Go home and get some sleep," Vanessa said.

Lydia nodded, and Griff led her out of the bar. As he left, he glanced back over his shoulder to give Joan an indecipherable look. It made her exceedingly aware that she and Vanessa were alone now. The beers she'd had were swirling around her head, which made it easier to look Vanessa in the eye.

"Lydia's drunk," Joan said. "But do you see what I'm saying, that she means well?"

"I see that she's lonely," Vanessa said, leaning back.

"I mean, everybody's lonely."

Vanessa shook her head. "No, not everybody. Are you lonely? You have Barbara and Frances."

"Sure, no, I know. I'm not lonely."

"That was unconvincing."

"Well, are you lonely?"

"I don't know how to answer that question," Vanessa said.

"Why not?"

"You know why not."

Joan didn't want to respond, but she couldn't stop herself. "I can't imagine you ever being lonely," she said. "I can't imagine that everyone's not begging to stand next to you all the time."

Vanessa looked at her but said nothing. Joan was losing control of what came out of her mouth.

"Tell me what you're thinking," Joan said.

"You do not want me to say what I'm thinking."

Joan knew that this was true. But she also couldn't resist the temptation. "I don't know about that. I feel like I could know you forever and still be curious about what you're going to say next."

Vanessa leaned forward and lowered her voice: "I thought the same about you, the first time I saw you," she said.

Joan's chest began to feel heavy and leaden, like there was an anchor sinking into the tenderest parts of her heart.

"We should go," Vanessa said. "I'll drive you home."

• • •

THEY DROVE IN SILENCE. JOAN was unsure what to say that felt true.

When they pulled up to Joan's building, Vanessa said, "Can we talk inside?" and Joan nodded.

A silence overtook them again as they made their way to Joan's door and went in.

When Joan shut the door of her apartment, she felt like she could breathe again.

"I need you to understand something," Vanessa said.

They both stood by the threshold.

"Okay."

Vanessa looked at her and frowned. "I don't know how to . . ." Vanessa exhaled. "I have a recurring dream," she said finally.

"About what?" Joan hoped it was her.

"It's my funeral. And I'm in the casket, but I'm alive—I'm actually completely fine. But no one can see that, or hear me. So they are all just crying. My mother is there. The other people change, but my mother is always there. And she's always sobbing into a tissue. And she always talks about something that I never got to do. Sometimes it's that I never had a family. Or I never got married."

"Do you want those things?"

Vanessa shook her head. "It's more about what my mom wants for me. But it's always about how short my life was. And when I'm in the casket, I realize how little I did on Earth. That I didn't get a chance to do something with the time I had."

"Do you think it's about your father?"

Vanessa shook her head again. "No, what I'm saying is that . . . Joan, you live in a world where time is on your side. But I don't live in that world, Joan. You live there alone."

"What do you mean?"

She inhaled deeply and blew out her next words like cigarette smoke. "I mean, don't confuse my respect for you with patience."

Joan felt the heat of Vanessa's gaze. She understood that the real Vanessa had never looked right at her until now.

The real Joan could not look back. "I don't think I understand what you are saying."

"You spend a lot of time pretending you don't understand what I'm saying."

Joan looked away. She didn't know how to be the person she knew she was.

"I don't have a recurring dream, exactly," Joan said. "But there is a type of dream that I keep having, ever since I was a teenager."

"Okay . . ."

"I'm happy and doing something really simple," Joan said. "I make dinner. Or I read a book. Or I hang up a picture. It's always different houses. Sometimes it's my parents' old house. One time it was this mansion I saw in a movie. I'm always different ages, doing different things. There's never anything risky about it, or dramatic. Nothing big happens. I'm just at home. Living my life."

"But?"

Joan looked Vanessa in the eye, then. Forced herself to not look away. "I'm always alone, Vanessa."

Vanessa looked down. Their hands were just an inch apart and Joan wanted to move her pinkie, to reach out and touch her. But she couldn't bring herself to.

"I do understand what you're telling me," Joan said. "You won't wait forever."

Vanessa shook her head. "No, Jo. You don't get it at all."

The amber of Vanessa's eyes was almost gold when the light hit it. The look of them, especially in this moment, was so complex that they reminded Joan of what her mother always said about her favorite landscape painting, which hung above the dining room table at their house. It "rewarded your attention." Joan could stare into Vanessa's eyes for hours and still never tire of all that they held.

"I'm scared I *will* wait forever," Vanessa said, her voice a whisper. "And it will kill me."

Joan's heart began to pound.

"I'm begging you to tell me not to," Vanessa said. "Please. Tell me

I'm wasting my time. Tell me I'm crazy. Put me out of my misery, Joan. Can you do that?"

Joan looked at her. "I can't tell you that."

Vanessa stared at her.

"And I don't want to tell you that."

Vanessa held her gaze a moment longer and then pushed Joan up against the door and kissed her. Joan put her hands on Vanessa's face and kissed her back. And, in that second, almost everything Joan had known about herself became untrue.

And everything she never thought she'd want or have was in her arms.

Vanessa tasted like salt. And she smelled the way she always smelled, but richer, the scent thicker. Joan pulled her closer, as hard as she could. For a moment, she worried that she was hurting her, pulling her that tight. But Vanessa sighed. And Joan's arms went loose as she let go of her weight against the door and sank into her legs in a way she never had before.

Vanessa pulled away then, but Joan pulled her back. And it was partially because Joan was afraid to look at her, to face what she was finally letting herself do. But it was more that she had to have Vanessa's body against hers, had to feel the weight of her. She wanted to be trapped between Vanessa and the door. To be asked to surrender to her.

Joan let her go, finally. And Vanessa pulled back slightly but did not go far. She looked at Joan, and Joan felt herself blush. Vanessa took her thumb and grazed it across Joan's jaw. Joan's muscles melted, and she felt like she could dissolve.

Joan knew then that Donna was not an idiot. And the Beatles were not nonsense. And that there had always been a place for her in this world. She had just been walking past it over and over again, never noticing that there was an unmarked door, waiting for her to discover it.

OH, BUT WHAT NOW?

Joan did not know what she was doing!

She did not know when it was okay to smile at Vanessa at work and when she should hide her feelings. She did not know if she was standing too close to her when everyone was out together at a bar.

And so, instead, Joan spent over a week with her pulse racing, desperate to find herself alone with Vanessa as if by accident. Which was not an easy feat.

"We should go away," Vanessa said in a low whisper, one afternoon when the two of them finally ran into each other alone on campus. Vanessa moved so effortlessly, appeared to know where to look with such ease.

"Okay," Joan said, aware that her tone sounded eager but unable to hide it. "Where?"

THEY DROVE DOWN TO ROCKPORT separately, so that they would not drum up suspicion. That had been Vanessa's suggestion. And Joan was starting to get a sense of how this would work.

Joan got to the hotel early, and so she sat in the grand lobby having an iced tea, watching the brass revolving doors. Families and couples walked in, a few businessmen. When a girl Frances's age walked in the door, Joan felt the pang of missing her. She'd called Barbara to make plans so she could be sure to see her the following weekend, but it still felt uneasy, choosing to go away.

Joan finished her iced tea quickly and a waiter brought her another. After she finished that one in two big sips, she declined a third. Her bones were already jumping within her skin.

Joan saw Vanessa's car pull up at the front entry. She stood up, as if to greet her, then felt silly and sat back down.

Vanessa got out of her car, put the top up, and then handed the valet her keys.

As Vanessa walked through the revolving door, she did not see Joan. And so Joan waited, watching Vanessa walk toward the reception desk to check in. Vanessa smiled at the woman behind the counter. And then, as the woman looked up Vanessa's name in the records, Vanessa scanned the lobby and her eyes landed on Joan. Vanessa's entire face lit up. She took the hotel key from the receptionist and walked toward Joan.

"Hi," she said when she got near.

"Hi."

Joan tried to hide her smile, but it just kept opening up across her face.

"Should we drop off our bags in the room?" she asked.

"Sure."

Joan grabbed hers and walked alongside Vanessa toward the elevators.

Joan simply could not stop smiling. She kept thinking about when Frances was four or so and got really into what she called "playing tricks." She would throw a blanket over herself or hide under the bed with both legs dangling out and Joan would say, "Jeez, I wonder where Frances went." And Frances would giggle, as if she was doing the funniest, most daring thing anyone had ever done. If the giant blob the size and shape of Frances under the blanket or the dangling legs didn't give it away, Frances's gleeful laugh certainly would have. But Frances could not contain her joy.

That's how Joan felt now.

How did people do this? How did they go through every single day with this kind of excitement inside them? *How how how how how.* Poor Donna. Having to hide this for so long. It was the single greatest feeling Joan had ever felt.

The elevator doors opened and Joan was relieved to see that the car was empty. When the doors closed, Joan hoped desperately that Vanessa would rush toward her. Instead, Vanessa reached her hand out and grabbed Joan's softly, as if they had held hands thousands of times before. It was so casual in its affection that for a sweet, soft moment, Joan felt light-headed.

But then the elevator stopped on the mezzanine level and Vanessa let go of her hand just as easily as she'd grabbed it. A woman in a Chanel suit got into the elevator.

"Oh, my," the woman said as the doors closed. "I meant to go to the lobby."

Vanessa smiled kindly at her, but they were stuck now. Certainly this woman could sense the tension. Couldn't she feel the way the space shifted as she intruded into this world of theirs?

The elevator's bell dinged and Vanessa calmly led the way down the hall, stopping in front of room 408. Vanessa opened the door with her key, and they walked across the threshold.

Joan loved the sound of the thick door clasping shut, all of its locks falling heavily into place. Had anything sounded better?

"Come here," Vanessa said.

Joan rushed to her. Vanessa put her arms around Joan and the two of them fell onto the bed.

Vanessa put her hands on the top button of Joan's shirt.

"Is this okay?"

"Yes."

Take off all my clothes, Joan thought. What had felt so necessary her entire life—to cover up—felt so restrictive now. She wanted everything gone. Her clothes, Vanessa's.

Joan lay back on the bed as Vanessa took off her own shirt and then lay on top of her, Vanessa's necklace hitting Joan's chest. Joan kicked off her shoes, unbuttoned her pants.

To touch Vanessa's bare skin with her own seemed vital, crucial. She'd never wanted anything more.

Vanessa took off Joan's bra and the cold edge of the air hit Joan's chest and the warmth of Vanessa's hand sent Joan into a shudder. Joan closed her eyes. She could not allow herself to question any of this, could not let the part of her brain in charge of judgment light up. There could be no embarrassment or shyness or hesitation. Not if she was going to get what she wanted. Not now.

She had to exist only in the base of her brain, the heavy putty of her heart. And so she put everything away except *Yes,* and *I want,* and *More, please.*

She instead focused on the buzz in her chest, the warmth and lightness of her lower belly.

If Joan had listened to what was happening outside that room, she would have heard people walking by in the hallway and the sounds of the waves outside the window. But all she could hear was the beat of her own pulse and the sound coming out of the base of Vanessa's throat. Then, soon, all she could hear was her own voice saying, over and over again, "Oh."

What ran through Joan made her call out, in a tone she did not recognize. And a thick peace overtook her.

Self-consciousness dared to creep up, but Joan would not let it. *Not now. Not yet. Don't take this from me.*

Did she fumble? Was she unsure of how to move and what to do? Yes, yes, of course. She did not care. For the first time in Joan's life, she knew how it felt to give in to someone and let go.

"I WANT TO GO OUT to dinner with you," Vanessa said, kissing Joan's neck as they lay together under the sheets.

"Can we do that?"

"Can we eat dinner?"

"In public? I'm just not sure how all of this works. With, you know . . ."

"Being with a woman in this world?"

"Being with anyone in this world. But yes."

"Do you want to get dinner with me?" Vanessa asked.

"I want to do everything with you. I want to be so close to you that I'm worried I'm being creepy about it."

Vanessa threw her head back and laughed.

"So then let's decide where to have a romantic dinner."

"What if someone sees us?"

"They will see two women having dinner and think nothing of it. We're in a busy hotel, in a city where no one knows us. As long as I don't lean over and kiss you, no one's going to notice."

"Okay," Joan said, nodding.

"Back home, we have to be careful. But there will also be times when there's nothing to worry about. No one will look twice at us here if we don't give them a reason to. I'm not going to pretend this is always easy, but this weekend, right now, it can be."

"Okay," Joan said, smiling. "I like easy."

Vanessa laughed as she got up and started unpacking.

"Which side do you want?" she asked.

Joan pointed to the right. "Uh, this one."

Vanessa nodded. "Good, that way I'll be by the door."

They each unpacked their things, one by one. Joan placed her T-shirts and jeans in one drawer. She hung her dress in the closet. And then she reached into the bottom of her suitcase. She'd bought a lavender bra-and-underwear set yesterday at the lingerie store. That's what the saleswoman at the store had said to do, to match her bra with her underwear if someone was going to see it. As Joan reached in to get them, she dropped them on the floor. She bent down to grab them and dropped them again.

"Oh, for heaven's sake!" she said.

Vanessa looked at her. "Are you nervous?"

Joan calmed. "Yes!" she said. And it felt good to admit it. To just get to be nervous without the extra effort of hiding it. "Aren't you nervous? What are we doing?"

Vanessa smiled. "I'm not nervous, no."

Joan's cheeks started to burn.

"I'm *excited*," Vanessa said, closing the gap between them. "I want to take you everywhere. And do everything with you. And ask you every single question that's been on my mind for months. And I want to know when you knew what was happening between us and I want to tell you when I knew. And I want to hold your hand in a quiet corner and I want to lie in bed and hear your heartbeat through your chest. I want to bring you coffee in bed. And I want to hear you tell me anything you've always wanted to tell someone. Because you know that you've met someone who desperately wants to listen."

Joan's heart was in her throat, and she could not swallow it down. "No one has ever . . . said anything that wonderful to me before," she said, trying to keep her voice level and failing.

Vanessa took the bra and underwear out of her hand. She placed them gently in the top drawer of Joan's side of the dresser. And then she stood in front of Joan and kissed her.

"Good. So finish unpacking and take me on a date tonight," Vanessa said.

VANESSA WANTED TO SWIM LAPS.

"It will be nice to spend time in a pool when I'm not wearing a three-hundred-pound suit, practicing fixing a latch with a ratchet wrench."

"That's a great idea," Joan said. "Why don't you bring a bag and shower in the locker room, and we can meet in the lobby at eight?"

"Like a real date?"

"Like a real date."

"See you then," Vanessa said. She grabbed her things and kissed Joan goodbye. The kiss was so small. So quick. It was a peck, really, a formality. But when Vanessa shut the door behind herself, it took Joan a moment to recover.

And then she went to the phone and called down to the concierge to make a dinner reservation.

When she was done, she put on her navy blue dress that tied at the waist. It had a lower neckline than her other dresses, and she liked how she looked in it.

She went over to the mirror and opened her sparse makeup bag. That night, for the first time, Joan picked up the mascara wand and took it to her eyelashes not just to fit in, but with the hope that someone might notice. When she was done, she breathed in and looked at herself. *Did* she look like Ingrid Bergman? The cheekbones and the lips . . . maybe. Maybe she did.

When Joan got down to the lobby, Vanessa was leaning against a column, wearing faded Levi's and a black belt, with a crisp white button-front shirt, the sleeves rolled up on her forearms. Her hair was still drying around her face.

She was the most beautiful person Joan had ever seen in her life.

Joan wanted to kiss her as she made her way to her. But she didn't. She just smiled. And this time, she was able to let the secret that existed between them live lower in her body, deeper under her skin.

Vanessa smirked, and Joan bit her lip to hold back too big a smile.

Joan had never felt this way about a man, so she'd never stood with one in public and held his hand. And maybe, if that had been available to her with Vanessa, she would have enjoyed it.

But for now, Joan could think of nothing sweeter than what she had.

"I'm going to drive," Joan said.

Vanessa raised her eyebrows. "Lead the way."

When they got to Joan's car, Vanessa took Joan's right hand in hers before Joan could even put the key in the ignition. She brought Joan's hand up to her lips and she kissed the underside of Joan's wrist.

No one had ever touched Joan so delicately there, and Joan knew that, while she could not predict what would happen to them, for the rest of her life she would think of that area of her body as belonging only to Vanessa.

. . .

HALFWAY THROUGH DINNER, JOAN WAS talking about how badly she wanted to help NASA develop a solar probe when she noticed that Vanessa was staring at her.

"Did I do something wrong?" Joan asked.

"No, of course not."

"Then what is it?"

"I love hearing you talk," Vanessa said, smiling at her.

Could you burn up from a gaze this bright upon you? "Oh."

"You're the first woman I've ever met who I feel like understands things about me before I even say them."

"Really?" Joan said. "How do you mean?"

Vanessa considered the question. Then she looked Joan in the eye. "How did you feel when you saw the moon landing on TV?"

Joan laughed. "Really?"

"Really. How did you feel? Because I felt something so intense, and I've never been able to explain it."

"I . . ." Joan tried to find the words to convey something that lived so deep in her chest. "I felt . . . left out," she said finally. "In this way that burned me up. Like I had been fine until humans touched the moon. But once somebody had, I had to, too."

"And now?" Vanessa asked.

"Now I will settle for the stars."

Vanessa laughed. "I knew you knew. I knew you knew it even better than me. For so long, almost no one understood how I've felt. Why I wanted to do this. I mean, they were impressed, don't get me wrong. But trying to explain that fire I feel to leave the planet, the one you're talking about? It is like trying to describe the color blue to someone who has never seen it. And then you come along and it's like you are describing the color blue to me and I feel such . . . relief. I'd have followed you anywhere just for that."

What was happening?

Joan's chest grew hot, and she did not know what to say back. And so she did not say, "I love hearing everything you have to say" or "I think I've been pulled toward you since the moment I saw you." She said, "I want to show you the way my mother serves bread."

"Oh," Vanessa said. "Okay."

Joan took a slice of bread from the basket and covered every millimeter of it in a very thin layer of butter. She sprinkled it with salt first and then pepper. Evenly, lightly. And then she handed it to Vanessa.

Vanessa took it and bit into it. And her eyes went just the littlest bit wild.

"See?" Joan said.

"How is it so much better with just a little bit of salt and pepper on it?"

"I don't know but I . . . I want to show you every good thing I've ever found," Joan said.

The way Vanessa's eyes crinkled at the sides . . . Joan knew that she would not need to find a way to tell Vanessa how she felt. Vanessa would understand it. Which meant Joan would not need to learn how to be anything other than who she already was.

Later, after Joan paid the bill and the waiter had left the table, Vanessa looked Joan square in the eye. "I love your dress," she said. And then, in a low whisper: "And I want to take it off you."

A heaviness took hold in Joan's hips.

Joan rushed them toward the car. They did not make it back to the hotel. They pulled over on the side of a dark road and, urgently, recklessly, Joan let Vanessa cure what ached her.

AT THREE IN THE MORNING, they were still awake. Joan's head was on Vanessa's chest as they lay in bed. It was hot, the blankets were off, the sheets barely pulled up to their waists. Joan was shocked at herself, how quickly she had learned to shed decades of inhibitions.

". . . and then when I saw those drawings you did," Vanessa said, laughing.

"The sketches were not of you!" Joan said. "They were of the stripper. What was her name? Raven!"

"Oh, I know. I could see that. They were of Raven . . ."

"Thank you."

". . . the one stripper in that joint who looked like me."

Joan was embarrassed in a way that reminded her of being tickled as a child. "Unbelievable," she said. "How would you even know what Raven looked like? You left early."

"I left early because I could not stand to watch you stare at those women."

Joan looked at her. "Oh."

"Yeah."

"I didn't know that."

"Well, now you do."

"You were . . . jealous."

"I was jealous."

Joan could feel her muscles starting to shake within her skin. She took Vanessa's hand. "I don't think anyone's ever been jealous over me before."

"They have," Vanessa said. "You just can't see half the things going on around you."

She pulled Joan's arm closer. "Wait, are you okay?" she asked as she put her hand on Joan's forearm. Joan was not sure what she meant, but when she looked closer, she could see there were hives all over her arms. Joan then looked down at her chest. It was also bright red.

Vanessa leaned over her and checked her back.

"You're breaking out," she said. She sat up and then sat Joan up. "Do you think it's something in the sheets? Do you want me to call the front desk and get new ones?"

"It's fine, I feel fine."

"You're covered in hives."

"I know, I can see that. But they don't hurt. I don't even feel them."

"Should we at least get you in the shower? Maybe cold water would help?"

Joan lay back down and gestured for Vanessa to as well. "I'm fine, Vanessa. Truly."

"Okay . . ." she said. "Does this happen a lot?"

Joan exhaled. "No, actually. It's only happened one other time that I can think of."

"When?"

Joan laughed. "I don't want to tell you."

"Oh, now you *have* to tell me."

Joan put the crook of her arm over her eyes. "It was my seventh birthday. My parents took me to Disneyland. And usually, even if it was my birthday, Barbara was the one who dictated what we would do. My parents were always saying, 'Well, your sister might get upset if . . .' But that day . . . well, I guess my dad knew someone who was in charge of scheduling the characters' appearances, and he set it up so that I got to meet Minnie, Mickey, Donald, and Daisy all by my-self. Just me. Even Barbara didn't go."

"And you broke into hives when you saw them?"

"I broke into hives walking over there. On the way across the park, I was walking just with my dad, and he explained where we were going and that it was a special thing, just for me and . . . I broke out into hives. And then I met them all, and I cried and could barely get up the courage to talk to them. I was just so happy. I remember it very clearly. That I could not believe I was talking to Minnie Mouse all by myself. That she was right there, and focused entirely on me. The hives went away later, after it was over. My parents called the doctor that night, and they said it was probably just excitement."

"Excitement," Vanessa said, with a small smile.

"Oh, it's mortifying," Joan said, just as the hives started to itch. She clasped her hands to stop herself from scratching her arms.

Vanessa got up and turned on the shower. She came back to the bed and put her hand out.

"Up you go," Vanessa said. "The cold water will help."

"But I'm so tired, I just want to fall asleep."

"Can you fall asleep with those hives?"

"No."

Vanessa tugged on Joan's arm, pulling her body up out of the bed. Joan breathed in deep. "Okay."

Joan got into the shower and the cold water calmed her skin, cleaned the sweat off her. She turned off the shower and pulled the curtain open to see that Vanessa was standing there, leaning against the sink, smiling and shaking her head.

"What's so funny?" Joan asked.

"This is dangerous," Vanessa said as she handed Joan a towel. "Those hives of yours might just be the most romantic moment of my life."

FALL 1981

JOAN BARELY SLEPT. NEITHER OF THEM DID. IF THE MOON WAS OUT AND the lights were low, they were together, wide awake in bed.

So many nights, Joan felt as if her heart might implode as she rubbed her leg against Vanessa's, felt the softness and bone of her, the way her upper thighs were smooth, her knees knobby.

Joan had had no idea how quickly you could learn another's body. How swiftly their legs become your legs, their arms your arms. She was no longer Joan, or no longer *only* Joan. She was also part of this larger body, this larger self. That could only exist when they were together.

And yet, when she was *only* Joan, that had changed, too.

Joan's body felt alive—an electric current running from her chest down her legs.

She felt it when Vanessa was close to her. She felt it when she was waiting for her. When she was thinking about her. When she was entirely alone.

Joan did not need Vanessa in order to feel this current. Because it now lived in her. It was hers.

On the nights when Joan fell asleep with Vanessa in her bed, she was grateful for that charge. But on the nights when Joan fell asleep alone, feeling the soft sheets against the skin of her legs, grazing her own fingertips across her own belly, she was so grateful that she now possessed it. That it had possessed her.

From the outside, her life looked the same. She kept her dates with Frances. Neither she nor Vanessa were ever late to work, despite how tempted they were to stay in bed.

Joan said nothing to Barbara, nothing to her parents. When she hung out with Donna and Griff, she rarely mentioned Vanessa. When they were all at the Outpost together, Joan and Vanessa always sat at least one person away from each other. When they ran into each other at JSC, they acted like they always had: two friends, catching up.

To everyone else except the two of them, nothing had changed.

Except on those perfect nights when, after saying goodbye at the bar or Frenchie's or driving home separately from a barbecue, there would be a soft, perilous knock on Joan's door an hour later.

God, that sound. The knowledge that the part of Joan's day that was in black and white had ended, and color was about to bleed in and flood her night.

Vanessa's voice, so smooth, so low. "Hi."

Joan's after, smaller, excitable. "Hi."

"CAN I ASK YOU SOMETHING?" Joan said one night as she gave Vanessa a massage. Joan was in her underwear and bra, Vanessa wrapped up in Joan's bedsheets.

It was so easy, to be this close to someone. Why had it ever seemed out of reach?

"You can ask me anything," Vanessa said without looking back at her.

"Does your mother know?"

Joan could feel Vanessa's shoulders tighten. She dug deeper into them.

"Does my mother know what?"

Joan knew there was no need to clarify.

"My mother is Catholic," Vanessa said, finally. "So no, she does not." Her flat tone made Joan think there was nothing more to say but then, after a moment, Vanessa spoke again: "I think she has her suspicions. But she will never ask me directly. In exchange, I never do anything to make it obvious."

Joan could not conceive of telling her own parents; she certainly was not going to tell Barbara. Sometimes, Joan felt as if the words were in her throat, desperate to leap out of her mouth. But she held them back.

No matter how easy it was for Joan to lose herself in this new life, she was constantly aware of the cold, hard borders of it. The world would not care for her and Vanessa as they cared for each other.

It wouldn't matter how pure the warmth in her chest felt. It wouldn't matter that Joan had loved and accepted so many others. There were people—many people—who would never return that kindness.

It was too early, in all of this, to know what the future held. But what Joan understood already was that what they had together was a lit candle, and the wind could be fierce.

"Are *you* Catholic?" Joan asked.

Vanessa turned over onto her back and pulled the sheets up over them both. "I no longer believe in God," she said. "If that's what you mean."

Joan grabbed Vanessa's hand and started playing with her fingers, grazing her own through the gaps in Vanessa's. She saw that Vanessa had a hangnail on her right middle finger, the skin reddening.

Joan thought of all the people she believed she had known well in her life. Her family, her old friends back in college, Donna and Griff. She would have said she knew everything about them. But it was only now, vulnerable in the intimacy of the middle of the night, that things turned granular. It was only now, in the quiet of this moment, that Joan's eyes could see the redness around Vanessa's cuticle.

"You don't believe in any god at all, or just the Catholic God?" Joan asked.

"The Catholic one is the only one I know. And I will fight against it until the day I die."

"How do you mean?"

"I mean . . . sometimes my mother and I go months without speaking to each other because I refuse to go to Mass, and she refuses to drop it."

"Months?"

"One time it was a year."

Joan's eyes went wide.

"She says I'm stubborn," Vanessa said. "But it's . . . it's hard to pick up the phone sometimes when I'm mad. And that doesn't come from nowhere—I got it from her."

"Don't you miss her? When you aren't talking?"

"Of course I do."

"Then why not just go to Mass when you visit her and ignore what they say?"

Vanessa turned onto her side, to face Joan. "Because I do not believe there is any original sin in any of us and I cannot sit there and listen to someone say there is. I don't want to believe in any being who would judge and punish like that. And I'll pay the price if I'm wrong and God does exist. Because I will not submit to a God like that willingly."

Joan cracked a smile.

"What's funny?"

"No, nothing's funny. It's just . . . you're so . . . dauntless."

"I'm dauntless?" Vanessa said.

"Yeah! I mean, you're so bold. You seem so unafraid. And . . . I don't know. I feel like I'm always trying to not cause problems, but you're not like that. You stand up for what you believe in, and I love what you believe in."

"You do?" Vanessa said.

"You're saying you don't believe in a God who would hate, right? And if that God does exist, you'll remain defiant."

"Yes, that's . . . yes."

"Yeah, that's incredibly daring! And it's beautiful."

"What about you?" Vanessa asked, her voice quieting. "Do you believe in God?"

"I think I do. In a different way than you're talking about, though."

Vanessa lay back on the bed, parallel to the headboard, and Joan did the same.

"Tell me," Vanessa said.

"Well, my parents are Protestant. They believe that God made the world in six days. Eve came from Adam. The Earth is six thousand years old."

"But that doesn't work for you."

Joan shook her head. "The Earth is at least four and a half billion years old. We know that, objectively. So I had to start asking myself different questions."

"Because science and God don't mix?"

Joan sat up. "No, no, no. Not at all. I don't feel that way at all."

"But why not? Why, when they tell you that God created man out of thin air and then you learn about evolution, why does the whole thing not crumble for you?"

"Because there are so many ways to define God and there's still so much unknown about the universe. I could never say that science has obliterated the possibility of God. Certainly I don't see that happening in my lifetime. And I think something would be lost, if it did. Or maybe I should say that I hope that if it did happen, it would only be because something even more incredible was discovered."

Vanessa smiled. "You're so passionate about the subject of God," she said. "I had no idea."

"I'm passionate about the Milky Way," Joan said. "And I think God's in it."

"I'm listening . . ."

Joan looked at her askance. "You really want to hear all of this?"

"Yes, I'm fascinated," Vanessa said.

"Really?"

"Desperately. I want to hear it all."

Joan beamed and tried to hold back her smile. In all of her time spent watching others, she hadn't picked up on this part of falling in love, that someone could look at you as if you were the very center of everything. And even though you knew better, you'd allow yourself a moment to believe you were worthy of being revolved around, too.

"Okay," Joan started. "Well, the larger questions we ask when we talk about God seem to be 'Why are we here?' And 'Is there an order to all of it? Is someone or something in charge?' But the thing is, science is largely about figuring out answers to those very questions."

"Science is about figuring out the meaning of life?"

"Science is about figuring out the order to the universe. Yes."

"Okay . . ."

"The theory of general relativity explains the rules of the physical world at large scales, the world we can see with our eyes. Quantum mechanics explains the subatomic world, like electricity and light."

"Gravity and electromagnetism—I'm with you."

"You combine them with the two other forces we know of in the universe, the strong force and the weak force—"

"I'm familiar."

"Well, okay then: that's already a pretty significant order to the universe right there! Everything that we know of since the Big Bang is ruled by those four forces. We are all connected by these four rules. That's the beginning, at least, of learning how we are here. Now, we still need a unifying theory—our understanding of the laws of gravity and quantum physics are not currently compatible."

"It's a big caveat."

"But the unifying theory *does* exist. It must. We just haven't figured it out yet. And I think the pursuit of finding one law to explain the universe is, yes, science, but it's also the pursuit of God."

"Not the God that most people are talking about," Vanessa said.

Joan considered this. "The Jewish philosopher Spinoza said that

God did not necessarily make the universe, but that God *is* the universe. The unfolding of the universe is God in action. Which would mean science and math are a part of God."

"And we are a part of God because we are a part of the universe," Vanessa said.

"Or better yet, we *are* the universe. I would go so far as to say that as human beings, we are less of a *who* and more of a *when*. We are a *moment in time*—when all of our cells have come together in this body. But our atoms were many things before, and they will be many things after. The air I'm breathing is the same air your ancestors breathed. Even what is in my body right now—the cells, the air, the bacteria—it's not only mine. It is a point of connection with every other living thing, made up of the same kinds of particles, ruled by the same physical laws.

"When you die, someone will bury you or turn your body into ashes. Eventually, you will return to the Earth. You already are a part of the Earth. What better reason do we have to take care of this Earth and everything on it than the knowledge that we are of one another?"

Joan thought about this so often that it startled her now to realize she'd never put it into words before. What a thrill it was, to say it all.

"The trees need our breath, and our breath needs the trees," she continued. "As scientists we call that symbiosis, and it is a consequence of evolution. But the natural consequences of our connections to each other—that's God, to me. I believe in it because I can see it with my own eyes. I know it exists. But I also believe in it because I want to believe in it. I want to spend my energy thinking not of how my actions might be frowned upon by a man in the sky, but how my actions affect every living and non-living thing around me. Life is God. My life is tied to yours, and to everyone's on this planet. How does that not instantly make us more in debt to one another? And also offer us the comfort that we are not alone?"

Vanessa smiled at her. "Is there more?"

Joan bit her lip. "I don't know. No?"

"You know," Vanessa said, "when you're flying a plane, you can't see people on the ground. All you can see are the towns they live in and the neighborhoods they fall asleep in. From up there, everyone is so alike, they have so much in common, and they can't see it. But I can, when I'm up there."

"That's exactly it! We *are* each other. I guess I'm too blown away by it all—too moved by it—to not feel a sense of awe that other people feel in a church."

Vanessa looked at her. "Someday, I want to take you flying over the Rockies early in the morning, when the sun is rising over the mountains and it hits the ridge just right and . . . it reminds me of the light coming through the stained-glass windows at the church my mother took me to every Sunday. And I just know you're going to say, 'That's God.'"

"I *am* going to say, 'That's God'! Not just because it's beautiful, but because sunrise over the mountains is part of the universe itself. Everything, all of us, is God."

She noticed Vanessa staring at her, smiling.

"I probably sound like I'm high," Joan said. "Not that I'd know."

Vanessa laughed. "Don't worry, I followed it perfectly." She folded both arms behind her head. "Have you told anyone this whole theory of yours?"

"It's not my theory! Einstein believed it. Many civilizations have considered some form of it. But . . . no, nobody's ever asked."

Vanessa looked at her and smiled. "Well, you're brilliant," she said. "You are wasted being a scientist. You should be an Evangelical preacher with that kind face and all this compelling proselytizing." She pulled Joan back down onto the bed.

Joan laughed. "I'm pretty sure they don't let people like me be Evangelical preachers."

"Yeah, you might have a few disqualifying attributes," Vanessa said as she buried her face in the crook of Joan's neck. Then she said something that took Joan a second to process: "I love you, you know."

Joan froze, trying to contain herself. She thought she might break out in hives again.

"I did not know that," Joan said back, as cool as she could.

"I've never said it to anyone before."

Joan pulled back and looked at her. "I love you, too."

"You do, huh?" Vanessa said with her lopsided smile. "Wow. Imagine being so lucky as to be the girl Joan Goodwin loves."

"Imagine that," Joan said, putting her arms around Vanessa's torso, holding on to her. She could hear Vanessa's heartbeat through her chest.

A few minutes later, Vanessa asked if Joan thought it was too early to get up and find a diner open for breakfast. But Joan did not move. She just held Vanessa tighter. All she could think about was how grateful she was that the Earth was ninety-three million miles away from the sun today, far enough to be warm but not too hot, just the right distance for life on this planet.

ON THE MORNINGS WHEN VANESSA SLEPT OVER AT JOAN'S, SHE SNUCK out of her apartment around four A.M.

When they were out at the bars, Vanessa often talked about an old boyfriend who didn't exist.

When Donna asked Joan, in front of everyone at Frenchie's, if she was open to going on a date with Hank's buddy, Joan said she would love to and then sipped her wine, knowing full well she'd never get around to calling the guy back. But when she caught Vanessa's eye, Vanessa did not need to have even the hint of a smile for Joan to feel it in her chest.

They were thoughtful about how often and where they spent their evenings together—more and more frequently at Vanessa's instead of Joan's. This necessary privacy had been the reason Vanessa lived so far off campus to begin with, Joan understood now.

It was not easy.

But, oh, was it good.

THAT NOVEMBER MORNING, JOAN WOKE up in Vanessa's soft bed and went out to the kitchen to see that Vanessa had made her a Gruyère soufflé.

Joan took a bite of it, warm right out of the pan, holding her fork over the sink.

"You can sit down, you know," Vanessa said. But Joan was too busy getting another forkful to find a plate and a chair.

"You're a good cook," Joan said.

"It's been a long time since I had someone to cook for," Vanessa said.

Joan leaned against the sink and wondered who else Vanessa had cooked a soufflé for. But she didn't know how to ask without making it obvious how much she cared about the answer.

"I have to pick up Frances soon. Barb is meeting with some matchmaking service," Joan said. And then: "Do you want to come with me?"

Vanessa started wiping up the countertop. "Oh."

Joan stared at her. "Oh?"

Vanessa stopped cleaning and turned to Joan. They were leaning against opposite counters now. Joan had to make a conscious effort not to fold her arms.

"I'm sorry," Vanessa said. "I'm not . . . I didn't take it as a given that we would meet each other's families."

Joan stared at her. She tried not to let the way her heart was sinking show on her face. It was very hard, Joan had learned these past few months, not to scream at someone sometimes. One moment you were vibrating with excitement, but quickly all that same energy could be funneled into fear or anger. She'd never lived this much on the edges of her own emotions, and it was exhausting.

"Okay," Joan said. "Is that . . . do you mean ever?"

Vanessa frowned. "I . . . I don't know. I've never done that."

"You've never been with someone and met their family?"

"I mean, I'm normally the person women *don't* want to bring home," Vanessa said, as if it were some hilarious joke they were both in on.

"You've never wanted to . . ." Joan asked. "Introduce someone to your mother?"

Vanessa scoffed. *"No."*

"Well, certainly you've met an old girlfriend's family . . ."

Vanessa considered the question. "I'm not really sure I've ever called someone my girlfriend. It feels . . . like something people do in high school?"

"Right," Joan said, unable to look at her. She nodded. "Sure."

"I mean, I've . . ." Vanessa sighed. "I've just always had relationships like what we have now. I never pictured myself as someone who meets somebody's niece. It's not like we're in a situation where I can come to a Sunday dinner and try to win over your family."

"I know that," Joan said, her jaw tight. But she wasn't sure if she did know that.

"But," Vanessa said. "I've also never felt about someone the way I feel about you."

Joan tried to hold back a smile. Vanessa could melt her so swiftly.

"I'm not asking you to meet Barbara," Joan said, finally. "Or my parents. I know that is different. But I have a life, and there are parts of it I want to share with you. Don't act like that makes me cuckoo."

Vanessa smiled and closed the space between them, putting her hands on the counter on either side of Joan. "Am I acting like you're cuckoo?"

Joan laughed and dodged Vanessa's kiss. "A little!"

Vanessa missed Joan's mouth and kissed her neck instead. "Well, I don't think you're cuckoo," she said.

"So you'll meet Frances at some point," Joan said, giving a firm nod. "Wonderful."

Vanessa laughed and pressed herself against Joan's body. She buried her face by Joan's ear.

"Ah, ah, ah," Joan said. "Just because you're chickening out doesn't mean I don't still have to go." She kissed Vanessa on the mouth. "I'm getting dressed and leaving, and you will just have to miss me."

Vanessa hung her head and groaned, as if it physically pained her for Joan to leave. "Can't you stay five minutes longer? Please?"

"No," Joan said. She could not wipe the smile off her face.

WINTER 1982

IT WAS ELEVEN O'CLOCK AT NIGHT AND VANESSA AND JOAN WERE AT Joan's apartment, lying on the floor, listening to records. Tonight, Vanessa said, was about Joan learning to fall in love with David Bowie.

"If you love me, you have to love this one thing I love," Vanessa said. "I can't be flexible about it at all."

"I told you I like *Hunky Dory.*"

"Of course you like *Hunky Dory*! I couldn't be with a woman who didn't like *Hunky Dory*! But you still have a lot to learn. Starting with the entire Berlin Trilogy."

Joan laughed. "Okay, but I didn't act this way when you told me you'd never listened to *Ladies of the Canyon.*"

"And I listened to every Joni Mitchell album you have, did I not?"

Joan nodded. "Yes, you did. Go ahead and play it."

"Thank you."

This was how they spent a lot of their nights together—with an ease and comfort Joan had never known alongside another person.

Whether they were seeing one of Vanessa's favorite black-and-white movies at an old theater miles outside of town, or the two of them were reading their books together on the couch, or Joan had convinced Vanessa to watch the evening news with her, it was always with a peacefulness that Joan had never experienced.

It was late January, and they had been together for almost six months, but Joan didn't want to mention it. She didn't want to feel like she was counting the days, even though she was. And she didn't want to feel like this could ever end, even though she understood that some love affairs did. Or, rather, that all of them did, eventually. Just the act of falling in love was to agree to a broken heart.

"Steve's not been around as much," Vanessa said.

"Because he's training for his mission?"

"Yeah, but that means I can't fly with him," Vanessa said. "I can go up with Duke. But he doesn't let me fly from the backseat."

"I mean, none of them do very much," Joan said.

"But I'm a pilot," Vanessa said, her voice carrying an edge Joan had not heard before. "And Steve sees that. And he lets me fly the T-38 as a backseater."

"Taking off and landing, too?"

"Yes! Of course. I know what I'm doing. It's the only thing I've ever truly been great at."

"I don't doubt it—I'm just surprised."

"Steve gets what I can do."

"Good," Joan said. "You deserve that."

"But now . . ."

"But now you're stuck with Duke."

"Yes," Vanessa said. "Do you know how frustrating it is? To have to get permission to do something I've been doing on my own my entire adult life? It's insulting. It would be like if someone said you could only use a telescope under supervision."

"I'm sorry," Joan said. "It's not right. And NASA should have ac-counted for the gap in military opportunities for women long before now."

Vanessa squinted at her. "Say more things like that—I'm feeling better."

"They're wrong, you're right," Joan said.

"Oh, wow, now I'm feeling almost entirely pacified."

"And you *will* be the first woman to pilot the shuttle," Joan said.

"I don't care about being the first, I just want to do it," Vanessa said.

"Yes, I know," Joan said, moving closer to her. "But we need someone undeniable in order for them to realize they can't deny it."

"And that's me?" Vanessa said.

"That's you."

Vanessa tried not to smile. "Well, okay! I am here to serve."

The two of them started laughing, then stopped when the doorbell rang.

"Maybe it's Griff?" Joan whispered.

As Joan lifted the needle from the record, Vanessa got up and slipped into the bathroom.

"Joan, open up, it's me."

Joan had heard that voice so many times through her bedroom door as a child: Barbara always trying to convince her of something. To hide some gift from a boy or lend her money.

"I'm coming," Joan said. When she opened the door, Frances was in Barbara's arms, her legs dangling down at Barbara's waist, her arms down Barbara's sides, her head on Barbara's shoulder. Sleeping. Frances was seven and a half now, so big, and so independent, but in moments like this, Joan was relieved at how young she still seemed.

"What's going on?" Joan said.

Barbara walked right into Joan's bedroom and put Frances in Joan's bed.

"Barb, what are you doing?"

"Shhh," she said, shutting the door behind herself. "I have to go, and I need you to watch her this weekend."

"Go where? What are you talking about?"

"There's this guy," she said.

Joan inhaled. "The new guy? Frank?"

"No, not Frank. Frank is terrible. Do you know that man expected me to start splitting the check? Every time? When he invited me out?"

"Well, he never struck me as that much of a stand-up guy, Barb."

Barbara glared at Joan and then moved past it. "I met someone. Someone very, very special. His name is Daniel."

"Okay, but why does that mean you need to leave Franny here?"

"I hate when you call her Franny."

"Just continue, please."

"Well, something amazing happened. Daniel called and asked me to go with him to New York for the weekend. We're staying at the Four Seasons, and he's taking me to a Broadway show. Anything I want to see. He'll get us floor seats. And he says he can get us a reservation at Le Cirque."

"I . . . don't know what that is."

"It's a restaurant, Joan. Read a magazine."

Joan frowned at her. Then there was a thud from the bathroom, and Joan tensed up.

"Look, I just really need this favor," Barbara said. "I know this is a lot to ask. I wouldn't ask if I didn't really, really need it. I like him. We've been on a few dates and it's going very well. And he's very successful and he has made it clear that he's looking to get married. This could really be it for me. This could be the chance to get my life together in a new way. For me and for Frances. This could be my do-over, Joan."

"A do-over?"

"To fix things."

"Are things so bad they need to be fixed?"

Barbara frowned at her. "Joan, really."

"I'm serious."

"You think I don't know how my life looks to people? Frances has no father. I'm barely making ends meet as a secretary working mothers' hours, borrowing money from Mom and Dad. This isn't how it was supposed to go for me."

Joan didn't know Barbara had been borrowing money from their parents, and she felt stupid for not realizing it. Of course she was.

"Joan, please. I really think this guy could be the one. And I don't say that often, do I?" Barbara didn't wait for a response. "Daniel's a contract lawyer, he comes from a prominent Houston family. Frances and I would have money. I just need some time. To show him that I can make him happy."

Joan shrugged. "I don't know why I'm even fighting you on this— I'd love to have her."

Barbara exhaled. "Thank you. You were taking her all day Sunday, anyway, remember? So it's really just tonight and tomorrow in addition, and I'll pick her up from school Monday afternoon."

"Okay, go, have fun."

"Oh, thank you, thank you, thank you, Joan. Thank you."

"Yeah, not a problem."

"I love you!"

"I love you, too."

"You are the best sister in the whole wide world, and the best aunt in the world, too."

"All right," Joan said. "I'll get her to school on Monday, and you will pick her up."

"Thank you, I love you."

And then she was gone.

Before Joan could think about much else, she went and opened the bathroom door. Vanessa was sitting on the closed toilet lid, reading the ingredients on the back of the shampoo bottle.

"How do you think you pronounce j-o-j-o-b-a?" she said.

Joan told her. "Frances is sleeping here tonight. She's with me all weekend."

Vanessa put the shampoo back in the shower. "Yeah, I heard. I'll get my stuff and get out of here."

"Thank you, I'm sorry."

Vanessa kissed her on the temple. "Please do not worry about it. Frances comes first."

Vanessa started packing her things up. Joan watched her.

"Frances and I will have fun this weekend. I just . . . I don't understand my sister."

"Well, not to overstep by agreeing too quickly, but from what I just heard, I don't understand her, either," Vanessa said. She put her arms around Joan, and Joan sank into her. "But it seems like Frances is very lucky to have you. To have someone as incredible as you to love her as much as you do."

Joan nodded, although she was tempted to shake her head. Frances wasn't the lucky one. Joan was. It felt so good to love Frances. Joan's love for her had not been Joan's gift to Frances, but *Frances's gift to Joan.*

"So do I take Barb at face value?" Joan asked. "That she's dropping Frances off with me because she's trying to make their lives better in the long term?"

"I don't know. Maybe you'll only know in time. But I can sit here with you, until you want to go to sleep. And I can rub your feet."

Joan chuckled. "I mean, *it would help.*"

"C'mon," Vanessa said. Joan sat down on the couch and Vanessa rubbed her feet, and soon, Joan felt the world go fuzzy and she could feel Vanessa putting a blanket on her.

IN THE MORNING, JOAN WOKE up to see that Vanessa was gone and Frances was standing in front of her, her hair sticking straight up in the back.

"Joanie, what am I doing here? Where is Mom?"

"I asked your mom if I could have you for the weekend," Joan said, her vision still blurry.

Frances jumped on top of Joan and startled her, Frances's knees hitting her in the ribs. Who cared? Who cared what hurt when Frances was this happy?

"Thank you, Joanie! Thank you!"

THAT MONDAY, JOAN DROPPED FRANCES off at school and then headed straight to the all-astronauts meeting. After that, she worked with one of the investigators on Spacelab through lunch. She'd need to get to the airfield by three—Hank had offered to let her fly with him that afternoon, and Joan was behind on her hours.

She went home to change and then head to the airfield, but just as she was about to leave—with her bomber jacket on, her aviator sunglasses in her pocket, her keys in her hand—the phone rang.

Joan almost ignored it. But she looked at the time and instantly knew exactly who it must be on the other end of that line.

"Hello?"

"Hi, this is Rhonda, the secretary at Olive Elementary. Is this Joan Goodwin? Frances Goodwin's aunt?"

"This is she."

"Are you able to come pick up Frances?" the woman asked. "School let out forty minutes ago and, unfortunately, her mother is not here. I tried the home phone but there was no answer."

Joan inhaled sharply. "Absolutely, give me twenty minutes."

"She's here in the principal's office with me," Rhonda said.

"Is there somewhere else she can go?" Joan asked. "Maybe I can grab her from the library? I don't want her to feel like she's in trouble."

"I understand, ma'am. But Frances and I have a good time when she's here. She helps me with my crossword puzzles, and she's really good."

Joan closed her eyes and took a breath. "Okay, please tell her I'll be right there and I'm excited to spend the afternoon with her."

Joan called over to the airfield and let Hank know she had to bail.

"All right, well, I'll see if Donna or Griff wants to join me."

"I appreciate it, Hank, I'm sorry."

"No, ma'am, nothing to worry about. Just don't have time later this week, and I know you're running into the end of the month."

"It's okay, I will figure it out. Thank you."

When Joan walked into the principal's office not long after that, Frances somehow looked older to her. She was wearing the same Wrangler jeans and baseball tee that Joan had sent her to school in. But her hair had been redone at some point in the day—Joan suspected by Rhonda—and was now in a low ponytail. She was cheering because she had just beaten Rhonda at tic-tac-toe.

"All right, come on, babe," Joan said. "We have a fun afternoon planned."

Frances said goodbye to Rhonda, and they walked to Joan's car. When Joan got in the driver's seat next to Frances and the two of them put on their seatbelts, Frances looked at Joan as if seeing her for the first time and said, "Wow, cool jacket."

Joan leaned over and kissed her on the top of her head. "How are you doing?"

"Stop that," Frances said. "I'm seven and a half now."

Joan nodded. "Noted."

Joan brought Frances to Barbara's house, and they headed into the kitchen, where Frances sat at the counter to finish her homework.

"Will you make Rice Krispies treats?" Frances asked. "Mom promised me last week she'd do it this afternoon. I was thinking about it all day."

Joan looked through the cupboards. There was a box of cereal right next to a bag of marshmallows in the baking cabinet, among the chocolate chips and sprinkles.

"Sure thing," Joan said.

She read the back of the box and then melted the butter and marshmallows. As she mixed the cereal in, she tried to piece together how, exactly, she was making dessert right now instead of doing an aerial flip in a jet.

When the treats had cooled, Joan cut them up and gave one to Frances as she finished her homework.

Frances looked at them. "Mom puts chocolate chips in them."

"Oh, I'm sorry, I didn't know that."

"Can you put them in now?"

"Um . . ." Joan looked at the treats, considering. "I can try to put some on top, or sort of push a few in?"

"No!" Frances said, growing angry. "I don't want them on top. I want them all throughout, like my mom makes."

"Franny, I can't put the chocolate chips in now," Joan said. "They've already set."

"Why did you do that?" Frances yelled. "Why would you ruin them?"

"I didn't mean to," Joan said. "You know that."

"You just don't want me to have them!"

"I do want you to have them, babe. But there's nothing I can do."

"Make them again, then!"

"Frances, please calm down."

"I can't calm down! I don't want to calm down! I want you to put the chocolate chips in them!"

And then Frances swung her foot from the stool she was on at the kitchen counter, directly into Joan's shin.

"Frances!"

Frances did it again.

Joan stared at her, completely shocked. Frances burst into tears.

At NASA, Joan's job was preparing for every single possibility. It was a system built to eliminate unknown variables. In her work life, she had never felt more *prepared* and ready to face disaster.

But all Frances had to do was kick her in the shin, and Joan had no idea what to do.

She bent down to Frances's eye level as Frances continued to scream.

"I want my mom! She knows how to do it! You don't know anything!" Frances began to flail her arms around and shoved her homework folder onto the floor.

Joan did not know what to do except lean over and put her arms around Frances, holding her tight against her body.

"Stop it!" Frances screamed at her. "Let me go."

Joan didn't. She held Frances as Frances thrashed against her. Joan was quiet and steady. Eventually, Frances relaxed into Joan and stopped yelling. She began to cry into Joan's shoulder. When she finally stopped, Joan pulled back and looked at her tears.

Frances's face was flushed, her eyelids swollen. But when Frances turned her gaze up from the floor, it was her eyes that gripped Joan.

Supposedly, children are resilient. But Joan suspected this was merely something we tell ourselves because we are terrified they are just as delicate as we are.

Joan put her thumb to Frances's cheek and softly wiped her tears away.

Frances did not say much after that. She never ate the Rice Krispies treats. But the two of them watched TV together until it was time for Frances to go to bed.

Frances got into the shower and bathed on her own.

Joan lay down on Frances's bed. As the shower ran, she looked up at the plastic stars on Frances's ceiling. They were disorderly, those stars. They had no relation to the actual night sky.

There was nothing she knew to do except take every single star down off that ceiling.

When Frances came out of the bathroom in an oversized T-shirt, her hair wet, Joan was still on the stepladder.

"What are you doing?" she asked Joan.

Joan got down. "Turn off the light," she said.

Frances did, and the stars began to glow. She looked up at the ceiling. "Did you move them?"

"Come here," Joan said, patting a spot on the bed. Frances got in. Joan tucked her in and then lay down next to her.

"Do you see those stars in a line there, right above you? And how it looks like there's a big basket at the bottom?"

"The Big Dipper," Frances said.

Joan smiled. "Exactly right."

"Part of Major Ursa," Frances said.

"Ursa Major. That's right—you've been listening. What's the one across from it? That looks similar but upside down?" Joan pointed just to the right of where they had been looking.

"The Little Dipper. Ursa . . . Minor?"

Joan kissed her forehead. "Smart kid."

"Show me the others," Frances said. And so Joan showed her the other two she had managed to arrange during Frances's shower, Cassiopeia and Lyra.

"I love it," Frances said. "Thank you."

And then Joan tried to say good night.

"Please don't go," Frances said. "Please just stay all night."

"I'll be here. I'll be right downstairs."

Joan heard the front door open then and relaxed, knowing Barb was finally home. She didn't say anything to Frances.

Frances shook her head. "No, I mean will you please stay here with me until I fall asleep."

"Okay, you got it," Joan said, laying her head down on Frances's pillow.

As she did, Frances moved her arm underneath Joan's neck, pulling Joan toward her with a confidence and authority that startled Joan. As if Joan were the child, and Frances the adult. And Frances kissed Joan's forehead, just as Joan had done to her. "I'm sorry for what I did, Joanie," Frances said as she began to drift.

"It's okay, honey. I know."

And then Frances was asleep.

When Joan got downstairs, Barbara was sitting at the kitchen table drinking a glass of wine. She looked absolutely gorgeous. Her dark hair blown out, her blue dress cinched at her waist. Her lipstick was a little faded but deep red. Joan could see that Frances was going to grow up to look a lot like her. That Frances would have that same glamour to her one day.

"Where the hell have you been?" Joan asked her.

"Oh, don't even get me started," Barbara said. "After the day I've had."

"The day *you've* had?"

"I called you ten different times from LaGuardia Airport, Joan," she said. "I missed my flight. What did you want me to do? I had to get on the four o'clock."

"I want you to make sure your kid isn't abandoned at school," Joan said, trying to keep her voice down.

"Well, maybe you should hook up the goddamn answering machine I bought you for Christmas!"

"The school secretary is on a first-name basis with Frances, did you know that? They have gotten into the habit of doing crossword puzzles together because of how often Frances is left there."

Barbara shook her head. "Here we go again, gearing up to recite the litany of ways you and Frances are both better than me—"

"I'm not—"

"No, please, do enlighten me. It's not enough that you were so perfect our entire childhood that if I made a single mistake, I looked like a screwup. And now our parents can tell everyone you're an astronaut and I'm nothing. Apparently, you also know better than me how to be a mom. Lovely. Please, tell me. I'm desperate to learn from Saint Joan."

Joan grabbed her jacket.

"She's hurting, Barbara," Joan said. "She misses you."

"She's fine," Barbara said. "Frances is special. Even though I'm sure you can't see that."

"Of course I see that."

"Mom says she's an old soul. She's capable of handling more than most girls her age."

Joan shook her head. "Good night, Barb. Do not do this again. I'm behind on my flying hours as it is. I can't be blowing off entire afternoons."

"Sorry," she said. "Here I was thinking family is the most important thing. I'll remember that's not true for you, next time."

Joan slammed the door and then instantly regretted it, worried she'd woken Frances up. She walked to her car, calming herself down as best she could, but then jamming her foot on the gas to peel away from the curb.

When she got home, she was up past midnight installing her answering machine.

A FEW DAYS LATER, JOAN AND VANESSA HAD BOTH HAD THEIR PILOTS fall through—there had been a last-minute trip for some of the astronauts up to Boeing. And so they had taken the afternoon off and gone out for fried chicken.

When they got back in Vanessa's car, Joan looked at the time. "That took longer than I thought. I have to go get Frances."

"Oh, okay, let me get you back quickly," Vanessa said.

Joan nodded. "Or you could pick her up with me."

She waited, quietly, for a response. She got none. Instead, when she looked at Vanessa, she could see that she had her eyes closed. Vanessa did that sometimes, Joan had noticed. As if she could escape somewhere Joan could not see.

"I don't know, Jo," Vanessa said finally. "I don't know how to talk to kids. I don't know how to do any of that stuff."

"How is it any different than talking to anyone else?"

"I don't know!" Vanessa said, throwing her hands up. "I told you this is not my thing. What if I say something stupid and Frances doesn't like me? And then you don't like me because she doesn't like me?"

Joan cocked her head. "How could someone not like you? That will not happen."

"You don't know that."

"You're making too big a deal out of this. Kids are easier than adults."

"I don't know what kids like. Or how they want to be spoken to. Do I ask her what subjects she likes in school? Or is that annoying? I don't know how to not be condescending."

Joan grabbed Vanessa's hand. "Don't you remember being seven?"

"I barely remember being a kid at all."

Joan nodded. "Sure," she said. "Fair. Okay, what's the most childish thing you like?"

"What?"

"What's the thing you like that most reminds you of being a child? Like, I love Christmas. I love going to bed on Christmas Eve and knowing tomorrow morning will feel bright and twinkly and exciting. And it doesn't matter that the presents aren't for me anymore—it still feels like magic is coming."

"You do realize there's no Santa Claus?"

"You do realize there is more wonder in the world than just Santa?"

"Wonder? Did you just say 'wonder'?" Vanessa said. "No."

"What about birthdays? Do you remember a really great birthday you had as a kid?"

"I remember that my mother got a clown for some birthday I had before my father died and the four girls I'd invited screamed and then we all had nightmares."

"Cotton candy?"

"Disgusting."

"Unicorns?"

"Imaginary."

"Who cares?"

"I do."

"Rainbows?"

"A function of wavelengths."

"Where is your inner child?" Joan finally said.

"Gone!"

"I can see that."

"Ground down to dust and blown away with the wind and now it's one with the clouds, by way of your God."

Joan laughed.

"Did I take it too far?" Vanessa said, laughing.

"No, I loved it."

"Look, I care about who you care about," Vanessa said. "But I feel like if you're a part of a kid's life you have to . . . take that seriously. You have to be there. You have to put them first. My life is not like that. And I can't let a kid down. I don't want to let anyone down."

"Has it occurred to you . . ." Joan said. "That you're bringing some real gloom and doom to something that is very simple. Which is that I need to pick my niece up and we're now late?"

Vanessa laughed.

"You're going to take a left at the light up there," Joan said. "When she gets in the car, you say, 'Hey, I'm Joan's friend Vanessa.' You ask her how school was. You ask her teacher's name."

"You make it sound so easy."

"It is easy. And it's important to me. Which is why you're going to do it."

Vanessa closed her eyes again and then opened them and put the car in gear.

"Wonderful choice," Joan said. "By the way, you're underestimating Frances. She has excellent taste."

THEY DROVE TO THE ELEMENTARY school, where they found Frances sitting on the ledge by the stairs.

"Hey," Frances said, with a disbelieving look at the sight of her aunt in a convertible.

"This is my friend Vanessa," Joan said, getting out of the car to fold her seat back.

"Hi," Vanessa said. "I'm Joan's friend Vanessa." And then she cringed slightly. "I think we actually met briefly on the camping trip last year."

Frances smiled sweetly. "Oh, yeah, nice to see you again."

"Hop in the back," Joan said.

Frances stepped into the back and shoved her books over. Joan got in, and Vanessa pulled away from the curb as Joan directed her where to go.

"Did you have a good day?" Joan asked.

"Kinda. But we played kickball in gym class, and I tried to get Nicky out and missed. It didn't even get halfway to the plate. It was so embarrassing. After, Phil Magnusson said I throw like a girl. And when I told him that was unkind, he called me a 'pansy.'"

They came to a red light and Vanessa turned her entire body around. "He doesn't know what he's talking about. Pansies are very hardy flowers."

"What does that mean?" Frances asked.

"It means only an idiot would try to use that as an insult. Pansies can literally survive a frost."

"What's a frost?"

Vanessa hit the gas when the light changed. She raised her voice to speak over the wind. "It's when the ground freezes. The point is that when many other flowers would die from being too cold, pansies can survive. Pansies can handle it. Pansies are tough. They are beautiful and tough as nails."

"Really?" Frances said.

Joan turned to see that Frances had lit up, entirely focused on Vanessa's next word.

"Yeah, so you *are* a pansy, I bet," Vanessa said. "And he's an idiot."

"Well," Joan said, "we try not to call people 'idiots.'"

Vanessa wasn't listening. "Next time he says something like that, you know what you say? You tell him that you can learn how to throw a ball farther if you want to, but he'll always be stupid."

"Frances, do not ever say that!" Joan corrected.

Frances was already laughing. "He *will* always be stupid," she said to herself, nearly wheezing. "It's true."

Joan looked at Vanessa like a teacher scolding the class clown. Vanessa bit her lip, then mouthed, "Too much?"

Joan nodded.

"Hey, I have an idea," Vanessa said. "Does anyone want to go out for milkshakes?"

Joan turned to the backseat to see Frances's reaction.

"YES!" Frances yelled. "OF COURSE!"

．　．　．

AT THE DINER, VANESSA ORDERED a strawberry milkshake and a peanut butter and jelly sandwich, which she cut into four pieces.

"When I was really little, even younger than you," Vanessa said,
across the table from Frances, "my dad would take me to this diner,
and do you know what he and I always got?"

"Milkshakes?"

Vanessa acted as if Frances were a mind reader.

"How did you know that?"

"It's what I would do."

"Well, yeah. That's what we did. A strawberry milkshake," Vanessa said. She handed Frances a piece of the sandwich. "And we also
always got a peanut butter and jelly sandwich to dip in it."

Frances laughed. "A sandwich in a milkshake?"

"Don't knock it until you try it."

Frances took the piece of sandwich and dipped it in her chocolate shake. She made a face like she thought it was just okay.

"I should have been clearer," Vanessa said. "A strawberry milkshake is what you need for a peanut butter and jelly."

She took another piece and dipped it in her own milkshake and
handed it to Frances.

When Frances tried it, her eyes went wide. Joan could barely
make out the words coming out of her full mouth. They were something along the lines of "Wow, that's really good."

Vanessa dipped hers and did the same thing. "See?"

"All right," Joan said. "Somebody let me try."

She grabbed a piece and dipped it in Vanessa's milkshake.

"See, Joanie?" Frances said.

Vanessa handed Frances the last piece of the sandwich and Frances took it. She dipped it and stuffed it in her mouth. "Next time, I'm
going to order this. And I'm going to call it 'the Vanessa.'"

Vanessa laughed and turned to Joan. "What a legacy to leave behind."

Joan laughed, too, but these were the moments of legacy she found the most compelling: the chance to share something of the past with a person who could bring it further into the future. She knew most of the world was focused on bigger triumphs—scientific discoveries, great works of art—but a peanut butter and jelly sandwich in a strawberry milkshake seemed to Joan, at that very moment, a grand thing to carry forward.

SUMMER 1982

JOAN AND VANESSA HAD GOTTEN IN THE HABIT OF TALKING ON THE phone before bed on the days they could not see each other. Those days were coming more and more often as they got more and more busy.

Vanessa had been working as a Cape Crusader—one of the members on the Astronaut Support Personnel team for the missions. They prepped the shuttle, assisted the crew with getting strapped into their seats, and helped close out the shuttle after the mission was over. It meant spending a lot of time on Cape Canaveral.

Which meant that time together was harder to come by lately. Joan would go whole weeks with just these stolen phone calls, whispering over the line to Florida.

But right now, they were both in Houston and Joan was grateful for it. Joan was setting the table at Vanessa's house as Vanessa came in the side door with the grilled kebabs.

Vanessa set the plate down and told Joan she had a question. "Hank says that if he changes his schedule, he can take me up in the T-38 tomorrow," she said. "But that means you'd have to find someone else to take you up on Wednesday. I'm really sorry to ask, but he says he'll let me take the controls the whole time. And I haven't been able to get up there much this month. Is it okay? If it's not, I swear I will back out. I don't want to leave you in the lurch."

"No," Joan said, shaking her head and taking a seat. "I mean, that's fine. Duke had said he could take me up sometime. I can just ask him, but . . ."

"But what?"

"But we both had the afternoon off tomorrow, remember? And you said you wanted to drive to that Tex-Mex place in the city before you take off for KSC again?"

Tomorrow was supposed to be their last chance to see each other before Vanessa headed out.

"Oh, right," Vanessa said. "No, I do want to do that. But . . ."

"You want to fly the T-38 even more."

Vanessa paused and then said, "I mean, yeah."

Joan had known Vanessa for over two years by then, had kissed her for the first time almost a year ago, had waded further and further into this intimacy.

Joan had given in to Vanessa in a way that still surprised her. Joan had not lost herself to Vanessa, but found herself in her. She had not cut off parts of herself to fit so much as learned to make room for someone other than herself.

Joan would so happily, even if she were a vegetarian, make Vanessa a meatloaf.

This surrender had not always been easy—it had shocked Joan just how much physical pain there was in loving someone like this.

It hurt Joan's hands not to touch her in front of people the way Donna could touch Hank.

There was a fire in her—a burning through her belly and chest— when they fought.

And they did fight. There was the time Joan lost her temper just before Donna and Hank's wedding, when Vanessa didn't want to go in the same car. And when Joan started crying after Vanessa introduced Joan to a woman she had dated once, without giving Joan a heads-up first. And the deadly silent treatments Vanessa would levy against Joan when Joan canceled on her one too many times. The fights they'd gotten into when Joan defended Barbara's questionable behavior.

They both had said awful things to each other. It was the first time in Joan's life that she'd said something untrue just to upset someone else—just to try to make her own sting go away. She'd been horrified by what could come out of her mouth. "Of course you're not as important to me as my niece!" "You don't know how to stand by anyone! You always have one foot out the door!"

And the things Vanessa had said: things that, no matter how many times Vanessa apologized, Joan knew in her heart she would never really let go of. "You're a doormat to your sister!" "You are child-ish, Joan. It's not your fault, because you're inexperienced, but some-times you are as mature as a teenager about this."

How was it, exactly, that two people could scar each other like that and keep going? In fact, go deeper? How was it that Joan could know that Vanessa did mean some of those things—that Joan could admit to herself in quiet moments that she meant some of what she'd said, too—but somehow the effect was to be tied together even more tightly?

Why was it that when you let someone that far in, you learned to be okay with all the ways they saw you, even if they weren't flatter-ing? Why, right now, talking to Vanessa, did Joan feel the most per-fect sense of safety?

Joan's scientist mind could come up with a series of explanations for this that had to do with the brain's talent for denial and compart-mentalization. But she suspected that the truth was that acceptance so powerful made everything else feel small.

Vanessa loved her. Would love her. Showed no signs of stopping. And did it at great risk to her own future.

"Yeah, of course," Joan said. "Obviously, you should fly the T-38 with Hank. It's not even a question."

"Are you sure?"

"Really," Joan said. "I get it. You have to do it. I will be mad at you if you don't."

Vanessa laughed, and just the sound of it made Joan happy. Joan wanted to love Vanessa in a way that never made her give up what she wanted. That never changed her.

BUT, MAYBE, THAT WASN'T EXACTLY true.

After Vanessa went flying the next day, she showed up late at Joan's apartment, when Joan was already in her pajamas, getting ready to go to sleep.

Vanessa took off her pants and her bra, brushed her teeth, and got into bed in her T-shirt alongside Joan, pressing her cold legs against the warmth of Joan's body.

As they were falling asleep, Vanessa said, "I haven't had a dream about my funeral in months."

"Really?" Joan said. "I wonder why."

And Vanessa, as she buried her head in Joan's neck, said, "You."

JOAN AND VANESSA WERE DRIVING BACK FROM DINNER IN VANESSA'S convertible with the top down, the hot August wind in Joan's hair.

Joan noticed that Vanessa had taken to driving with one hand on the steering wheel and the other on her knee. Sometimes, Joan would watch Vanessa do a reverse three-point turn, her palm flat as it moved against the wheel. It never failed to light something up in Joan.

Vanessa pulled into her driveway and cut the engine.

"I want to take you somewhere special," Vanessa said.

"I've always wanted to go away," Joan said, and then more quietly as she moved closer: "Somewhere far from here where no one can see us, and I can kiss you in the sunshine."

Vanessa closed the convertible top, and they walked inside. Once the door was shut behind them, Vanessa pushed Joan against the wall and kissed her. Joan never got tired of it, being pushed and pulled like that.

"Do you know what I want?" Vanessa said. "I want to be lying on a beach where we don't know a single soul. And you are in a bikini. And I lay out this big blanket. And everything smells like suntan oil. And there are waiters bringing us French 75s. And the water is warm."

"And we can go into the ocean together and I can put my arms around you as the waves come and put my legs around your waist and just rest there with you."

"And I can kiss you and no one looks, no one cares."

"I want that, too."

"You know, my friend Eileen has an airfield outside of Miami. Sometimes she uses her client's Hawker 400 and takes her partner, Jacqueline, down to Costa Rica. Maybe we could do that one day. Hitch a ride with them."

"Or borrow a plane and you can fly us."

"Well, it's funny you should say that . . ."

"Are you going to fly us somewhere?"

"Would you like that?"

"I want to watch you do it. I've never gotten to fly with you piloting before. To watch you up close. I want to see it."

"Well, I know we don't have enough time to take a big trip at the moment. But I had a more manageable idea."

"Tell me."

Vanessa smiled. "In a little over a month it's going to be Labor Day weekend."

Joan's heart throbbed.

"Last year, at that time . . . we went to Rockport."

"Yes, we did," Joan said.

"And it was great."

"Yes, it was."

"And I thought maybe to commemorate that, I could take you out to dinner."

"Okay," Joan said. "Labor Day weekend, take me out to dinner."

"But not just anywhere, obviously."

Joan copied her tone, smiling at her. "Well, obviously, it's an important dinner."

She laughed. "What if I flew you to Glacier Park in Montana, and we ate under the stars?"

"What if we did, Vanessa Ford?" Joan said. She could not contain the smile that was erupting across her face. "What if we did!"

VANESSA FLEW A PLANE LIKE she drove her car. Quiet, focused, and confident. There was an ease about the way she moved the controller.

They were flying over Big Bend National Park and Joan had her forehead against the window, looking at the immenseness of the mountain range below.

"I love it up here," Joan said. "I don't know how I spent so much of my life down there, quite frankly. What a chump I was."

Vanessa laughed. "Sometimes, with both feet on the ground I feel lost," she said. "Does that make any sense?"

"Of course it does," Joan said.

"I find it easier up here. It's quieter, there's less people. I can be myself in a way that I'm not sure I can down there."

Joan nodded. "That makes a lot of sense."

"But I think I also find flying to be really . . . hopeful."

"Hopeful?"

"Oh, yeah. I mean, right now you're in a machine that eighty years ago they said couldn't exist. In 1903, *The New York Times* declared that we were still one to ten million years away from a flying machine."

"They said ten million years?"

Vanessa nodded. "The article was called 'Flying Machines Which Do Not Fly.' Some of the most notable engineers in the world said it was impossible to create a flying machine heavier than air."

"I don't think I knew that."

"But then sixty-nine days later, the Wright brothers did it."

Joan laughed. And so Vanessa did, too.

"I know! It made them all look incredibly stupid. But the thing is, they had good reason to think it could never happen. So many people had failed. Samuel Langley had just crashed his Aerodrome into the Potomac. And engineers had been at it for a long time. They hadn't been able to achieve anything approaching powered flight."

"And then the Wright brothers just figured it out?"

"The Wright brothers figured out a lot of things that Langley and the others didn't. Three-axis control, balance, you name it. But one massive thing that the others hadn't understood that the Wright brothers did was that it wasn't just about the plane, it was about the pilot."

Joan smiled and then closed her eyes. "Of course."

"It's not just about making a machine that can fly. It's also about understanding *the way* to fly it. The pilot matters. Knowing how to be a part of the machine is what makes the machine possible."

"Ooooh," Joan said. "Okay. Okay, I get it."

Vanessa looked at her. "You do?"

"I do. You're bigger than just human," Joan said. "When you're flying."

Vanessa blushed and then looked forward again, nodding to herself. "The Wright brothers didn't have funding or even college degrees. They had a bike shop and a younger sister named Katharine, who deserves way more credit than she gets because she took care of everything for them as they tinkered around. But they just wanted to see if they could learn how to fly. And that's why they stuck with it, because they loved the pursuit. When I think about that . . . I guess that's what I mean when I say 'hopeful.' Because when I think about that, I wonder—"

"What else everyone has said is impossible that you could try to do just for fun?"

"Yes!" Vanessa said. "Can you fucking imagine what's possible if this is possible? Can you imagine what the shuttle can do?"

"I think you're going to be the one to find out," Joan said.

Vanessa bit her lip and did not look at Joan. "Do you really think that?" It was the smallest Joan had ever heard Vanessa's voice.

Joan put her hand on Vanessa's knee. "I really do."

Vanessa nodded and then inhaled. "Hey," she said, her voice back to normal. "Can I add a pretty big detour and fly you over the Grand Canyon?"

"A thousand times yes," Joan said.

And with that, Vanessa nodded and turned the plane so smoothly that if Joan hadn't seen her do it, she was not sure she would have known they were changing course.

Joan watched her some more, watched her change the controls, reset her sights. She watched Vanessa's chest as it rose and fell. So calm, so controlled, so free.

As they flew over the Grand Canyon, Joan pressed her forehead to the window and looked as far down as she could at the vastness of the chasms below. She marveled at the millions of years of time Earth had existed without humans on it, at how unhurried the Earth had been to unfold.

Joan looked back at Vanessa. She watched the smile erupt on Vanessa's face as she kept them steady just over the North Rim, the calm that took over as she pulled them up, back to altitude. Joan saw Vanessa's ears move back, her eyes soften, her shoulders drop, all nearly imperceptibly. This was the woman she loved.

And Joan could find no fault with her, no complaint that didn't, in that moment, feel so small. Joan had not ever believed that God sent down two halves of a soul in separate bodies, destined to meet. She did not believe in a God that *could*.

But she did believe in a God that had led them here. That led their lives to intersect. That led Vanessa to need what Joan had to give. That led Joan to have what she needed.

That led the North American tectonic plate to shift, causing the uplift of the Colorado Plateau, pushing former seabeds nine thousand feet above sea level. Joan believed in a God that, indifferent and unknowing, sent the Colorado River cutting through those rock formations.

She believed in a God that put a young girl without a father in proximity to a family friend with an airplane. She believed in a God that had pulled her to Joshua Tree to fall irretrievably in love with the stars. She believed in a God that had led them to this very moment: the two of them flying together, so safe, above the Grand Canyon.

And Joan loved that God.

Later, Vanessa laid out a blanket under the stars in Montana. She brought out Joan's telescope, which she had carefully packed up. And a picnic basket she'd picked up from a deli, and a glass bottle of sparkling water.

"I forgot cups," she said.

"I don't care," Joan told her.

They drank out of the bottle, passing it back and forth.

"There's Pegasus," Vanessa said, pointing east.

"Vanessa," Joan said. "I want to do this forever."

Vanessa turned to Joan and smiled. And then kissed her temple and said, "Wouldn't that be something?"

SUMMER 1983

THEY SPENT THE FALL, WINTER, AND SPRING OF THEIR SECOND YEAR together, shifting from desire into comfort.

That rush and ache that Joan had once felt at the graze of Vanessa's hand along her arm had muted. There was less newness between them, almost no mystery.

But Joan knew she felt less buzz because she also felt no fear. There could be no danger between them when they made each other this safe.

This wasn't romance—Joan was sure of it. It was something much deeper. Something that, unlike every other thing in the known universe, Joan suspected, could last forever.

THAT JUNE, JOAN AND VANESSA were at a bar with Donna, Lydia, Griff, and Hank. It was two nights before STS-7 was supposed to launch— two nights before Sally Ride was to become the first American woman astronaut to fly on the space shuttle.

Tomorrow, Vanessa and Hank would head out to Edwards. Donna and Joan were heading to Cape Canaveral.

But Joan always liked this moment best—this liminal time right before a launch where no one had anything to do just yet. Even if Vanessa was growing unnecessarily heated about what was the best song about space.

"Griff," she said. "I am glad we agree that it's Bowie. But it's 'Space Oddity.'"

Griff shook his head. "I stand by what I said."

Hank laughed.

"You're standing by 'Starman'?" Vanessa said. "Are you fucking kidding me?"

"I don't want to rock the boat with y'all, but it's 'Rocket Man,'" Hank said.

Both Vanessa and Griff looked at him.

"That's number two," Vanessa said.

"She's right."

And then they looked back at each other. "'Space Oddity' is a tragedy!" Griff said. "It's heartbreaking. 'Starman' is hopeful, it's embracing the future."

Vanessa shook her head. "You *would* be a sucker for that."

"Okay, let's not get personal."

"I like 'Space Baby,' by the Tubes," Donna said. "Or what's that one by the Kinks?"

"All right, at least Griff is smart enough to know it's Bowie," Vanessa said.

Joan put her hand on Donna's shoulder. "It's better, when Vanessa is talking about David Bowie, to not get involved. She's insane."

"Hey!"

Joan sipped her beer. "You know, one time, when Frances was over, she was watching *Sesame Street,* and this song came on called 'I Don't Want to Live on the Moon.' Ernie sings it. And it's all about how he wants to go to the moon, but he doesn't want to live there because he would miss all his friends."

"Are you serious?" Griff said. "Is this your honest contribution to the best song about space? Bert and Ernie?"

Bert wasn't in it, but Joan could tell that wasn't the point. "I'm just saying . . . I found it moving."

Vanessa and Griff shared a smile. "She found it moving," Vanessa said.

"You guys are making jokes like you don't understand what's at stake on Saturday," Lydia said.

Everyone turned to her. "One day it will be you on the shuttle, Lyds," Donna said. "Don't worry."

"It's not that," Lydia said.

"C'mon," Vanessa said. "That's always what you're worried about."

Lydia shook her head. "Not this time. It's really not." She pushed her beer away from her. "Guys, if anything goes wrong on Saturday, anything . . ." she said. "If Sally so much as sneezes at the wrong time, everyone will blame it on the fact that she's a woman. And then none of us will go up there for a very long time."

Griff and Hank sat back.

Lydia grew more animated. "Little girls across the country will be made fun of at recess when they want to grab the ball, and teenaged girls who get straight A's in science will be told to have a backup plan, and no one will dress up as Sally for Halloween. Girls' understanding of who they can be will be smaller. If this does not go well. Whether we mean to or not, we will have done that to them."

Donna put her hand on Lydia's shoulder.

Lydia was entirely right. There were four men on that shuttle. But every American woman was. Joan and Vanessa and Donna and Lydia—and so many people at NASA—were steadying themselves on the edge of a coin. It could be so easy for it all to go sideways. If it did, the backlash would be swift, and brutal. A wave overtaking all of them, each lost in the riptide.

To Joan's surprise, Vanessa reached across and took Lydia's hand for a moment. Then she let go and sat back.

"But then again, it's also the first time jelly beans are going to space, so pray for the jelly beans," Lydia said.

Joan choked on her water.

"I told you I'm funny," Lydia said.

TWO DAYS LATER, STS-7 LAUNCHED without a hitch. And six days later, Joan pushed her way into the theater at Mission Control to watch the shuttle land, safely, at Edwards.

When Joan got home to Vanessa that night, neither of them said it, but Joan knew both of them felt it.

Sally had done it. Any of them could be assigned now. Their moment was coming.

IN AUGUST, NASA WAS HOSTING THE BICENTENNIAL BALLOON MEET. Joan had called and asked Barbara if she could take Frances to see some of the balloon launches.

"Sure. Can I come, too?" Barbara said.

"You want to come with us? It's just a picnic at JSC."

"Yeah, I want to see what you do. Where you work."

"Oh," Joan said. "Yes, I would love that."

When Joan got off the phone, she turned to Vanessa. "Barbara wants to come."

"Well, that's nice, right? She's trying. I feel like she's been nicer to you lately."

Joan considered it. "Yeah, she seems happier, I think."

Joan had met Daniel. She'd joined Barbara, Frances, and him out for dinner one weekend. When Joan had shown up in the parking lot of the restaurant, he'd taken off his ten-gallon hat and put it to his chest as he shook her hand and smiled. Joan noticed that he was about ten years older than Barbara, hair graying at the temples. He seemed perfectly nice, albeit arrogant in exactly the way Barbara would confuse for confidence.

"Well, she's getting laid consistently, so that's probably it," Vanessa said.

Joan shook her head. "Would you stop?"

"Still such a prude," Vanessa said as she kissed Joan's neck and dragged her into the bedroom.

JOAN DID NOT KNOW WHAT to expect that evening, but then, when she met Barbara and Frances at the main parking lot at JSC, she immediately spotted the giant diamond ring on Barbara's finger. She decided not to say anything.

"Hey, babe," Joan said to Frances.

Frances was nine now and had taken on an air of maturity that Joan both celebrated and mourned. There was no sitting on Joan's lap anymore, no smushing their noses together, no carrying Frances across a crowded parking lot. Those things had been replaced by talking about pop music, and wanting to see a lot of the same movies, and less being asked of Joan in the taking care of her.

When Frances had been younger, Joan would sometimes carry her such long distances that it hurt her back. Back then, Frances would hang on so tight that sometimes she would press on Joan's windpipe or kick her in the ribs. Now Frances would barely hold her hand.

Joan felt, so acutely, that the incurable problem with life was that nothing was ever in balance. That she could not have toddler Frances and fifth-grade Frances at the same time. She could not meet adult Frances and have a moment to hold baby Frances all at once. You could not have a little of everything you wanted.

Joan tried to remind herself that when Frances had been younger, she had held Frances's little hand every single chance she got. When Frances had been a baby, she had smelled her hair sometimes for whole minutes at a time. She had been present for all of it. Didn't that mean that she would not grieve its loss, since she had voraciously and self-indulgently taken all of it that was offered?

No. It did not.

She still ached for every version of Frances.

But to love Frances was to be always saying goodbye to the girl Frances used to be and falling in love again with the girl Frances was becoming.

She missed every Frances she had known. *But oh, this Frances.* This lanky, gangly, whip-smart Frances, with her ears pierced and a Cyndi Lauper T-shirt on, this Frances was a gift Joan would one day miss, too.

"This is how they used to launch astronauts into space," Joan said as she pointed to the Mercury-Redstone on display. "This was the rocket that launched the very first American in space. And this one"—she pointed to the Saturn V—"launched the first astronaut to the moon."

"Neil Armstrong," Frances said.

"That's right."

"Are you going to the moon?"

Barbara cut in: "Joan is doing something even more important."

Joan looked at her.

"One day, she is going to go into low-Earth orbit and put up a satellite or a telescope—or something else that is going to help everyone learn about our universe better."

Joan was taken aback. She had not told Barbara any of that.

"We're very proud of Auntie Joan," Barbara said.

"Of course we are!" Frances said.

For a moment, Joan couldn't speak.

"We should get going," she finally said. And then: "Thank you both. That means a lot."

The grass was packed, but Joan found them a spot a ways back, far from the action, so they could relax and talk. There had been heavy rain for weeks, but tonight was clear and dry.

Joan put a blanket out on the lawn. She rolled up a sweatshirt and used it as a pillow for Frances. Barbara sat down with her legs to the side and covered herself with the skirt of her dress. They watched the sun begin to set.

"Two hundred years ago, in France, the first man flew. He went up in a hot air balloon, invented by the Montgolfier brothers. It was made out of paper, but it was pretty similar to the ones they have on the ground over there."

"Wow," Frances said.

Joan told neither of them that some of the balloon teams had asked members of the astronaut corps to accompany them in the air, and that Vanessa had eagerly raised her hand. So only Joan knew that Vanessa was just off in the distance, preparing to go up.

"And here is something else," Joan said to them. "This is commemorating twenty-five years of spaceflight, too."

"Like what you do?"

"Like what I'm trying to do. But there are a lot of us astronauts, and we all want to go. There's only so many spots at a time."

"You will get picked one day," Barbara said. "I bet it's soon."

Joan had long known that if you're unhappy, it's hard to watch other people be happy. So it stood to reason that the opposite was true, too. That if you were happy, you wanted others to be happy alongside you. This was the only reason Joan could think of for why Barbara suddenly seemed so immensely proud of her.

If that was the case, then maybe Barbara had been right. She had needed to set up her future with Daniel in order to take care of the people around her. In order to be her best self for Frances.

"Thanks," Joan said. "I hope so."

Barbara inhaled sharply. And then she held out her hand for Joan to see. "I'm surprised you haven't congratulated me yet," she said.

Joan looked at the ring and pretended to see it for the first time. "Oh, my God, Barb, it's gorgeous."

"Thanks—it's five carats."

Joan did not know much about diamond rings, except for what she knew about diamonds themselves. Which was that scientists had long thought it was possible that there were diamond-like minerals on other planets. In fact, in 1967, a substance named lonsdaleite was discovered in the Canyon Diablo meteorite in Arizona—a fragment of an asteroid that had struck Earth—and it is theoretically harder and purer than any diamond ever known.

Which meant that the rock used in Western civilizations to express romantic love and steadfastness was not the strongest material in the universe, but merely the strongest thing humans had ever found on Earth. The hardest, strongest thing humans knew of at the time.

Language is what allows us to communicate. But it also limits what we can say, perhaps even how we feel. After all, how can we recognize a sentiment within ourselves that we have no word for? And perhaps, Joan thought, science is the same. Even the way we tell one another we want to live alongside them is limited by what we understand is possible in the world. What more could we say if we knew more about the universe?

"I'm happy for you," Joan said. "I know this is what you wanted."

"He's a really good man," Barbara said.

Joan nodded. "I believe that. And I'm thrilled to hear it."

"What are you talking about?" Frances asked.

"I'm getting married, honey," Barbara said to her. "Daniel and I are getting married."

"Oh."

Joan squeezed Frances's hand, trying not to let it show on her face that she was stunned that Barbara had not told Frances all of this before, at home, just the two of them.

"He'll be your stepdad. We are all going to be a family. And we'll move in with him. Into his big house with the pool—remember when I brought you over there?"

"I'll have a pool?" Frances asked.

"You'll have everything you ever wanted," Barbara said, rubbing Frances's cheek with her thumb.

The balloons started to lift, one by one. "Look!" Barbara said. "There they go!"

There was a red-and-yellow one, one with blue and green stripes, and a few were rainbow-colored. They all started to lift.

Vanessa had said she would be in the American Express balloon, but Joan couldn't quite make out which one that was. And so, as they all began to take off, Joan felt thrilled by each one lifting, all of them potentially holding Vanessa. If she was not exactly sure where Vanessa was, then Vanessa was everywhere.

"You know, Frances, it took us one hundred and twenty years to go from a man in a hot-air balloon to the invention of the airplane,"

Joan said. "But then only fifty-eight years to go from the first airplane to the first man in space."

Barbara looked at her.

"I'm reading a book about the Wright brothers," Joan said. It was the closest she could come to saying to Barbara, *I love a pilot.*

"Well, then imagine what we will do in the next fifty-eight years," Barbara said, smiling. She started French-braiding Frances's hair as they watched the sky.

Joan looked up. Vanessa was in the air somewhere. And if Joan was looking up, trying to find Vanessa, it stood to reason that Vanessa was looking down, trying to find her.

"Wow," Barbara said.

"I want to fly," Frances said. "Someday."

"Then someday you will," Joan said.

"Who knows," Barbara told her. "Maybe one day Daniel will buy you a plane."

"I can't wait until you get assigned to a mission, and I can tell everyone at school that my aunt is going to space," Frances said.

As the hot-air balloons floated above their heads and the sun had set and the stars dared to come out, Joan grabbed Frances's hand. It was not as tiny as it had once been, but it was still so small compared to hers. Frances was still so young. Joan could not wait to meet the adult she would be, but also wished she could pause here, in this moment, forever.

Joan kissed the top of Frances's hand. "I'm glad you're both here," she said.

And then she bent her head back and looked up at the sky with the wonder of someone who'd never seen it before.

IT WAS A BALMY SEPTEMBER NIGHT, AT SIX O'CLOCK IN THE EVENING ON a Monday.

Vanessa and Joan were at Joan's apartment, about to head out to Frenchie's for dinner with Donna, Lydia, and Griff. But then Joan's phone rang.

Joan picked it up in the kitchen.

And there he was. That voice that ruled over the astronauts as if they were mere gods and he was Zeus.

"Can you come see me tomorrow morning?" Antonio said. "First thing?"

"Of course," Joan said. "Is something wrong?"

"Nothing's wrong," he said. "Just please come see me when you get in."

Joan hung up and then looked at Vanessa, who was leaning against the refrigerator, watching her.

"Antonio?" Vanessa asked.

"He wants me to see him first thing in the morning. He won't say why."

Vanessa cocked her head. "How did he seem?"

"Very casual, like it was nothing at all. Like he always summons me to his office."

"Maybe you're getting a flight assignment."

"Before Lydia or Griff? C'mon."

Vanessa shrugged. "It's not impossible."

"It's not likely."

Vanessa didn't respond. Instead, she grabbed a bottle of wine off Joan's counter and began to open it. "Let's stay in tonight and drink this bottle and listen to records and make out," she said.

Joan had become a flake since falling in love. "Yes," she said, "Let's."

THE NEXT MORNING, JOAN WAS outside Antonio's door at seven forty-seven, despite knowing he usually didn't get to the office until after eight.

She waited patiently by his door until she saw him coming down the hallway, holding a briefcase.

"Come on in," he said, opening his office door.

He had a corner office in Building 1, the large windows giving him a view of the campus. And Joan saw a future, in a flash, of who she might be when she was no longer an astronaut. Might she be Antonio one day? She did not want to go back to academia. She wanted to be here at NASA for as long as they'd have her. But that would require her getting this part right first, the astronaut part.

She sat down as she waited for him to get settled.

Antonio put down his briefcase, hung his suit jacket over the back of his chair. When he sat, he situated the notebooks on his desk and then looked at her.

"Joan Goodwin, always a pleasure."

"Thank you, sir."

"Tell me, how would you feel about going up into space?"

"What?"

Antonio started smiling and leaned back. "How would you feel," he said again, this time slowly, "about going up into space?"

"I would feel . . . great about that," Joan said. "I would love that, sir."

"I thought you might."

He took a long pause, and Joan felt herself leaning forward. A smile spread across his face and crinkled his eyes.

"We are assigning you to STS-LR7. Your commander will be John Donahue, who I know you've spent some time with during training."

"Yes, sir, he was one of the survival-training instructors."

"This will be his second mission, so you'll be in good hands. And your pilot will be Greg Menkin. The mission specialists will be you, Mark Simons, and Harrison Moreau. You'll be flying on *Discovery*, slated for launch November of '84, which gives you more than a year to train."

"I . . . I don't know what to say."

"Say that you accept."

"I do, I absolutely do," Joan said.

"Good. You'll be assigned to Spacelab on the shuttle. You have become absolutely crucial to the inner workings of the pallet. We have a series of experiments that will be conducted by all of you, but we are planning on moving forward with the solar investigations, which we believe you are best suited to execute. But more than that, we feel you will be a great asset to the crew in terms of expertise and demeanor. We need a calm, steady hand on any crew, someone who understands that we all succeed or fail together. And we believe for STS-LR7, you are the best fit. That's why we've selected you."

"I am honored, truly."

"The assignments on STS-LR7 will be announced shortly. As I know you are aware, the entire astronaut corps is eager to be assigned a mission. I ask that you keep your assignment between us and your crew until I have time to formally announce. And when it is announced, that you help me to keep morale high for those not assigned yet."

"Of course, sir. I would consider that my highest priority until training."

"I know, Goodwin. That contributed to my decision. You are exactly who NASA needs on the mission. And we are lucky to have you in our service."

He stood up and put out his hand. Joan stood up and shook it. "Thank you, sir. I will make you proud."

"Of that, I have no doubt."

When Joan left his office, she had trouble composing her face.

Finding it impossible to steady her hands, she walked into the bathroom and closed the door behind herself. She was overcome. And it came bursting out of her.

She sobbed.

Crying in the office felt so good. Holding it in felt so terrible.

As Joan inhaled and blew the air out of her lungs, she let the tears fall down her face.

She'd done it. She'd been assigned a mission. The first mission of her group. She was going to space.

When she was all cried out, she left the stall and washed her hands at the sink. She looked at herself in the mirror.

Her eyes were puffy, her cheeks splotchy. Her hair was falling out of its ponytail. Her mascara had run.

This probably wasn't what an astronaut looked like to most people. But she was one, and she was going up into space. So the definition was going to have to change.

She waited until some of the redness went away, caught her breath, and then left the bathroom. As she was walking back to her desk, she saw Vanessa coming down the hallway.

Vanessa was trying, covertly, to read her face. She raised her eyebrows inquisitively.

As they passed, Joan said, "November '84."

Vanessa beamed.

And then the two of them walked on in different directions, not skipping a beat.

THAT NIGHT, JOAN WENT TO Vanessa's house and knocked on the door.

Vanessa opened it and they both walked inside. But just as Joan shut the door behind them, she took Vanessa by the wrist and pulled her close.

"You're sure you're okay with me going up there first?" Joan asked. "It would be okay if you were struggling with it."

Vanessa shook her head. "Every day I don't have an assignment,

I'm on pins and needles waiting to hear," she said. She pushed her body into Joan's and took Joan's face in her hands. "But that has nothing to do with you."

She kissed her and then looked her in the eye.

"I fell for the coolest astronaut at NASA," Vanessa said. "What did you think I thought would happen?"

THE ANNOUNCEMENT ABOUT THE FLIGHT crews was made the following Monday at the all-astronauts meeting.

Donna put her hands on Joan's shoulders and squeezed them. Vanessa clapped softly while smiling at her. Lydia's jaw tensed. She would not look at Joan. She just kept nodding, intensely, rapidly, in a way that was almost pathological.

Later, in the hallway, Joan chased Lydia down.

"Are you okay?"

Lydia turned to her. "I'm fine, Joan."

"I know you wanted it to be you."

"I'm fine, Joan. Congratulations."

But three days later, at nine o'clock at night, when Joan was alone in her bedroom, there was a knock on her door.

Vanessa had gone to Alabama, where she was working in the dunk tank. Joan had been sketching, trying to draw Vanessa's face. In all of their time together, Joan had not once captured it right. Every so often, Vanessa would ask Joan if she could see whatever Joan had come up with. Joan had yet to show her a single attempt.

This evening was no different. It wasn't right. It was the hair—it was always the hair. How could you capture something like that with a pencil? The way it was always in motion? You couldn't.

Before Joan could put the pad down, the person knocked again. She tucked her things in her nightstand and walked to the front door and answered it.

"Can I come in?" Lydia said.

"Uh, sure," Joan said, opening the door wider.

Lydia looked at Joan's apartment. Joan could now see it through her eyes: a little messy, a little lived in, a little quaint.

Lydia stood by the couch. "Can I sit?"

"Of course—do you want water or something?"

"No."

"Okay."

Lydia sat down. "You need a new couch," Lydia said. "The springs are soft."

"I like it just fine," Joan said, as she sat in the chair opposite Lydia. "What's on your mind?"

Lydia said nothing for a moment. There was an awkwardness to Lydia that some people found off-putting. But it did not unnerve Joan at all. Joan found it easier to be around Lydia one-on-one, when she did not have to contend with Donna's or Vanessa's discomfort around her.

Lydia put her elbows to her knees, looked down at the floor. When she looked back up at Joan, her eyes were soft, just a hint of glassiness to them. Joan could hardly return her gaze.

"Why wasn't it me?" Lydia said.

Joan blew the air out of her lungs. "I don't know."

"It should have been me," Lydia said, her voice breaking slightly.

"No, Lydia, that's not true."

"I understand you deserve it," Lydia said. "I'm not saying you don't."

"Good," Joan said.

"But I work harder than you."

"No, you don't."

"Well, I'm smarter than you."

"No, you aren't."

Lydia considered this, looked down at the floor again.

"Why are you here, asking me this?" Joan said. "Instead of going to Harrison's door and asking him why he got assigned before you?"

Lydia nodded and continued to stare at the floor. And then looked up at her. "I'm . . ." She hung her head again. And then quickly worked up her nerve again. "I'm not confronting you. I'm . . ." She looked Joan in the eye. "I'm asking your advice."

Joan's entire body softened. "Oh."

"I want to go up there—" Lydia said.

"And you will," Joan said.

"Stop—please let me finish."

Joan backed off.

"I want to go up there first and, sure, that is part of why I'm upset. But, Joan, even more than that, I . . . I want to be good at this. Not just because I want the gold pin. I want to be good at it in the sense that I want to be helpful. I want to use what skills I have to be of service to this team. I want to be what NASA needs. I really want that."

Joan nodded.

"They need you for Spacelab, and I get that. But also, if they wanted me, they would have just assigned Marty to Spacelab and given me Harrison's spot. I have the most hours on the RMS of anyone from our group, so it doesn't actually make sense to give it to Harrison first. There must be another reason. Something I didn't get exactly right yet. Or there is something else I need to learn," Lydia said. "So that I can be a great astronaut, someone Antonio knows he can trust."

"I can't speak for Antonio," Joan said. "But I do think you're already learning it."

Lydia looked up at Joan, her eyes a little brighter. "Learning what?"

"That it's not about you," Joan said. "Choices like this are dictated by what is best for the mission, not the individual. And if you're asking my advice, I think that's where you sometimes go wrong. You're not smarter or harder working than anyone here. Yes, you're brilliant and driven, but you're surrounded by people who are just as brilliant and just as driven. You're not better than anyone on this crew. You cannot be. And you cannot *want* to be. If you are, you won't be prepared to do the hard stuff, if you're too worried about whether you're winning some imaginary race. It's about the collective, not the individual."

Lydia closed her eyes and nodded. She did not speak for quite some time.

"You're saying be less American, be more Soviet."

Joan laughed. "I absolutely did not say that!"

"Yeah," Lydia said, laughing. "You did. I'm going to tell everyone you said I needed to be more Soviet in my mentality, and you're gonna get kicked off LR7 for being unfit to serve and I'm gonna get your spot. I finally figured it out."

Joan was still laughing when Lydia stood up. "This is so much easier than I thought! I don't have to learn anything!"

Joan stood up too and then, without thinking, walked over to Lydia and hugged her.

"What is happening?"

"I'm hugging you."

"Why?"

"I don't know."

Lydia didn't pull away. She relaxed into it. "I hate this."

FALL 1983

THAT FALL, FRANCES TOOK UP BALLET, AND BARBARA AND DANIEL BEGAN throwing Sunday night get-togethers for the neighborhood at Daniel's house.

Which was why this Sunday afternoon, Joan and Barbara were at the grocery store across from the children's ballet center, picking up cocktail mixers and ice.

"You know, Daniel and I just decided that as exhausting as it is to host so many people, we have to make a point to do this every week," Barbara said to Joan in the beverage aisle. "It's come to mean a lot to the neighbors."

Joan smiled and nodded. Barbara was already rewriting her place in the world, but Joan had to admit that she was touched to see that Frances had made a friend on the block.

Joan grabbed the grapefruit juice Barbara had asked for and put it in the cart as Barbara picked up bottles of soda. "It's so funny because a lot of the neighbors are angling for an invite to the wedding, but we've had to say it's a little late for that!"

"Oh," Joan said, rearranging things in the cart so the bottles didn't roll. "I meant to tell you that I haven't gotten my invitation yet."

Barbara pushed the cart forward. "Sorry about that. The invitations are very expensive, and I didn't think you needed one because I talk to you every day."

"Oh," Joan said. "All right."

"You'll need to be at the church at noon for makeup. I put you down for the chicken, not the fish, because you hate halibut . . ."

"Thank you."

"And you don't have a guest, obviously. Just you."

"I can't bring a guest?" Joan said. "I'm the maid of honor."

Barbara cocked her head at Joan. "You haven't been on a date in twenty years."

Joan stared at her. "I'm not allowed to want company?"

"Who would you bring?" Barbara laughed as she grabbed a bag of ice. "You're just going to sit with Mom and Dad all night."

Barbara put the ice in the cart and started walking to the register. Joan followed her, each step growing heavier.

"I am not just going to sit with Mom and Dad all night," Joan said.

"Do you have any male friends?"

"I have friends, Barb. What do you take me for?"

"You have a man you want to bring to my wedding?"

"Yes, maybe," Joan said. "Or I could bring a girlfriend. Someone to have fun with."

"You want to bring a *woman* as your date?"

Joan felt her shoulders tense, her gut turn.

"What you're asking is not only preposterous, it's also tacky," Barbara said. She walked up to the cash register and then leaned in and whispered to Joan: "You do realize bringing a woman as your date will make you look like a . . . you know . . ."

Barbara smiled as if this was hilarious, and then turned her attention to the cart. She unloaded the groceries onto the conveyor belt and made small talk with the cashier.

Joan simply stood there, staring at her, wondering how it was so easy for Barbara to stick a knife in someone and then carry on with the mundanity of her day. She did not move until Barbara stared back at her with all the groceries packed in bags and in the cart. "Joan, what are you doing? Let's go."

They picked up Frances from ballet. Joan could not look at her sister the entire way home.

When they got back to Daniel's house, Frances ran into the family room to watch TV. Daniel was in the kitchen, grabbing things for the grill.

"Good trip?" he said.

"We got everything we went for," Barbara said. "But somebody got a little touchy about not having a guest at the wedding."

Daniel looked at Joan and then at Barbara. "What do you mean?"

"We don't need to talk about this," Joan said.

"You're the maid of honor," Daniel said. "Of course you can bring a guest."

"It's fine," Joan said.

"But she doesn't have a date," Barbara said. "She has never had a date to a single wedding. She used to ask me to go as her date . . . and, listen, I'll be busy." Barbara laughed.

"Barb is right about that," said Joan.

"She was asking to bring a girlfriend," Barbara said to him, as if this was the funniest thing in the world.

"A woman who is my friend, but it's not important, really. Let's drop the subject."

Daniel looked at Barbara and nodded toward the dining room. "Can I talk to you in the other room?" he said.

Barbara looked shocked as the two of them went into the other room. Joan put away the ice.

When they came back in, Barbara had a fake smile on her face.

"Joan, we would love for you to invite whomever you would like to our wedding," Barbara said. "As your guest."

Daniel walked by Joan and put his hand ever so briefly on her shoulder.

Joan was confused. Because while the change of pace was nice, this person standing in front of her wasn't really Barbara.

"Well, um, thank you," Joan said.

"I think I forget sometimes," Barbara said. "That your life is different than mine. It must be very hard seeing so many happy couples while you are on your own. You deserve to have a great night."

Never mind. She was still Barbara.

ON THE DRIVE HOME, DESPITE knowing it was an absurd fantasy, Joan kept picturing Vanessa asking her to dance at Barbara's wedding.

Joan would say yes. And it would be a fast song when they stood up, but by the time they got to the floor, it would have changed to a slow song. So Vanessa would pull Joan close, and they would sway. And Joan would lead. And Vanessa would say something like "I think your parents like me," and Joan would say, "I think so, too." And they would know that everything that was happening that day could happen for them, too.

When Joan pulled up to Vanessa's house, she resolved not to ask her. It was not a smart thing to do. To go to a wedding together. They *couldn't*.

BUT THEN AS THEY WERE brushing their teeth, Joan recounted her day to Vanessa, and it just came out.

"You asked to bring me?" Vanessa said, spitting her toothpaste into the sink.

"I didn't say your name, just asked to bring a friend. It went about as well as you'd expect."

Vanessa considered this, but did not say anything.

"I'm not asking you to go," Joan said. "I know we can't attract that much attention. I also know that meeting my family isn't high on your list of priorities, and I completely understand it."

Vanessa wiped her face with a hand towel and then turned and leaned against the counter.

"I do sometimes wonder," Vanessa said. "What your mother is like."

Joan laughed. "She's not one to really wonder about, honestly. She's pretty . . . expected. A little vanilla, even—but in a very, very nice way."

"Oh, if anyone ever said that about me, I'd murder them."

"Yes, I know, but my mother would not be offended by me saying that. And that should tell you everything."

"Well, now I have to meet this milquetoast woman."

"I didn't say she was milquetoast! She's just a person who does what society expects of her in a way that makes it look easy. I don't think she's milquetoast at all."

"Well, I'm still curious. About her and your math-teacher dad."

Joan laughed.

"I think we should go," Vanessa said.

Joan looked at her. "Are you serious?"

"Do I think it's a particularly smart thing to do? No, I don't," she said. Then her eyes lit up. "But, fuck your sister. And I want to."

Joan laughed. She could not quite wrap her head around the moment in front of her.

"Frances will be there for a lot of the night, too, right?" Vanessa asked.

"Yeah," Joan said. "She will be."

"So even better. She can dance standing on my feet."

"I don't know," Joan said. "She's got some pretty great moves herself."

"Great," Vanessa said. "I'll dance on hers, then."

Vanessa walked toward the bed, turned the blanket down.

"You aren't worried what people will think?" Joan asked as they got into bed. "The two of us there together?"

Vanessa turned out the light and Joan moved toward the center of the bed. Vanessa's arm was tucked in the crook of Joan's neck.

"Plenty of women bring friends to weddings," Vanessa said. "It's not like we're going to slow dance with your head on my shoulder."

Joan did not say anything for a moment. And then: "It's not fair," she said, finally. "That part is not fair."

"No, honey," Vanessa said. "It isn't."

Later, before they fell asleep, Joan said, "Happiness is so hard to come by. I don't understand why anyone would begrudge anyone else for managing to find some of it."

"That's because you're too good for the world you love so much," Vanessa said.

FRANCES WAS THE FLOWER GIRL. Daniel's friend Robert held the rings. Vanessa wore the one dress she owned. It was a navy blue shift that she wore under a blazer, with a pair of loafers.

Joan stood at Barbara's side, quietly holding her and Barbara's flowers. When the preacher was speaking about love not being boastful, Joan's heart seized. She looked at Vanessa in the second-to-last row, and smiled as she caught her gaze.

As Daniel and Barbara made their vows, Joan smiled at Vanessa, hoping that Vanessa understood what Joan's smile was trying to say.

I would promise you all of this, too.

DURING THE RECEPTION, JOAN SAT next to Vanessa at the table. Frances was on her other side. Joan's parents were across from them. As the waiters came around with wine, Joan saw her father kiss her mother on the temple. How had she not seen it before? Been taken in by it? Her parents' love story.

"Introducing," the bandleader said, "Mr. and Mrs. Davenport!"

Barbara and Daniel came out, and Joan could see that Barbara had changed from her princess-style wedding dress into a sleeker long-sleeved lace gown.

"Mom looks beautiful," Frances said.

"Yes, she does," Joan said.

"You two look so much alike," Vanessa whispered into Joan's ear. Joan's chest flushed.

Barbara beamed as she stood at the center of the dance floor with Daniel. She had landed one of the most notable bachelors in town, she'd been able to quit her job and become a housewife, she was getting the big house, the country club membership. Of course she was happy.

This was Barbara's low-Earth orbit, Joan realized.

But just as Daniel pulled Barbara toward him, Joan saw something else pass across Barbara's face. It was a look she'd never seen in Barb before, but it was easy enough to recognize: she loved him. Daniel smiled as he put his cheek to hers, and Joan could see that he loved her, too.

Joan closed her eyes, flooded with joy. She looked at Vanessa, who clearly could see it, too.

"I hate him," Frances said.

"What?" Joan asked.

"He's such a dork. And I hate him."

"Frances!" Joan's mother said, as she shook her head. "My dear, we don't say such things."

Vanessa leaned across Joan and whispered to Frances, "Hey, I saw the wedding cake over in the hallway. Do you want to go see if we can get a tiny bit of frosting off it, without anyone noticing?"

"You can't do that—" Joan said.

Frances was already up and giggling. "Yes!" she said. Vanessa winked at Joan as she and Frances scurried away conspiratorially.

Joan's mother leaned over to Joan. "I'm worried about her behavior. Barbara said she's been rude to Daniel."

Joan shook her head. "I'm sure it's just an adjustment. It's hard to have your mom all to yourself your entire life and then watch some guy come in and take her attention."

Joan's mother nodded. "Elaine did say her grandson threw tantrums the whole first year after her daughter remarried."

"Hopefully they'll all find a little balance as a family sooner than that," Joan said.

"Vanessa is a delight. Good friend you got there," Joan's father said.

Joan swallowed and nodded. She wanted so badly to tell her parents that Vanessa was more than a friend. She wanted to open her mouth and say that lying in bed next to Vanessa at night was the only way Joan knew she'd had a good day. That the touch of her hand in Joan's made Joan's heartbeat slow down. That Joan did not know why everyone was so goddamn happy all the time until she met her.

But the Moral Majority was campaigning again for Reagan. Anita Bryant had come through Houston just a handful of years ago to convince voters that people like Joan should not be allowed to be near children. A couple of years ago, Billie Jean King had come out and lost $2 million in endorsements overnight. At that very moment, people all over the country were convinced that AIDS was a punishment for moral failing.

Sure, her parents weren't from Texas. They were from Pasadena, California, and had gone door-to-door for Kennedy and then Johnson. But Joan knew that they had never known a person like her, at least that they had been aware of. So how could they truly understand this part of Joan at all? Her parents misunderstood her, the same way she'd misunderstood herself for so long.

Joan wanted to tell both of them that they *thought* she didn't want to get married, but the truth was that she wanted exactly what Barbara had. She wanted what *they* had. She wanted what Donna and Hank had. And what every marriage in the whole godforsaken country had.

The right to exist and to love and be proud and happy.

The right to *live*.

"Yeah, Vanessa is really sweet," she said.

When Frances and Vanessa came back to the table, Frances seemed to have forgotten all about hating Daniel.

"Couldn't find the cake," Vanessa said, smiling. "But we did find a tray of brownies and we snuck one."

"It was so good!" Frances said.

Joan laughed.

Barbara and Daniel danced all night. Soon Barb's high heels were off, and her makeup started to smear, and Daniel drunkenly, joyously, put Barb's garter in his mouth. Which was when Joan and Vanessa volunteered to take Frances to her room at the hotel.

Frances walked on her own across the hotel lobby, and into the elevator. But once they were on the right floor, Vanessa picked Frances up and carried her. Frances was too big for Joan to carry. But she smiled to herself as she watched Frances close her eyes and let Vanessa take her the rest of the way.

Vanessa put Frances down on one of the beds. Joan took Frances's shoes off and they both put the blankets on top of her.

"I'll stay with her," Joan said to Vanessa in a low whisper. Eventually, Joan's parents were going to sleep in the room with Frances. But Joan didn't mind waiting for them. "You can head home."

"No way," Vanessa said. "I want to stay, too."

There was a balcony with two chairs and a mottled-glass coffee table. Joan grabbed two beers from the minibar and the two of them went out there. There was no bottle opener.

"I got it," Vanessa said. She lined the first beer up along the railing of the balcony at an angle and then swiftly, confidently, slammed her hand down and popped the top off, handing Joan the bottle.

"Wow," Joan said, standing next to her, leaning against the railing. "I feel like I know everything about you, but I didn't know you could do that."

Vanessa did it again for hers. "I try to remain a woman of mystery."

"I don't need any mystery," Joan said.

They were quiet for a moment until Vanessa cleared her throat and said, her voice cracking halfway through, "I'm sorry that I can't give you all this. What they have."

Joan looked at her.

Vanessa closed her eyes. "I feel like I . . ." She shook her head.

"That maybe you could have had more—had an easier life—if I hadn't convinced you to love me."

Joan took Vanessa's hand. "I don't think you had any say over whether or not I loved you," Joan said. "I don't even think I had any say in it. It happened without me even giving myself permission."

Vanessa looked at her and smiled, but Joan could tell she was serious.

"I would give you anything I could," Vanessa said. "But I will never be able to give you what your sister has, or what Donna and Hank have."

"I don't think that's necessarily true," Joan said.

"I can't hold your hand as we cross the street," Vanessa said. "I can't pull you into the crook of my shoulder when we go to the movies. I can't ask you if you want to dance."

Joan nodded.

"I can't stand up in front of everyone we know and announce how good it feels to love you," Vanessa said.

When Joan was a kid, she learned that her father's father had left him when he was a baby. She could not imagine this, being raised without a father. She had asked her father if he had missed him. And her father had said, "You can't miss something you never had." It had sounded good at the time. It had a finality to it that she had liked.

But it wasn't true, was it?

Joan missed what she'd never had every time Donna and Hank arrived for the all-astronauts meeting in the same car on Monday mornings.

"I've always known I could never have that," Vanessa said. "But . . . I hate to think I took that opportunity from you."

For a moment, Joan couldn't look at her. But that's what was so nice about talking about big, deep things outside at night. You just looked up at the stars.

"Why are you saying all of this now?" Joan said.

"Because today, at the wedding, I realized I would marry you," Vanessa said.

Joan turned to her. My God, who could care about the stars when there was her to look at?

"I would marry you in a second," Vanessa went on. "I've never felt that way about anyone. In my entire life. What am I even doing here? At your sister's wedding? Meeting your parents? This was a stupid thing to do. To come here. But I . . . want to be a part of your life in every way I can."

Joan nodded. She opened her mouth to say something and then, at the last moment, thought better of it and, instead, looked around at the trees and the other balconies. And she saw, far to the left, outside a corner room, a man and a woman standing on their balcony. The man was resting his hands on the railing, and the woman was behind him, resting on him. As he'd felt her come up, he'd taken his arm and put it around her and pulled her toward him. Joan wondered if that man felt for that woman half of what she felt for Vanessa.

It cost him nothing. Nothing! It cost him nothing to hold her like that where everyone could see. The man kissed the woman on the top of her head. Had they been together for over two years? Or did they meet last week at a bar?

"I know our life will look different, does look different, than other couples'. But there are plenty of women who make this work."

Vanessa nodded. "Yeah, but most of them aren't employed by a government agency in careers that put them in the public eye."

"No, I know," Joan said. "I know."

"I just . . . I don't want you to think I don't want all those things. I mean, I didn't. Ever. Before. But I do now, with you."

"You do?"

Vanessa looked at her and took her left hand. "I want to live in a little bungalow with you and if the cabinet door started to feel loose, I would tighten it the moment you said something. And I'd make you anything you wanted for breakfast every weekend morning. And I'd take your name, if I could. Or give you mine."

Joan's eyes began to water and her mouth began to quiver. What was the point of this? To be told exactly what you couldn't have?

"I would give you anything," Vanessa said, "if it wasn't going to cost us everything."

"I would never ask it," Joan said, shaking her head. Her tears began to fall, and she dried them.

"Which is how I know that you'd be worth giving it to," Vanessa said.

Joan closed her eyes.

"I love you," Vanessa said. "And I'm sorry."

"I know," Joan said. "It's okay."

"It's not," Vanessa said. "The whole situation is not okay. But . . . I guess I'm saying that I can accept the trade-off. And I want to make sure that you can."

"What do you mean?"

"I can wake up every single day and choose you, over and over and over again. If you're in bed next to me, I will take your hand. If you are not, I will *go find you*. I will spend the rest of my life, if I get that lucky, seeking you out. Not because I promised you or because you're *there*. But because I will want to. I will want to be beside you. Every day. Forever."

"You will?"

Vanessa tucked a strand of Joan's hair behind her ear. "Every morning, I wake up and I think, 'God, yes, her.'"

Joan smiled and dried her tears.

"If that can be enough for you," Vanessa said, "it's yours until the day I die."

A WEEK LATER, JOAN GOT a stomach virus and had to call in sick. She forbade Vanessa from coming over because Vanessa was supposed to leave for Cape Canaveral the next day. And so, that night, there was no knock at the door. But her phone did ring.

"There is homemade chicken noodle soup at your doorstep. With crackers, ginger ale, and a cookie," Vanessa said.

"What?" Joan asked. "Were you just here?"

"I'm at the pay phone."

Joan stretched the phone cord as close to the window as she could to sneak a glimpse of Vanessa across the street. Vanessa looked toward the window and waved at her.

Joan waved back.

"I have something to tell you," Vanessa said.

"What?" Joan said.

"Antonio called me in this morning."

Joan's eyes went wide. "No! What did he say?"

"STS-LR9. Steve's my commander. It's him, Hank, Griff, Lydia, and me. Right after Christmas '84, six weeks after you."

"You're going up into space," Joan said, smiling.

Vanessa laughed. "I'm going up into space."

SPRING AND SUMMER 1984

FOR THE NEXT FEW MONTHS, JOAN'S TRAINING FOR HER MISSION BE-
came so intense that she was not always able to see Frances. Meanwhile, Vanessa's parallel training had her in the dunk tank in Alabama
so often that she and Joan would go weeks without seeing each other.

But Joan threw herself into it.

She was running simulations with the crew, going through vari-
ous physical tests, and preparing Spacelab to run the solar experiments. Joan sometimes hit the bed at night like she'd been knocked
out, sleeping heavy and hard, the morning feeling more like coming
to than waking up.

Still.

As stretched thin as she was, she walked into Antonio's office and
asked for more.

"I'd like to be assigned time in Mission Control," Joan said, once
she sat down.

Antonio appeared surprised.

"You've had someone on each crew do it for the past few missions," Joan said. "And I see immense benefit in that. We all need to

know how best to communicate with Mission Control, and having at least one of us actually having worked the job is the best training. I think I should be that person."

All of that was true.

The thing she didn't tell Antonio was that lately, she ached to be in that seat.

As they had run their simulations the past few months, Joan found herself drawn to the lone voice on the other side of the speaker. It reminded her of being in college, listening to the teacher but also unable to resist imagining herself teaching one day. What would it be like to be that steady voice for someone?

"I will consider it," Antonio said. "I'm not sure it is necessary for you, specifically."

"Respectfully, sir," Joan said, leaning forward, "I am exactly who you need."

"And why is that?" Antonio asked. He seemed neither impressed nor doubtful.

Joan inhaled. She'd prepared all of her arguments in the shower that morning.

"Because out of everyone on the crew, I am the most unflappable. Look at my heart rate and blood pressure stats during our sims—you can even go back and look at my stats from the initial assessments four years ago. I am also the person on the crew with the most consistent relationships throughout the astronaut corps. I am friendly and on good terms with everyone. From pilots like Hank and Duke to mission specialists like Lydia. And I can think on my feet. You've seen it yourself in our simulations. You saw it yourself in our assessments when we applied. And I will do what needs to be done for the team. I follow orders. I have always displayed that here.

"In that CAPCOM chair, you need someone who is trusted, can remain calm, think quickly, and do what they are told. That's me."

. . .

"PEOPLE THINK YOU'RE SO EASYGOING," Vanessa said when Joan told
her that Antonio had agreed. "But you're surprisingly intense about
things. Nobody sees you coming."

"I don't give up," Joan said. "When I want something."

Vanessa nodded. "Persistence. Highly underrated in women.
Overrated in men, but underrated in women."

Joan laughed.

ONE FRIDAY AFTERNOON, JOAN PICKED Frances up from camp and took
her to the mall. They stopped at the food court and split an order of
french fries.

Which was when Frances asked if she could spend the whole
weekend at Joan's place.

"The whole weekend?" Joan said.

Already the impossibilities of it were piling up. There was a barbecue at Antonio's that she was expected at on Saturday night that
kids weren't invited to. She had told Harrison she'd get lunch with
him on Sunday to discuss what was going wrong during the sims.
Jack, the flight director she got along with best, had offered to have
her in on Monday to observe. But the biggest issue was that there
was no way to have Frances at her house and still be close with Vanessa. The two things were incompatible.

"We can make a plan for that in the future, but probably not this
weekend. Aren't you excited about your new room?"

Daniel had brought home paint chip samples from the hardware
store, and Frances had chosen a lavender gray. Barbara had picked
out a matching bedroom set from Macy's. A full bed, a nice dresser.
It was a beautiful room.

"Not really," Frances said. "My bedroom is boring. I just read
books alone in there. Mom and Daniel are never home, Joanie."

"What?"

"They are never home. They go out to dinner every single night.

Mom feeds me a grilled cheese and then tells me to get ready for bed and I do, and then they leave. I don't see them again until the morning."

"Oh," Joan said. Frances was ten years old, having just finished the fifth grade. Joan tried to remember how old she'd been when her parents left her at home and in charge of Barbara. She had been older, certainly. But maybe it wasn't the same.

After they finished eating, Joan took Frances to get a birthday present for her new friend, Rebecca.

After that, Joan was supposed to bring Frances home, but instead, she took Frances's hand and said, "Should we see a movie while we are here?"

Frances jumped up and down. Joan called Barbara from a pay phone.

"I was wondering if I could keep her tonight," she said. "Bring her back in the morning."

"Oh, please do," Barbara said. "She's killing me."

"What do you mean?"

"What do I mean? She's terrible, Joan! She's rude to Daniel. She's crying all the time for no reason. I've been very clear—Daniel's been very clear—that we expect respect in this house. 'Yes, sir,' 'No, thank you,' simple stuff. And she won't listen!

"Last night, he called home and offered to bring her dessert from the restaurant we were at and she said she'd 'rather die' than take anything from him. This, to the man who made sure she had the perfect bedroom. And has opened his home to her. Do you know he has been planning on buying her a stereo? Not even for her birthday, just to be nice. But I'm not sure she deserves it now. I swear I raised her better than this. Do you remember when she was little? She was a dream."

"Do you think maybe she's just feeling left out? Of your new life?"

Barbara was silent for such a long pause that Joan thought the line had disconnected. "Hello?"

"She's ten years old," Barbara said. "She's not part of my adult life."

"Okay," Joan said. "I'll try to talk to her."

"Thank you. I really need to make this work."

Joan shook her head and got off the phone. "Okay, your mom said she will miss you, but she's okay with it," Joan said. "Ice cream, movie, dinner, you sleep at my place—what do you think?"

"Can Vanessa join?" Frances asked.

Joan smiled. "I'll call her right now."

Joan did not know how to have Frances with her all weekend and still be with Vanessa. But this, tonight, would work beautifully.

"It was Frances's idea," Joan said as Vanessa considered it.

"Well, I do what Frances Emerson Goodwin asks," Vanessa said. "I'll meet you at the movie theater in twenty."

The three of them saw *The NeverEnding Story*. When they came out of the theater, Frances and Vanessa were teary.

"You two are a bunch of softies," Joan said, smiling.

"You're like Atreyu," Frances said to Vanessa.

"I am?"

"Yeah, you're just like him."

"How is Vanessa like Atreyu?" Joan asked.

"Because," Frances said, looking at Vanessa, "you are the sort of person who would do anything to save the kingdom." And then: "Don't you think, Joanie?"

Joan looked at Vanessa and smiled.

"Can I have change for the gumball machine?"

When Joan gave her a coin, Frances ran ahead.

"Good God," Vanessa said. "Kids can just knock the wind right out of you, huh?"

Joan laughed. "They just tell the truth without any agenda, that's all."

"Well, I'm not sure it's the truth but . . ."

"But what?"

Vanessa shook her head. "It would just be nice to be the person she thinks I am. That's all."

Afterward, the three of them went out for Italian food. And Frances again brought up how much she liked being with Joan and Vanessa, and how little she wanted to be at home.

Joan wasn't sure what to say, but Vanessa spoke up first: "Listen to me, kiddo. For some people, childhood is the best part of their lives, and later, all they are trying to do is go back to it. But for people like us, it's different. The good part hasn't started yet. But it's coming. It's just ahead, when your life is in your own hands and, listen to me, you are going to soar."

Frances leaned forward. "You really think so?"

"I know so," Vanessa said. "I can see it in you."

"Do you think I could be an astronaut?" Frances asked.

"If you want, baby girl," Vanessa said. "You may just land on the moon."

JOAN SPENT ALL OF HER TIME WHEN SHE WASN'T TRAINING FOR HER mission taking shifts in Mission Control.

It was the highlight of her days and nights.

She loved the hum of the room, getting to know the engineers at each console. It was like being surrounded by mission specialists. All nerds, no cowboys.

But it also meant she'd been packing her schedule too tight. After work tonight, she had to drop Frances's books off at Barbara's, and she was already late to meet Donna and Griff.

They were supposed to meet at the bar, and while Joan did not particularly want to go, she felt needed. She had to be there to order a club soda and then let Donna swap it for her vodka and tonics. That way Donna could seem like she was drinking and no one would pick up on the fact that she was almost six months pregnant. Vanessa and Joan were the only ones at NASA who knew other than Hank.

Surprisingly, Donna wasn't showing much. It was certainly concealable in a flight suit or a baggy shirt. Which was good. Because the moment the higher-ups at NASA learned she was pregnant, they were going to restrict what Donna could do, even if there was no medical reason for it.

Namely, they wouldn't let her fly in the T-38s anymore, which meant she wouldn't qualify for missions until after she had the baby. Donna getting pregnant was going to directly and indirectly ensure that she did not get assigned to a crew for *years*. Meanwhile, Hank was going up in less than six months.

Joan really wanted to get to the bar in time to order Donna's drink. It felt like an honor to be trusted with such a secret, and she wanted to come through. But she was already running late when Barbara pulled her into the formal living room to have a "chat."

"What is it, Barb?" Joan said. She did not sit down.

"Please sit," Barbara said, sitting down on a white leather uphol-stered sofa in front of a glass coffee table.

Joan sat.

"I owe you an apology for something."

Joan tried not to cock her head and look at her sideways, but she had middling success.

"I don't think I've given you enough credit for everything that you have done for Frances and me these past few years. Well, no," Barbara said. "Not the past few years. Her entire life."

It was like being handed a gift you had wanted desperately five years ago. One that Joan had taught herself how not to yearn for any-more. And, therefore, did not know what to do with now.

"Oh," Joan said.

"When she was born, I was so lost. I was so angry," Barbara said. "I was angry at the world for finding myself in that position. And I . . . I knew, in those moments, that I could rely on you. I have relied on you for such a long time, and I think, well . . . Daniel has helped me see that I was embarrassed. For needing you. So I acted like it was nothing. That was wrong of me. I'm sorry."

"Wow," Joan said. "That's—"

"And you have been an extra parent to Frances in many ways. Ways not every sister would have been. So thank you. Because of that, I want to include you in our news."

Joan could sense something was coming, and she felt stupid for not seeing the punch before it landed.

"Frances is going to boarding school."

Joan felt the breath pulled out of her lungs. "What? Barb, no."

"Yes, she is."

"She's not even in junior high."

"Some of these schools start in sixth grade. She'll begin the school year at Landingham Prep after Labor Day. It's in Dallas. Lots of kids go there and love it."

"Why are you doing this?"

"Because the current situation is not working."

"You have to give it time."

Barbara shook her head with a patience that enraged Joan.

"I cannot believe you are doing this to her," Joan said.

"Plenty of children go to boarding school, Joan. Don't be dramatic."

"She is ten years old. She's young for her grade. She's not ready."

"She's certainly old enough to cause trouble."

"She's hurting and confused about you getting married and her life changing. This is not the time, even if boarding school were right for her."

"Joan, please—"

Joan's heart rate was rising. "And the worst part is, you know better."

"I know better? Excuse me. You have no idea how she speaks to him, Joan. It's unacceptable. And that's not even getting into how she speaks to me. Daniel is honestly worried about her. That she needs some discipline. Maybe I did wrong by her, up until now. I felt so guilty about being a single mother that I babied her. She needs structure, and she's not accepting the structure we are giving her. So this is how she's going to get it. It's good. It's good for her."

"Does she want to go?"

"Of course she wants to go. What do you take me for?"

It sounded impossible to Joan. She marched right up to Frances's bedroom. Frances was sitting at her desk, finishing her homework.

"Your mother told me you're going to Landingham. Is this what you want, babe?"

"Yeah," Frances said. "Mom says there's a lot of other kids there. I'd eat dinner with my friends every night."

Joan looked at her and sighed. How could Joan make any better argument? Frances had been eating dinner alone most nights.

"I'll have a roommate, which I think will be fun. And we'll go on field trips all the time. I read in the brochure that we get to go to Washington, D.C., in seventh grade."

Joan nodded. "You're sure you want to do this?"

"I'll miss you, but Mom says that I will be back a lot of the weekends, like every month. And I was thinking maybe a few of them could be at your place?"

"Of course. Of course."

"I'm excited."

How had Barbara done this so masterfully? Joan had no way to stop it.

Joan put on a smile. "I know you're old now, but can I still kiss you on the top of your head?" she asked. "This once?"

Frances laughed and then bent her head down.

Joan kissed the part in Frances's hair.

"I love you, Frances," Joan said.

"I love you, too."

Joan shut the door. She tried to regain her composure before going downstairs.

"So that's it?" Joan said as she put her hand on the door handle. "The decision has been made? There will be no further discussion?"

"I appreciate everything you've done for us. I really do. Like I said, I know I haven't always made that clear. So thank you. But my child is unhappy. I want her to find a place in the world where she feels she belongs."

Joan wanted to take her hands and thrust them into Barbara's shoulders, to knock her down on the ground. She wanted to yell at her. Shake some sense into her. She wanted to go upstairs and tell Frances that she deserved a home where she felt she belonged.

Instead, she gritted her teeth and walked out the door.

THE DAY FRANCES WAS LEAVING FOR BOARDING SCHOOL, JOAN WOKE UP in Vanessa's bed and started crying before she was even alert.

Ever since Frances had been born, Joan had not gone more than ten days without seeing her for at least a few minutes. Now Joan was approaching a future where she saw her only on holidays. Even if this was good for Frances, like Barbara claimed, it would break Joan's heart to miss her this much.

Vanessa handed Joan a tissue. Joan dried her tears.

"She will be home some weekends," Vanessa said.

"I know," Joan said. "I'll miss her, but I'll be okay. I'm just . . ."

"They're shitty parents," Vanessa said finally.

Joan looked at her, shocked.

"You talk *around* it," Vanessa said. "Even your mother seems to know it but is unable to say it. But just say it. It's shitty, what Barb and Daniel are doing."

"Barb thinks it's what's best for Frances," Joan said.

Vanessa frowned. "Do you think it's what's best for Frances?"

"Of course not."

"Do you think if Barbara thought about it for one second, she would still think it's best for Frances?"

Joan shook her head. "For some kids it *would* be a good idea. But if Barb were honest with herself, she would see that her child is acting out because she's lonely and needs to feel cared about and pulled in. Not sent further away."

"Exactly."

"But I'm not Barbara," Joan said. "At the end of the day, Frances is not my kid. She's my niece."

"Yes, but also, who cares what word you use? Some aunts are completely irrelevant, and some aunts have been there since the day their niece was born. I had one grandmother I never saw and one who, when she died, I cried for three days. The word isn't what matters. It's the specific relationship. You love that kid more than anything on this planet. She knows that. And that's what matters."

Joan nodded. "I don't know how I'm going to say goodbye to her."

"You'll tell her what you have to. That you'll be fine, even if you won't. And she'll be fine, even if you're not sure. And that you're always there."

JOAN WENT OVER THAT MORNING and had breakfast with Barbara, Daniel, and Frances. They were leaving in an hour to start the drive.

As Barbara and Daniel packed the car, Joan sat with Frances in her room.

"I'm in Clarefield Hall," Frances said. She picked up the brochure she had from her first visit to campus. "You can see it in the background here."

Frances pointed to a large brick dormitory behind what looked like a campus square.

"It's the building all the girls want to be in," Frances said. "Because it is next to the cafeteria and it's the newest one, so it has individual bathrooms and more phone booths. That means I can call you anytime I want, I bet."

Joan nodded. "It looks gorgeous."

"My roommate's name is Tabitha. She's eleven. I think most of the other kids are eleven. Tabby and I decided we are going to pick out posters to hang up together. She likes Cyndi Lauper, too. So I think that will be cool."

Joan kept watching her face, looking for signs of sadness that weren't there.

"And Mom and Daniel are coming for parents' weekend in just a few weeks. Mom says they are going to send really huge care packages all the time. Like every Friday."

"Well, good," Joan said. "I'm glad."

"And I'll be home for Thanksgiving."

"Oh, I can't wait."

"I wish I could come see your liftoff," Frances said.

"I know, but you're gonna be having so much fun at school, you're not even going to be thinking about it. I'll be up there and back before you know it. In time for Thanksgiving, too. So I can come get you and take you to the movies that weekend. You can think about what you want to see."

The minutes were speeding by and Joan ached to slow them down. It had been that way for much of Frances's childhood. *Stay. Stay. Stay right here. Don't go so fast.*

Barbara appeared in the doorway.

"Listen, babe," Joan said. It was getting harder and harder to keep her composure, and she didn't want to cry in front of Frances. "I think I should get going—you all are about to get in the car."

"Come on down in two minutes, okay, my love?" Barbara said.

Frances nodded.

When Barbara left, Joan hugged Frances as hard as she could, as if it would make up for all the time ahead of them.

"I love you, make good decisions, I'll see you at Thanksgiving," Joan said.

"Joanie," Frances asked as Joan reached the door.

"Yeah?"

"I'm going to have so much fun, right?"

Joan choked back the lump in her throat. This didn't feel right to her. Any of this. But what could she do? She didn't have the ability to stop it. She was leaving on a mission in just over two months. She closed her eyes and reset herself. "You're going to have a great time. And I'm always a phone call away. Day or night. I will always pick up. Okay?"

Joan rushed in one more time and kissed Frances on the top of her head and said goodbye.

*   *   *

THAT TUESDAY, JOAN'S CREW HAD a full-scale simulation to prepare for their mission.

She strapped into her seat in the mid-deck. She listened to the commander and pilot as they prepared for liftoff. She was there, ready for anything that came at them.

But part of her brain was with Frances.

She was thinking about how it must have felt to arrive at the campus, whether Frances and Tabitha were getting along. Were the upperclassmen intimidating? Had she been okay saying goodbye to Barbara and Daniel?

Joan tried to imagine Frances free and happy and surrounded by friends, that the school was everything Frances had dreamed of.

After eight and a half minutes, they were "in orbit" during the simulation. Joan unstrapped herself and began to pretend, as best she could, that she was in microgravity. Pretending to solve problems while floating, even though the gravity of Earth kept them all weighed down.

So much pretending.

FALL 1984

JOAN AND VANESSA WERE AT THE OUTPOST WITH DONNA, WHO WAS going to have the baby any moment.

"How are you feeling about liftoff?" Donna asked Joan.

Joan downed half her beer. It was wild to think there was a time when she did not look forward to the taste of an ice-cold beer.

"Are you scared?" Donna said.

"Me?" Joan asked.

"Yeah. It's only six weeks away. I know all the men say they aren't scared to go up there, but I think they are lying. And I think you'll tell me the truth."

Over the past few weeks, Joan had become intensely aware of the fact that she was getting into a spacecraft attached to a massive fuel tank and two solid rocket boosters that were alarmingly delicate. If anything went wrong, she might never touch land again.

"Yeah," she said. "I think I'm scared."

"Being scared is . . . the rational response," Vanessa said.

"I'm scared," Donna said. "I don't even have my assignment yet. But I'm scared."

"I'm scared, too," Vanessa said.

Vanessa's mission had been scheduled for two days after Christmas. And as it got closer, her training had picked up rapidly. She and Joan were used to going weeks without seeing each other. Now sometimes they couldn't even talk on the phone.

Joan found it hard to remember how to be that alone. Without Frances. Without Vanessa. She'd taken up running again. It had not been helping much.

"But I also feel *ready*," Vanessa added. "I guess I feel like I'm ready to face whatever it is. I'm ready to pay whatever price is asked of me. I'm scared, but I'm ready."

"Courage," Joan said. "You have courage."

She looked at Joan and smiled. "I guess I do."

Joan held her gaze for a moment too long, smiled a little too earnestly.

Donna stared at them. When they snapped out of it—when Joan finally saw Donna's face—she could see that Donna was holding back a smile. Donna had a brightness in her eyes that Joan interpreted immediately.

Donna *knew*.

Donna knew and she had, perhaps, *long known*.

And she didn't care.

Donna sipped her club soda and bitters as she glanced at the two of them. Suddenly Joan felt as if her heart were so swollen it might burst open.

Donna knew! Donna would love Joan *anyway*, would love Joan *still*, maybe had even loved Joan *because*.

Joan was safe with her. Joan was okay.

God, Joan's entire life she'd been asking that question, hadn't she? Was she okay? She had been looking around every room she was in to survey the people around her, compare herself to the way she saw them, trying to gauge where she didn't fit, trying to find where she could. Trying to see if she was okay.

And she was.

She was.

Joan wanted to say something—anything—but there was no air in her throat.

"You should be more scared of what's happening to you and Hank," Vanessa said, raising her eyebrows. "That gorgeous miserable bomb that's going to blow up your life when it arrives, any minute."

Donna laughed. "I'm not scared of that. I'm scared of what NASA and everybody else in the world is going to try to tell me I can't do once I'm a mother. 'How can you leave your child at home while you're in space,' even though fathers have been doing it for, let's see, over two decades. 'Should mothers even be in space?' 'Who takes care of your child when you're at work?' *That* I'm scared about. But I'm not scared of being a mother."

"Why not?" Joan asked her.

"Because it feels good to love someone," Donna said. "It feels better than anything on this Earth. And I bet better than anything up there."

DONNA GAVE BIRTH TO THEA four days later, after only eight hours of labor. Hank called everyone that night. By the time he called Vanessa, it was two A.M. Vanessa answered it bleary-eyed as Joan sat up next to her.

"Aw, congrats, Hank. Tell Donna we're proud," Vanessa said. "That I'm proud, I mean."

Joan knew she probably had a message on her answering machine.

That weekend, they drove over to Hank and Donna's with an oversized teddy bear and a frozen lasagna.

When they pulled into the driveway, Jimmy was leaving the house.

"Oh, nice," Jimmy said when he saw Vanessa get out of the car with the lasagna. Joan was trying to get the teddy bear out of the back. "It's good how you women do that, the 'taking care of each other' thing."

"You could have just as easily brought food," Vanessa said, and Jimmy laughed.

Vanessa was holding the lasagna, and Joan waved her off, encouraging her to go ahead inside without her.

After Vanessa walked away, Jimmy stopped at his car door and turned to Joan.

"It's early," Jimmy said, "in the morning, don't you think?"

It was nine A.M. on a Sunday.

"What do you mean?" Joan asked.

"No, nothing," Jimmy said. "Just that you two are always together. Early in the morning. Late at night."

Joan looked at him. "Oh, no," Joan said, her voice as condescending as she could muster. "Little Jimmy Hayman has never had a friend."

Jimmy squinted at her, got in his car, and left.

Joan finally pulled the teddy bear out of the backseat and tried to lower her heart rate. She planned on telling Vanessa later. But Donna looked so happy, and Hank and Vanessa seemed to be having such a great time talking about their upcoming mission, and Thea felt so good in Joan's arms. It reminded her of when Frances was so light that Joan kept worrying she would drop her.

The day was such a good one that Joan just put it out of her mind. There was so much to do. She could not be worried about Jimmy Hayman.

THE REST OF OCTOBER PASSED by so fast she felt dizzy. It was wild to Joan how long you could wait for something—how much you could ache for it to hurry up and happen—and then how it could come too quickly.

The simulations the crew had tackled over the past months had gone well. Joan felt as prepared as she could imagine herself being.

But in early November, she also felt like each moment was carrying more and more weight, the closer she got to the day.

The night before Joan went into quarantine, Joan was waiting for Vanessa to come over when the phone rang.

When Joan realized it was Barbara, she assumed her sister was checking in one last time before Joan's mission. But no. Barbara had called to talk about Thanksgiving.

"Barb, I have other things to focus on right now other than what I'm bringing to Thanksgiving."

"Joan, that's what I'm trying to tell you. We aren't hosting Thanksgiving this year. Mom and Dad aren't coming. We're not doing it."

"What?"

"Daniel is taking me to Gstaad."

Joan blinked. "I'm confused."

"I don't have to host Thanksgiving for the whole family, you know. That's not my responsibility."

"I know, but why are you bringing Frances to Gstaad for the few days she has off for Thanksgiving? You can't drag a kid that far across the world and back in four days."

"Don't be absurd. She's staying at school."

Joan gripped the receiver. "What do you mean, she's staying at school?"

"She has asked to not come home," Barbara said.

"I don't believe that for a second."

"Well, I don't care what you believe. I asked if she wanted to abide by my rules or stay there and she said stay there. So we booked a trip to Gstaad instead."

"You can't leave her alone for the holiday. Even if she said to."

"Okay, first of all, it's Thanksgiving, not Christmas. No one likes Thanksgiving. We do it because that's what people do. And she's not alone. There's a whole program there where kids have Thanksgiving together. Lots of her friends will be with her. That's why she wants to stay."

"I don't buy that. Something must have happened for her to make that choice. What was it?"

"I mean, ask her. We went for a parents' weekend and it was horrible, Joan."

Frances had told Joan that Barbara and Daniel had left early, but Joan hadn't been able to get much more out of her than that. "I don't care if it was horrible!"

"She kicked me in the shin!"

"But why did she do that? She wouldn't do that for no reason."

"I don't know, but I'm really getting tired of you always taking her side. She kicked me. And she told Daniel she wished I'd never married him. I really don't understand it, because she's getting glowing reviews at the school. Her grades are good. She finishes her work early most of the time. Her teachers say she has a lot of friends. Everyone loves her. Apparently, she won an essay contest that included the entire middle school. She actually won!"

"Well, that's great."

"So I don't get it. And I'm not going to waste more time trying to. She's perfectly well behaved when she's there. So let her stay there."

"Of course she is well behaved there—she isn't mad at them."

"Well, why on Earth would she be mad at Daniel? He hasn't done anything to her."

"But she can't see that. All she can see is that he showed up and you suddenly stopped paying attention to her."

"I swear, sometimes you act just like a child," Barbara said.

"Hey."

"No, I mean it. It's like you can identify with a child's point of view because there's still something very childlike about you."

"That's completely out of line."

"I'm really not trying to be mean. But think about it. You've still never even gone on a date outside of high school, have you? Have you even had a real kiss? Do you know how adult life goes? Of course you don't understand what I have with Daniel. Because you've never had it.

"And you could certainly never understand how to actually raise Frances. I don't mean to hurt your feelings. It's just that I've felt judged by you for such a long time. Such a long time. And I'm finally seeing the situation as it really is. Which is that you judge me because you don't understand what it is like to be in an adult relationship. You don't understand what it means to love. You may never understand that. You're probably just not built for it. And that's not your fault. I just have to stop letting you get into my head."

"Barbara, that is completely . . ."

"What? You may not like it, but nothing I said is factually incorrect."

"Yes, it is."

"Which part?"

Joan wanted to tell her that she knew exactly what it meant to love someone. That she'd had kisses and dates and a whole life that Barbara knew nothing about. But that—also!—her opinion would still matter even if she hadn't. Even if Joan had never fallen in love, she would still matter. She wasn't a child just because her life looked different from Barbara's. She wanted to tell her that there were many, many people in this world who had full, rich lives the likes of which Barbara could not fathom because of her tiny little brain.

But when she played it out in her mind, it was so clear how such a conversation would go that there was no need to see it through.

"Forget it, it's not worth it," Joan said.

Barbara had done so many things society said were "wrong." And Joan had stood by her, cared for her, taken her side. How many nights had Joan wiped away Barbara's tears while she was pregnant? How many times had she made Barbara feel better after someone made a disapproving remark about the absence of a father?

The rules of society came for everyone eventually: the too big, too small, too wild, too quiet, too strong, not strong enough. When Barbara had been kicked out of the main group, she'd never stopped to question the injustice of it all, she'd just been so desperate to get back in.

There would be people who loved Joan for exactly who she was. Donna, Griff. Maybe her parents, hopefully Frances. But Barbara would never be one of them.

The world was full of Barbaras. That was the whole problem.

Joan hung up without saying goodbye. She called Frances's hallway phone three times but kept getting a busy signal.

Later, Barbara would make a remark about how she could never forgive Joan for hanging up on her.

But Joan would never be able to forgive Barbara for not loving Joan as Joan had loved her. For not knowing how to love Frances as Joan loved her.

THE NEXT MORNING, JOAN FOUND it difficult to drag herself out of bed. It was so comfortable, Vanessa's body so warm as it clung to her.

"I have to go," Joan said.

She had to go to the airfield and get into a T-38 to Cape Canaveral. She would not—could not—see Vanessa or anyone other than her crew for over a week.

It would be her and the guys in the crew quarters until the morning of liftoff.

As Joan lay in bed, her legs sinking into the welcoming mattress, her pillow so soft, she kept trying to understand how she'd gotten here.

Hadn't she been an associate astrophysics professor, teaching freshmen about Copernicus, just yesterday? She would go home each night and heat up her dinner. Frances was six and slept over every weekend.

But as Joan had taken each small step forward, the world had kept spinning on its axis. Days had formed into weeks and months and years, which people marked with watches and calendars, all based on the only thing they had to tell what time it was: the stars.

As the Earth orbits the sun, it shifts toward the sun's warm embrace. Then summer turns to fall, fall to winter. Soon it loops back around, and winter thaws to spring, spring to summer. Through it all, babies are born from stardust and grow taller. They begin to walk and talk and learn the days of the week, the months, the seasons. Then they look up at the sky, to see where they came from.

And the adults spend most of their days looking down. They fall in love and make mistakes and learn new things and feel tired. They lose people they love, and fail themselves, and change or never change. They get new jobs and fall out of love and convince themselves that if they just get this one thing, they will finally be happy.

Day in and day out, the Earth keeps spinning and revolving and sailing through the Milky Way. That is why time never stands still.

And that is why, small as they were, Joan's choices had added up to something magnificent. In the changing of seasons these past four years, Joan had found it all.

Something she loved, someone she loved, the parts of her she had hidden within herself.

"Goodbye, my love," Joan said as she kissed Vanessa's temple.

"Come home soon," Vanessa said.

It felt so good to Joan, to hurt to leave her.

"T MINUS TEN . . . NINE . . . EIGHT . . . SEVEN . . ."

Joan was in her flight suit, her helmet on. She was strapped to her seat in the mid-deck, lying on her back. The four guys on the crew, including Harrison, were sitting in the flight deck. She did not have a view out any window during ascent. All she could see were the lockers in front of her.

"Six . . . five . . . main engine start . . ."

The shuttle ignited, her bones vibrating as the ship came to life and began to quake. And it was a great relief to her—to shake like that.

She'd barely been able to sleep the night before—adrenaline running through every limb of her body. But the morning had been so slow, so methodical. She could not rush or indulge her excitement. Each item had to be checked off one by one, cross-referenced with Launch/Mission Control.

The difference between the outside of her—so controlled—and what ran inside her—such thrill—was jarring and hard to reconcile.

Until, now, finally, the outside was matching the inside. Joan felt an intense sense of equilibrium for the first time in days.

". . . four . . . three . . . two . . . one . . . zero . . . and liftoff of the space shuttle *Discovery*."

The ignition of the rockets hit her like a bang, her body hurling into the air.

Joan tried to think of how to explain the feeling to Frances. It was like being dragged through a hurricane, all the blood in her brain rushing to the back of her skull.

Discovery dropped its solid rocket boosters. And as the ship ascended higher and higher, going over seventeen thousand miles an hour to fight against gravity, Joan felt an intense lift in her belly. They hit main engine cutoff, and then there were two loud blows, which she knew to be the dropping of the huge external fuel tank, now emptied of its liquid hydrogen and oxygen. Then everything went quiet and still.

The cacophony, the quaking of the ship, the pressure—gone. Replaced with an eerie sense of calm.

Joan's body started to catch the air and she felt suddenly, excruciatingly alive—somersaults overtaking her chest and lower body. She detached from her seat.

"And we are in orbit," she heard Commander Donahue say.

Joan's stomach was in her feet, her head in her chest. She took off one of her gloves and let it go, remembering just in time to grab the tether attached to it as it began to float away. She removed her helmet and took a deep breath.

She tried to swim to the window, to look out across the expanse of space to spot the terminator line, dividing dark from light across the Earth's surface.

But she was seeing double, her vision looping, as if replaying a bad videotape. Her stomach felt both full and hollow. Her throat constricted. She could feel bile coming up through her chest.

Within the first hour of being in space, as the majority of the crew got to work, Joan vomited three times.

This continued through revolution after revolution around the Earth. She puked through each of the many sunrises and sunsets, what she usually used to measure days now coming in ninety-minute revolutions. The only thing that made her feel better for the first twenty-four hours was that Harrison was puking, too.

He puked for one day.

She puked for three.

Sometimes, during those days, as she made her way into the Spacelab module and conducted her experiments, she was fighting against a haze of confusion. Joan could not always focus her eyes, could not count her fingers. In fact, at one point, she lost the ability to recognize where her arms were or how to control them. She, twice, could not swim out of Spacelab until she summoned all of her strength—as if lifting a car on Earth—to pull herself through the hatch. On the third day, she developed a headache so painful she could not keep her eyes open.

What are we doing? Joan thought. *Believing we have any right to be up here?*

"Look at the smallest thing you can, and don't move," Harrison told her as they hung in their sleeping bags.

Joan moaned. She was determined to finish her experiments. But it was making her feel even sicker to think about them.

"Don't look out the window—it's not like being carsick," Harrison said.

"I know," Joan said. "I'm trying to just keep my eyes closed."

"No," Harrison said. "Do what I did and look at your fingernail. For as long as you can stand to."

She stared at her fingernail for six and a half hours.

"You hanging in there, Goodwin?" Donna said through the earpiece at some point on day four. What a joy it was, to hear Donna speaking to her as CAPCOM. Joan knew that it could not have been easy to get everyone on board with her coming back to work so quickly. But Donna, clearly, had pushed it through. How delightfully unsurprising. Joan was not sure that she herself would have that in her. But it thrilled her to know that Donna did. That Donna would make the world give her all the things she wanted all at once. "Feeling any better?"

She wanted to tell Donna everything. She wanted to say, *I don't think humans are meant to be up here.* And *I'm worried I've spent my entire life hoping for something it turns out I can't stand.* And *I don't know who I might be anymore if I don't want to do this ever again.*

But there would be time for that later. Instead, she said, "I'll survive."

. . .

ON THE FIFTH DAY, NOT long before the end of the mission, Joan felt well enough to look out the window.

As she stared ahead, at the big, bright, deep blue of the oceans of Earth, she took a full breath for the first time in days.

There it was.

Earth.

Daytime over the Pacific Ocean.

She looked at the western coast of the United States—all green and fading brown, cloud patterns across it in the starkest white. She could spot Baja California, but she could not tell where the border between the United States and Mexico was for certain. She could not see countries, with firm lines and borders. She saw only land-masses, undivided.

It was so funny to her, in that moment, to think that only American-trained space explorers were called "astronauts." That if you were trained in the Soviet Union you were a "cosmonaut." How utterly silly to make that distinction, when Russia kissed North America the way it did.

She thought back to *Sputnik 1.*

She'd been seven years old, looking up at the night sky with her father, when she had seen the satellite overhead in her binoculars. It rocked something in her, that humans had sent something up into the sky. That week, on the news, she kept hearing that "the Russians" put a satellite in space and that America must catch up.

But as Joan watched the Earth through the window now, it struck her as monumentally absurd that any of this had been a race with any opponent. Whatever the stated or unstated goals of the Apollo pro-gram, the achievements of everyone in space were shared, she thought, among us all.

Humans had figured out how to put a satellite up there.

Humans had gone to the moon.

And sure, they were all Americans in that shuttle at that very moment. But for the space shuttle program to be an American victory felt so small compared to the victory that it could be, should be.

Look what we humans had done.

We had looked at the world around us—the dirt under our feet, the stars in the sky, the speed of a feather falling from the top of a building—and we had taught ourselves to fly.

It was as beautiful an achievement to Joan as anything Rachmaninoff had written, as Leonardo da Vinci's *Vitruvian Man,* as monumental to her as the Great Wall of China or the pyramids of Egypt.

Space belonged to no one, but Earth belonged to all of them.

"It's so small," Harrison said, having just floated up beside her.

Joan nodded. "It's a midsize planet orbiting a midsize star in a galaxy of a hundred billion stars. In a universe of one hundred billion galaxies."

"With almost five billion people on the planet," Harrison said.

Joan nodded.

"Hard to believe any one person has any significance," he said. "I knew that before, but I never *knew* it, until now. Human life is . . . meaningless."

Joan looked at him.

How was it that two people, right next to each other, given the rarest of perspectives, could draw two totally opposite conclusions?

When Joan looked back at the Earth, she was overwhelmed with her own life's meaning—and the fact that the only meaning it *could* have was the meaning she gave it.

Joan studied the thin blue, hazy circle that surrounded the Earth. The atmosphere was so delicate, nearly inconsequential. But it was the very thing keeping everyone she loved alive.

Intelligent life was her meaning.

People were her meaning.

Frances and Vanessa.

Harrison swam away, but Joan stayed at the window and tried to spot Dallas. She thought of Frances, and what time it was there, and whether she was with her friends or playing field hockey. She thought of Vanessa, in Houston, at JSC, doing her own flight preparations.

Were they happy? Had they had a bad day? Did they need her?

Nothing happening across Texas mattered to the universe. Joan had always known that. But, oh, how it mattered to her. It made the whole Earth look bright and vital and urgent to her. It made that thin line of the atmosphere the most beautiful thing Joan had ever seen.

But as beautiful as it was, she wanted to feel it, and smell it, and taste it. She wanted to touch it in her hands.

Joan wanted to go home.

THE DAY BEFORE
THANKSGIVING 1984

"JOANIE, I SAW YOUR LANDING IN CALIFORNIA. I WAS SO HAPPY TO SEE that you got home okay. I know it's safe to go up there, but I just feel better knowing you're home. I love you."

"Joanie, I thought maybe you'd be back by now, back home I mean. Maybe I could call you on Thanksgiving Day, if you're around."

"Hey Joanie, it's me again. Sorry for calling so much. I think I'm just . . . can you call me back? I—"

WHILE THE REST OF THE crew needed some time to acclimate to the hard ground under their feet, it took Joan no time at all to readjust to the pull of gravity.

But when she stepped foot in her apartment that first morning back, something felt off. It was as if she'd come home to her childhood bedroom or tried to drive the old sedan she had in college. They had been hers, yes. But they belonged to a version of her that she'd grown out of.

It wasn't until she hit the answering machine and heard Frances's voice that she finally felt truly grounded again.

Before Joan had even finished listening to the third message, she'd grabbed the phone and dialed Frances's dormitory. It rang for so long.

"Hello?"

"Frances?"

"Joanie?"

"You picked up!" Joan said.

"Yeah, I'm the only one in the hall."

"You're the only one there?" Joan asked. "Your mom said lots of kids are staying at school for Thanksgiving. She said there was a whole big to-do there in the cafeteria."

"Um . . ."

Joan could hear Frances's voice start to waver. "They do have it every year. But none of the other kids stayed. It's just me."

"What do you mean, it's just you?"

"It's just me and Ms. Green. But she's very nice. And she's not my teacher, so it's not like I'm in class or anything. We are going to meet up at three tomorrow to have turkey sandwiches."

"You're kidding me."

"No, but it's okay, it's okay," Frances said, her voice so upbeat that it betrayed her. "She said they have cranberry sauce in them."

"Franny . . ."

"I'm fine, Joanie."

Then Frances burst into tears.

"Babe, I'm coming."

"No, you don't have to."

"Frances," Joan said, her voice stern. "I'm coming to get you, and I'm taking you home."

Frances was quiet for a moment and then, finally, said in barely more than a whisper, "Okay."

"Listen to me," Joan said. "I was circling two hundred miles above the Earth, and all I wanted was to get home and see you. Do you understand that? Do you understand that I don't care how big or small this world is, that you are the center of mine? Do you understand that, to someone, you are everything that matters on this entire planet?"

"Okay," Frances said again. This time Joan could hear the lump in her throat.

When Frances was younger, her problems had been tough but simple. She couldn't sleep. She cut her lip. She couldn't write uppercase *B*'s.

But Frances was ten years old now, a few months into sixth grade. Her problems were heavier and darker. Joan couldn't fix them with a sweet word or a joke or some ice. To hear Frances alone and crying so far away, it made Joan feel absolutely helpless. And she could not live with that.

"I will be there in less than four hours. Pack your stuff."

"I can't leave without Mom signing me out."

Joan sighed. "Goddammit."

"I'm sorry."

"It's not you."

Joan considered the situation. "Okay, it might take me a bit longer. But I'll be there. Have your stuff packed."

"Okay," Frances said. And then: "Joanie?"

"Yeah?"

"I love you."

"I love you, too, babe. More than you will ever know."

JOAN'S EARS WERE RINGING AS she knocked on Barbara's front door with the side of her fist, pounding so hard she shook the windowpanes.

"Jesus, Joan," Barbara said when she came to the door.

"Barbara, I swear to God . . ."

Barbara rolled her eyes. "I assume she's performed some sob story for you?"

"You said she wanted to stay there with a bunch of other kids."

Barbara left the door open and walked back into the house. Joan followed her.

"Joan, what do you want from me?"

"Where's Daniel?"

"He's picking up the traveler's checks."

"What are you thinking, running off to Europe? Don't do this. Let Frances come home."

Barbara inhaled and then shook her head. "No."

"She's having Thanksgiving with a teacher. They are eating club sandwiches."

"They are eating turkey sandwiches with cranberry sauce. But there the two of you go, making it seem worse than it is. She's being a manipulative brat. And I'm surprised you're falling for it. But you always do. You're such a mark, Joan, honestly."

Joan could not control the ferocity that came out of her. "What is the matter with you?" she yelled.

"What do you want from me?" Barbara shouted.

"I want you to take care of your daughter!"

"I am! She has a roof over her head and food to eat and a good education!"

"She's alone!"

"Joan, what am I supposed to do? Daniel has never wanted kids, but he said he was happy to try to be a stepdad. And he tried. He really tried. She made it impossible!"

"Why would you marry a man who doesn't want kids? You have a kid!"

"I am doing my best! Before I met Daniel, I spent most nights crying myself to sleep because I was so lonely and so tired. Do you know how hard it was just trying to take care of her and make enough money to keep us eating canned beans? You think this world is easy on a single mother with no college degree?"

"I could have lent you money."

"I didn't want your money! I wanted a life! I want a life with a man who loves me and pays the bills and provides a beautiful home and makes sure my kid gets an incredible education so that she never ends up like me! That's what I want, Joan! I don't want your charity."

"And so that's it? You're shipping her off—and she's never allowed to come home—because you picked a guy who doesn't know how to deal with her?"

"*I* don't know how to deal with her! She's insufferable!"

"She's hurting!"

"Well, I don't want to deal with her anymore!"

Joan pulled back. Barbara blinked a few times and then she sank down on the sofa and sobbed. Joan stared at her, shocked that she had the audacity to cry.

Joan marveled at how easy Barbara's inner life must be. How entirely undemanding of yourself it was to believe that everything happened *to you*. And everything was *about you*. And that *your* feelings were the only ones that mattered. Worse yet, to afford yourself the role of the victim always—regardless of how grotesquely it required you to twist reality—so that you never had to look in the mirror and admit you were the perpetrator.

"She's your daughter," Joan said, finally.

"I know," Barbara said as she continued to cry. She buried her face in her hands. Joan refused to comfort her.

"You are going to find a way to fix it," Joan said.

"I can't. Daniel doesn't want her here after the way she's acted."

"Well, tell him that's not realistic. Even if she stays at school the rest of the semester, what are you going to do? Not have her come home at Christmas?"

Barbara pulled a tissue from her pocket to dry her eyes. "Daniel wants to stay in Europe for a little while."

"What?"

"Copenhagen for Christmas, Paris for New Year's. He has a few meetings in London at the top of the year, so we'd stay until then."

Joan dropped her head. She was so stupid. So incredibly stupid not to see what had really been going on. But it was hard to admit just how low your own sister could go. Joan's own moral code had felt so innate as to be genetic, intrinsic to the DNA they both shared. And perhaps that's why, until now, she had been unable to see just how little they had in common. "What kind of meetings?" Joan said finally.

"What?"

"What kind of meetings does he have in London, Barbara?"

Barbara looked away. "They are transferring him there. In the spring."

Joan shook her head and then closed her eyes. She stared at darkness and then opened her eyes and her mouth at the same time. "Please tell me you're making this up."

"I'm not."

"What is your plan?"

"I don't know."

"I will not let you abandon her. What is your plan?"

"She's at boarding school, Joan. For crying out loud, no one has abandoned her."

"She's crying. Alone up there. She thinks no one loves her."

Barbara shook her head in her hands. "Of course I love her." She began to howl in tears.

"If you love your daughter, then you need to show her. By taking care of her," Joan said. "There is no other option."

Barbara stood up and snapped, "It's not that simple!"

"Yes, it is!"

"It's not! I've been doing it on my own since I was twenty years old, and I'm sick of being treated like some sort of screwup because I'm trying to create a life out of this mess!"

"She's not a mess! Stop talking about her like that!"

"She's my daughter, I can say anything I like about her!"

"I'm not sure you ever deserved her, you know that? I've tried to avoid thinking that for years, but I don't know what other conclusion to draw anymore. She deserves better than you give her."

"Then take her!" Barbara said. "You think you're so fucking smart, Joan. *Oh, the mom you'd be!* If only you had a love life or a man interested in you enough to give you a child. Please. You take care of her. The two of you would probably love that."

"Barbara, don't say things like that. This is not a game."

But it was a game, wasn't it? And Barbara had been winning for a very, very long time.

"I mean it!" Barbara said. "She has never liked me as much as she likes you. The two of you, with your special bond. You can have each other, as far as I'm concerned. You can go be happy together, without me to look down on."

"She doesn't look down on you. She worships you."

Barbara laughed and shook her head. "She hates me. She thinks I'm a selfish fool, just like you do, and she makes it perfectly clear. Oh, you'll see, Joan. Once she's really yours. It's no picnic. She hates me. One day she'll hate you, too. You'll finally see it then. And it will be too late, because I won't accept your apology. But in the meantime, go for it. She's all yours."

Joan stared at her. But Barbara's face did not seem sad or angry so much as unflinching. Her eyes had gone dead.

This was Barbara's whole plan. Joan was her get-out-of-jail-free card.

"You are seriously going to let this child be alone on Thanksgiving?"

"I am going to let her learn that it's not always about her and that it's time that my life starts, too. Yes, I am. But you seem to want to be her mother, so go right ahead."

Part of Joan felt like she could not give Barbara the satisfaction. She was going to abandon her child and flit off to Europe, leaving Joan to handle all of the responsibilities. Joan shouldn't participate in that.

But Frances deserved better than anything she could make Barbara begrudgingly give her. Frances needed someone to truly care and to show it. Someone to be there.

In that moment, all Joan could think of was the joy of having

Frances back. Of getting to spend each evening helping her with her homework. Of taking her to the movies each weekend. Of seizing those rare times when Frances would still let Joan kiss the top of her head.

Joan would do anything to get more of those moments. They were already slipping away so fast.

She would never let that go—never let Frances down—just to teach Barbara a lesson.

"Write a letter to the school giving me the power to make decisions for her and take her from the school," Joan said. "Do it now."

"You think I don't mean it? Because I will do it."

"Do it, Barbara! Now!"

Barbara went into the kitchen and scribbled on a piece of stationery with Daniel's name at the top. Then she handed it to Joan. "I don't want to see either of you before I go," she said. "She threw a tantrum. And you played right into it."

"You will call her tomorrow to wish her a happy Thanksgiving from the airport. If you don't, I will call your hotel every hour on the hour until you get on the phone. Do you hear me? I think we both know Daniel won't be happy with you if this gets messy. So if I were you, I'd call before noon and I'd stay on the phone for ten minutes and I'd make it count."

"Thanks, Joan. Thanks for treating me like I wouldn't call my own daughter on Thanksgiving. Wow, I'm such a monster."

"I think that maybe you *are* a monster," Joan said. And then she slammed the door so hard that it bounced back open. She did not look back.

WHEN JOAN GOT TO THE school, Frances was sitting in the lobby of her dormitory with a woman who looked to be in her late twenties.

"Hi," Joan said as Frances stood up and smiled.

"You must be Joan," the woman said. "We are all very big fans of you and everything you do. I suspect our physics teacher, Marlon Ryan, will be sad to have missed the chance to make your acquaintance. It is a true pleasure to meet you."

"Oh, thank you. I appreciate that. I'm assuming you're Ms. Green?"

"Indeed."

"Well, I would love to take Frances home," Joan said as she handed over the note.

Ms. Green looked it over. "Okay," she said and then she turned to Frances. "Happy Thanksgiving, Frances. We will see you Monday."

"Um," Joan said. "No, you won't."

"What?" Frances said.

"We will talk about it in the car," Joan said to Frances. "But for now, let's pack up your things. Not just for the weekend."

They went to Frances's room. Joan was taken with how neat everything was on Frances's side. She'd made her bed with sharp corners, and her books were lined up on her desk at right angles.

Joan looked at Frances. "Do you have any duffel bags we can use?"

Frances nodded and grabbed three bags and a box from under her bed.

"Great, you pack your clothes. I'll get your pillow and blankets."

When they were done, Frances asked if she should bring her books and Joan said no. "But your mom said you won an essay contest."

"Yeah," Frances said. "I did."

"Do you have the essay? Is it here?"

"Um, yeah," Frances said.

"Well, we can't leave that behind. Grab it."

"Okay . . ." Frances pulled a drawer open and took a few pages out and tucked them into the open bag in her hand.

"All right, kiddo," Joan said. "T minus zero. We're outta here."

And Frances laughed. It felt so good to make her smile.

"That was so cheesy, Joanie."

. . .

ON THE WAY HOME, JOAN and Frances stopped at a diner and split a peanut butter and jelly sandwich and a strawberry milkshake.

It was almost nine at night by that point. Frances looked tired. Her eyes were red, the skin around them puffy. Her lips were chapped. Joan wanted to hug her but worried that if she did, she herself might fall apart. Returning to Earth was exhausting.

There was an ache in Joan's chest looking at Frances.

But there was also a sadness that Joan could not name. A disappointment, perhaps. Maybe a reckoning. Certainly a recognition. She had tried so hard to have faith in Barbara. Now it was clear that Barbara was never going to put in much effort to be worthy of her faith.

Barbara had shown who she was. If Joan continued to not see it, well, that would be Joan's fault.

"Listen, babe," Joan said, over a plate of french fries that neither of them were eating. "Some stuff has happened."

"I figured, since you said I'm not going back to school."

"Your mom and I talked, and I finally got her to come around," Joan said. "On something that I think could be very exciting."

"What is it?"

"What do you think about coming to live with me?"

"For the weekend?"

"Permanently."

"Live in your house?"

"Yeah. I'll have to get a two-bedroom, obviously. So at first you'll be on the sofa or we will get a mattress. I'm not sure. But I'll figure that out quickly."

"I don't care where I sleep," Frances said. Her face started to bubble up, the tears coming to the surface quickly. "You'd . . . want me there?"

"Oh, honey," Joan said. She reached across to hold her hand. "I want you with me more than anything."

Frances put her face down into the crook of her own arm and her body started to shake. Joan moved to her side of the booth and held her. Eventually, when Frances's crying did not stop, Joan put cash on the table, stole the silver tin holding the strawberry milkshake, and led Frances to the car.

"I'm going to re-enroll you in public school, okay?" Joan said once they got to the car.

Frances nodded.

"And I don't know exactly how it's all going to work, but you and I, we will figure it out."

Frances nodded at that, too. "Joanie," Frances said. "Thank you."

"Don't thank me, babe. I should be thanking you, for the gift it is to be around you."

Frances leaned toward Joan and Joan pulled her in, across the gearshift. If Frances had spent the first ten years of her life unsure of where she belonged, Joan knew she would spend the next ten knowing she firmly belonged to her.

"Listen, Frances Emerson Goodwin," Joan said, holding Frances by the chin and making her look at her. "I will love you until the day I die, do you hear me? There is nothing you could do or say or think or feel that would change that. I am yours to fall back on, forever.

"You make my life worth something. And I can promise you with my entire body that you will never be alone. Every day, you can wake up and go to bed knowing there is someone whose heart is bursting, barely able to contain how much they love you. I know you're my niece, Frances. But you have always, too, been *mine*."

THE NEXT DAY, BARBARA CALLED AT ELEVEN-THIRTY.

"Happy Thanksgiving," Frances said, standing in Joan's kitchen. "I hope you have fun with Daniel. And you both have a nice vacation."

Joan watched from the stove, standing over a pot of boiling cranberries. How was it that Frances had this much character at ten years old? Or maybe it wasn't surprising at all. If character was built through bones breaking and healing, Frances had earned some.

"Thanks, I love you, too, Mom," Frances said as she got off the phone.

So that was how this would work. Barbara would pretend it was normal. There would be no taking it back, no apology. Joan could only hope, for Frances's sake, that one day Barbara would regret it. That she would, in the future, attempt to fix this, to win Frances's trust back.

But if not, then Joan would be honored to step in for the rest of Frances's life. It would not be easy. Already Joan was building contingencies for how every facet of her life would have to go to plan B. But Joan would do it all joyfully, despite the heaviness that loomed in the background. She could already feel the full weight of all the ways, both big and small, that this would forever alter her life.

THAT AFTERNOON, VANESSA PICKED JOAN and Frances up and the three of them went to Donna and Hank's for the holiday.

Donna had invited Joan and Vanessa before Joan had left for her mission. And had gotten so excited when Joan called her and asked if Frances could join.

"Yes!" Donna said. "Because I need a babysitter to come over here and hold this fuckin' baby. I need a break, and Hank is going to be smoking the turkey all afternoon."

When they got to Donna and Hank's, they could smell the smoker from the driveway. Donna greeted them with huge hugs. Thea was napping. Donna immediately put Frances to work folding napkins.

Griff was standing at the stove wearing a plaid apron that said, "Who Invited All These Tacky People?" And then over at the table, snapping green beans, was Lydia.

"What is Lydia doing here?" Vanessa whispered.

Donna waved Vanessa off. "Hank says that because she's part of your mission, I had to invite her. Steve and Helene are stopping by later, too, so it's the right thing to do. I tried to keep an open mind today. But when she got here, she said our house smelled like mold and we should look into that, so I've closed my mind again."

Joan laughed and went over to Lydia to help snap the beans, while Frances folded napkins right next to her. Lydia barely acknowledged Joan's presence.

When Hank walked in to grab a beer, he put a hand on Joan's shoulder to greet her and introduced himself to Frances.

"Nice to have you back Earthside," he said to Joan.

At which point, Lydia dropped the green beans in her hand.

"Okay, I'm just going to say it," Lydia said. "I heard you puked the whole time."

Donna laughed. Vanessa bit her lip. Griff stopped stirring and turned toward Joan.

"I heard that, too," Griff said with an embarrassed look.

Donna put both hands up. "I'm staying out of it."

"Joanie, is that true?" Frances asked.

Joan looked around to see that everyone was waiting for her to respond. "Well, if you must know," she said, finally. "That is correct. I puked straight into the air."

Frances threw her head back and cackled. All of the adults in the room started laughing with her.

"No, I used barf bags. Many, many, many barf bags," Joan said, delighted by Frances's reaction. Frances laughed so hard she went silent and her face turned red. "Let the record show I did not let it stop me! But I am very happy to be home now with you fine people," she added, putting her arms around Frances's shoulders and giving her a squeeze.

"Hear, hear!" Vanessa said, raising her glass.

LATER, THEY ALL SAT AROUND Donna and Hank's dining table, Frances crammed in between Joan and Vanessa. Griff told everyone he'd met someone and was thinking of introducing her to all of them. Donna made fun of him.

Lydia kept asking people to pass the potatoes, and when people didn't hear her one too many times, she stood up, walked to the other side of the table, took the casserole dish of mashed potatoes, and walked them back to her seat, where she put them in front of her plate.

"There," Lydia said. "If anyone wants them, they can ask me."

"Lydia," Vanessa said, her tone completely dry. "Can I have the potatoes?"

When Thea woke up, Frances sat in the living room with her and rocked her over and over. Hank went in there and sat with them.

Joan overheard Frances ask Hank what it was like to fly the space shuttle and he said, "Dunno, kid, but I'm excited to find out."

When Steve and Helene showed up with their kids, everyone cheered. Vanessa gave her seat to Steve; Joan gave hers to Helene. Hank and Griff gave theirs to the kids. And Joan smiled, to watch them.

Once again, there was a table in the center of the room and most of her group stood on the edges, looking on. Joan looked at Griff and smiled. "It's just like the all-astronauts meetings," Griff said.

Joan laughed. "You always know what's in my mind before I do," she said.

They all shared pecan pie and banana pudding. Vanessa let Frances have both when she thought Joan wasn't looking. Joan smiled and shook her head at her. Vanessa laughed.

Griff taught Frances a magic trick. Hank told the kids knock-knock jokes.

Later, when Joan and Lydia were doing the dishes, Lydia thanked Joan for her advice.

"Things are going really well with this team," she told Joan as she cleared plates. "And I'm not sure that would be the case if it weren't for you."

"Well, I'm glad," Joan said, beginning to load the dishwasher.

"You're . . ." Lydia said. "You're my best friend here, Joan."

Joan looked at her and then touched Lydia's arm, but Lydia did not look at her.

"You're loading the plates wrong," Lydia finally said, taking a plate from Joan's hand and pushing her out of the way. "Who taught you how to load a dishwasher?"

Joan shook her head and turned to see that Vanessa had caught the whole interaction. Vanessa raised her eyebrows and shrugged. Joan laughed.

When it got to be late, and it was time to go, Joan found Donna in Thea's room, rocking her to sleep. Donna seemed so content, as if she had everything she'd ever wanted.

Joan did not want to go up to space again. And perhaps that had made room for Frances. But Donna would not need room. Donna would find a way. One day, Donna would come home from space and tell her daughter all about it.

Donna looked up at Joan in the doorway and smiled. Joan waved her good night.

It was the first Thanksgiving Joan had ever had without her parents and Barbara.

But it was the first time she'd ever felt this at home.

. . .

LATER THAT NIGHT, VANESSA WALKED Joan and Frances into Joan's apartment. Frances headed to brush her teeth and get ready for bed. Boarding school had abruptly matured her. Frances now did so many things on her own, insisted on reading books that struck Joan as perhaps a bit too advanced for her age, and had started wearing shorter skirts and dresses, almost never wearing T-shirts. But she still wanted to be tucked in. And for that, Joan was grateful.

"I'll be in in a second," she said to Frances as Frances headed to the bathroom.

"Today was a good day," Vanessa said once Frances was out of earshot.

"Yes, it was," Joan said, holding Vanessa's hand. "Though I missed you, even when you were right there in front of me."

"I missed you, too," Vanessa said softly.

They looked at each other. Vanessa could not sleep there that night. There could be no more of that for a long time. Soon they would need a plan.

"Good night, Franny!" Vanessa called out.

"Good night!" Frances called from the sink.

When Vanessa walked out the front door, Joan grabbed her hand for a moment.

"I don't know how this is all going to work now," Joan said. "With Frances always here."

"I know. But we will figure it out," Vanessa said. "People like us have always had to find a way. And so we do."

And she then kissed Joan on the cheekbone.

Joan closed her eyes and inhaled.

THAT MONDAY, JOAN HEADED TO ANTONIO'S OFFICE TO REQUEST A MEETing. She wanted to discuss moving to Mission Control permanently, and no longer being assigned missions in space.

To her surprise, Antonio was walking past his assistant's desk when she came by. He invited her right in.

"Tell me what's on your mind," Antonio said, leaning forward.

Joan did not say that she had just taken in her niece and was now, effectively, a single parent who couldn't leave the planet for long stretches. She said the other thing, the one that was more relevant, and possibly even more true.

"I belong on the ground," Joan said. "I have learned that I am supposed to have both feet on Earth and look up at the stars. Not the other way around."

There was so much to learn about the universe from Earth. So much she wanted to do from this very ground, here at NASA.

Antonio considered her. "To be honest, I was hoping we could send you up a few more times. Despite your space-adaptation issues, we were very happy with your research."

"I understand, sir," she said.

"But I have heard from Jack that you've been a great help on previous missions," Antonio said. "I think he'd be very open to integrating you into Mission Control."

"I would be grateful," Joan said. "If you would consider it."

Antonio nodded. "I will," he said. "I will."

"Thank you," she said. Joan stood up, and Antonio walked her to the door. But he only put his hand on the door handle. He did not open it.

"I wondered if you could help me," Antonio said. "With something."

"Of course," Joan said.

"As you know, being assigned any mission requires a certain level of security clearances," Antonio said.

"Sure," Joan said.

"And security clearances cannot be granted to anyone who we believe is . . ." He appeared to be searching for the words. "Morally compromised," he said, finally.

It hit Joan like a sucker punch.

"Yes, sir."

"Not as a matter of judgment, mind you, but because it opens people up to the potential for blackmail. People with large debts, for instance, or gambling problems would be a good example of the type of person we would have to rescind a security clearance from, rendering them unable to fly. People who have family members with ties to organized crime would be another example. Also, the appearance of sexual deviation would make any of our astronauts vulnerable to such a blackmail."

Joan and Vanessa had asked for too much, pushed too hard, believed too naïvely that they could have what they wanted.

Wasn't that the story of so many of the gods up there among the stars? She'd been looking at them her whole life and had never really listened, never learned from their stories. They were always punished for their hubris.

"I want to be very clear about something: I have never felt it is my personal business to know what any of my astronauts do on their own time. My purview is only as it relates to what is of concern to the U.S. government and to the public interest."

"Of course," Joan said.

"I want to protect my team here. You did tell me once that you hold particularly special relationships with many of your fellow astronauts. I wonder if you would be willing to convey this to anyone within the corps who needs a reminder?"

"Yes, sir."

"The loss of security clearances for any of our astronauts would be a devasting blow to the department and would reflect poorly on NASA as a whole," he said. "And I am . . . well, Goodwin, I am hoping it never comes to that."

"I understand, sir," Joan said.

"Thank you," Antonio said as he opened the door. "I would be very eager to recommend you for Mission Control, including any classified missions that lie ahead. I know you will ensure that you hold up to any such scrutiny."

"Thank you, sir," Joan said.

She picked Frances up from her first day back at school that afternoon, but could not remember anything else she did that day.

FOR TWO WEEKS, JOAN PRETENDED, WITH EVERY CELL IN HER BRAIN, that she needed time to figure out a plan.

But she knew what she had to do.

Instead, she hid.

She dropped Frances off at school every morning and then scheduled as much time as she could flying. She took any meetings she could off campus. She made appointments to see two-bedroom apartments in Frances's school district so that she and Frances could be moved in by the new year.

When the phone rang, she let Vanessa leave messages on her machine. And then she called Vanessa only when she knew she'd be out, and left messages on hers.

She took Frances to pick out a Christmas tree, to buy ornaments. The two of them decorated it together. As they did, Frances asked if Joan would be willing to talk to her class about going to space.

Joan was thrilled to be asked, thrilled by the idea of making Frances proud. "Of course!" she said. But she could not *feel* the joy she knew was in her.

She was numb to almost everything.

Except for those moments in the middle of the night, while Frances slept but Joan could not. It was only then that she gave in to the profound sorrow, and wept as quietly as she could.

She had known from the moment she'd left Antonio's office what had to come next. And she could not bear it.

It had been easy to avoid Vanessa at first, because Vanessa's schedule was incredibly intense. She was only weeks out from her mission. But then, as Vanessa got more insistent about seeing Joan before leaving, it suddenly wasn't easy at all.

"So I'll come over the night before I leave," Vanessa said when

Joan finally picked up the phone. "Because I have to see you both just one more time."

"Right, of course," Joan said.

"Is everything okay?" Vanessa asked.

"Yeah, everything's great. We're excited to see you," Joan said as she found herself agreeing to what felt like her own execution.

That night, Vanessa cheerfully brought over a pizza and helped Frances with her homework as Joan's heart raged in her chest.

Tomorrow morning, Hank, Griff, Lydia, Steve, and Vanessa would all fly to Cape Canaveral to begin preparations for their mission at the end of the month. Maybe this could wait until Vanessa came back.

The three of them played a game of Scrabble in which Joan could think of no good moves and Vanessa kept looking at her, confused.

"You didn't notice you could put the *q* in 'quit' on the triple letter score?" she asked Joan.

"Oh," Joan said. "Sorry."

"Better for me!" Frances said, using Joan's *q* to play "queue" with the rest of her tiles and win the whole thing.

"All right, babe," Joan said. "Brush teeth, get your pajamas on, and I'll be in to kiss you good night in a moment."

Frances went into the bedroom.

"Okay, what's going on?" Vanessa said.

"Hm?" Joan cleared the table. But as she walked by Vanessa, Vanessa took her arm.

"Joan, what is going on?" Vanessa said again.

"I'm not sure what you mean," Joan said.

"Joanie!" Frances called out. "Can you help me roll out my bed?"

Joan went into the bedroom and set up the futon. She tucked her in and said good night.

When she shut the door behind herself, Vanessa was leaning against the kitchen counter, staring at her.

"Jo," Vanessa said. "What is going on? I'm serious."

Joan closed her eyes. When she opened them, her jaw was tight. "I think, with Frances here, this is not going to work," she said finally.

The sound of the words coming out of her mouth shocked her, even though she had rehearsed them for days. She threw her head into her hands.

"What are you talking about?" Vanessa said.

"How are we going to do this?" Joan said. "I will never be able to spend the night at your house. You won't be able to spend the night at mine. I think . . . it's not realistic. Anymore. You and me."

Vanessa tensed her jaw; her eyes went glassy, and Joan wanted to die.

Vanessa pursed her lips and nodded. "And when did you decide this?" she said.

"I've been thinking it since Thanksgiving," Joan said.

"You're lying," Vanessa said.

"I just wasn't sure how to tell you," Joan said.

"So you've been avoiding me? Because you didn't have the decency to break up with me?"

"No," Joan said. And then: "Maybe. Either way, it's not going to work anymore."

"I don't agree," Vanessa said, crossing her arms.

"What are we going to do? I'll get a babysitter once a week and you and I can go out to dinner three towns over? And then I'll rush to be home before the sitter has to leave?"

"Yes!" Vanessa said, shouting in a whisper. "That's exactly what we'll do. And I'll drive you home. And I'll stay in your room with you that one night a week and then I'll sneak out before Frances wakes up. Yes!"

"That's not a relationship!" Joan said, doing her best to keep her voice down.

"That's what we can have!" Vanessa said. "And I'll take anything I can have with you! Don't you see that?"

"Well, I can't ask that of you."

"I'm asking it of you! I'll sneak into your house just to kiss you once a week if that's what I can get. I'll wait until Frances is in college if that's what I have to do. Are you insane, Joan? I want you. Forever. I told you that. I don't care what it takes."

Joan could barely catch her breath. She slumped herself down onto a kitchen chair and rested her head on the table.

"Jo, I don't understand," Vanessa said. "Why are you doing this?"

Joan looked up at her. Vanessa's eyes were teary, her voice catching, her mouth turned down. "Please don't do this. Please."

All of Joan's body went limp, and she began to sob.

"They know," Joan said, finally.

"What?"

"They know. NASA knows."

Vanessa blanched. "No, they don't."

"Yes, they do. I don't know if we were too obvious. Or someone told them. A couple of months ago, Jimmy made a comment. I didn't give it enough attention at the time. I can see now that I should have. He might have gone to Antonio. It doesn't really matter how—they know."

"That's impossible. Steve told me Antonio had no idea."

"Well, Steve was wrong."

"But how?"

"Maybe Antonio knows the same way Donna or Jimmy figured it out," Joan said. "I mean, we have been in a relationship for three years and it's probably incredibly obvious. In ways we can't see."

Vanessa shook her head. "Maybe you misunderstood him."

"I went to his office to talk about Mission Control, and I was about to leave, but before I got to the door, he calmly reminded me of the importance of security clearances for astronauts, and that they require no appearances of 'sexual deviation.' He said it leaves one open to blackmail."

Vanessa flinched. "Well, yeah, it leaves us open to blackmail because people act like who we are is shameful. If we didn't have to keep it a secret, then people wouldn't be able to blackmail us," she said. "Did he ever think about that?"

Joan shook her head and sighed.

Vanessa pushed on: "Did he say why he was telling *you* this, specifically?"

"He said it was because he knew me to have good, *special* relationships with many members of the astronaut corps, and that he trusted me to get this information to anyone who needed to hear it."

"He meant me," Vanessa said.

"Yes, he meant you."

Vanessa put her knuckles to her mouth.

"What do we do?" Vanessa said.

"What I am doing," Joan said. "This is what has to happen."

Vanessa closed her eyes. Joan watched her chest rise and fall.

"You have to leave us," Joan said. "With Frances here, the three of us spending time together, it's only going to become more obvious. You have to leave us."

"No—"

"You have to," Joan said firmly. "I'm sure you're okay for this mission because it's happening so soon. But everything after that is at risk. You have to leave, or you will never fly the space shuttle."

Vanessa did not say anything. She started tapping the counter with her fingers, over and over and over again. Joan buried her head in her arms on the dining table.

"Is that what you want me to do?" Vanessa said. "You want me to leave?"

"Yes," Joan said. "That is what I want you to do."

"Maybe you don't want to lose your own job," Vanessa said. "I wouldn't blame you if you're afraid to be unemployed, now that you've got a kid to take care of."

Joan scoffed. *"No."*

"Well, then why didn't you tell me about this sooner?" Vanessa said. "Instead of avoiding me?"

Because I do not know how to live my life without you. Because I don't even recognize the person I was before I loved you. "Because . . ." Joan said. But she had no words.

"Then—"

"But this is final," Joan said. "You have to go. I knew I couldn't talk to you about it until I worked up enough nerve to see it through. But this is how it has to be. That's never been clearer to me."

Joan closed her eyes. When she opened them, Vanessa was standing in front of her, crying.

"Jo, please—"

"Vanessa, this is not up for debate. I will not allow you to give up everything you have worked toward. It's over."

Vanessa hung her head.

"Please do not call me," Joan continued. "Please do not come back here."

"How could you—"

"You will meet someone else," Joan said. "Someone who is not in the corps. And you will be able to keep it a secret. A better secret than we have. You will be able to have everything you deserve. But you cannot have that with me."

"I—"

Joan could not bear another second of this conversation. It had to be over. She stood up.

"Vanessa, just go," Joan said.

"Joan—"

"You need to go. I'm asking you to leave my house," Joan said.

"But Frances . . ." Vanessa said, a tear falling from her face. "You're not even letting me say goodbye to Frances."

"I know," Joan said. "I will explain it all to Frances as best I can. She will be okay."

Vanessa stared at her.

But Joan was right. And they both knew that.

Vanessa's eyes narrowed, her lips tight. "I deserve to at least have a say in this," she said.

Joan shook her head. "There is nothing left to say."

"What an incredibly fucked-up thing to do," Vanessa said.

"I don't care," Joan said.

Without saying another word, Vanessa grabbed her keys and left. For a moment, Joan thought she was going to slam the door, but she shut it quietly. And Joan knew it was so as not to wake up Frances. She wanted to run to Vanessa and tell her that she could not live without a woman who cared about her niece that much.

Instead, when the lock finally clicked, Joan fell to the living room floor and sobbed. She let it shake her body from her chest down through her legs. She was still crying when she pushed herself up to a sitting position. And through her tears, she could see that while she had been on the floor for only a few minutes, her tears had left a mark on the carpet.

And then the phone rang.

When Joan picked it up, she heard just one word.

"No."

Joan's breathing slowed, and she tried to dry her tears.

"No, Joan," Vanessa said.

"Where are you?" Joan asked.

"I'm in the pay phone across the street because I assumed you would be a moron and not let me in," Vanessa said.

Joan ran to the window.

There, at the phone, was Vanessa looking up at her. "No. Do you hear me?" Vanessa said. "No."

"Vanessa, they won't—"

"I listened to you. And you wouldn't let me talk. But now it's *my turn*. And *you* don't get to talk. My answer is *no*. Absolutely not. I don't care what Antonio said. I don't care what they can take from me. I don't care if they never let me set foot in the fucking space shuttle ever again. No. I will not leave you and Frances. I *will not*. And you don't get to tell me what to do."

Joan wiped a tear from her eye and watched Vanessa yell at her from the pay phone.

"You have no right to tell me I don't get a say in this," Vanessa said. "And you have no right to do to me what you did tonight."

"I'm sorry," Joan said, "But—"

"I didn't ask for this!" Vanessa shouted. "I didn't ask to meet your niece and help you deal with your stupid sister and meet your parents and imagine a life where the two of us could have things that I never dreamed the world would let me have! I didn't ask for that! That was you!"

"I—"

"And now, when one asshole scares you, you're going to give it all up? No! I don't accept it. I love you. And I love Frances, too, and you don't get to take her away from me. Just because you're scared. Or just because you think you know what's best for me."

"All you've ever wanted is to fly the shuttle," Joan said.

"All I ever want*ed*—past tense," Vanessa said. "But you changed what I wanted, and what I thought was possible."

Vanessa started losing track of her breath as she broke down. "What an awful thing to do to a person! To make them believe they can have the things they never believed they deserved. And then take it away. What an awful thing."

"I'm sorry," Joan said. "I'm so sorry."

Joan, staring out the window, saw Vanessa looking at up her. "Please don't make me go," Vanessa said, crying harder now. "Please."

"But you might lose everything you dreamed of."

"Then I'll lose it," Vanessa said. "Let them take it. Just don't let them take you."

Tears fell down Joan's face.

"Will you come back up here?" Joan asked.

"Will you let me in and let me talk?" Vanessa asked.

"Yes," Joan said. "Of course."

Two minutes later, Vanessa was at Joan's front door. Her face was red. Joan hated herself for ever making Vanessa cry like that. But denial wasn't going to fix any of this.

"I'm not the one I'm worried about here. I don't care if I lose my job," Joan said. "I will find another one somewhere. At some university, if I have to. I'll teach freshmen again if it comes to it. I don't care. But you. You can't give up what you've been working so hard for."

"I told you," Vanessa said. "I don't care."

"But I do," Joan said. "Maybe you don't care about yourself

enough to do what's smart, but I won't be able to live with myself if I don't look out for you."

Vanessa wiped the tear from Joan's face.

"You don't know what's best for me," Vanessa said. "As much as you may think you do."

Joan sighed. "But . . ."

"I don't know what's going to happen," Vanessa said. "But if it's you or the space shuttle . . . fuck the space shuttle."

Joan dropped her head and laughed. Then she looked back up at Vanessa. "The woman I fell in love with would never have said that," Joan said.

Vanessa smiled her lopsided grin. "Then I guess I'm not the woman you fell in love with."

It was more than three years ago that Vanessa had pushed Joan up against the very door they now stood in front of.

Joan had told her that she thought she'd always be alone. Vanessa had told her that she thought she'd never have the things other people had.

But maybe they'd both been wrong.

Joan pulled Vanessa toward her and kissed her up against the door.

"We're idiots, you know," Joan said.

And Vanessa smiled. "I know."

"So what's your plan?" Joan said.

Vanessa shook her head. "I don't have one. Yet. But I will figure it out."

"Oh, you will, will you?"

"I will."

"Well, why don't we start with this?" Joan said. "Sneak out of here quietly. Don't call me while you're in quarantine. That way, they won't have any good reason to stop you from getting on LR9. Then, once you're back, we will find a way."

"Okay," Vanessa said, kissing her neck. "At least you're CAP-COM. So pretty soon I'll be able to hear your voice."

"I'll be waiting for you," Joan said. "On the loop."

DECEMBER 29, 1984

"HOUSTON, DO YOU READ? I ASKED HOW MUCH TIME DOES LYDIA HAVE," Vanessa says from the payload bay. She is counting her breaths to keep herself calm. But the realization that the payload bay doors may not fully close is bearing down on her. *How. How. How did we get here?* It was only hours ago that Hank and Steve were joking about who had a better barbecue smoker. And Griff had been complaining about drinking breakfast from a pouch. And now everyone is gone but her and Lydia. *How?*

"If we miss our deorbit opportunity, can Lydia survive?"

Joan does not respond. But Vanessa knows the answer. They all know the answer.

Finally, Joan speaks up. "We do not know if Lydia can survive," she says. Then, lower, in a tone that feels to Vanessa like Joan is confessing: "But the flight surgeon does not believe so."

Fuck.

Vanessa slams her hand against her helmet. *Thud. Thud. Thud. Thud. Thud.*

"So Griff is gone," she says. "And if I spend any more time trying to fix the payload doors, I may lose Lydia, too."

"Yes," Joan says. Vanessa can hear how much Joan is straining to keep her voice level. "But we believe it is the only way for you to survive."

"But we have no guarantee that I can fix the doors," Vanessa says.

"Understood. But we also do not have firm testing on how many open latches the shuttle can maintain through reentry. And we cannot risk losing you."

Vanessa shakes her head. *How the fuck can this be happening?*

"Do you read, Ford?" Joan says, her voice rising. "I said, *we cannot risk losing you.*"

"I want to get something very clear," Vanessa says. "If I stay and try to fix the doors, there's still an excellent chance the shuttle will not make it. Is that your estimation as well?"

"We believe our best chance of landing *Navigator* is for you to attempt to fix the doors."

There's an excellent chance, Vanessa understands, that she is going to die here in orbit. On the space shuttle *Navigator*.

She thinks back to every single moment of her teenaged years when she thought she was courting danger, daring God to take her. What a little snot she'd been.

In this moment, she is closer to death than she has ever been. And she wants to fight against it with every fiber of her being.

When she'd been messing with drugs and flying planes too low across the mountains, her mother had once asked her if she was trying to die. She'd sobbed one night at the kitchen table and begged Vanessa to care about her life, begged her not to leave her childless.

Vanessa wishes, so badly, that her mother could see her now. To see and feel how incredible the life is that she has made for herself, and how desperately she wants to live it.

She wants nothing more than to go home. To go home and say she's sorry to her mother. To find Joan and Frances.

Joan. Joan. Joan. Joan. Joan.

"If I stay to fix the payload bay doors, even if I get them to lie flat, Lydia will almost certainly die," Vanessa says.

"We understand that. But if you do not fix the payload bay doors, it is most likely that the shuttle will not make it. Which means Lydia will not make it, either," Joan says. Vanessa admires the strength and directness in her voice.

There's not really any branch of statistics that can weigh her chances of closing the latches against Lydia's chances of surviving another rev. There is no concrete answer. Everyone listening knows that.

"Lydia saved me," Vanessa says. "She saved the shuttle. She tried to save us all."

"Affirmative," Joan says.

Vanessa waits and then Joan speaks up again, in a tone softer than she has used all day: "We know. We know." And then: "But we cannot lose you."

Vanessa closes her eyes. She can feel her breath quickening. She wants to try to fix the shuttle doors. She wants to get home and smell the dirt and oil of Earth. She wants to find her mother. She wants to see Joan's face again.

She wants so badly to see Joan's face again.

Please, God, let her see Joan's face again.

JOAN UNDERSTANDS WHAT IS GOING TO HAPPEN BEFORE VANESSA says it.

She understands what is going to happen before anyone in Mission Control does.

She understands that it is the only thing that *can* happen.

There is commotion on the floor. Ray and Jack are going back and forth about how much time Lydia has. RMU is running through possibilities for what the shuttle can withstand upon reentry.

But Joan stares straight ahead at the telemetry.

Her muscles go limp for a moment, and she can feel her soul retreat into the core of her body.

She cannot love Vanessa without understanding why she will do what she does next.

But she is also *furious*.

VANESSA CLOSES HER EYES. SHE STARES AT THE DARKNESS WITHIN HER-
self. The fact that Joan is not speaking, Vanessa understands, is because Joan is giving her a chance to think this through . . .

When the answer comes—so clear—she knows that her only
course of action is the cruelest thing she could do to the woman she
loves.

And she hates the fact that she would not be able to live with
herself if she made any other choice.

She had made Joan a promise. That she would wake up every
single day and choose her. Forever.

And now she must break that promise.

"I cannot leave Lydia to die," Vanessa says.

"I know," Joan says in a whisper. "I know."

Vanessa can hear the breathlessness in Joan's voice, and she
wants to reach through the microphone and hold her and apologize.
She wants to tell her that given the choice, she would deny herself
the joy of having met Joan, just to keep Joan safe from what she has
to do now.

She wants to say, "I'm sorry, honey," in between hyperventilating
sobs. "I'm so sorry."

But she cannot do that.

What Vanessa is about to do will end her NASA career, if it does
not end her life. But Joan's life will go on. And Joan is great as CAP-
COM. She can't ruin that for Joan now.

So instead, she says, "Houston, I deeply regret any pain that will
be caused by what I must do."

There is no immediate response, so she keeps going: "But I could
not live with myself if I didn't try to get Lydia home in time to save
her."

If she has secured the payload bay doors just enough, she can save them both. If she keeps trying, she can only save herself.

"*Navigator,*" Joan says. Her voice sounds strong, but Vanessa can sense that it is cracking at the edges. "We are asking you to please continue to work on the payload bay doors in the hopes that we can at least get you home. That is what Jack is commanding right now. Do you read, Vanessa Ford? This is *Jack's command.*"

Vanessa nods to herself and closes her eyes.

The way Joan says it reverberates in her mind.

This is *Jack's* command.

Vanessa begins gathering the tools and securing them in the tool kit. "Roger that, Houston. Understood," she says. "But I believe that trying to land the shuttle with the doors as they are now is Lydia's best chance of survival."

"*Navigator,* the entire—"

"Tell NASA to do whatever they have to do to me if I survive," Vanessa says. "Censure me, fire me, arrest me. I do not care. I'm going back into the flight deck, and I'm starting deorbit procedures."

"*Navigator,* you do not have the approval—"

"Everybody down there, listen to me. It's not a discussion," Vanessa says.

She needs to make Joan understand that there is no way to change her mind, or else Joan will blame herself for everything that happens today. She will replay it in her head for the rest of her life to see if there was anything she could have said to convince Vanessa otherwise. Vanessa cannot allow that to happen.

Vanessa needs Joan to understand that this was always inevitable.

From the moment Vanessa was born, this moment has been inevitable.

"I know a lot of people are listening right now," Vanessa says. "I know you all know that I'm breaking protocol. For anyone reviewing this later, the transcript will show that I am doing this alone: I'm making this decision. Joan isn't. Jack isn't. No one at NASA is.

"There is one person who can land this thing and potentially save any of the lives on board. And that's me. So I will be deciding. And what I am choosing to do is to attempt to save the life of Lydia Danes. This decision has already been made. I will not consider any other arguments."

Joan is crying now. Vanessa can hear her gasp. *"Navigator—"*

"Joan," Vanessa says, her voice soft. "We do not know what is going to happen, okay? We don't know what the next few hours hold. We do not know the aerodynamic effects of the warp in the payload doors. We do not know, for certain, what will happen on reentry. The shuttle has withstood plenty of things we didn't believe it could. That's my gamble right now. Because I will not tinker away back here when Lydia needs me to get her home. I won't do that. So do not ask me again. We have less than a rev to get her home. If you take any more of my time, you threaten both of our lives even further."

She waits.

"Roger that," Joan says, finally.

Vanessa knows that it is not Joan making that call. She knows that in Mission Control, Jack looked at Joan, and nodded.

Still, Vanessa knows it killed Joan to say the words.

And that Joan did it for her.

JOAN IS SITTING AT HER CONSOLE IN MISSION CONTROL AND SHE CAN-
not breathe. Her body has stopped taking in air as an involuntary
process. Instead, every few seconds, she gasps and abruptly exhales.
And then holds her breath again.

It's been happening for the past half hour, as everyone in Mission
Control has tried to figure out how to address the unprecedented
insubordination of the only conscious astronaut aboard a damaged
shuttle.

Jack and the rest of the team have resigned themselves to what
Joan knew well before Vanessa said it.

"We have no choice but to support the premature deorbit," Jack
announced when Vanessa got into the airlock against orders. "And do
what we can to ensure that *Navigator* survives reentry under the current conditions."

Right now, there are teams of engineers trying to calculate to what
percentage the shuttle can withstand reentry with the vague specs
Vanessa has reported.

And Joan is sitting at her console, trying to catch her breath.

She has never experienced this in her body before.

But she's also never sat in a chair and pretended she was only
worried about losing a colleague when, really, her entire life was at
stake.

They have to start the deorbit burn in the next few minutes. All
of the final preparations are being made. Joan looks around the room
as she gasps again.

Antonio has come onto the floor. He is standing to the right, with
both hands behind his back, looking up at the telemetry.

He looks at her and nods, his eyes glassy. From his frown, she can
tell he is worried about her.

She feels so much anger. At him. At the shuttle. There is a tiny spark of fury building to a bonfire within her.

But more than that, she has never felt sustained terror like this before, as if she is falling with no end. Her pulse beating against the confines of her neck.

But no one needs her anger and terror and panic right now. They need her composure.

They need her to be CAPCOM.

When Vanessa gets home, Joan is going to scream at her with such venom she might go hoarse. Then she will fall into her and sob.

But for now, she will be the CAPCOM Vanessa Ford needs.

She can do that for her. She has to do that for her.

It is the only real way to love her.

VANESSA IS LOOKING OUT THE WINDOW AT A STAR THAT JOAN WOULD know the name of. But her vision grows blurry. In microgravity, her tears don't fall; they cling to her eyes, pooling under her eyelashes.

She raises her arm and rubs the sleeve of her launch reentry suit across her face, to clear her sight.

She turns to see Lydia, unconscious, in the seat next to her. Vanessa takes her hand for a moment and squeezes.

"Here we go," she says to Lydia.

"*Navigator*, this is Houston," Joan says. "We need to start the deorbit burn right now."

There's that voice.

That calm, serene voice.

It is possible that Vanessa has asked too much of the world, pushed it too far beyond its limits.

But if Joan's voice is the one with her now, she must have done something right.

"HOUSTON, THIS IS *NAVIGATOR*. I AM READY TO START THE DEORBIT burn."

Joan reminds herself that the burn is the easy part. They might as well be preparing for Vanessa to start the car. It is what happens after that, as the shuttle approaches the atmosphere, that Joan doesn't want to consider yet.

"Let's go," Jack says. He points into the air, signaling he's ready. "Ground Control, are we go for the deorbit burn?"

"We are go."

"Guidance?"

"Go."

"FIDO?"

"Go."

"PROP?"

"Go."

"GNC?"

"Go."

"RMU?"

"Go."

"EECOM?"

"Go."

"FAO?"

"Go."

"DPS?"

"Go."

"INCO?"

"We're go."

"Booster?"

"We are go."

"Surgeon?"

"Go."

Jack nods at Joan. "They have a go for the deorbit burn."

"*Navigator,* this is Houston," Joan says. "You are a go for the deorbit burn."

"Copy that," Vanessa says. "Go for the deorbit burn."

Everyone in Mission Control—on the floor, in the director's suite, in the theater behind them—watches the telemetry with a sense of unease.

First, Vanessa needs to get *Navigator* into the proper position. She needs to fly it upside down and backward, with her tail pointed in the direction she wants to go.

Barely a breath can be heard as all of Mission Control watches the data on the screens.

The orbiter slowly moves into place.

"Flight, PROP. We've got a good config for the burn."

There's a collective exhalation.

Joan: "*Navigator,* we've got a good config for the deorbit burn."

"Roger, Houston. Good config for the burn."

In the three minutes it takes for the burn, the future dares to seep into Joan's mind. She stares straight ahead, her eyes wide, trying not to picture what comes next.

When it ends, she forces herself to redirect her attention back to the present moment.

"Flight, this is Guidance, good burn, no trim required."

"Roger," Joan says. "Good burn, *Navigator.* No trim required."

"Copy that, Houston. No trim required."

Joan allows herself a moment to picture it: Vanessa's feet back on Earth.

Jack is on the main loop: "All right, everybody! Good work. We are in the post-burn. PROP, any deltas?"

"Negative, Flight. No deltas."

Jack nods.

The shuttle knows what to do from here. The onboard guidance will direct the firing of the RCS thrusters to maneuver *Navigator* from the upside-down and backward position to nose forward for reentry into the atmosphere.

Even with everything operating optimally, the entry into the Earth's atmosphere is dangerous. The pressure of reentry can cause the skin of the shuttle to reach temperatures up to 3,000 degrees Fahrenheit—enough to burn up an unprotected spacecraft and everything in it.

But the shuttle, with its coat of thermal tiles and blankets, is built to withstand this heat—provided reentry is executed perfectly and the payload bay doors are closed tight.

Joan reminds herself that the shuttle is capable of more than their conservative estimates. They've already seen that on other missions. That's what Joan is holding on to.

"Houston, this is *Navigator*."

Joan sits forward. "We read you, *Navigator*."

"I'm over the Indian Ocean."

"Affirmative, we read that you are over the Indian Ocean."

"Reentry will be in less than an hour."

"Affirmative, *Navigator*."

"Goodwin, can we . . ."

"Ford, do you read? We lost you."

"No, I'm here. I just . . . Look, I want to say something. Before . . . I know people are listening. I know they can hear me say it, but . . . Will you tell everyone I'm sorry?" Vanessa says.

"Roger that," Joan says.

"No, please, listen to me," Vanessa says. *"I'm sorry."*

Joan closes her eyes.

"Do you remember when we were arguing about the best song about space?" Vanessa continues.

"Of course I do."

"I was so intense about it," Vanessa says. "I feel so silly. I got so mad at Griff."

"He understood," Joan says. "You know he understood you, right?"

"I know. I know he did."

Joan's chest begins to cave in. She snaps herself out of it.

"I think both of us—Griff and I—should have been listening to you," Vanessa says. "You had the right idea the whole time."

"Ford, my song was from *Sesame Street*," Joan says.

Vanessa does not laugh. "Yeah, but . . . it's kind of that simple, isn't it? You get up here, and then for one reason or another, you realize you want to come home."

Joan does not answer for a moment. Jack moves closer to her, standing just behind her. She cannot bear to look at him. To see how much of this he understands.

"Goodwin, do you read?" Vanessa says.

"Of course." Joan nods. "Yes, of course. Roger that."

"I want to come home."

"We know you do," Joan says. "We know."

"It's just that I can't do it without Lydia. I couldn't live with myself."

Joan does not know what to say back.

How could I say I loved you if I didn't love this about you?

"Tell her when we see her again," Jack says, "I'm going to slap her on the back to congratulate her, and Antonio is going to fire her—all in one fell swoop."

Joan looks at him. His eyes are bloodshot. The smile plastered on his face is so superficial she can already see the frown underneath it.

But she relays the message.

Vanessa tries to laugh. "Who all is there?" she asks. "At the flight center. You must have a lot of guests by now."

Joan looks around the room. She's unsure how to answer, unsure what a good answer would be.

Jack speaks up: "Tell her everyone. We are all here for her. Tell her Donna and her baby girl are in the theater. Tell her Helene is here. Tell her the entire astronaut corps is with her in spirit right now. Tell her everyone here is rooting for her."

Joan nods and gets back on the loop. "Well, Ford, just about anybody you've ever met is here."

"Does my mom know?" Vanessa asks. Joan can hear the jovial tone Vanessa is trying to hold on to slip away.

Joan looks to Jack, who nods. "Affirmative," Joan says. "Your mother knows."

"She's probably scared."

Yes, she's probably terrified. She's not sure how she's going to live through the next hour.

"I don't think she is scared at all," Joan says. "I think she knows what her daughter is capable of. I think she knows exactly who her daughter is."

"Yeah," Vanessa says. "Maybe."

The future bleeds in again, and Joan can't deny what may be coming. She won't be able to live with herself if she doesn't tell Vanessa this one thing.

"You are courageous, Vanessa Ford," Joan says. "Beyond all measure. You have proven yourself to be of stunning character. And I believe your father would be proud."

Vanessa does not respond for a moment. But then: "Joan, can I ask you a question?"

"Roger that," Joan says.

"No, *Joan*," Vanessa says. "I need to ask you something. Is it okay to *ask you something?*"

Joan looks to Jack as if he can help her, but he can't. Only she knows what Vanessa is intimating.

"Affirmative," she says. "Yes. Anything."

Vanessa blows air out of her lungs and then says, "Will you tell Frances that I really wanted to fix the payload bay doors? Will you tell her that I was deeply conflicted?"

Joan has to bite down on the inside of her cheek to stop the tears from forming in her eyes.

"Joan? Did you hear me?" Vanessa asks.

"I heard you," Joan says. And then: "Vanessa, I heard you." She tries to steady her voice. "I will tell her. Of course I will tell her."

"I don't want her or anyone—I don't want anyone out there who can hear this right now—to wonder if it's that I didn't have anything to live for. I do. Okay? Do you think everyone knows that?"

Joan takes in a deep breath, and Jack catches her eye. She begins to cry. Then Jack nods to her with a downward motion that is so quick, she could swear it never happened. But as he holds her gaze, she understands.

He need not choose any words to convey it. The sentiment—perhaps beyond language—is strong enough.

He puts his hand on Joan's shoulder. "Tell her what you need to tell her," he whispers.

VANESSA IS WONDERING IF SHE'S LOST THE CONNECTION, BUT THEN Joan's voice comes back.

"Do you remember when you told me you felt like you'd never met someone who had also seen the color blue before?"

Vanessa smiles. "Yes, I do."

"Well, this is what I think the color blue looks like right now," Joan says. "I think that you want to come home and sleep in your warm bed. I think you want to go out for milkshakes and peanut butter and jelly sandwiches. And watch Marlon Brando and Paul Newman movies. I think you want to know what David Bowie is going to record next. I think you want to listen to Joni Mitchell albums with the stereo on low, staring at the ceiling at midnight. And lie down on the grass with a picnic blanket and look up at the stars and wonder if all the answers are up there. I think you want to play Scrabble at a kitchen table with a ten-year-old girl. I think you want to go to weddings and slow dance. I think you want to live in a two-bedroom bungalow, and when the hinges on the cabinet are broken, you'll fix them. I think you want to take the people you love flying over the Rockies at dawn. I think you want to be here to find out which, of all the things we believe to be impossible, we figure out next.

"And I think the only thing you want more than any of that," Joan says, "is to know that you did everything possible to save the lives of your fellow crew members."

Vanessa is trying not to cry, not to break down over the loop.

"And I think that you have to do this," Joan says. "Because you come from a long line of heroes. And we are lucky that today, we have a hero on board STS-LR9. That's what I think. Okay? That's what I am . . ."

Joan can't finish her sentence. She tries again: "That's what I am . . ." She stops once more.

"It's okay," Vanessa says.

But now Vanessa is crying and unable to speak as well.

She can see that *Navigator* has made it over most of the Pacific, and the California coastline is just ahead. Any moment, the shuttle will hit the dense atmosphere and enter ionization blackout. There is not much more time to set everything right. To make sure everyone can live with whatever happens.

"Will you do me a favor?" Vanessa says. "Please tell my mother that I love her. Tell everyone down there that I loved them. That we loved them—I know Hank and Steve and Griff and Lydia would all feel the same way. Can you tell Donna and Helene and everyone that? Don't let this hang too heavy, don't carry it with you all too far down the road. We wouldn't want that."

"Vanessa, you . . ." Joan can't finish her sentence again.

"Listen. It's okay. We asked for so much, didn't we? We wanted to touch the stars, and look what we did. There's nothing more we could ask from the universe, or this God you always talk about, than that. So it's okay. It's fine. Okay, Joan? For me, as long as you all know what you meant to me, it all worked out fine."

She knows that Joan is crying. She doesn't know how she knows, but she knows. But, for once in this godforsaken day, Vanessa doesn't feel sad at all.

How could she?

She had asked the world to please let her earn the love of that gorgeous, brilliant astronomer with that beautiful smile. She had asked the world to let her leave a legacy she could be proud of.

She'd been given everything.

"Do you know why I kept saying the best song was 'Space Oddity'?" Vanessa asks.

"Because of your favorite part."

"When he says, 'Tell my wife I love her very much . . .'" Vanessa says.

"And then he says, 'She knows,'" Joan says.

"Yeah," Vanessa says. "That's it. That's the best part of that song. But do you think she knows? Do you really think she knows?"

"She knows," Joan says. "She absolutely knows."

"Okay," Vanessa says. "I can live with that."

THEY LOSE COMMUNICATION WITH *NAVIGATOR* SEVENTEEN SECONDS later.

Joan puts her head in her hands. Jack places his hands on her shoulders.

It is routine. The communications—both the telemetry and voice—cannot penetrate the plume of ionized plasma formed by the hot atmosphere around the shuttle. And so, with every landing, there is this period, which usually lasts for around ten minutes, in which there is charged silence.

Everyone at Mission Control remains speechless, staring up at the screens, waiting for any sign.

Voice and telemetry have not kicked back on. C-band tracking data isn't coming in. The radar shows no signs of the shuttle in the atmosphere.

"We should have them back by now," Jack says.

Every single person in Mission Control is now standing up, their hands covering their mouths. This is the moment they have been fearing for hours.

This isn't right.

Joan isn't breathing.

"*Navigator,* this is Houston, do you read?" Joan says.

Nothing.

Jack: "Try them on UHF."

Joan switches to the analog frequency. "*Navigator,* come in. Come in, *Navigator.*"

Again, nothing.

Joan's stomach starts to sink.

This was not supposed to happen. No. *No.* Vanessa was supposed to do the right thing and survive it! That's what was supposed to happen!

No, there is still so much Joan needed to say.

She should have told her that she loved her. She should have said the exact words. No matter who was listening, or what NASA might have thought about it.

She should have told her that Frances needed her.

Joan should have told her about everything she'd been thinking since the day Vanessa left for quarantine. That she would quit NASA if she had to. That the three of them could be a family, taking care of Frances together. That once Frances went to college, the two of them could move to some small town and keep to themselves, or maybe live together in a house out in the country. Or they could move to San Francisco and hold hands on certain street corners.

Joan should have told Vanessa about this idea she'd had a few days ago. That when they were in their sixties, Joan would spend nights in the backyard with her telescope, and Vanessa would spend early mornings taking out her prop plane. They'd get a dog.

Vanessa had been right; Joan should have told her that. They could not back down. Joan should have told her that she was determined to rail against the world at every turn. She would scream and she would fight against how the world treated people like them, treated anyone on its edges.

Because Joan knew they would win in the end, they all would. They would hold on long enough to see the world change. To make it accept what Joan knew to be true.

That her life was complete only if lived next to Vanessa's.

They say love isn't always enough, but Joan knew, in that moment, that it could have been. It could have been for them. She should have told Vanessa that.

And that nothing—not even Vanessa not making it home—would ever be able to stop how much Joan loved her.

She should have said that.

Oh, she should have said that.

"*Navigator*," Joan says, through her tears, standing up. "*Navigator*, please. Please come in. Please. Please, *Navigator*." She is begging now. She's not sure whom.

There is silence. Jack touches her shoulder again, but Joan pushes him off. *No! No!* "*Navigator!* PLEASE! Do you read? *NAVI-GATOR!*"

Joan's is the only voice that can be heard on the entire floor of this building. Everyone else is looking down, silent.

"Please, Vanessa, don't go."

She listens for anything, a single vibration. Anything at all. The soundlessness feels so sharp it could cut her.

And then she understands what everyone else does.

They are gone.

They are gone.

Vanessa is gone.

Vanessa died somewhere over California, having proven herself to be the exact sort of person she had always hoped she was. And now Joan is left to bear it.

Joan's legs buckle underneath her. She falls to her desk, the ground underneath her disappearing. She cannot hold her own weight. She can feel her heart begin to implode.

But then, in a shock, Joan feels the most perfect peace overtake her.

What a gift. To have known Vanessa, and to have loved her.

The way the universe had developed—*the way God itself unfolded*—was that Vanessa had been here for thirty-seven years.

But Joan had been given four of them.

She had been given so much of Vanessa when so few ever understood her at all. She had been given that face to sketch for the rest of her life. To spend her days trying and failing to capture her hair.

In this one moment of brilliant clarity—a clarity Joan knows she will lose her grasp on within seconds, and have to fight like hell for years to come back to—Joan understands that God gave her something spectacular. A love, and a life, beyond the confines of her imagination.

Small, slight, unimportant Joan. Just one person of five billion, on a small planet orbiting a small star, in a humble galaxy, one of billions of galaxies. Joan is so insignificant and yet, look what God had given her. Look at all that God had given her. Look at what no one will ever be able to take away.

Vanessa has gone into the ether.

And it will make Joan even more eager to take each breath.

What a world.

Joan hears a crackle in her headset. She lunges forward.

She watches Jack turn his gaze to the screens. All at once, they begin to update.

"—ston, this is *Navigator*. Do you read?"

The air rushes into Joan's lungs. "Vanessa? Vanessa, are you there?"

And then Vanessa's voice comes through, loud and clear.

"Houston, this is *Navigator*. Lydia Danes is alive. I'm about to land at Edwards."

The entire room erupts into such loud cheering that Joan jumps.

"*Navigator*," Joan says. "We read you."

Vanessa lets out a wild sigh, sharp and whistling.

"Hi," Vanessa says.

Joan takes a breath. "Hi." She closes her eyes and smiles.

Maybe they had not asked for too much. Maybe they would get everything they wanted.

ACKNOWLEDGMENTS

For the past few years, I've been joking with my family that I should dedicate this book to "artistic license." It was incredibly challenging to get close to historically accurate in order to create Joan and Vanessa's world. So much of my growth as a writer was in accepting that my work cannot and will never be flawless. I am flawed; my scope of understanding the world is limited. And thus, so is this book. But, with any luck, within the flaws there is something that can mean something to somebody.

What technical accuracy this story has is thanks to the books I've read—a selected list of which follows these acknowledgments—and to the people who agreed to help a stranger with a crazy idea.

Paul Dye, it speaks to what a generous person you are that you took so much time guiding me through the details of life on the space shuttle and in Mission Control. I have learned so much from you throughout this process, not only about how to create a monumental life-threatening disaster in space but also the way the people at NASA approach the world. Thank you.

Jeffrey Kluger, I am so grateful for your time. A large part of Joan's love for space travel was formed that day we spoke about the value of exploration. Corey Powell and Mike Massimino, thank you so much for your help with the science and day-to-day details.

Kari Erickson, I am exceedingly grateful for your expertise at every step of the way in crafting this book. It is better because of you.

Jennifer Hershey, you have changed my life and changed me as a writer. Your support, not only in helping to get this book into shape but also in understanding me and what I've needed, has made all the difference. Kara Welsh, Kim Hovey, Jennifer Garza, Emily Isayeff, Taylor Noel, Wendy Wong, Bonnie Thompson, Robert Siek, Susan Turner, Angela McNally, and the incredible team at Ballantine, thank you for everything you do. I am exceedingly lucky to get to work with such talented, passionate people.

Theresa Park and Celeste Fine, there is a fierceness to both of you that I admire greatly. Thank you for always being the steady hands that have never steered me wrong. To Andrea Mai, Emily Sweet, Abigail Koons, Ben Kaslow-Zieve, Kathryn Toolan, John Maas, Charlotte Sunderland, and Haley Garrison, I get excited every single time I get to see you—and you all know how much I hate leaving the house, so that is saying a lot.

Brad Mendelsohn, you endure so much complaining from me! And you make it seem as if you don't mind it at all. Thank you for everything you do to realize my wild visions. Sylvie Rabineau and Stuart Rosenthal, I am so fortunate to have you both, and I never take that privilege for granted. Stephen Fertelmes and Michael Geiser, thank you for understanding what I need, as unorthodox as it may be sometimes. This team is an incredible one.

Julian Alexander, Venetia Butterfield, Ailah Ahmed, and the incredible teams at Soho Agency UK and Hutchinson, I am so lucky to be repped and published by such a sincere and passionate team in the UK. To Leo Teti, Joaquín Sabaté, and the team at Umbriel (hi, Facu!), your dedication to my work means the world to me.

To my brother, Jake Jenkins, who never lets me say a bad thing about myself without staunchly defending me, thank you. I hope one day I'm as good of a writer as you see me as.

To Rose Reid and Sally Hanes, thank you for everything you do for Alex, Lilah, and me. You so often make it so that I have the time I need to write. And you have listened so much these past few years as I've figured things out.

To Julia Bicknell and Kate Sullivan for reading this book early on. You have always seen me in the full complexity of who I am and made me feel exceedingly safe to be my true self. And to Julia Furlan, Ashley Rodger, Colin Rodger, and Emily Giorgio, thank you for never seeing me as an author first. It means more to me than I could have ever known.

Sigh And now for you, Alex Reid. You went through the NASA documents with me, read the books, talked things through, and gave me so many ideas. But more than that, you read every draft of this love story between two women and always understood why I wanted to write it. You cheered me on every step of the way. I have never had to bury or deny any parts of myself in order to make sense to you. What a gift it is, to be loved like that.

And finally, as always, to Lilah. I told you the story of Joan and Vanessa the day I finished it. And you listened to every word. You gasped, and you swooned, and then, at the end, you cried. Nothing I've ever done creatively has been as satisfying as that. How lucky am I? To be the one to tell you a story. I will tell you stories forever, my love. And eagerly listen to all of yours. Because while the great expanse of space may be enticing, I belong here, with you, looking up at the stars from afar. You are, forever, my Frances.

FURTHER READING

If you are interested in learning more about NASA, the space shuttle program, astronomy, or astrophysics, here are some of the books I loved reading during the writing of this novel.

Shuttle, Houston: My Life in the Center Seat of Mission Control by Paul Dye

Apollo 13 by Jim Lovell and Jeffrey Kluger

The New Guys: The Historic Class of Astronauts That Broke Barriers and Changed the Face of Space Travel by Meredith Bagby

The Six: The Untold Story of America's First Women Astronauts by Loren Grush

The Milky Way: An Autobiography of Our Galaxy by Moiya McTier

Cosmos by Carl Sagan

The Art of Stargazing by Dr. Maggie Aderin-Pocock

The Science of "Interstellar" by Kip Thorne

ABOUT THE AUTHOR

Taylor Jenkins Reid is the *New York Times* bestselling author of nine novels, including *Carrie Soto Is Back, Malibu Rising, Daisy Jones & The Six,* and *The Seven Husbands of Evelyn Hugo.* She lives in Los Angeles with her husband and their daughter.

taylorjenkinsreid.com
Instagram: @tjenkinsreid

To inquire about booking Taylor Jenkins Reid for a speaking engagement, please contact the Penguin Random House Speakers Bureau at speakers@penguinrandomhouse .com.